ALSO BY EMILY MCINTIRE

Be Still My Heart: A Romantic Suspense

THE SUGARLAKE SERIES
Beneath the Stars
Beneath the Stands
Beneath the Hood
Beneath the Surface

THE NEVER AFTER SERIES
Hooked: A Dark, Contemporary Romance
Scarred: A Dark, Royal Romance
Wretched: A Dark, Contemporary Romance

TWISTED

A Never After Novel

EMILY MCINTIRE

Bloom *books*

Copyright © 2023 by Emily McIntire
Cover and internal design © 2023 by Sourcebooks
Cover design by Cat/TRC Designs
Cover image by tawan/Shutterstock
Internal design by Ashley Holstrom/Sourcebooks

Sourcebooks and the colophon are registered trademarks of
Sourcebooks. Bloom Books is a trademark of Sourcebooks.

Published by Bloom Books, an imprint of Sourcebooks
P.O. Box 4410, Naperville, Illinois 60567-4410
(630) 961-3900
sourcebooks.com

Cataloging-in-Publication Data is on file with the Library of Congress.

Printed and bound in the United States of America.
KP 10 9 8 7 6 5 4 3 2 1

Playlist

"Devil on My Shoulder"—Faith Marie

"Changes"—Hayd

"In the End"—Beth Crowley

"Boyfriend"—Dove Cameron

"Love Is Madness"—Thirty Seconds to Mars (feat. Halsey)

"idfc"—blackbear

"Under the Influence"—Chris Brown

"Demons"—Imagine Dragons

"Girls Like Us"—Zoe Wees

"Infinity"—Jaymes Young

For the people pleasers.
Sometimes, it's okay to be a little selfish.

"It is amazing what women in love will do."
—Anonymous, *The Arabian Nights*

Author's Note

Twisted is a dark contemporary slow-burn romance.

It is a fractured fairy tale, not fantasy or a literal retelling.

The main character is a villain. If you're looking for a safe read, you will not find it in these pages.

———————

Twisted contains mature and graphic content that is not suitable for all audiences. **Reader discretion is advised.** I highly prefer for you to go in blind, but if you would like a detailed trigger warning list, you can find it on EmilyMcIntire.com.

PROLOGUE

Julian

MY MOTHER USED TO HAVE ME PICK MY OWN switches. I'd traipse through the small, wooded area at the back of our house and find the smallest branch I could: one that was thick enough to replace the belt but wouldn't hurt quite as bad.

Then she'd whip me until I bled.

"It will only hurt for a little, piccolo," she'd always murmur.

Afterward, she'd apologize and take me for gelato.

Dark chocolate raspberry. Her favorite.

Sometimes, I deserved the whippings. I was a boy who rebelled at the idea of following in my father's footsteps, taking over the dry-cleaning business started from the ground up by my grandparents when they immigrated from Calabria, Italy. Other times, you had to look deeper for the cause.

Any time my father would come home, after being ridiculed and talked down to by the customers he cleaned stains for, he'd beat my mother black and blue. Our walls were thin, and I'd lie awake to the sounds of a broken woman's whimpers and an angry man's curses. I'd always know that not long after, she'd come into my room, her midnight-black hair so similar to mine, pulled back as tight as her smile while she passed along the torture.

My family has always been predictable that way—taking power from those too weak to keep it.

Maybe that was why I started sneaking away and watching the hapkido classes that took place at the end of our block. I'd see them train and wonder what it would feel like to be so powerful. To have such control over your opponent that you had no fear of being hurt.

I'd imagine learning how to use the short stick or the staff and beating the hell out of my piece-of-shit father, making sure he could never touch my mother again.

If she found some peace, maybe I could as well.

It will only hurt for a little.

I snap out of the memory, allowing it to fade into the recesses of my mind where I keep it locked up tight and straighten from where I'm leaning against the wall in the dimly lit hidden room of my house. The plastic tarp that I hung earlier from the ceiling covers the floor, creating a cocoon around the man currently bound to the chair in the middle of the space.

His breathing is heavy, the sound accompanied only by the hissing of Isabella, my twenty-three-foot python, as she slithers her way around his feet and up his legs. The second she hits his calves, he jerks, his once perfectly pressed suit soaked through with perspiration.

"Careful," I tsk. "She likes when you put up a fight. It *excites* her."

I rub my palm over my jaw, the three-day stubble rough beneath the pads of my fingers, and then I sigh, reaching into my pocket and gripping my custom-made compact metal staff.

Pulling it out, I press a button on the side, and it elongates until it's full size, the silver ends shimmering against the black metal. I twirl it in my hand as I step toward him.

"Pl-please," he begs.

A chuckle escapes my chest as Isabella continues to curl her way around his body.

"Your manners are *impeccable*, Samuel. I suppose that's expected of the son of a wealthy businessman," I drawl. "But I don't have any use for them." My footsteps halt when I stop in front of him, my muscles tight with anticipation. "Do you know why you're here?"

His brows furrow, small beads of sweat trickling down the sides of his ashen face. "I'm just here for the girl," he rasps, his bottom lip trembling. "They told me to come. I—"

"The girl and everything that comes with her are *mine*," I say, my eyes flaring.

I bring the staff upward in my grasp, spinning it around sharply, reveling in the fear percolating through his dark eyes.

"Don't worry." I grin. "This will only hurt for a little."

CHAPTER 1

Yasmin

"HE DOESN'T LOOK SICK."

The words slice through my clothes and prick against my chest. If I weren't brought up to remain politically shrewd and cordial, I'd snap and say something out of turn like…

"Read the room, Debbie. You sound like a clown."

Instead, I chew the inside of my cheek and pick up my water, allowing the weight of the crystal in my palm and the cool bite of liquid against my lip to keep me quiet.

Besides, I'm confident that Debbie, the young, shiny wife of New York's governor, didn't *mean* for me to hear what she said. Or maybe she did. Rude of her, considering we're at *my* house, but I guess we can't all have manners.

I follow her stare, down the length of my espresso-stained dining table, until my gaze hits my father at the head, his dark skin looking sallow and worn. Deep bags line his tired eyes, the splotches of purple indicating the fact that he *is*, in fact, quite ill. But I guess if someone hasn't spent years of their life memorizing the minuscule changes of every one of his features, I could see how he might look simply overtired. And for a man who owns and runs a multibillion-dollar empire that controls most of the world's jewels, being *overtired* is synonymous with normal.

I'm sure he will be thrilled people can't see the change in his health.

Jealousy squeezes my middle, and for just a moment, I wish I could trade places with someone else in the room, *anyone* else, if it meant I could pretend he was still okay.

The tilapia from our last course threatens to surge back up my throat, nausea tossing my stomach, because I know my wish is impossible to grant. Maybe *they* don't see the difference, but I do.

I see it in the way his movements are stiff and stilted, like there's concrete coating his bones that he can't seem to shake off.

I see it in the downturn of his lips when he thinks no one is watching, the way he soaks in small inconsequential details that we all take for granted every day.

And most of all, I see it in his absence, every time he locks himself away, sparing me from having to watch as the radiation and chemo burn through his veins, destroying everything in their path.

That's what cancer does. It ravages you from the inside out without caring who you are. It doesn't matter whether you keep the world in the palm of your hand or if you have more money than God.

It just feeds on death.

And death always wins, one way or another.

My gaze moves from my father to the French doors that line the far wall and open to the back of our estate. I focus on how the stars twinkle against the black sky and how the deep blue lights of the expansive swimming pool create a haunting glow over everything they touch.

Anything to keep me from focusing on the problems I can't seem to outrun.

Debbie giggles and draws my attention away to where she's practically purring at the man sitting next to her.

Julian Faraci.

His dark eyes, as black as bottomless pits, are already on mine, searing through my mask of polite quiescence and stripping me down until I feel like a small, worthless girl primed and ready to be squished beneath his shoe.

I remember when he first came around, hired on as the COO of Sultans when I was fifteen, and like the naive girl that I was eight years ago, I developed a crush. He was a power-hungry twenty-eight-year-old man, and whenever I'd come home from boarding school for the holidays, I'd hero-worship him, blinded by his appearance and sucked in by the commanding nature that bled from his pores.

But it only took one time of me overhearing him try to convince my father to keep me locked away that my stomach stopped fluttering in his presence.

She's bad for business. You shouldn't let your daughter show up and distract you when you're supposed to be focused on things here. Shame she isn't a boy. Who will you leave everything to?

That last line was the nail in the coffin of my crush on Julian Faraci, and anything I've felt since has been little more than hatred.

No loss, really. By then, I'd turned my sights on my best friend anyway.

My gaze narrows on Julian, irritation stabbing at my skin like needles. He smirks, lifting up his wine and tilting it toward me, the tattoos on his other hand shifting with the flex of his knuckles as he brushes it through his disheveled black hair.

A small drop of water from my drink splashes on the back of my wrist, and I set down my glass quickly, tearing my eyes away from his taunting gaze while I shove my trembling fingers beneath my thighs.

My phone vibrates in my lap, and I bend my head down, seeing a notification from the boy who's held my heart since we were kids.

Aidan: You're beautiful

My heart flutters and I grin despite myself, glancing around to see where he is. His mom is standing in the corner of the room, her blond hair pulled back in a tight bun, the way every member of the staff in our house is told to wear it, and her gaze is pointed down. *Is he working with her tonight?*

"Yasmin." My father's harsh voice cuts through the fog, and I snap my gaze back, meeting the eyes of the twenty people around the table who are now focused on me.

"I'm sorry." I force a smile and bring my hands up to clutch my silverware. "I must have missed what you said."

"The governor asked what you think about your father's newest acquisition." Julian's voice is cold yet smooth as butter, and a chill skirts down my spine. It's rude for him to have a voice like that and a face like he does when his soul is so rotten. He looks over to Governor Cassum, smiling sardonically. "Yasmin has no clue about the ins and outs of *our* business. She's been busy frolicking in…" He glances at me. "Where was it? Oregon for college?"

My fork clinks against the plate as I set it down and turn my attention to Governor Cassum, my teeth gritting from the control it takes me not to throw my knife across the table and hope it stabs Julian in his cold, dead heart.

Despite what everyone seems to think, I *do* know what goes on in my father's business. He may try to shield it from me, but growing up around a man who is as powerful as him means I've seen and heard more than my fair share of under-the-table deals.

Besides, having Memfi Romano, a rumored capo of the Italian Mafia, stop by to *personally* drop off gifts for the holidays every year doesn't really scream aboveboard.

To the majority of the world, though, my father simply specializes in selling the idea of love through overpriced jewels. The brand name alone is enough to wow, but add on the catchy taglines and the millions of dollars dumped in marketing every year that plaster Sultans diamonds all over TV and billboards, and he's the quintessential poster boy for elegance and sparkle.

"Turn your love from in the rough to spectacular with a Sultans diamond."

"I wouldn't presume to know the ins and outs of *my* father's business," I say, emphasizing the word *my* purely for Julian's benefit. "But if you're asking for my opinion on the moral implications of continuing to trade diamonds in conflict areas, then I'm more than happy to give you my thoughts."

Someone scoffs to my left, and my eyes are drawn back to Julian. His sharp jaw twitches, highlighting the five-o'clock shadow that accents his tan face.

Now it's my turn to smirk, and I do, lifting the corner of my mouth as I glare at my father's right-hand man. His eyes narrow, irritation splashing across his features like the flash of a camera. It makes me extremely satisfied to see that I've gotten under his skin with my remark, just the way I had hoped it would.

After all, I said the quiet part out loud, the part you're never supposed to actually *say*.

Everyone at this table knows that regardless of slapping a "conflict-free" label on the diamonds Sultans sells, it doesn't mean they're actually conflict-free. They're just...*regulated*. And I know my family's business well enough to know that regulations are more of a smoke screen than an actuality. They have been ever since my grandfather immigrated from Lebanon and built Sultans from the ground up, forging relationships with whomever he needed in order to gain access to the diamond industry.

My father breaks the tension, chuckling. "These days, kids run off to university and think they're ready to take on the world. This is just another example of why men should run the country and women should stay at home and care for the children."

Heat sears my cheeks, and I peer back down at my lap as chuckles ring out around the table. I'm not truly embarrassed. I'm used to my father's misogynistic rhetoric, and despite what he says, I know he loves me. He may not be a *good* man, but he's always been good to me, and I love him despite his outdated ideas and less-than-savory business tactics.

It's amazing what we're capable of overlooking—what we're willing to do—when it comes to those we love.

My father's eyes soften as they take me in. "You'll make a wonderful mother with that caring heart, habibti."

The truth is, I don't even want to *be* a mother. All I want to do is take pictures. But that's not an acceptable career for the daughter of Ali Karam. I'm not sure *any* career would be acceptable. My father is happy as a peach knowing that I'm home for good and done with the "experience" of higher education.

Julian leans in and speaks to my father while the other

dignitaries start up their superficial conversations that mean nothing and *do* nothing other than stroke their own egos, and just like that, the attention is off me.

My phone vibrates again.

Aidan: I can't wait to touch you

My fingers drift over my lips, excitement bubbling in my middle as I think of ways to escape this boring dinner and find Aidan. My foot taps against the marble floor of the dining room and I glance around, my insides fidgety.

I could probably leave without anyone even noticing.

But I don't, because no matter how much I want to, the etiquette that's been bludgeoned into my psyche since birth reigns supreme. It isn't until dessert is finished and the men excuse themselves to my father's cigar room that I press a hand against my head and feign a yawn.

"Are you all right, Yasmin?" Debbie asks, her copper brows drawing in.

The few other women left at the table—mostly wives, a few mistresses—look at me in mock concern.

"A headache, I'm afraid. Nothing a good night's sleep won't fix." My eyes glance toward the hallway. "If you'll excuse me."

My fingers curl around the wood as I push back from the table and walk past the few estate staff clearing the dirty dishes, scanning to see if Aidan is one of them. He isn't. I pull out my phone the second I'm around the corner, my fingers flying as I type out a message of where to meet, butterflies fluttering in my stomach.

CHAPTER 2

Julian

I SWIRL THE JOHNNIE WALKER BLUE IN MY GLASS, the smell of books and tobacco filling the air as I lean against the ornate wooden table in Ali's cigar room. The clock to the left chimes eleven times. It's late, and everyone has finally left. Blowing out a breath, I sip my whiskey, a headache throbbing between my temples at having to wear the face of a dapper host.

Even though it isn't *my* estate and it wasn't *my* dinner, everyone knows that wherever Ali Karam is in name, I'm there in the background, pulling the strings. It's tedious to put on soirees like the one tonight, but they're essential. And never-ending.

This week, it was the governors and the CEOs of the world. Next week, it could be the capos or the jefes, depending on who it is we need to have in our immediate pocket. It's a tenuous game we play, being masters of the universe, but it's one I enjoy.

Controlling most of the world's diamonds means you control most of the world, and a diamond is never *just* a diamond.

That's not to say Sultans isn't a reputable company. It is.

We're unique in the way we operate. Where most diamond

retailers are the bottom of the food chain, Sultans has built itself
as a stronghold in every facet of the industry. We have jewelry
stores in every major city across the United States, several in
other countries, and we're expanding every year.

It's only once you pull the curtain back from all the stores and
sales numbers that you get to the truth. And the truth is that we
also control a large majority of the diamond black market.

No one can deny that I've done more to advance our
position both politically and socioeconomically in the past
eight years than Ali accomplished in a lifetime. And it's been
my goal to take over Sultans ever since I was a young boy, when
I was watching Ali Karam on TV being lauded as the most
powerful man in the world after his father died and left the
company to him.

He's everything I wished I could be.

There's only one issue.

For some reason, he doesn't *want* me to take the reins. Not
officially anyway, which is complete bullshit considering no one
else has poured their blood, sweat, and tears into his legacy more
than I have.

With his declining health—the extent of which he hasn't told
anyone other than those in his closest circle—there's an under-
current of anxiety that taints the air, specifically when he speaks
of his daughter, Yasmin. She came back six months ago, a fresh
graduate from whatever university he had her stashed at, and he
started calling in suitors for her hand immediately. Like it's the
eighteenth century and he's on borrowed time.

Part of me almost feels pity for the poor fool who will end up
saddled with the spoiled brat. She has no attributes other than
looking nice on an arm and being the heiress to a billion-dollar

fortune, and all that is ruined by her desperation to have her *daddy's* attention.

When Ali told me he was bringing in suitors, I grew suspicious. A quick trip to his personal lawyer and a flip of my staff later, I learned the ins and outs of Ali's will. He's leaving everything to his daughter, provided she marry someone "suitable."

Ridiculous.

I have no doubt in my mind she'll jump at the chance to take over her family's legacy, to make her father happy, even if it means marrying someone she has no interest in. She's never been the type of person to go against something Ali wants, especially if it gains his favor.

She'll be its ruin. She'll be *my* ruin.

Unless *I* become the man she marries.

The thought makes my stomach curdle.

Samuel, the poor fool who thought he'd be introduced to Yasmin this evening, was the first of what I assume will be many unfortunate casualties. But after careful consideration, I've decided that until I have a plan in place, no one will get near Yasmin Karam.

Ali lets out a sigh, sinking into the deep burgundy leather of his oversize chair. He coughs suddenly, surging forward. The sound is jagged and rough, as if it were forced from his lungs by steel hands and dragged through barbed wire on its way up his throat.

My brows crease, something tightening in my sternum. "Do you need water, old man?"

His eyes tear up as he waves me off. "No, no. I'll be fine." He pauses, his finger running over his trimmed and patchy salt-and-pepper beard as he stares into space. "Did you find out what happened to Samuel?"

I try to adopt a sympathetic face. "Never made it on his flight, I'm afraid. I've tried to get in touch, but no luck so far."

"Hmm," he hums, his body slouching. "And the lamp? Any news?"

Frustration bleeds into my middle, spreading like molasses. This blasted lamp is quickly becoming the bane of my existence, especially considering *everyone* is after it, but no one knows if it even exists.

If it does, then I need it in my hands and under my control. You can wield a lot of power with a lost relic said to be a spelled lamp of an ancient Egyptian pharaoh, and there's a rush of people trying to find it first.

The idea that it's actually spelled is ludicrous, of course, but the myth combined with the history are enough to make it priceless. And if I have the lamp, then I can finally center Sultans as not only a powerhouse in the diamond trade but also antiquities, which is the one area of the black market we haven't yet entered. It's not enough to be one of the players in the game. I want to control it all.

Convincing Ali of its importance was easy. It's finding the damn thing that's giving me problems.

I purse my lips, fingers tapping against the rim of my tumbler. "Still looking."

Ali jerks forward but stops as another harsh cough pours from his mouth.

I blow out a breath, setting down my tumbler of whiskey on the table and walking over to where he sits, reaching out my arm. "Come on, old man. You don't need to put on a brave face for me. Let's get you to your room so you can rest. Everything else can wait until tomorrow."

His eyes flare, and I can see the way I've offended him by the stark lines that burrow deeper with his frown. But then yet another coughing fit overcomes him, his thin skin showcasing the bulging blood vessels underneath.

I dig into my breast pocket, pulling out a handkerchief and passing it to him. He grabs at it quickly, shoving it against his mouth, his eyes scrunching in the corners as his free hand curls around his stomach.

I stand by silently, my jaw tensing as the man who I've looked up to since I was a child disintegrates in front of my eyes.

Finally, it eases, and he drops the cloth in his lap.

It's stained with red.

My stomach twists at the sight.

He reaches out and uses my arm as leverage to pull himself to his feet, shaking his head as he pushes past me and into the hall. I don't follow, knowing he needs to maintain every ounce of dignity he has left. I can't say I wouldn't do the same.

Glancing around the room, I walk back to my whiskey and drain the last few drops before making my way down the darkened hallway of the expansive estate, following the twists and turns I know by heart so I can go home for the night.

It's a large building, well over twenty thousand square feet, and I parked in the private lot off the staff's quarters, not wanting anyone to see me arrive or leave.

I've just hit the hallway that leads to my car when a muffled moan hits my ear.

My footsteps stutter.

I spin on my heels, head tilting as I try to pinpoint where the sound is coming from. Another moan, this time slightly louder, and my abs tense with a delicious sensation. I move toward the noise without a second thought, wanting to see who's responsible for the arousal suddenly spinning through me. The last door at the end of the hall is closed, but I reach out, testing the handle, my heartbeat ratcheting higher in my chest. I continue to twist slowly until it unlatches, creating a sliver of light that filters from the room into the dark hallway.

My eyes scan the scene, my cock jerking immediately when I see the side profile of a naked woman laid out on a small twin bed on the far side of the room. It takes a few moments to realize who it is, and by then, I'm too invested to leave, the perverse pleasure racing through me and making me rock-hard.

Yasmin.

Her breasts are large and full, dark areolas puckered in the air and begging to be sucked as a young man thrusts into her.

Well, this is interesting.

She moans again, and my dick strains as I soak up every greedy inch of her skin, seeing her in an entirely different light than ever before.

Granted, in the past, she was young, and I wasn't interested in a teenage girl with a silly crush.

But now I can't help but appreciate the soft curves of her body and the sharp angles of her face, despite the disgust that slips into the mix when I think about who she is.

Pampered little rich girl, with a cushy life she's never had to lift a finger to attain.

I have plenty of people to keep me satisfied, so there's never been the slightest temptation, even if she has grown into a stunning woman.

The boy above her grunts, his movements growing jerky and then stopping altogether, and amusement filters through my chest when I take in the unsatisfied look that floats across Yasmin's face.

"Did you come, princess?" he asks.

If you have to ask, the answer is no.

She gives him a small smile and shakes her head. "It's okay."

"Let me take care of you," he murmurs, slipping his purple-condom-covered dick from inside her and dipping his face between her legs.

Yasmin lets out a small gasp, but even from here I can tell his movements are that of a boy, not a man.

She has no clue what it could be like for her. The pleasure that could be wrought from her body. My cock pulses as the image of her tied and bound to my bed, her swollen and bruised cunt on display while she begs for mercy, whips through my mind.

I bite back a groan, palming the front of my pants, pressing the heel of my hand against my erection. It sends a burst of pleasure through me and my chest spasms when Yasmin's head turns in my direction. I should hide myself before she sees.

Maybe if I were a better man, I would.

But I've never been a gentleman.

Instead, I toe the door open more, just enough to ensure she has a nice view of me standing here, watching, waiting, my palm rubbing against the thick length of my cock while it strains against the zipper.

Her gaze locks on mine and widens, her cheeks flushing, mouth parting into the perfect O.

My balls tighten when she sees me, the urge to walk into the room and give her lips something to latch on to so strong it makes me dizzy, but I hold back, choosing to grip the outline of my cock and stroke myself through the fabric.

Fuck.

My stare burns through hers, a drop of precum leaking from my dick when I take in how vulnerable she is, splayed out for another man and clearly unsure of what to do when she sees me watching.

I expect her to scream. To stop the pathetic attempt of her boy toy and cover up.

But she doesn't.

Instead, her back arches and her eyes roll, her chest heaving as she chokes on air. I bite the inside of my cheek because I'm so fucking hard, I can't see straight.

Does it turn her on, knowing that someone who's thirteen years too old for her, someone who's the closest thing to her father's best friend, is watching her get fucked? That boy may have his tongue inside her, but it's *me* she's thinking of right now, whether she wants to be or not.

Her eyes open again, locking onto mine immediately, like we're two sides of a magnet drawn together by force. Then her gaze drops down the length of my body, searing a path all the way to where I continue stroking myself to the sight of her.

I smirk, and her tongue swipes out to run along her bottom lip.

My stomach tightens, imagining what that tongue would feel like running up the length of my cock while she stared up at me from her knees.

I'm two seconds away from saying *fuck it*, undoing my belt, and letting her see what she could have, but just as my hand brushes against the buckle, my mind catches back up to my body, and I wonder what the hell I'm doing.

Ripping myself away, I spin around and leave, my body screaming and revulsion worming its way through the arousal from my lack of control.

I have no interest in Ali's daughter, sexually or emotionally, and I'd never *once* thought of her as anything other than a nuisance, a silly girl who gets in my way and thinks she deserves the world simply by being born into it.

Only now, she's burned into my brain.

And I'm not sure how to get her out.

CHAPTER 3

Yasmin

IS HE GOING TO TELL MY FATHER?

It's the first thought that races through my head after I've come back down from the most intense orgasm of my life.

Julian Faraci was spying on me. And I let him.

"Are you okay?"

Aidan's voice is muddled, both because my ears are fuzzy from how hard I just came and because my mind is a fog trying to compartmentalize what just happened. Nausea curdles my stomach when I meet Aidan's deep brown eyes.

Is it considered cheating if I couldn't control it?

I didn't do anything wrong, but the way my thighs are still slick from what *his* eyes caused has disgust and guilt mixing and sinking like a rock in my gut.

"Princess," Aidan continues.

Shaking my head slightly, I reach up and press my palm against his cheek. "Yeah, I'm fine."

I almost tell him what happened, the words sitting heavy on the tip of my tongue, but at the last second, I swallow them back down, deciding to bury the memory somewhere deep inside me where I won't be able to reach it. After all, it'll never *happen* again.

Julian really has nothing to lose, but if he tells my dad, then I'll be loud too and force him to admit he was watching me. And I can't imagine he'd want anyone to know he was rubbing his dick while watching his boss's daughter get eaten out. I'm not even sure why he *was* watching me when he's spent most of his time actively trying to get me out of his sight.

A sick feeling washes over my skin and pricks at my insides like needles when I think again about how I got off because he was there.

About how much I liked it.

It was only because he's attractive. A temporary lapse in judgment, caused by the heightened senses of my arousal and the unfortunate picture-perfect features of Julian's face.

A shot of *something* strikes between my legs and my pussy spasms.

Dammit.

"When can I see you again?" Aidan whispers, leaning in and pressing his sweat-slicked forehead against mine.

Warmth spreads through my chest and I press my lips to his. "As soon as I can sneak away."

I hate that it has to be this way with Aidan, hiding in dark corners and whispering promises of when and where. But the thought of even bringing it up to my father makes my hands clammy and my heart sink.

How do you tell a man you're terrified of disappointing that you've been sneaking around beneath his nose with a boy who's worked in your house for years?

He'd never be okay with it. He's always been vocal in the past about me protecting myself from people without money because they'd be the first ones to try and take it from me. He wouldn't understand that Aidan doesn't care about any of that.

And honestly, disappointing my father is the least of my fears of what he would do. He could send Aidan away. Fire his mom. Leave them out on the streets with no job and no opportunities.

I'm under no illusion that Baba is an upstanding citizen. His morals are flimsy at best and nonexistent at worst. And I couldn't live with myself if something happened to Aidan or his mother because of me.

Aidan's jaw clenches, a tumultuous emotion flitting through his gaze. "Let me go to your father, Yas."

Panic seizes my throat and makes my hands clammy, the way it does every time he brings it up. "N-no. Not yet."

Aidan shoves himself back, jumping from the bed and rummaging through the pieces of clothing on the floor until he finds his pants, pulling them roughly up his thighs. I watch him in silence, the guilt feeling like a thousand boulders tied to my middle, dragging me down until I drown.

"He wanted me to meet a man tonight at our dinner," I force out.

I'm not sure why I bring it up now or why I bring it up at all, other than maybe if I tell him this, then I won't feel so bad about keeping what happened with Julian close to my chest.

It isn't until he's fully dressed, throwing his basic white T-shirt over his head, that he speaks again. "And…did you?"

I shake my head. "He never showed."

Aidan sighs. "You can't let your father control your life forever."

A spike of rage flashes through me, and I lick my lips, turning my head to the side. "You don't understand."

"Because you won't let me!" He spins to face me fully as his fists ball at his sides.

"He's *sick*, Aidan!"

He scoffs. "Believe me, I know."

My gaze softens as I stare at him, wishing I could wipe the hurt look from his face. But what Aidan's asking isn't something I can give.

Sighing, I run a shaky hand through my tangled hair, the thick, curly black pieces fighting against my fingers. "I don't want to cause him any stress. It's not good for him to be stressed."

A little slice of anger wedges its sharp edges into my chest from having to verbalize it. Saying it out loud makes it *real*, and I'm still trying to pretend that it's not.

My dry tongue sticks to the roof of my mouth. "I'll tell him, okay? I just need time."

Aidan stares at me, the smooth planes of his face drawn tight before he finally blows out a breath and walks over, sitting next to me. His hands cup my cheeks, and he wipes away the few stray tears I couldn't keep in. "Princess, how much more time do you *have?*"

His words smash through the grief like a wrecking ball, spreading the shattered pieces until they splinter my skin. "Don't use his lung cancer as a weapon to get your way, Aidan."

"I'm not."

My bottom lip trembles and I pull it between my teeth, twisting my head from his grasp.

His grip tightens and he brings me back to face him. "I'm not. I just… I've loved you since I was thirteen, and I've respected your wishes, waiting on the sidelines, having you in secret all these years while you figured out a way to tell him. I don't want to lose the chance of getting his blessing. Let me prove to you I'm good enough, Yasmin. For him *and* for you."

My stomach churns.

"I can give you the world. But you have to let me actually be with you in public." He peppers small kisses along my jaw, causing goose bumps to sprout down my neck. "I love you, Yas. Surely, your dad will see that you love me too."

Nodding, I push down the fear and run my fingers through his silky brown hair. "Okay. I'll talk to him tomorrow."

But the next morning, when I'm sitting in my father's office...I *don't* talk to him.

Despite what Aidan may think, it isn't that easy. I've tried a thousand times over the years to make the words pass my lips: *"Baba, I'm in love with Aidan Lancaster."*

But they never come.

At first there was nothing truly to tell. It was just a deep friendship, one that blossomed soon after he showed up at the estate, his mother becoming the head of our household staff when he was six years old. We were two kids spending our free time together in the summer and sneaking out to make snow angels in the winter. And when it turned into something more, I became protective, afraid of what I'd do if I lost Aidan all together and, if I'm honest, afraid of making my father upset. There's a need for my dad's approval that spawns deep in my gut, bleeding through every single one of my good intentions until it snuffs out all the light. He's not a coldhearted man—at least not with me—but he expects a certain type of person to exist in our circle, and people in a lower income bracket don't fit the mold. They're staff members, meant to be seen and not heard. And definitely not meant to sweep in and steal his daughter's heart.

I'm not sure where the insecurity stems from. Maybe it's because my mother died in childbirth, leaving him to be the only one in my orbit, or maybe it's because despite the less-than-ideal vision he has for me, he's loved and supported me every day of my life.

He's never *not* been there.

I would give my dad the world because it's what he's given me. I'd be selfish to pretend otherwise.

"Habibti, are you okay?" My father's voice coasts through the air, skating along the tops of his dark wood furniture until it settles heavily on my shoulders, forcing me deeper into the rich burgundy leather of his oversize chair.

We're in his home office, the place he spends most of his days now that he's ill, and flashes of my time as a young child sitting in my father's lap behind his desk while he taught me about the four C's of diamonds—cut, color, clarity, and carat weight—come to the forefront of my mind. A warm feeling of love fills me up when I remember the way he'd bounce me on his knee while I stared into a magnifying glass and looked at the jewels he'd bring home.

"Yes, Yasmin," Julian cuts in. "You look positively flushed. Care to share?"

I cut my gaze over to him, annoyed that he's always here and clearly trying his best to get under my skin. I've always known that he's my father's sidekick, but until I got back from university, I didn't realize that meant he would be forever lingering like a bad habit.

He stares at me with a challenge, his tall frame fitted in a perfect suit and his shoulder leaned against the wall like he doesn't have a single care in the world. As if he didn't become the world's worst Peeping Tom last night as he watched Aidan fuck me, then get me off with his tongue.

"Don't you have your own house to go to?" I snark. "Your own family to bother?"

He chuckles. "Why be there when there's so much to *see* where I am?"

Embarrassment flows through me, my blood pressing beneath the surface of my skin.

"Does me being here bother you?" He tilts his head.

I shrug. "You're like a roach, always lurking in dark corners."

He smirks, straightening off the wall and sauntering toward me, leaning down slightly as he picks up my hand and presses a small kiss to the back. "I could teach you a lot about what happens in dark corners, gattina," he murmurs.

My heart shoots to my throat.

"You two are like siblings," my father says with a laugh.

Julian frowns as he stands up straight again. He smooths down the front of his black suit jacket, the veins on his hands pronounced from the ink that weaves around them. Squinting my eyes, I realize it's a tattoo of a snake peeking out of his sleeve, and I track my gaze along his arm, wondering how far up the art goes.

A snake.

Fitting, I think.

A tingling sense of foreboding slithers up my spine and wraps around my neck.

"Baba," I say, tearing my eyes away from Julian. "Can we talk in private?"

I keep my attention on my father, but the side of my face burns, and I can tell just from the feeling that Julian hasn't taken his gaze off me.

"I was just leaving," Julian states. "Rest up, old man. I'll call you with any important news."

My father nods as he watches Julian leave, and my fingers dig into the sides of the leather chair to temper the urge that's whirling through me, telling me to follow him and make sure he never speaks about what he saw. To ask him who the *hell* he thinks he is.

"I wanted to speak with you too," my father says. "I'm not sure how much time—"

"No," I cut him off, panic suddenly filling up my chest like wet cement. "I don't want to talk about this."

His gaze softens. "We *have* to talk about this. There's no cure here, sweetheart, and there are things I need to say before I... before I can't."

My fingers curl into fists until my nails break skin, hoping the sharp bite of pain grounds me.

"I need you to listen with an open mind," he continues. "Can you do that for me?"

The knot in my throat swells until it feels like it will burst through my esophagus. I swallow around the pain. "I would do any..." I suck in a shaky breath. "Anything for you, Baba."

A dark emotion hits his eyes, and even through the ashen skin and the dried-up lips, I see a spark in him, one that I thought was gone forever.

"Do you mean that?" he asks.

I nod, straightening in my chair, desperate to make him see the truth. "With my whole heart."

"Then I do have one request." He stops, a heavy cough breaking free. It makes *my* lungs cramp tight as I watch him struggle through the harsh sounds and rattly breaths before he pulls himself together. He gives me a sad, small smile. "Consider it a dying man's last wish."

My heart aches.

"Anything," I whisper.

"I need you to marry."

Shock rushes through my middle like a flooding dam.

"Wh-what?" I stutter.

He smiles softly, sitting back in his chair. The clock on the wall is ticking audibly, muddling up my already-racing thoughts as I try to figure out what it is he means. It must be a metaphor or a euphemism, because I *know* it's not what it sounds like. He wouldn't ask this of me. *Not this.*

My father nods and stands up from where he was sitting behind his desk, walking slowly around the edges and making his way toward me. My heart is beating so loudly I can hear it in my ears, and the sound makes me sick to my stomach.

Am I going to throw up all over his Persian rug?

Sighing, he sits in the chair next to me, reaching out and grabbing my fingers, his frail thumbs smoothing over the backs of my hands.

I glance down at the movement, my chest tightening from the affection. From the way his grip isn't as strong as it used to be and the fact that every single thing he does is another reminder of just how sick he is.

"You're my daughter, Yasmin. The most important thing in my life. I need to know you'll be taken care of," he murmurs.

I swallow around the dread that's creeping through my pores. "I can take care of myself."

"Listen, I…" He pauses, his gaze flicking from my face to something behind me and then back again. "I don't trust outsiders.

My legacy is you and what our family has built. Sultans has been ours since my father came here with a dream to build an empire, knowing one day it would pass down to me and then to a son of my own."

His words slap me in the face and are a stark reminder that for all the things I *am* to my father, there's also one thing that I'm not.

A son.

"Sultans belongs in the family," he continues. "Everything I have is yours."

"Then let me have it," I say, my voice growing strong. This is my moment to prove to him that I'm more than what he sees. It's not my dream to run a multibillion-dollar conglomerate. My degree was in psychology, not business, and I'd have no clue what in the hell to do, but I could learn. I'll do anything to make sure his name lives on, that our family's legacy lives on, if that's what he needs me to do.

He chuckles, but it's an empty sound. "You're the light in my life, Yasmin. But you aren't meant to live in my world."

"That's not fair, Baba. I—"

"No," he interrupts. "I've done everything I could to shield you. To…*protect* you from the unsavory side of my life. And there are things you couldn't possibly understand and things you could never forgive me for if you knew."

My brows raise and I sit back in my seat, pulling my fingers from his. "I know more than you think."

He chuckles, reaching out to pat the back of my hand.

Irritation pulls my chest tight. If I were a man, this wouldn't even be a conversation. He'd probably have had me in all his meetings from the time I was little, teaching me about the "unsavory" things, expecting me to listen and learn. The fact that he doesn't have the person he's searching for—someone to take over Sultans that has Karam blood in their veins—is his own fault.

I'm not the delicate flower he wants to believe I am.

"If you marry, your husband can make the decisions on your behalf as the sole shareholder, and I can die peacefully, knowing the two most important things in my life are left in good hands. In the hands of *family*."

My chest hurts from how quickly my heart is beating, and my head feels like a rubber band is being wrapped around my skull and tightened. But despite all that, I realize, this is *it*. This is the moment I can tell him about Aidan. I suck in a deep breath and steel myself through the nerves. "I actually have some—"

Before I can finish the sentence, he coughs. And coughs. And coughs. It's loud and grates against the rough edges of his diseased lungs before it explodes from his mouth. His hands leave mine suddenly.

I watch as he hacks until his eyes water. He grabs a handkerchief from his pocket, and the red that stains through the fabric has me swallowing back the words like bile, allowing them to singe my throat instead of taint the air. I can't tell him about Aidan right now. I can't disappoint him with a choice he'd never want for me. Not when he's like this.

My nostrils flare, despair wringing through me as I watch my father fight through his pain to ask this one last thing of me.

But how can he ask this of me?

How can I say no?

Slowly, he wipes his mouth, a single teardrop rolling down his face and hitting his patchy beard, the one that just started to grow back when he came home on hospice and stopped his treatment for good.

In any other circumstance, his hair would be a sign of hope, of resilience. Now, it's just another reminder that his days are numbered.

"Please," he whispers, his voice weak.

A thought flares in my head, spreading through my brain like acid. *This* is why he wanted me to meet that man at dinner. He was *matchmaking*.

Betrayal sits on my tongue like dry powder. All this time, all these years, I've nodded and said yes to anything he's asked, I've gone away like a good little girl to all the boarding schools and the etiquette classes, and I've never spoken out of turn. I went to college and got a "respectable" major instead of doing a bachelor of fine arts in photography like I wanted.

And when he became sick, I rushed home without a second thought, knowing that there was time for me to figure out my own life after.

After.

He's dying, I remind myself.

I glance up, looking at his face, the weight of what he's asking from me feeling like the world was just plopped on my shoulders.

His eyes won't meet mine, and I know it's hard for him to be like this in front of me. He's always been the pillar of strength in my corner, and I owe it to him to give him this back.

I owe him *everything*.

"Okay, Baba. Whatever you wish."

CHAPTER 4

Julian

MY JAW CLENCHES AS I EAVESDROP AT THE DOOR, listening to Yasmin and her father. I'm not surprised to hear Ali say she needs to marry, since I already knew it was coming, but it burns all the same.

Honestly, I'm a little insulted that he hasn't thought of proposing *I* marry Yasmin. I assume it has to do with our age difference, or the fact that he "sees me like a son." But there's a thought that's taken root ever since I learned that he was bringing in suitors, whispering that maybe, just like everyone else always has, he doesn't think I'm good enough.

My chest smarts at the idea.

Doesn't matter.

There's still time to snip the strings and rearrange them until the marionettes move to my liking. Once Ali has passed away, I won't have a need for a princess who thinks the blood that runs through her veins and the money she's been fortunate enough to grow up with make her better than everyone else.

My heart jumps into my throat when coughing rings out from

behind the heavy wood of the door, and at the same moment, my phone vibrates against my leg, causing me to jolt back.

Taking a deep breath, I shake my head and pull the cell from my pocket.

I spin around from where I was eavesdropping and make my way down the ornate marble hall, decorated with oversize paintings by Monet and van Gogh, and lit with dim thousand-dollar lights. It's cliché to have them hanging here, but that's kind of the purpose. Well-known art that even a layman would recognize. That's all any of this is, really—the lavish furnishings and the flashes of money—a show.

But it's one I enjoy starring in.

I dreamed about being in places like this since I was a kid, growing up with next to nothing.

It gets old fast, being powerless and penniless.

When my piece-of-shit father died, I stepped in and sold the dry cleaners, using the money to take night classes in business while I snagged a low-paying job in the mail room of Sultans as a fresh-faced eighteen-year-old.

It took five years to make my way into the executive offices after getting my degree and another five to become Ali's right-hand man. It was tedious killing all of the people who were in my way, but after the previous COO's *unfortunate* demise, I finally made it.

They didn't all die in vain though. They're memorialized forever as artwork on my skin.

Trophies, if you will. A reminder of all I had to sacrifice in order to get where I am.

My phone vibrates again, and I glance down, *Mamma* flashing across the screen.

I clench my jaw, my body warring between the duty I feel to pick up and speak with her and the absolute dread of doing so. A heavy sensation settles in the center of my stomach and drops like a lead weight as I stop in the middle of the hall, watching it light up over and over.

At the last second, I silence it, the heavy burden immediately lifting off my shoulders when I send her to voicemail.

She's a battle for another day. And until then, I lock her up tight in the recesses of my mind, where I don't have to think about her at all.

I don't put the phone back in my pocket, instead pressing the number one to speed dial my assistant Ian.

"Boss." His voice is high, brash, and rough around the edges, the type of sound that makes me want to duct-tape his mouth shut and rip out his vocal cords until he's a mute puppy that's not allowed to bark.

If he weren't so damn good at his job and so unfailingly loyal to me both personally and professionally, I probably would have. But it always serves to have someone in your back pocket when you need them, and I've worked hard over the past five years, ever since Ian came on board, to ensure that he's *mine*. Nobody else in my life has ever been so faithful, and I reward loyalty regardless of the source.

"Are you at the office?" I ask him.

"Of course."

"I'm on my way."

"Excellent," he squawks. "I'll be here for anything you need."

"I need—"

"Hey!"

My voice cuts off at the sultry yell, and I pause, twisting

around from where I'm making my way down the hall, my brows lifting as I see Yasmin speed walking, fire in her dark eyes as she catches up to me.

"I'll be there soon," I say, my gaze never leaving Yasmin as I hang up the phone and slip it back in my pants. My hands follow, sliding into my pockets as I rock back on my heels.

She stops in front of me, her arms crossed over her breasts, causing them to rise and fall with her heavy breathing. My gaze begins to flick down, remembering the way her nipples pebbled while she came on another man's tongue, but I steel myself against the temporary lapse in control.

"I want to talk to you about last night," she rushes out.

A smirk pulls at the corner of my mouth. I wasn't sure she'd ever mention it. Surprisingly, I like that she is. "Don't you have more important things to worry about?"

Her eyes narrow, those dark amber jewels spearing through me. "Did you have something to do with putting this ridiculous idea into my father's head?" she hisses.

"You'll need to be more specific," I drawl.

"I think you know exactly what I'm talking about." Her finger reaches out and pokes my chest, her perfectly manicured red nail striking against the black of my dress shirt. "You've been whispering bullshit in my father's ears for years. Don't play dumb now."

Removing my hand from my pocket, I reach up and brush her away like a piece of lint, adopting an air of boredom, even though my nerves are vibrating with discomfort. I don't like to be touched unless I initiate the touching. "If he's done something to upset you, I promise, gattina, it has nothing to do with me."

A dark cloud flashes through her features.

"What is it, Julian?" she purrs, her body a hairsbreadth away from mine. "Can't handle a little competition from a woman? Afraid of what I'll do when Sultans becomes mine and I take out the *trash*?"

A laugh bubbles from my throat even as annoyance pricks at my edges, her words stabbing at wounds I don't want to acknowledge are there.

She must see the change in my demeanor and has realized she's stepped too far, because her confidence drops when I move in close until our bodies are almost flush against each other, angry little breaths puffing out of her perfect little mouth. She gasps, stumbling back like she needs to get as far away as possible.

My hand reaches out and grasps her wrist tightly, pulling her in until my shadow towers over her ample frame, engulfing her in darkness. I'm not sure why I do it, other than the fact that I can't *not*, as if something has suddenly tethered us together, urging me to touch her or fuck her or shut her the hell up so she never speaks about Sultans again.

She's infuriating in a way that I can't control, but touching her makes her uncomfortable. I can see it in the way she squirms. It makes me want to do it often, just so I can assert my power and make sure I keep the upper hand.

I glide my fingers slowly up the bare skin of her arm, across her shoulder, over her exposed collarbone, up the expanse of her neck.

She swallows, her throat moving beneath the pads of my thumb.

"If I wished for it," I murmur, leaning in until our noses touch, "I could make you need nothing *but* me."

She scoffs, turning her face away.

The urge is there to pull her back, to force her to stay still until *I* allow her to move, but I resist the temptation, releasing her and straightening as I run my palm down the front of my shirt. "I promise…" I pause, reaching out and tapping my fingers against her cheek. "I'm not someone you want on your bad side."

"You're not someone I want on *any* side," she retorts.

"No?" I lift a brow. "Silly decision for such an educated girl."

"You know, I think you might be the most arrogant man I've ever met."

I laugh. "You don't even know me."

"I know enough," she retorts. "I know that you're a creep."

"And you're a spoiled brat." I shrug. "But I'd still use you to my advantage if I could."

Her head tilts to the side. "What?"

My heart speeds in my chest, making the cavity tighten as the thought that's been itching my brain solidifies into a full-fledged idea. One that could solve everything.

Ali wants her to marry, not willing to leave anything to his *perfect* daughter unless she has a man to claim it, and I…

I could be the one she marries.

I've thought of it before but brushed it off instead of allowing the plan to take root because while it wouldn't be a hardship to have her in my bed, I'm afraid my ears would bleed from the annoyance of her voice, and my short fuse at putting up with her obnoxious attitude might not let her survive a single night.

But it would be a temporary annoyance and one that would solve almost all my problems. And now that she's standing here in front of me, with my cock at half-mast and my mind whirling at the plan taking shape in my head, it sounds almost appealing.

Marry the girl, let the old man die, and then kill her and be done with it, inheriting everything without the bitch of a daughter attached to my side.

My spine straightens and I let my eyes drop down the length of her, looking at her for the first time as if she's my prey and I'm ravenous to eat.

"Clearly, Ali's done something to upset your fragile ego. And you said it yourself. He listens to me."

"His biggest flaw, in my opinion." She smirks.

"Cute." I smile. "A smart woman would see me as an opportunity."

"I…what do you mean? Are you saying you want to…help me?"

"I'm saying it seems advantageous to have me in your corner. Me, the one who holds sway with the most important man in your life." I quirk a brow. "Assuming he *is* the most important man in your life?"

Her body folds in slightly. Clearly, she gets the insinuation of me bringing up her secret lover, and she doesn't want to talk about it.

"Of course he is," she murmurs.

Humming deep in my throat, I nod and reach in, pressing my thumb and forefinger against the bottom of her chin, pinching slightly. "Then I suggest you put away those claws, gattina. Why make me an enemy when I can be an ally?"

Fire rages behind her eyes and I spin around, a sick satisfaction at leaving her without the chance to respond spreading through every vein in my body.

CHAPTER 5

Yasmin

I'VE KEPT AIDAN A SECRET FROM EVERYONE IN MY life for years. To the outside world, he's nothing but a childhood friend. And at first, they were right. I was lonely when I was home, and he was just *there*. But then before I knew it, he had stolen my heart like a thief, and when I wasn't sure what the feeling was, he told me it was love.

As I sit across from my best friend, Riya, watching her sip on raspberry Bellinis and moan around twenty-dollar chocolate croissants, I can't help but wish that she knew. That I hadn't kept this secret from everyone and had allowed her to be my rock.

Maybe, if I had someone to talk to about everything, I wouldn't feel so alone—wouldn't feel like I'm suffocating on air.

"These croissants are nothing but sugar and carbs," she says as she leans back in the metal patio chair, her black-painted fingernails scratching her stomach. "Worth it though."

I hum, grabbing my Canon EOS R3 camera, snapping a quick photo of her.

She grins and flips me the bird.

I snap another one, already imagining how good it will look in black and white. Riya's sass doesn't need color to bleed through the lens.

Photographing people in their element is my favorite part of taking pictures. There's something so cathartic about candid photos, capturing a single solitary moment and keeping the emotion alive forever.

"God, I hoped you'd grow out of that after college." Riya nods to my camera as I set it down beside me.

I grin, picking up my Bellini and taking a sip, letting the bubbles sit on my tongue and mix with the sweetness of the raspberry. "Well, I'd hoped you'd grow out of being a bitch, but we can't all get what we want."

She guffaws, tossing a napkin across the table at me. I grin, placing my drink back down.

Riya and I have been meeting for Sunday brunch since our college days out in Oregon. We were roommates there just like we had been for years, having had plans to go to college together since we were little kids running around in the boarding school our parents threw us in.

We connected instantly when we met, both of us coming from wealthy upbringings with strict parents and invisible walls to keep us from straying too far out of line. But where my father gives me everything I could ask for and all the spare attention he has, hers treats her like a ghost, something that can be stowed away and kept quiet with cash. But Riya learned that even bad attention is *attention*, and she became a troublemaker quickly, craving the acknowledgment it provided.

So when we got to university, she acted out. She was known

as a party girl who was hanging on to her diploma by the skin of her teeth and the numerous donations in her parents' name.

As a result of our differing lifestyles, when we had our first taste of freedom, Sunday brunches became our fail-safe, our weekly check-in. Mainly so I could make sure she made it through the week alive after not coming home to our dorm more than once or twice in a seven-day span.

In Oregon, we were able to find little hole-in-the-wall pubs—hidden gems with bad sanitary habits and killer Bloody Marys. Now that we're back home in New York, we've had to adapt. I had more freedom when I was far away, but my father likes to know I'm safe.

He's an important man, and important men have lots of enemies.

So we meet here at Bazaar Treats. It's an upscale place known for their delicacies and overpriced menu, hidden away in the ritzy hills of Badour, New York, where we live.

I've never begrudged my father the things he needs to do to take care of me, but just once, I'd love to break through the cocoon and get lost in the streets of New York City. It's difficult to do when I have to depend on the drivers provided by my dad. I've never learned how to drive; there wasn't really a need, and my father preferred for me to be driven rather than do the driving.

Maybe in another life. Or maybe after he's gone.

Shame coats my insides when the thought crosses my mind, nausea tossing my stomach like a ship in a storm until buttery flakes of croissant surge up my throat.

How could I think that?

Anger at his request isn't a reason for selfish thoughts. *Evil* thoughts. But I'm having a hard time coming to terms with my emotions.

It's been three days since the conversation with him when he turned my world upside down. Seventy-two hours for anxiety to fill up every vein until they're humming, high-pitched, and tight. And I'm no closer to a solution than I was.

My phone vibrates against the top of the table to the right of my empty plate, and I look down, guilt flip-flopping through my chest when Aidan's name flashes across the screen. I've been avoiding him, not sure what to say—what to *do*—and not wanting to hear the heartbreak in his voice when I have to tell him what's going on.

I had hoped to have thought of something by now, something that could save me from this nightmare without hurting every single person that I love, but clearly, that's not the case.

"What's up with you?" Riya asks, snapping her fingers in front of my face.

I shrug, flipping my cell over until it's facedown. "Nothing. Why?"

Her brow raises until it touches her dark hairline, and she leans over the table, her hand shooting out like she's going for my phone.

Trepidation surges through me and I grab it clumsily, shoving it in my lap.

I'm not sure why I panic the way I do. She knows Aidan exists. She knows we've been friends and that I care for him. In fact, they've been friends for just as long, because more often than not, Riya would come to my house for the holidays while her parents were vacationing in the south of France. The three of us bonded the way any kids of the same age with nothing but time and boredom on their hands would.

She just doesn't know exactly *what* he means to me. I've wanted to tell her a thousand times, but it's just...too risky. Sighing, I attempt to run a hand through my hair, my fingers getting caught in the curls.

"Mm-hmm," she snarks, her back slamming into her chair. "You're a shit liar, you know?"

I grab my champagne flute and gulp back more of my Bellini. She smirks. "You're really not gonna tell me?"

Again, my secrets skim the surface of the deep place where I keep them locked up tight, the war inside me weakening my defenses until I can't fight anymore, especially considering my father's demand and my promise to Aidan.

"I hooked up with Aidan," I admit.

It's not the whole truth, but it assuages the weight of keeping it inside all these years at least.

"And?" She rolls her eyes, barking out a laugh. "What else is new?"

"What's that supposed to mean?" I squint.

She leans forward, resting her elbows on the white linen of the patio table. "I'm your best friend, Yas. You don't have to tell me you're in love with someone for me to know. You two have always been absolute shit at hiding anything."

My heart stutters, teetering on the edge of a cliff and deep diving through my middle. *How long has she known?* And if she knows, then does anyone else?

"Yeah, well, my father's bitch boy caught us the other night." My cheeks heat and I groan, dropping my head into the palms of my hands, pressing until white dots scatter behind my closed eyelids.

Riya sucks in a breath. "Who, Julian?"

I let out a heartless laugh, my stomach souring at his name. "The one and only."

"Oh, *shit*."

"Yeah." I chew on the corner of my lip until the skin starts to break. "I don't think he'll say anything though. He seemed to like what he saw."

Riya's deep eyes widen, her dark gaze sparking and a devious grin spreading across her face. "You slut! You let him watch?"

"I didn't *let* him do anything," I say. "I just…didn't stop him."

Once again, revulsion tears its way through my insides, because how the hell could I have possibly let this happen?

She throws back her head and laughs so loudly, the other people on the patio glance our way.

I ball up the napkin she threw earlier and toss it back, shoving away the guilt once again. This time I hope the memory stays away for good. It's done, and just because I liked the way it felt to have someone's eyes on me doesn't mean that I like *him*.

She sits forward again and brushes her hair off her shoulder. "If I were you, I'd take the opportunity. I bet he fucks like a god. Older men always do."

"That's because you're a selfish bitch." I grin.

"There's nothing wrong with putting yourself first." She shrugs, looking at me with an accusing glare. "You should try it some time."

Her comment sobers the amusement buzzing through my chest, and I frown at her.

"So that's what has you zoning out every couple of seconds like you're drugged?" she continues. "You're thinking about Julian Faraci?"

"My father wants me to get married." I rush the words out so fast,

I choke on the sudden knot in my throat. I reach out and grab my glass again, downing the last few sips of my Bellini before twisting my head around to scan the room for our server to ask for another. I'm already buzzed, but not nearly enough for this conversation.

"Oh." Riya's voice is flat.

My heart squeezes. "Yeah. *Oh.*"

"Like...to a stranger?" Her head tilts with her question, but there's no point in pretending we don't both already know the answer.

I swallow and nod, a flash of Aidan running through my mind. The guilt settles thick on the back of my tongue. "Well, I don't know," I amend. "I was too busy trying to breathe through the shackles being placed on my arms and legs to ask questions."

"What's he going to do, line up suitors and have them duel for your hand?"

"I'm not a prize at a fair." My stomach burns.

She scoffs. "Tell him that."

My palms grow clammy and I wipe them off on my lap, unsticking my tongue from the roof of my mouth. "He's *dying*, Riya. He's never asked much from me, and I..." Blowing out a breath, I pinch the bridge of my nose. "He just wants to make sure I'm taken care of."

Riya hums, her head bobbing. "So you give up your life for his?"

"He's my only family," I whisper, my fingers tightening until they feel like they might break. "He's all I have left."

"You still have yourself," she answers back. "You shouldn't have to give that up too."

Her words cut like a serrated knife slicing through my gut, because it feels like there's nothing I can do to keep my world from free-falling off its axis.

But that's not exactly true.

If I can just get my father to see that Aidan is a good man, that he's *the* man for me, then maybe I can keep everyone happy. And in order to do that, I need to suck it up and go ask for help from the last person on earth I want to deal with.

I need to go see Julian.

CHAPTER 6

Julian

I PINCH THE BRIDGE OF MY NOSE AS I LISTEN TO Tinashe Moyo, the man who runs the other side of the world for Sultans. Right now, he's in our compound right outside Girga, Egypt, spearheading the effort to keep on archaeologists who have been preapproved from the Egyptian government to dig. To find the lamp, we need to first be able to get into the places where it could be, and it's far easier to bribe the people already there than try to sneak in people and keep them under the radar. It's hard enough smuggling things *out*.

But there's no one else I'd trust. Tinashe first started working for me when Sultans took over the artisanal mines in Kimberley, South Africa.

Over the past few years, I've brought him in to lead all our new operations, to be my eyes and ears when I can't physically be there to see or hear myself. He ensures that everything goes according to plan, that the rough diamonds make it from beneath rock all the way to one of our warehouses. Some end up here at our headquarters in New York, and others end up around the world in our smaller manufacturing houses, being cut and polished before being formed into beautiful jewelry that's sold to the masses.

Tinashe has become paramount to Sultans running like a well-oiled machine, and I don't think we'd be as overwhelmingly in control of the percentage of the diamond trade that we are if it weren't for him.

Since he's come on board, we've grown to controlling fifteen of the twenty major diamond mines left in the world, and once we find the lamp, I'm going to shift his focus to Russia, which is the one country Sultans has no presence in at all.

"I've got a few personal family things I need to take care of," Tinashe starts, his voice strong over the speaker phone. "I'd like to go deal with them in person, but we've also been running into problems with Da—"

"None of this shit matters," Ian bursts out from on the other side of my desk. The nostrils on his wide nose flare as he taps his foot against the wooden leg of his chair, his dirty-blond hair mussed from where he's run his fingers through it. His rough voice stops Tinashe from speaking, and I grit my teeth to keep from lashing out.

Ever since I've clued Ian in on the fact that Ali is one foot in the grave and I'm nowhere in the will, he's been…*tense*.

I squint my eyes, running my hand over my jaw.

"Apologies for the interruption, Tinashe," I finally say, my eyes never leaving my petulant assistant's. "Take the time with your family. I'll send someone over to take your place."

Ian swallows harshly, his Adam's apple bobbing as I press the button to end the call. I lean back in my chair, steepling my fingers in front of my mouth, hoping my displeasure is coating the air and strangling him. He knows better than to speak out of turn with important people. He's supposed to be seen, not heard.

"Remind me again," I start, pressing my hands down into the arms of the chair and pushing myself to a stand, "when I gave you the idea that you were allowed to have a voice?"

Slowly, I roll up the black sleeves on my button-down shirt until they're above my elbows, showcasing the tattoos I've accumulated over the years. Ian is the only person in the world who knows what they stand for, and right now, I use them as an intimidation tactic. He's never above being another trophy on my skin.

Reaching into my pocket, I remove my compact staff, twirling it around in my hand as I make my way toward him. A strand of my hair falls from its place, tickling my flesh as it sweeps across my forehead when I look down at my favorite weapon.

"Boss, I didn't mean—"

"Shh." I stop in front of him, resting the top of the metal stick over his thin, pasty lips. "You need to trust me."

He swallows thickly. "I am. I do. I just hate to see you work so hard for that chump, Ali. And now we're supposed to woo his daughter?" He shakes his head. "You're better than that. Better than *them*."

"I agree." I smile, straightening up and slipping the staff back in my pocket, deciding he's groveling enough to not need a lesson. "Soon, this will all be ours and no one will stand in our way. But we have to play the game in order to get the spoils. My instinct has never steered me wrong. This is our in."

Ian nods. "Marry the Sultans princess, so we get the Sultans legacy."

I open my mouth to reply, but voices suddenly filter through from the front room to my office. My eyes flick from Ian's face to the door, and I try to make out the blurry figures through the frosted glass.

Nobody is set to see me in person today, and even though my receptionist, Ciara, is new, just recently hired on by Ian, she knows better than to let random people in. "Precisely."

"And after?"

Smirking, I press a hand against my chest. "I'm sure she'll be devastated after the old man dies, longing to see her father again. What kind of a husband would I be if I didn't take care of her every wish?"

Ian's smile grows, his chipped front tooth gleaming with his slimy grin. "A family reunion."

I laugh. "You've got a foul mind, Ian. But you're not wrong."

If she annoys me in the meantime, I'll just shove her in the farthest wing of my house and maybe let the boy come around. Keep her satisfied enough so she doesn't bother me. It won't do me any favors to have her miserable, even though the idea sends a personal thrill through me at the thought. Instead, I'll keep her agreeable, convince the world we're *desperately* in love, and then play the part of the grieving widower.

Of course, after the way I'd left her the other night, I assumed she would have come running by now with her tail tucked between her legs, begging for my help, and since she hasn't, I may have to reassess how things are handled.

The noise from the reception area becomes louder, and irritation winds its way down my spine that Ciara still hasn't handled it. I walk closer to the door, pressing my ear against the wood so I can listen to the conversation.

"Miss, there's nothing else I can do," Ciara says.

"What's your name?" the other person responds.

My brows shoot up at the voice. *Yasmin.*

Delight swims through my veins and I spin around, unable to keep the smile from spreading across my face at the coincidence. "Luck is on our side, Ian."

I move to the door and open it, expecting the two women to turn toward me when I do, but they're locked on to each other as though they didn't hear me at all.

Ian steps up behind me, his face hovering above my shoulder as he peers at the scene. I can feel his presence and see him in my peripheral vision, but I ignore him, moving slightly away and leaning against the doorframe, uncomfortable with how close he was standing.

I slip my hands in my pockets, my fingers running along the length of the metal staff.

Ciara and Yasmin stand on either side of the small white desk that's against the left-hand wall of the reception area. Ciara's dull brown hair is pulled back in a sleek bun, her eyes sparking with annoyance, her small wiry frame tense.

"Again, Mr. Faraci is a very busy man," she says through a pinched smile. "You can set up an appointment, but that's all I can offer."

Yasmin sighs. "Fine."

Ciara bobs her head, leaning down to tap on her computer. They still haven't noticed me, and I take the time to really soak in Yasmin's appearance. She's dressed impeccably, as she usually is, her baby-blue pantsuit a gorgeous contrast against her brown skin. Her hair is down, wild and curly, and every time she moves, it bounces. Her teeth sink into the corner of her lips, her eye makeup accenting her expressive gaze, which is trained on Ciara as she taps away on the keyboard.

"Unfortunately, there's nothing coming up right now." Ciara smiles up at Yasmin. "Maybe you should give us a call later and we can try to work something out."

"This is ridiculous," Yasmin snaps. "I know he's here, and I only need to see him for a second. He'll most likely be at my house tonight. I—"

Ciara's face drops in a flash, her mouth parting as she sucks in a breath.

I smirk, knowing that Yasmin just inadvertently implied we were sleeping together.

"Look." Yasmin sighs again, pinching the bridge of her nose. "I don't want to have to go above you, and I *really* don't want anyone to get in trouble."

She leans in, resting her hands on the top of the desk. Her back arches slightly with the motion, and the side profile of her bent over my office furniture sends a rush of heat through me. I could walk up behind her right now, press into her while I grasp her curly hair in my fist and feel her ass grind against my dick. I could rip off her pantsuit and take her right there, just like that, hitting spots inside her that the boy could only *dream* of.

I turn my eyes away, annoyed that once again, I've lost control of my thoughts.

"I know you don't believe me," she continues, her voice lower than before. "But you will get in trouble if I decide to make a scene. If you'd just tell him Yasmin is here—"

"Then he'd be more than willing to clear his schedule for the rest of the day," I interrupt, standing up straight and moving farther into the room.

Both of the women jerk their attention to me.

"Mr. Faraci, sir," Ciara mumbles, her back going ramrod straight.

I pay her no mind, keeping my eyes on Yasmin as she straightens from where she was bent, crossing her arms over her chest as she looks at me. Something coasts across her features, making them soften ever so slightly, like she's relieved I'm here.

Good. She's needing me already, even if she doesn't want to be.

I walk across the marble floors until I'm directly next to Yasmin. I glance down at her, breathing in her soft vanilla scent. My abs tighten and I move my gaze from her over to my receptionist. "I expect my employees to know when the daughter of Ali Karam is standing in my office."

Ciara's eyes widen. "Sir, I—"

"This woman," I cut her off, "is allowed to interrupt me any time of the day. For any reason. Understood?"

She swallows and nods.

"Good." I smile, reaching out and placing my hand on Yasmin's back, twisting her in the direction of my office and pushing lightly.

Ian, who has been standing and watching silently, scrambles out of the doorframe, his eyes calculating as he watches me lead her.

Surprisingly, Yasmin doesn't fight my touch, and it isn't until I close the door behind me, shrouding us in privacy, that she jerks out of my hold, her eyes narrowed into slits as she presses her back against the closed door.

"Stop looking at me like that," she demands.

A grin tugs at the corner of my mouth. "Like what?"

She tilts her head, staring at me. "How long were you just standing there like a creep, watching me struggle?"

"A while." I shrug. "I was curious."

"About?"

"Maybe I was waiting to see if the two of you would get into a sexy cat fight." I wink. "My money's on her, although I'd enjoy watching your claws come out."

She scoffs, tapping her foot on the floor and crossing her arms. "You're disgusting."

I move toward her, wanting to rile her more because I like the way it makes me feel to see her on edge and bothered. Leaning down, I reach around the side of her body, so close I can feel the heat from her skin.

"And you're pretty when you come," I whisper.

Her breathing stutters, and I flick the lock on the door, then turn around and walk across the room until I'm leaning on the lip of my desk, facing her.

"I was also curious about whether you'd use your name to see me," I continue.

She takes a step toward me. "I don't use my name to get my way."

"What a waste," I reply.

She huffs, shaking her head. "You would think that."

"Your name is your power, gattina. If you wanted to, you could rule the world."

Her brows draw down before a laugh pours from her mouth. "Oh my *god*. You're fucking delusional."

My smile drops, something dark hitting me in the chest with her insult. "I prefer the term 'visionary.' Regardless, you're here, so I assume you've decided to lick your wounds and play nice?"

"I don't have any wounds to lick," she replies.

I slip my hands into my pockets. "I could give you some if you'd like."

She points a finger at me, indignation flaming behind her eyes. "Quit doing that. It makes me uncomfortable."

"Oh?" I tilt my head. "You don't like honesty?"

"I don't like *you*."

Nodding, I wave my hand toward the door. "Then leave."

She doesn't speak, a contemplative look flashing over her face as she stares at me, and I don't push her for a response. The key to manipulating someone into your favor is to make the other person think it's their idea, so it's important that she comes to me.

"You said you would help," she finally murmurs.

"I said I *could* help," I correct.

"My father..." She pauses and swallows, her delicate neck moving with the action. "My father wants me to marry."

She looks up at me from under her lashes, as if she's searching for a reaction.

I give her none.

"You knew," she deduces, her voice dropping in disappointment. "I figured as much."

Again, I don't react.

She sighs, twisting her fingers together. "Well, not that anyone asked, but I don't *want* to marry a stranger."

Now I move, standing up straight and taking a step toward her. "Ah, your lover boy. Of course."

She frowns. "He has a name."

"Don't we all?"

She groans, dragging a hand over her face. "You're impossible to talk to."

"Please. I'm incredible at conversation."

Her lips twitch and she leans forward, like she's trying to peer deep into my eyes. It makes me uncomfortable, as if I'm losing control of the situation, so I step closer to try to gain it back.

"I'm assuming you want your father to give you his blessing to marry this…" I lift a brow, urging her to fill in the blank.

"Aidan."

"*Aidan,*" I echo.

She chews on her lip, and my hand reaches out without a second thought, tugging on her chin gently, releasing the abused skin from her teeth and pulling her head up until her neck is craned.

Her breath hitches as our gazes lock, but she doesn't move from my touch. Energy buzzes in the space between us, and my hands tingle with the urge to reach out and wrap my hand around her curls, tugging until she bows before me, begging for me to be her savior from her unfortunate fate.

The image of her on her knees sends a shock through my system, heat collecting at the base of my spine as our eyes remain on each other.

Her mouth parts, her tongue peeking out to swipe across her bottom lip, *so* close to the tips of my fingers that I can almost feel it.

"And why *should* I help you?" I ask.

She jerks then, the tense buzzing in the air dissipating as she shoves herself away almost violently. "This was a mistake."

"Maybe." My heart thuds against my chest. "But if you want to be with your boy…"

"He isn't a boy," she bites out.

"Trust me, he's a *boy.*" I step closer again. She steps back.

A thrill zings up my middle and I repeat the motion, enjoying this cat-and-mouse game we're playing.

"Quit it," she demands, continuing to walk backward until she hits the wall next to the door.

I ignore her plea, stalking toward her until there are only centimeters between us. I lift my arm up and rest it above her head, caging her in. Her body goes stiff.

"And will you do anything to keep him?"

The air grows silent and still, nothing but the sound of our breathing filling the quiet hum.

"I don't want to lose him," she finally whispers.

I bend down until my lips brush across the shell of her ear. "Then, tell me you need me, gattina."

Her body stiffens like a piece of wood, and she speaks through gritted teeth. "Get away from me, *pig*."

I don't fight her, backing away and spinning to walk across the room until I'm standing behind my desk. I grab my wire-frame reading glasses from where they're perched on the corner and slip them on, reaching down to rustle through the papers next to my computer, my eyes briefly scanning over the profit margins from our diamond production department. I try to focus on the words, spending the next few minutes ignoring her, but she doesn't move from her spot, instead choosing to keep her heated glare trained on me.

Glancing up at her from over the rim of my glasses, I say, "If you're done wasting my time, you can see yourself out."

She still doesn't move from where she's pressed against the wall, and I wait for her to work through whatever pathetic crisis she's having in her head.

Finally, she does. And then she's surging forward, stalking toward me.

"You're a dick," she spits when she gets close, her closed fists pressing onto the top of my desk. "But I need your help." She hesitates, and then, "I *need* you, Julian."

The papers drop from my hands. "What's the magic word?"

"Please," she grits out.

I grin broadly. "Well, since you asked so nicely."

Her eyes flare but she doesn't bite back. Part of me is almost disappointed. I've been enjoying the way she riles so easily.

"Bring the boy here to meet me," I command.

She shakes her head. "It's not that easy. No one knows. We can't just—"

"Does your little secret rendezvous spot have room for one more?" I quirk a brow.

Her tongue swipes across her bottom lip as she stares at me and nods slowly.

"I'll find you tonight then." I jerk my chin toward the door. "Now leave. I'm a busy man and you're wasting my time."

She spins around, leaving in a flurry, but despite me telling her that I have things to do—which is true—I stand still behind my desk, my thumb grazing my lower lip, wondering what it will feel like when I force her to be my wife.

CHAPTER 7

Yasmin

I WASN'T SURE HOW I WOULD FEEL AFTER TALKING to Julian, but I *didn't* expect it to make my anxiety skyrocket. Yet here I am, sitting in the vacant bedroom in the staff's wing—the same one Julian found Aidan and I in the other night—more nervous than I can ever remember being in my life.

Ever since I left his office at the Sultans headquarters, there's been this gaping, pulsing *ache* in the center of my gut, one that sends tremors of anxiety through my limbs until my whole body shivers. You'd think that knowing someone was in my corner would calm me down, but Julian Faraci is about as calming as a fire alarm, so it's having the opposite effect.

I can't get rid of this feeling, and it's bothering me.

Or maybe it's because I haven't talked to Aidan in days, despite all the times he's called and texted me. If I'm honest, I was hoping that maybe if I ignored everything, it would just disappear on its own. I know avoiding problems never makes them disappear, but for some reason, I continue to test the theory, hoping that eventually I'll be surprised and things will magically get better.

That I won't feel like I'm drowning from everything I always want to say but don't.

That I'll be free to love Aidan openly and in public without disappointing everyone who matters.

That my father won't be sick.

But life never works that way, despite all the times I've wished for it to be so.

So after I left Julian's, disgusted with myself for letting him affect me the way he does, for letting him *touch* me, I texted Aidan and asked him to meet me here.

Julian and I never set a specific time for our meeting, but I want to make sure that I've cleared the air with Aidan beforehand.

United front and all that.

My leg jumps in a steady, nervous rhythm as I sit on the corner of the twin bed in the small room, the cashmere of my blue pantsuit gliding over my skin with the antsy movement. I can't sit still. My eyes bounce from the blank tan wall opposite me to the small window on the right, where there's a rickety old wooden chair that I'm not sure can actually hold weight, and then back to the blank wall again. Over and over, I repeat the track of my gaze, my mind moving over possible scenarios as quickly as my leg taps against the ground.

No one has occupied this room for years. Well, nobody except for Aidan and me when we started to sneak away, needing to be alone somewhere people wouldn't see. There's still a slight level of risk, but it's an inconspicuous place, the very last room in the wing of the staff's quarters, hidden away in the far corner.

I think about the first time we came here all those years ago, when I was a bumbling fifteen-year-old girl and just coming home for summer break.

I peer around the corner at my father and his new employee, my eyes drinking in the man like I'm starved for the sight. It will be the most embarrassing moment of my life if I get caught, but I can't stop myself from peeking any chance I get, regardless.

They're arguing about whether it's a good idea to switch over to synthetic diamonds for industrial use, which means they're the lower-quality diamonds that get used to cut and polish the ones high-end enough to sell.

Personally, I think it sounds like a good idea, but my father is stuck in his ways and rejects even the notion of a synthetic diamond. But just from eavesdropping on this conversation, I can tell the man at my father's side will get his way.

My father's been busy spending all his time with this new guy ever since I got home from summer break three days ago.

Julian, I think his name is.

I can't wait to tell Riya about him. She's been boy crazy since last year when she stayed with me for the summer and went out one night while I was sick, letting a random guy from New York City pop her cherry.

But I doubt that guy looked like this though.

I'm so mad I don't have my camera, or I'd sneak some pictures to send to her.

Ever since my father introduced Julian and I when I first got back, I haven't been able to stop looking for him everywhere. And when I look, I usually find him. It's a sprawling estate, almost as big as the boarding school I attend, but I'm convinced Julian's moved in and has made himself at home while I've been gone.

At first, I kept "casually" running into him whenever I had the chance, but it only took a few times of him either sneering down at me like I'm annoying or ignoring my existence altogether for me to take to hiding in dark corners and watching from the wings.

It's confusing, my fascination with him.

I don't feel butterflies like when I stare at Aidan. More like fire that's sizzling beneath my skin, Pop Rocks exploding in my stomach one by one until they make my body tremble and heat flare between my legs.

"What are you doing?"

Aidan's whispered voice sends my heart into my throat, and I spin around, my hands moving out to grab his shirt in my fists as I push him back violently.

"Shh!" I press my finger to his mouth.

Aidan smiles, his dimples creasing the apples of his cheeks, and my heart starts to calm into a smoother rhythm.

"Who were you spying on?" he asks.

I narrow my gaze. "None of your business."

Footsteps sound from where my father and Julian just were, and I panic, grabbing Aidan's hand without thinking and hauling him down the hallway.

Julian Faraci already looks at me like I'm an annoying bug that needs to be squashed; I don't need for him to find out I've been stalking him in my spare time.

Aidan follows easily, his fingers tightening around mine as he lets me lead him blindly. We race through the halls and don't stop until we've made it back to the rooms where our live-in staff stay, including Aidan and his mom.

I stop, out of breath from running.

"Now what?" Aidan laughs, squeezing my hand before releasing it.

Shrugging, I take a second to stare at him. It's the first time I've seen him since I've been back, and until I met Julian, Aidan was the one who took over all my thoughts. I could barely wait to see him again after so many months of being gone at school.

Now that he's standing here in front of me, that familiar flutter-ing takes flight in my stomach, and a slow smile breaks across my face.

He steps in close, his gaze growing darker. "You look good, princess. All grown up, huh?"

My cheeks heat.

A woman's voice rings out from the staff break room a few doors away, and Aidan tilts his head, grabbing my hand again and pulling me with him.

"Come on," he says, dragging me along until we reach the last door on the left. "No one will find us in here."

And nobody ever did. At least no one until Julian.

I glance down at my lap, the phone screen jostling with my shaky legs. It's open on my text conversation with Aidan. I cringe when I see the numerous strings of messages he's sent over the past few days, all of them going unanswered. Then there's my latest one asking him to meet me here. But he didn't respond.

Maybe he didn't get the message? Or maybe he's so mad he won't show up.

My stomach rolls and tightens, sending a shot of nausea up my throat.

I close my eyes and count back from ten, telling myself that everything is fine and there's no reason to worry, repeating the phrase like a mantra. It's a tactic my guidance counselor taught me when I was in primary school, back when I used to have anxiety attacks before tests, terrified I would fail and have to face my father's disappointment.

To be honest, it's never really worked. The only thing that's ever calmed me enough to quiet the racing thoughts is my camera.

The door swings open, the sudden noise in the quiet space causing my eyes to shoot open and my heart to jump.

Aidan flashes me a wide grin, showcasing the dimples in his cheeks. He glances behind him into the hallway before closing the door and walking toward me. The hem of his purple shirt lifts slightly as he runs a hand through his bouncy brown hair, and when he reaches the bed, he sits down next to me and grasps my hand in his.

"Hey, princess." His eyes are cast down as he rubs his thumb across the back of my knuckles. "Everything okay?"

Guilt makes my stomach cramp, and I squeeze my fingers around his. "I'm sorry I've been avoiding you, I just..."

He winces at my words. "Avoiding? I was hoping you'd have a better excuse."

And now it's my eyes that won't meet his, choosing to focus on our linked hands instead. "I talked to my father."

Aidan sucks in a breath, his head snapping up. His gaze is searing the side of my face, and the hope I can *feel* permeating off him burns through my skin.

"You *did?*" he asks.

My mouth goes dry as I force the words out. "He wants me to get married."

Aidan's eyes darken and he drops my hand like it's lava, running his fingers through his hair as he lets out a humorless chuckle. "I'm guessing not to me?"

I purse my lips, my eyes dipping again.

"So you tell him no." His voice is firm. Like it's just that simple. Yes or no. This or that. My father or him.

But life isn't black and white, despite how much he might want it to be.

"Aidan..." I start, my voice breaking on his name. "It's not that simple. It's his dying wish."

He laughs again and stands up, the mattress creaking from how fast the weight shifts. "So what, just fuck me then, right? Fuck everything we've talked about for years? Fuck *everything* I feel for you and all the promises we've made?"

His cheeks flush, and my chest throbs as I shake my head, trying to force the words I need to say off my tongue.

"I know you're upset—"

"Upset?" he interrupts. "You just told me you're going to be marrying someone else, Yasmin. What the hell am I supposed to feel, gratitude?"

"I have a plan," I mumble, my teeth sinking into the corner of my bottom lip, unease swimming through my veins.

I'm conflicted over what to do. I don't *want* to use Julian for anything, especially considering who he is and how his new favorite pastime is to apparently belittle me every chance he gets. He makes me so angry that my fingers shake, but I'm just going to have to put that aside and accept that he's my only option.

"What?" Aidan leans forward. "Don't get shy now, princess. Speak up so I can hear."

I suck in a breath at his harsh tone, biting back the tears that are trying to bleed from my eyes. "I said I have a plan."

He puffs out his cheeks, his hands resting on his hips as he leans his head back so he's staring at the ceiling. "Let's hear it then. What is it?"

I open my mouth to reply, but before I can, another voice cuts in.

"It's me."

CHAPTER 8

Julian

THE BOY REALLY IS INSUFFERABLE. HE'S GROANing over what Yasmin is telling him without offering any valuable input and figuring out a solution, which makes him worthless. After all, problems that show up are nothing more than puzzles asking to be solved.

That being said, the fact that this is the second time I've been able to waltz into their "secret" rendezvous spot without them even realizing I'm here doesn't give me much hope for either of their ingenuity.

The boy—Aidan—spins around, his dull brown eyes meeting mine before he whips his head to Yasmin. "You talked to *Julian Faraci* about this?"

I chuckle at the way my name rolls off his tongue like battery acid.

"My father listens to him," Yasmin rushes out, her voice tinged with desperation. "He can *help* us, Aidan."

Aidan looks back at me, his brows rising. "And you're willing to help...just like that?" He snaps his fingers.

Smiling, I move farther into the room, taking my time as I walk, my dress shoes clicking on the wood floor. I don't close the door behind me, just to see if either of them notice and say something about keeping this a private matter.

They don't.

I glance to Aidan, nodding toward the door. "You might want to close that."

His eyes widen as he rushes to it, slamming it shut and turning the lock before jogging back to Yasmin, who's standing in front of the small twin bed, and wrapping his long, lanky arms around her.

"I'm willing to help, but I'll admit it's not for selfless reasons." I brush a small piece of lint from my suit jacket's sleeve.

Yasmin snorts. "Who would ever think *you* were selfless?"

Her eyes flick to the small twin bed, just for a moment, as if she's remembering the last time I saw her here. And that makes *me* think of it, my cock twitching at the memory.

"I can be extraordinarily giving, gattina. Maybe one day you'll be lucky enough to experience it." I grin at her. "But in this case at least, you're right. Let's consider this a business deal."

Aidan perks up, his spine straightening like a dog with the promise of a treat. "Business deal?"

I nod, looking around the cramped room before meeting his gaze. "I assume you have higher aspirations than…this? Working alongside your mother can't be good for your ego."

Yasmin makes a noise, but I keep my eyes on Aidan. Body language gives away secrets mouths won't say, and right now Aidan's body is leaning forward, his attention rapt and his eyes gleaming.

And I know hunger for power when I see it.

"My ego is fine," Aidan replies.

Lie.

He reaches out, grasping Yasmin's hand in his.

"But I love her," he continues. "I'll do anything to be the one to marry her."

Yasmin stares up at him with stars in her eyes, leaning into his side with a soft smile.

I don't miss the way he doesn't lean into *her*.

"And if you needed to disappear for a while in order for that to happen?" I ask, tilting my head.

"*What?*" Yasmin gasps. "You never said anything about him leaving."

Aidan looks over at her, dragging her even closer and pressing his lips to her forehead. His jaw tenses before he meets my stare again. "Like I said, I'll do *anything*."

I nod, slipping my hands in my pockets, envy swirling through my middle. I'm not sure why I'm suddenly experiencing the emotion, but I assume it's because I've never known what it's like to have someone willing to put you first.

To choose you over everybody else.

Clearing my throat, I crack my neck and brush off the feeling. I wasn't sure how this would go, but having him so agreeable will only work in my favor. The easier it is to get him under my thumb, the faster he'll be out of my way when it comes to Yasmin. "Then you'll come and work for me."

"Can we be serious for a second?" Yasmin cuts in again. "This is *my* life we're all talking about, and—"

"Princess, shush." Aidan's voice is sharp.

My brows lift as I glance to Yasmin, ready to see that fire she brings so readily for me, sure it's about to explode from her pores at being hushed like a child throwing a tantrum. But instead of that rambunctious flame, there's nothing. Just her biting down on the corner of her bottom lip and moving her gaze to the ground like a docile pet that's been brought to heel.

The same way she does around her father.

"There's something her father wants," I say.

It's a tiny, little white lie. Ali doesn't care about the lamp half as much as I do or about expanding Sultans into other avenues outside diamonds, but it will work in my favor if they think it's *Ali* with the motivations. Easier to get Aidan out of the way so I can move in and steal his little prize pussycat for myself.

Moving my hand from my pocket, I bring it up to my face, staring at the cuticles on my fingers. "Unfortunately, the man overseeing the operation has to go home for some personal issues. And I can't find the will in me to care enough to travel myself."

"Diamonds?" Aidan asks, curiosity brimming the edges of his voice.

I flick my gaze to meet his briefly. "No. We're expanding beyond the diamond trade, or at least we're attempting to. There's a lamp. A relic. One that Ali is *desperate* for but hasn't been able to find. It's priceless really, worth hundreds of millions easily in a black market auction. If we secure it for ourselves, then Sultans will gain footing in the antiquity market. You can imagine how appealing that is, I'm sure, considering it's Ali's legacy we're talking about."

My legacy.

"I'll find it," Aidan is quick to reply.

Fool. As though he'd be able to find the most wanted lost relic of the ages with no experience and no one to guide him.

"I can't guarantee you ever will. You don't have any of the skills necessary, and people will absolutely talk about how you aren't qualified to oversee the digs. You'll need to rely on Jeannie, our lead archaeologist, who's there, and my assistant Ian, who I'll send with you." I quirk a brow, leaning in slightly. "But if you *do* find it…"

Aidan's body mimics my movements, hanging on to my every word like they're his lifeline. "I'd gain Mr. Karam's favor," he concludes.

I lick my lips and gesture toward Yasmin. "Find the lost lamp, and you'll get the girl."

Aidan's face lights up, his eyes wide as he nods, but Yasmin is looking at me with suspicion. She's dropped Aidan's hand to cross both arms over her chest, her heeled shoe tapping against the floor in an irritating rhythm, that obnoxious little glare marring her otherwise flawless face.

I ignore her glare and the way my hand tingles with the need to flip her over my knee and show her what being a brat gets her.

It's not quite that easy, of course. Aidan will need to be integrated into the system we already have in place. He'll need to meet Jeannie, our lead archaeologist on-site, and get her to allow him to shadow her, even though he has no clue what he's doing and will most likely only get in her way. But my goal isn't for him to actually *find* the lamp, although if by some miracle he does, even better. I just need him far away and out of Yasmin's reach, yet still under my thumb so I can use him to control her.

"So I'll be basically working for you? For Sultans?" he asks.

"Under the table, of course. You'll be paid in cash similar to the other people we have at the compound in Egypt. Can't have you on official payroll for something like this. But if you find it, then…" I lift a shoulder. "Who knows what the future could hold."

The boy's face is lit with promise, and I wonder how much Yasmin really knows about him.

"Do we have a deal?" I press, reaching out my palm.

He stares at it for a few seconds before placing his hand in mine.

My eyes flick to Yasmin. Her head is tilted to the side, and her gaze is bouncing from the boy and back to me, like a seesaw, unsure of where to focus.

There's something going through that normally empty little mind of hers, but I can't find it in me to care what it is. Let her think I'm either up to no good or her savior; it really makes no difference either way. Once I have her lover boy in my grasp, she'll bow to my demands whether she likes it or not.

———

I've just entered the lobby of Sultans' headquarters, which sits in the largest skyscraper directly in the center of Badour, New York, but before I can make my way to the elevator that leads to the eighty-ninth floor, which is exclusive to my offices and those who work directly beneath me, I see a blacked-out Maybach pulling up to the curb.

It's still incredibly early, the morning sun just rising beyond the horizon, the yellow headlights of the car cutting a muted glow through the dewy mist that fogs up the quiet city streets.

I'd know the car anywhere, but even if I didn't, there's only one other man who would arrive at an office before anyone else is even awake for the day, and that man promised me he'd be staying home in the future, allowing his body to *rest*.

Something pinches in my stomach when I see Ali's driver exit the front of the car and walk around to the back, opening the door and allowing Ali himself to step out of the vehicle.

I'm tempted to head over there and demand he go back home, allow his nurse to tend to him while I continue to do the heavy grunt work here, but then I think of what I'd feel if the situation were reversed. No amount of words will stop a man when there's determination thrumming through him like blood in his veins.

Still, I'm annoyed enough at the disregard for his health that I don't want to speak to him yet, and then I get even more frustrated that I care about him at all, so I spin around and press the elevator button, stepping inside and making my way to my own floor.

An hour later and I'm still lost in my head, even though I'm sitting at the end of a long rectangular table in the marketing floor's conference room, surrounded by a dozen other people. Glancing down, I skim over the quarterly report on macroeconomic trends, trying to focus on the voice of the pipsqueak who is standing in front of a PowerPoint, his tone shaking slightly as he spouts off about the state of the consumer and what our vision is to stay ahead of the market.

"Sir?"

I lift my head up from the pages, peering around and seeing everyone's eyes on me. Clearing my throat, I lean forward, resting my elbows on the table and steepling my fingers in front of my face.

Honestly, I have no clue what they've just said. My mind is still wandering to the hallway, wondering if Ali is going to make a surprise appearance.

Is he still here? I should go talk to him, put a hint in his ear about Yasmin and me.

I look over to Ian, whose eyes are wide and mouth drawn down while he stares at me, and I quirk a brow.

His hand smacks the table, clearly understanding that I'd like him to speak. "All this looks decent. Get the sales projections for the next quarter on Mr. Faraci's desk by the end of the day."

Right. Sales projections.

Standing up, I button the front of my suit jacket and glance down one more time at the papers. "Since these numbers clearly show the United States is dipping closer to a recession, I think it's advantageous for us to assume that we'll need to market differently until we're on the upswing. Show me how you plan to do that."

And then I'm out of the meeting, not waiting to hear their murmured replies, and I'm heading to the floor a few above mine where Ali's office sits.

His floor is similar to mine in grandeur, the white marble tile gleaming with swirls of sparkled gray, cream chairs, and gray couches scattered along the receptionist area with natural oak tables. I walk past the empty assistant's desk and head straight back until I'm standing at Ali's office door, my hand poised to knock. But something stops me in my tracks, and I lean my ear against the wood grain instead, holding my breath when I hear his muted voice.

"How long?" Ali's voice is strained and weak. Weaker than I've heard it before.

Silence.

"Two months?" he continues. "That's it?"

My heart pounds against my ribs, the breath that escapes me shaky.

He's closer to death than I thought. A punch of sadness hits me in the center of my chest, cracking through the concrete wall I've built around it, making my ribs tremble.

It's…conflicting, the way I feel about Ali's sickness.

In the beginning, my goal was to learn everything I could from him and then gift him the honor of living on through the artwork on my body, killing him off so I could step in effortlessly to take his place.

Maybe he'd die in an unfortunate accident, or perhaps he'd suffocate in his sleep.

But as time wore on, something happened that I hadn't accounted for.

I started to look up to him as more than someone I longed to be.

He has been the first man in my life to treat me like I'm worth a damn, the only one who's ever taken me under their wing and showed me a path to success that didn't involve a drunk dad and abusive mother. There have been plenty of opportunities for me to end his life, but every opportunity I had was squandered by the smaller piece inside me that was desperate for his attention, reveling in his approval and twisting it into a type of fatherly love that I've never experienced from anyone else.

When he confided in me that his cancer was terminal and he wasn't going back for another round of treatment, I was relieved. The burden of having to watch the life leave his eyes beneath my hands was weighing heavily on my soul, and this way, it could happen naturally.

I took it as a sign from God that I was destined to be great. The most powerful. And the universe is moving Ali out of the way in order for me to run Sultans.

Still, that small boy inside me who aches for love breaks a little more whenever I think about what life will be like once he's gone.

Ali sighs and says goodbye to who I'm assuming is his doctor, and I pull back from the door, overwhelmed by the mismatched emotions warring inside me.

I had known that he didn't have much time left, but I didn't realize he was this close to the end.

My throat tightens.

Two months. It's not enough time for my plans.

I spin around and head back toward the elevator, my leg muscles burning from my long, hurried strides. I jam my finger into the button for my floor, resting my hand on the elevator wall as the doors close and it starts to lower.

The soft jazz music flows through the speakers and feels like razor blades against my eardrums as I try to get control of my tumultuous feelings. I don't *like* the way they seem to keep sprouting up unwanted. Emotions lead to messy decisions and stupid mistakes, and I don't have time for either.

A ping sounds and the doors open to my floor, Ciara just getting settled behind her desk. She stands up straight when she sees me storming across the floor.

"Afternoon, Mr. Faraci."

I barely glance at her, giving her the slightest nod before I continue to my door. "Get Ian in my office," I say to her. "*Now.*"

I march into the room, stripping off my suit jacket and tossing it on the back of a random cream chair, continuing to my desk, which sits in front of the panoramic view of the city below. Running my hand through my hair, I tug on the roots until they sting, walking back and forth.

"Oh god, you're pacing." Ian's voice cuts through my thoughts as he walks into the room and closes the door behind him. "What's wrong?"

I spin toward him, noticing that his suit is slightly crumpled like he threw it on too quickly. "The old man is dying."

Ian sighs as he drops into a wingback chair in front of

my desk, crossing one leg over the opposite knee. "Not soon enough, in my opinion. Is that why you were so distracted in the meeting?"

His words shoot into my stomach, irritating the lining and sending a flare of anger through me. I tamp it down, not wanting Ian to know about my confused emotions regarding Ali.

"This isn't a joke, Ian," I spit. "I will not lose everything I've worked for to some nobody who doesn't belong or the obnoxious daughter who doesn't deserve it. I took care of that first fool who was sent here to meet her; I don't want a thousand more to waltz through Ali's doors in the next couple of weeks. I can't kill them *all*. Not so quickly at least. It would be incredibly suspicious."

Ian nods, running his fingers underneath his chin. "So we move up the timeline. Get Yasmin's boy out of the way sooner. I can have him on a flight to Egypt in less than a day."

His idea has merit, and I slow my pacing as I revise the plan in my head. "That's not enough. We have to push Yasmin into marriage sooner. Now, before it's too late."

Ian nods. "Shame we can't just kill her and be done with it."

Blowing out a breath, I rest my hands on the back of my chair, bending my neck until a satisfying crack runs up the side. "That would be entirely unhelpful. Stick to the plan: take the boy to Egypt, and we'll use him to control her."

Ian sits forward in his chair, a menacing gleam flitting through his eyes. "Can I kill *him*?"

"Your obsession with murder is disturbing." I give him a disapproving stare. "And no, you can't. It takes finesse, and you'll be too messy."

He groans, throwing himself backward. "Fine."

I rub my finger along the stubble on my chin, a new idea forming. "You may not be able to kill the boy yourself, Ian. But we'll make Yasmin *think* you will."

CHAPTER 9

Yasmin

IT'S SATURDAY AFTERNOON, AND IT'S BEEN LESS
than ten minutes since Aidan texted me that he was on the way
to meet Julian at some hole-in-the-wall restaurant in the middle
of Badour to talk more about his new employment.

And I'm…irritated.

His employment, like I'm supposed to just take a back seat
and let the men in my life handle everything. Besides, Aidan
doesn't have any clue what he's really getting himself into. My
father may not tell me anything about what it is he does, but
I know enough to know that danger goes hand in hand with
diamonds and money, and while I was brought up in this world,
Aidan wasn't. He was sheltered, treated as nothing more than
staff. He's too innocent and good to be mixed up in the seedy
underbelly of whatever it is Julian and my father get up to.

If it wasn't for the fact that I'm a course deep into lunch with
my father, I'd be putting up more of a fuss, demanding to know
where they are so I could sneak away and meet with them. Just

to keep an eye on things and feel like I'm still taking part in huge decisions that affect *my* future too.

But since time with my baba is more important than literally anything else, I have no choice but to give in and allow myself to trust. And I *do* trust Aidan. It's just that snake Julian who puts me on edge.

I don't even really have a basis for my suspicions other than the general vibe he gets off on giving, the way he's always so easily gained my father's favor over me, and the way he gets attention and praise when I have to work *so* hard to be treated as more than just a shiny beloved trophy my father can put on his shelf.

Plus, until very recently, he's always been mean to me at best and downright cruel at worst.

He's a prick. And I don't believe for a second that he's doing this out of the goodness of his heart. I just don't know what he's trying to accomplish, so not being there to hear every scheme that he's going to try to rope Aidan into makes me sick.

"You okay, habibti?" my father asks, keeping his eyes trained on the view and not on me.

I snap a quick photo of him as he stares out at the yard from his private room's Juliet balcony and then set down my phone, reaching across to grasp his hand in mine. "I'm perfect, Baba. Just making memories."

"Always stuck with your head in the clouds," he chuckles. "Just like your mother."

He doesn't talk about her often, I assume because it's still too painful. All I know beyond the few photos I've seen as a child is they met years ago when he was visiting Iran on business, and she left to come to the United States with him only weeks later.

Something hits the center of my chest. It doesn't hurt. It

never does when he brings her up. It just feels incomplete, like a gaping hole that's never been filled, so I don't know what I'm supposed to be missing.

But beyond that feeling, there's something else sneaking into the moment. A whisper of opportunity, telling me to use his past with my mother to make him see that what he's asking from me isn't right. Isn't *fair*. If I can just get him to see things my way and open him up to the idea of Aidan and me.

I'd do almost anything *not* to have to depend on Julian.

"Tell me again how much you loved her," I say.

"I still love her." He blows out a breath, gripping my hand tighter for a moment before releasing it completely and leaning back in his chair. "Your mama is in everything I do. Every breath I take, every thought that crosses my mind." He pauses, and I soak in his look, the way his eyes are tense with longing and his soul seems tired and worn.

"Every time I look at you, I see so much of her," he continues. "She was a strong woman, and I'm proud to call her mine."

I swallow over the rocks in my throat, words begging to drip off my tongue. "Then, Baba, how can you ask this of me? How can you have the love you did with Mama and ask me to give up on that chance?"

His eyes grow dark and he shakes his head. "Your mama was the love of my life, but you're mistaken if you think we weren't arranged."

Shock pummels through my middle, the string of hope slipping through my grasp. "What?"

He nods, a slight cough pouring from his mouth. He tries to cover the noise by taking a sip of his tea. "Sometimes the greatest love comes from the most unlikely of places."

I sit back in my seat, not knowing what to do or what to say. This was my ace in the hole, the way I was going to segue into Aidan, into making my father see reason. But this whole time, his wish for me was borne from his own experience, not in spite of it.

"Don't you think it's possible that you and Mama were just lucky?" I try again, testing the waters without diving in headfirst.

He hums as he takes another drink of tea. "There are a lot of people in this world who would do anything to live the life you do."

"I know," I reply.

"Do you?" He tilts his head. "The blood in your veins makes you a very valuable person. People, even the ones you think you can trust, are blinded by greed and seduced by the promise of power."

My stomach tenses. "And the one you marry me off to won't be?"

"No," he replies simply. "I would never pair you with a man in need of money or power. Just someone who will treat you well and carry on my legacy. Someone who will protect you from the harsh world of my business and take care of you while he does, because I won't be here much longer to do it." He leans forward again, reaching out to pat the top of my hand with his. My eyes follow the movement, locking on the dark bruises from IVs that linger on his skin. "You've never let me down before, Yasmin. I know you won't let me down in this."

My eyes burn and I grit my teeth, but I don't speak up again, choosing instead to nod and flip my hand around, threading our fingers together. But my heart splits, desolation smashing against it like a wrecking ball because this means that Julian's already won, and I haven't even figured out what game he's playing.

I have to depend on him. I have to *need* him.

Just the way he wanted.

I expected Aidan to check in with me hours ago, but it's evening now, and he still hasn't. I'm soothing my anxiety, telling myself repeatedly that he's busy, and it's okay if we don't always talk. I left him on read for three days, so I know it's hypocritical for me to be mad. But I can't help how I feel. I chew on the inside of my cheek as I glance at my cell that I threw haphazardly on the mattress.

Maybe I should try to call him.

Moving from where I'm pacing a hole in the carpet of my room to the bed, I swipe my phone from the top and sit down, my leg brushing against the cream drapery hanging from the corner of my four-poster bed. I open immediately to my texts to Aidan. Still nothing.

I try to call him, the phone ringing in my ear one, two, three times before it's sent to voicemail.

My chest twists. I text again.

Me: Everything ok?

Silently, I stare at the screen, willing the three dots in a bubble to appear, showing me that he's responding. But watching the blank screen is like waiting for water to boil, so I groan, tossing my phone down again and walking over to the full-length mirror tucked in the corner of the room next to the bay window. My hair is thrown up in a messy bun, the large silk scrunchie doing a terrible job of keeping my curls contained, and I'm dressed down in my black sweats and a baggy shirt that says Oregon State across the chest. I look tired. Stressed. *Thank god for makeup.*

My phone pings and I spin quickly, rushing to my bed and

grabbing it, disappointment pricking the hope that was swelling in my chest like a popped balloon when I see it's Riya.

Riya: What's the word, bird?

She's my small sliver of light in this mess. It feels good having her on my side, finally not keeping secrets from her the way I have for years.

I spin around and take a selfie showcasing my sweats.

Me: Trying on outfits for my potential hubby. Think this one will work?
Riya: Wow. Really sticking it to the man there, Yas. You should break a couple nails to complete the look. Show them what they're getting with the daughter of Sultans.

I scoff, looking down at my almond-shaped red manicure, wincing at the thought of not having them well-maintained. *Pass.*

Someone knocks on my bedroom door, and I drop my phone and rush to answer it, hoping that somehow Aidan has slipped into my wing of the estate. But I know it's a pipe dream. Aidan *never* comes to my room. There're too many people who could see; it's too risky.

I swing the door open, and Julian is standing on the other side, his head cast down, inky black hair on full display, one of his arms propped against the right side of the doorframe. His eyes slowly move from the top of my bare feet, up my legs, over my baggy shirt, until he finally meets my gaze.

"Of course, it's you," I sneer.

"Ciao." His forearm flexes as he forces his way into my room, tattoos peeking out from beneath his rolled-up sleeve.

"Please." I wave my arm dramatically before shutting the door behind him. "Make yourself at home."

He plops down on my bed, his body bouncing slightly on the mattress. "Such a wonderful host. Do you always welcome men into your bed so lovingly?"

I squint my eyes, irritation stabbing at my middle like a dull knife. "Are you implying I'm a whore?"

His head jerks back. "That's a pretty wild conclusion to take from what I said. Are you sure you don't have something heavy weighing down your conscience? Guilt, perhaps, over your harlot ways?"

My cheeks puff out with my breath as I close my eyes and try to keep from walking over and smacking him in the face. "Are you sure you're thirty-six? You act like a prepubescent boy who isn't getting his way."

He doesn't reply this time, simply cocking his head, his dark eyes sparking as he stares at me with a maniacal grin on his face.

"Quit looking at me like that," I demand, fidgeting from his gaze. "Where is Aidan?"

His playful smirk drops, and he leans back on his elbows, the mattress bowing slightly underneath him. I cringe at the sight of him on my bed, side-eyeing the sheets and making a mental reminder to have them changed so they don't smell like him when I try to go to sleep.

He shrugs. "Busy packing, I assume."

My stomach drops. "I'm sorry, he's *what?*"

"He didn't tell you yet?" His face shows genuine surprise. "I'm sending him to Egypt with my assistant, Ian."

"He wouldn't leave without telling me," I reply.

"Of course not." His voice is sarcastic, and he stands, moving toward me, waving his arms in the air. "They're going to hunt down the lamp that will grant all your wishes, giving you both your happily ever after."

I back up, not wanting him to get close.

He smirks, his footsteps halting. "Are you *afraid* of me?"

"Please," I scoff. "Don't give yourself so much credit. I just know you have a nasty habit of coming into spaces where you're not wanted."

His smile drops completely then, and he walks forward, doing the exact thing I just told him he would. Getting into my space.

My breath hitches in my throat at the dangerous glint in his eyes, so similar to the fire that was burning in them the night he watched me get fucked by another man, and I curse my stupid, traitorous body for reacting to him at all.

He doesn't miss the action, and I hate the way it makes me feel like he, once again, has gained the upper hand.

"Oh, gattina." He chuckles, ghosting his finger down the apple of my cheek until he's cupping my jaw. "If I come, I promise, you'll be *begging* for it."

My heart trips.

"You better get used to me here," he continues. "Your father only has a couple of months left, and I'd hate to see what happens if you aren't under my protection once he's gone."

Maybe I should take more stock in the thinly veiled threat, but the words "couple of months" and "my father" in the same sentence have me suddenly struggling to breathe too much to focus on anything else.

I reach up, my hands brushing against his broad chest as I push him away.

He goes willingly, backing up a few paces and running his tongue over his bottom lip.

"What do you *mean*, a couple of months?" I force out.

"I mean your father is a very sick man, Yasmin. Or are you living in a delusional world where he isn't going to die any day?"

His words attack my chest like splinters, plunging deep and sharp. "I don't..." I shake my head, pressing the back of my hand to my overheated face. "He has more than a couple of months, Julian, please."

Julian blows out a breath, his eyes calculating, as though he's trying to decide whether I really believe what I'm saying. But why wouldn't I? I know he's sick and that he'll eventually get worse until he passes, but to pretend he's worse off than he is, it's just cruel. I know realistically, hospice is a six-month death sentence at best, but...a couple of months?

Slowly, Julian steps back in again, his hand reaching out and cupping my cheek, lifting my face until I meet his solemn stare. "He doesn't, gattina."

I blink rapidly to clear the sudden fogginess from my eyes, the warmth of his touch sending ripples of unexpected comfort through me.

The feeling catches me off guard and I rip my face away. "How the hell would *you* know?"

He smirks. "Upset that Daddy didn't tell you first? Looks like you're not the favorite after all."

I stuff down the storm that brews at his words and shake my head. "It doesn't make any sense. He wouldn't expect me to get married in..." I pause, my brows furrowing. "He only has *a couple of months*?"

Julian nods. "Listen, we can hope that Aidan will find the lamp in time. I'm sending him to Egypt with my best people. But if I haven't been able to uncover it by then…"

He trails off, but I know what he's saying. Odds are low that Aidan will find it at all, let alone within the amount of time we need.

"So I'm fucked," I deduce. "This is *your* fault. You're the one sending Aidan on this stupid mission that he isn't even qualified to be on instead of helping me find a better solution."

"You could always just tell your father the truth."

Silence rings through the air. That seems so simple, doesn't it? But after our meal together, the thought of it sends me into a tailspin. My breaths start coming quicker and my stomach cramps until I'm resisting the urge to physically curl into myself.

"I can't," I whisper.

Julian slips his hands into his pockets and rocks back on his heels. "There is another option." He shakes his head. "No, never mind. You wouldn't be interested."

Annoyed, I hiss, "Don't assume you know anything about me."

"Fine." His brows rise. "If Aidan doesn't find the lamp in time, you could marry *me* instead."

My mouth drops open in shock, and I stare at him blankly, waiting for the punchline. Only he doesn't give me one.

Uncontrolled laughter bubbles in my chest and surges up my throat, escaping into the air. "Are you kidding me right now? Why would I ever marry *you?*"

"I told you that you wouldn't be interested," he replies. "But it does make the most sense, in my opinion. You convince your father you're in love with me. It gets him off your back and keeps you from having to tie yourself to someone who's expecting the world."

I tilt my head and watch him. "And what about you?"

"What *about* me?" he replies.

"I mean…you're just willing to go along with it? I don't believe there's a selfless bone in your body, Julian Faraci. What do you get out of this? What's the trick?"

He tsks, shaking his head. "No tricks. Just me wanting to get Ali's attention off you and back on things that matter."

My chest cramps, but I push the jealousy over Julian's relationship with my father to the side. "I'm not marrying you."

"I'm not asking you to. I'm just saying we pretend. For a little while, until the boy returns with the lamp. Unless, of course, you'd rather be paraded in front of suitors until your father takes his last breath."

"And when he wants a wedding before then?" I ask.

Julian grins. "Then we give him one. Doesn't mean it has to be signed on the dotted line."

What he's saying is ridiculous, but I can't deny the idea has some merit. I open my mouth to respond, but no words come out, because I genuinely have no clue what to say.

He wants to *pretend*.

Make believe that I'm in love with Julian? The thought alone makes me want to choke.

But what other choice do I have? I already know that my father has been setting up suitors, and I'm not naive enough to think that Julian wouldn't know the ins and outs of his plans, especially knowing that my father confided in *him* over the extent of his illness when he won't even let me be on the sidelines giving support.

My stomach cramps when it sinks in that *Julian* was the one who told me about my father, when I was just with him this morning and got nothing but silence and a pat on the hand.

I suck in a stuttered breath, steeling my spine for what I know I have to do.

I can't fall out of my father's favor, not when there's so much at stake, but if I have to go on dates like I'm a prized broodmare, I think I might lose my mind.

And it's just pretend.

I can fake anything for a while. Especially if I know I'll get Aidan in the end.

Julian walks toward me, using his fingers to tip my mouth shut. "Think about it. You know where to find me. But I'd urge you not to waste too much time, because you don't have very much left."

CHAPTER 10

Julian

THE FIRST TIME I THOUGHT ABOUT MURDERING somebody, I was five years old.

There had been an antsy energy swirling in my stomach all day, even though my papà had disappeared over a week ago, which meant the house was calm for the first time in my life.

When he wasn't around to beat Mamma, then she didn't have any reason to beat *me*.

It was peaceful.

But I wasn't used to the feeling of not being on edge, and the peace was a foreign sensation filling up my body, one that caused my fight-or-flight mode to go on the fritz, just waiting for the other shoe to drop.

Mamma was in the kitchen making my nonna's famous marinara, her shiny hair pulled tight in a low bun like it always was and a white apron wrapped around her with red trim and strawberries decorated along the front.

She didn't normally wear such light colors, and the contrast of the apron against her tan skin and dark hair made her look almost ethereal to me. I remember being confused that she wore the white apron so easily, when I had heard her complain so many times before about how difficult it was to scrub out bloodstains from light fabric.

But that day, she put it on without a care, resting it over her cream top, and she handed me my favorite teddy bear, Abe—the one Papà always yelled at me for having—thrusting it into my hands and humming under her breath as she danced along to the radio and stirred seasonings into a pot.

I stared down at Abe, the seams unraveling on his ear from me pulling him out of his hidden spot beneath my bed and sleeping with him curled in my arms every night, and pure happiness filled my chest. Maybe Papà was right, and boys shouldn't have teddy bears, but I didn't care.

If Mamma was wearing white and I had my favorite stuffie out in the open, maybe he really *was* gone for good.

But as soon as the good feeling showed up, it was overshadowed by the thick and jagged feeling of anxiety that coated my insides, imagining how quickly things could change.

Still, the days continued to pass without a beating in sight, and little by little, I let my guard down. The fight-or-flight feeling receded, and I realized that maybe good things really *do* stick around if you wish for them hard enough.

But I was a silly child.

One night, after about two weeks of bliss, it ended.

I was lying in bed, listening to random cars honk on the busy city streets outside our small apartment, holding Abe close to my chest. I was *so* close to falling asleep until the sound of a car got closer.

Too close.

My heart jolted, dread pouring through my stomach like thick sludge.

A car door slammed.

I shot out of bed, heading immediately toward Mamma's room, but right before I hit the hallway, I glanced down at Abe, who was gripped tightly in my fist. Sadness filled up my throat and bloomed behind my eyes. Taking him would only cause more problems. I spun around quickly, racing back to my bed and shoving him in the small space between the slats of my mattress frame, hiding him from view, and then sprinted to Mamma's room.

It wasn't new, me going to her room to try to protect her from him. For some reason, he never took his anger out on *me*, so I'd stay next to Mamma whenever I could, hoping that my presence would be enough to keep her from turning black and blue.

Sometimes it worked.

Other times, I'd have to lie still with my eyes closed, pretending I didn't hear him drag her away from me while his fists met her flesh and her whimpers hit my ears.

That night, I threw open her door, closing it behind me just as the front screen slammed open and shut. My breaths quickened as I ran to her bed, stopping at the side.

She was awake. Her body was still as stone and her head was flat on the pillow, but her dark gaze was locked on me.

"Mamma," I whispered, my eyes wide.

Silently, she stretched out her arms toward me.

And like every other time before and all the times after, I went, curling into her embrace and allowing her to hold me close.

I was her shield the same way I was often her burden, holding the weight of her pain that she couldn't bear alone.

Heavy footsteps rumbled through the tiny apartment,

making the seconds feel like hours, until they stopped right outside the closed bedroom door.

Mamma's grip tightened around my small frame, her breaths ghosting across the back of my neck.

The door opened and Papà walked in.

"Anita…" His voice trailed off, and silence draped across the room like a weighted blanket.

I slammed my eyes shut, pretending to be asleep and praying that he wouldn't hear my heart thudding heavily against my chest. But I could feel his eyes on me even when I couldn't see.

He sighed deeply, and then he turned around and left, the muted sound of local television bleeding through the thin walls.

Slowly, my sweaty palms opened from where they were curled into fists, and my breathing evened out.

Mamma was safe from him, which meant *I* was safe from her.

At least for that one night.

I spent days after praying he would leave again. But he never did, and that small bit of happiness that had taken root inside me curdled and began to rot until it was nothing more than a pipe dream. After a while, it became something I couldn't even grasp the memory of.

So I held on to a vision instead. One where I was bigger and stronger than Papà and could make sure he never hurt Mamma again. I started sneaking off down the street to watch the hapkido classes until one day the instructor opened the door and let me come inside. I was never *technically* enrolled in the courses, so I never got a belt. Never had someone there to cheer me on. But I didn't care about the accolades. I just wanted to feel strong. Powerful. Like I could protect myself and Mamma from the people who wanted to hurt us most.

I didn't understand fully back then that it was my mother who was actually causing the deepest wounds. I only knew that she was *mine* and that meant I had to take care of her, because that's what you're supposed to do for people you love.

You choose them. You put them first.

And then one day, I *did* become bigger than my father. Stronger than him. And he made the mistake of gifting me my most prized possession to celebrate the fact.

A python for my sixteenth birthday. The only gift he's ever given me, in honor of me becoming a man.

"You know the thing about snakes?" he'd said. "They're feared. And that makes them powerful."

I named her Isabella.

And then I stole one of the wooden staffs from the hapkido dojo and used it to beat him until he couldn't stand.

One strike for every bruise he put on Mamma.

Another for every bruise she put on me.

I dragged him out to the back alley in the middle of the night, put rats on his broken body, and let Isabella out to play. She sniffed out her prey with her tongue, mistaking him for food, courtesy of the rodents, and started to curl her scaly body around him. I stood back and watched, twirling the staff around in my hand, enjoying the way his blood vessels burst and his eyes bulged as she coiled around his neck, squeezing until he died.

"Don't worry, Papà. It will only hurt for a little."

And you know what? In the end, he was right. I did feel powerful.

I got my first tattoo in honor of the moment so I'd never forget the feeling. A replica of Isabella, starting at my hand and curling up my arm.

The biggest lesson my father taught me was that in all things, you must have patience.

Something that's becoming increasingly hard for me to remember with every day that goes by and we're no closer to finding the lost lamp.

I stare at the email on my computer from Jeannie, our head archaeologist in Egypt, as Isabella curls around my shoulders, the disappointment feeling thick like sludge.

Mr. Faraci,
Nothing yet on the lost lamp, although I'm going to check
out a new dig spot one of the locals told me about. It's
in the middle of the Western Desert and is off-limits to
civilians, so I'd rather go alone and scope the area. If I take
people with me, we're going to draw attention and we
definitely don't want that.
But I didn't want to do it without you knowing, and
since Tinashe left yesterday to go back to his home, I didn't
know how else to reach you directly outside of email.
Hope you don't mind. I'll keep you updated.
—Jeannie Grants

I don't mind, but this proves that I need to get Ian and the boy out there, if for no other reason than to have Ian overseeing things since Tinashe is needed elsewhere.

Sighing, I close the screen and reach up, running my hand along the top of Isabella's head. She feels warm and dry, and her tongue flicks out as she nuzzles into my palm.

"You're a good girl," I coo.

Despite the fact that she was a gift from my father, Isabella has become the most important living being in my life. She's loyal to a fault, and she cleans up my dirty work, aiding me in my kills and swallowing them for dinner whenever the opportunity should arise.

She doesn't talk back, and she doesn't ask for much, but she can give love in the way only an animal can. By providing a gentle, calm companionship that doesn't expect anything outlandish in return.

I feel guilty that I haven't been spending as much time with her as I should.

Standing up, the weight of her body heavy on my shoulders as I do, I walk out of my home office and up the staircase until I'm in the hallway where my bedroom sits, going to the room next door and placing Isabella back in her enclosure, which runs along the entirety of the far wall.

"I'll be bringing home a new friend," I tell her. "So play nice. She's a *friend*, not food."

Isabella ignores me, curling up in the bottom of her enormous glass cage.

I spin around but then pause before leaving, adding one last thing.

"She's temporary, so don't get attached."

I rap my knuckles against the heavy oak door of Ali's home office, then twist the handle to walk in, expecting to see him working hard behind his desk. We have a new line of Christmas jewelry that's a few months out from dropping, and I sent him the mock-ups for approval. What he doesn't know is they're already approved and on their way to our advertising team, but that's something he can live without finding out.

Since he's been in hospice, I've been sending him details of things after having already taken care of them, just to make sure he still feels like he's being useful.

If I were in his position, it'd be what I would want someone to do for me. It's hard enough accepting death; feeling as though you're useless while you're still around would be a bitter pill to swallow.

Instead, I see him sprawled out on the sofa in the far corner of the room, his hospice nurse, Shaina, at his side.

"What's wrong?" I ask, walking over quickly.

Shaina shakes her head, shushing me as she moves around the bed to check his vitals.

Ali's eyes are closed, which causes a twinge of panic to pinch my gut. I sweep my gaze over him, locking on the even rise and fall of his chest, and then shake off the feeling, reminding myself once again that it's a *good* thing for me if he's closer to death.

"What's wrong?" I repeat, more forceful this time.

"I'm okay," he rasps. "I just…I'm feeling a little tired today."

Nodding, I purse my lips and turn my attention back to Shaina. "Get out."

She lets out a humorless laugh and shakes her head again before standing up straight. "You better check your tone with me, Mr. Faraci. I don't work for you."

Annoyance at her disrespect winds its way through me, and I have to blow out a steady breath to calm down the burning energy that's filling me up, urging me to lash out. *She's doing her job.*

"It's fine, Shaina. Give us a few minutes," Ali replies, his bloodshot eyes peeling open.

She purses her lips before sighing. "I'll go make you some tea to settle your stomach. *You,*" she says, turning to me. "Don't do anything to raise his blood pressure, you understand? He needs *rest*."

I nod curtly.

She quirks a brow before finally spinning around and leaving us alone.

I walk across the room and grab one of the chairs sitting in front of his desk, dragging it until it's placed by the couch, and then sit down, leaning forward with my elbows on my knees.

"Shaina's overprotective," he complains.

"She's doing her job," I reply, the same reassurance I just gave myself.

He scoffs. "I can work just fine."

I shoot forward when he moves, placing a hand on his back and propping up the pillows behind him.

"It's Sunday," I say, urging him back down. "And nothing I have to tell you is more important than you getting the rest you need."

He shakes his head, a cough surging through his throat, although he tries to smother it. "I don't have time for this. There's someone coming for dinner tonight to meet Yasmin."

Leaning forward in my seat, I lower my voice. "I hate to be the one to tell you this, old man, but...you don't have time left in general."

Ali laughs. "You're a prick."

I chuckle as I lean back in my seat. "The point is, you should save your energy for things that matter."

The amusement drops from his face, and he twists to meet my gaze. "This is important, Julian. I want to know Yasmin is taken care of, by a man who won't tarnish our name and everything I'm leaving behind."

I blow out a breath, running a hand over my hair, a little taken aback that he's stating it so plainly. That he doesn't even care how much it might burn that he isn't leaving anything for *me*. "Okay… so I'll go for you."

Ali laughs, and my fingers flex to keep from balling into fists.

"What's so funny about that?" I ask. "Who better to make sure someone won't tarnish what you've built?" I lean in. "We both know I keep Sultans running smooth, Ali. You can trust me with your daughter the same way you trust me with your diamonds."

Ali opens and closes his mouth a few times before finally nodding his agreement. "His name is Alexander Sokolov."

"Russian?"

He nods.

"Are you sure that's smart?"

I don't need to elaborate, because we both know what I mean. Russia is our biggest competitor in the diamond trade and the one country where we haven't gained a stronghold. I'm sure Ali is attempting to kill two birds with one stone here, aligning his daughter with a husband who can get Sultans in the door finally and be knowledgeable about the business enough to take over all the shares.

And that's unacceptable to me.

"Make sure she gives him a fair chance," Ali says. "I want them to hit it off, Julian. He's a good match for her. And a good match for Sultans."

Smiling, I rest a foot over the opposite knee. "I promise, Ali. I'll make sure she knows *exactly* what kind of man he is."

CHAPTER 11

Yasmin

Aidan: Can I see you tonight?

It's the first I've heard from him since yesterday afternoon when he went to meet with Julian. I can't be mad at him for it, since then I'd be a hypocrite, so this is just something like karmic retribution. But it does sting to know that he agreed to go somewhere and do something that affects us both without talking to me.

Did he tell his mother first?

Me: Yes!! I have dinner with my father, but I can sneak away when I get back.

Chewing on my lip, I debate telling him that it's with a suitor or that Julian is now trying to get me involved in a fake engagement with him for whatever reason, but I hold back, figuring that I can just let him know once we're together. Things like this usually go over better in person anyway.

Aidan: I'll be waiting, princess. I love you. Have a good
dinner with your dad.

Groaning, the guilt surges like it always does these days
whenever I have something I'm not telling Aidan.

"What the hell kind of noise was *that*?" Riya asks, laughing
from where she's sprawled in the middle of my four-poster bed,
flipping through a magazine.

"I don't know what to do." I sigh, pressing my finger to the
side of my eye and running kohl-black eyeliner against my lid.

Riya makes a humming noise, the judgment pouring through
her vocal cords and tugging at me from across the room.

I pause, my hand halting as I glance at her from my vanity
mirror. "What?"

She licks her finger before flipping a page in the magazine.
"Nothing."

My chest smarts. "That's *so* fucking annoying, you know
that, right?"

She cackles, dropping the magazine entirely and sitting up
in the middle of the mattress. "*Excuse* me, bitch? Forgive me for
trying to spare your hurt feelings. Trust and believe you won't like
what I've got to say."

I smirk as I finish the winged eyeliner, moving on to grab
mascara. "When has that ever stopped you before?"

"Fine." She smacks her thighs, moving to the edge of the bed.
"You're being dramatic as *fuck*, Yasmin. You're playing this 'woe is
me' card when all you really need to do is tell your dad how you feel."

A sick feeling sinks in my gut. She was right. I should have
let her keep her mouth shut. "I've told you it's not that simple."

She lifts both of her hands in the air like she's weighing

something in her palms. "Tell your dad the truth, or shackle yourself to a stranger." She shrugs. "Seems pretty simple to me."

I shake my head. "And have him react by firing Aidan and his mom, throwing them out on the streets? Making it so that I'd never see him again? No thanks."

She lets out a humorless chuckle before standing up and walking across the room until she's hovering behind me in the vanity mirror. Her hands reach out, squeezing my shoulders, our eyes meeting in the reflection. "If *anyone* understands you, it's me. You think I want to be in law school? That my lifelong dream is to become a lawyer? Forced academic marriage is its own type of hell that I wouldn't wish on anyone. If I didn't think my dad would cut me off, leaving me destitute on the streets somewhere, I would be doing literally anything else."

Her brows are high on her forehead, and I shrink into myself, feeling bad that I even thought for a second she wouldn't get it. We're cut from the same cloth, just with different parents and different visions of what they wanted for their daughters. Where my father is in diamonds, Riya's is in oil. My father wants me married and barefoot in the kitchen. Riya's wants her to become a "force of power" in the world.

I reach back and grip her fingers. "Yeah, but...I think you'd probably tell your father about Aidan just to see the disappointment on his face. I'm not like that, Riya. I don't want him to hate me."

"Can't argue with you there." She winks, squeezing my shoulder. "But in this situation? I'd probably marry Julian Faraci just so I could get free rides on what I'm sure is his monster cock for the rest of my life."

A laugh pours out of me, and I shrug out of her grasp, scrunching my nose. "Bleh. Pass."

"Well…you *do* still have a choice. You either wait for Aidan to do whatever it is he's doing to win your dad over, or you control what little you can."

"Choosing between Julian and a random stranger is hardly a positive outlook," I reply, dread pricking me like needles.

She leans forward, her arm brushing mine as she grabs a matte lipstick from my vanity. "At least with Julian, you know what you're getting into. And if nothing else, pretending to be with him buys you some time, right?"

My stomach twists until it aches, and I bite the corner of my cheek.

"I don't envy you, sister. Here." She hands me the lipstick. "Wear the red. It's a power color."

I've been at the restaurant 1001 Arabian Nights for the past fifteen minutes, trying to work up the courage to go inside and meet my first official suitor.

Maybe I'm overthinking things. My anxiety has always bled into my decisions, making the worst possible outcome take center stage in my brain, but despite how much I try to work through the situation, it doesn't make it any more palatable. It's like the farther I dig the hole, the longer the climb out is, and somewhere along the way, I've lost my voice completely, becoming docile. a mute trophy for people to lug around.

Eventually I work up the courage to head inside, wondering idly if my father is already there. I thought we were driving together, but when I slipped into the car waiting at the front of the estate, it took off without him.

The turquoise silk dress is soft against my thighs as I exit the car, my heels aching as soon as I take my first step onto the sidewalk. The stilettos are an unfortunate discomfort that I couldn't pass up because they match the outfit so well. There's a small chill in the air, making goose bumps sprout along my skin.

This restaurant is known for its high-end clientele and pricey menu, so I'm not surprised to see a doorman holding open the door as I make my way inside. When I step into the building, the rich smells hit my nostrils. Distant sounds of clinking from plates and the low murmur of voices from the other patrons assault my senses and make my palms sweat.

I swallow back the unease of being in a crowded public place and walk toward the hostess stand, noticing the pretty blond girl with a bored look on her face and a white button-up with a small black bow tie around the collar.

Her eyes lock on mine, but before I can say a word, someone touches my lower back, sending a shock through my body. I jolt immediately, twisting around and coming face-to-face with Julian.

I roll my eyes, sidestepping his touch. "Of course you're here. Being my father's lap dog again?"

The corners of his lips twitch as he moves to stand beside me, his hand coming back but this time wrapping around my hip possessively and pulling me into him.

My stomach flips.

Jerk.

The hostess beams up at him, her eyes glazing over when he flashes her a dazzling smile. "Mr. Faraci."

I roll my eyes again, because *of course* he comes here enough to be recognized.

"Andrea, you're looking beautiful. I believe we have a gentleman waiting for us already by the name of Alexander Sokolov."

I watch him from my peripheral vision, annoyed that he's putting on such a show, acting all suave and charming when he's anything but.

The hostess—*Andrea*—glances down at her computer system and then back up. "He's already here. I'll take you both back."

We start to follow her, but it's difficult to walk with the way Julian's arm is *still* around my waist, making me stick to him like glue.

"Quit touching me," I murmur out of the side of my mouth. "You look like a skeevy predator."

It's not true. He looks incredible, and any other woman would most likely be thrilled to be seen on his arm regardless of the age difference, but I'll die before I admit it out loud.

He glances down at me as we walk. "And you look fucking sinful in that outfit. I'm not allowing anyone to think you're here by yourself."

My brows shoot to my hairline, the shock of his words making me lose any retort I had. Did he just *compliment* me? Backhanded, of course, because I can take care of myself, but still, I don't think he's ever so much as said thank you, so this is a shift in demeanor I wasn't expecting.

It puts me on edge, this stark one-eighty in his personality, and despite what he seems to think, I'm not clueless. I know he's buttering me up, trying to play the angle of a doting fiancé.

"You make me sick," I hiss.

His fingers tighten around me, squeezing so lightly I'm not sure if I imagined it, and then we're at the table and a tall blond man with broad shoulders and a dark suit is rising from his seat, his gaze flickering to Julian and then to his arm around my waist before they stop on me.

I shift in my spot, uncomfortable with the attention. It feels slimy, like I'm a prize he's set his eyes on and is determined to win. I stand there in limbo, wondering if I should introduce myself or sit down first, and then the choice is taken from me as Julian pulls out the chair next to me, prodding me lightly so I move to sit. He waits until I'm settled, his hand never leaving the back of the chair, and then he pushes me in.

My mind spins at the chivalry, and my eyes narrow up at him. *I know your tricks, asshole.*

He moves to sit next to me and props his ankle on his opposite knee, adopting a casual air as he waves over a waiter and orders a Glenlivet neat and a glass of cabernet for me.

Maybe I should be annoyed that he ordered for me, but the truth is that public places and people I've never met make me uneasy, and by the end of the night, I always have a headache from masking my anxiety and holding my jaw too tightly. The direction from him is soothing, and I hate to admit it makes me relax, even just the tiniest bit.

"Where's my father?" I ask, suddenly realizing he still isn't here.

"That's a good question," the man across the table cuts in. "I was under the impression I'd be meeting not only Ali's beautiful daughter"—his eyes run up my torso, resting on my breasts before meeting my gaze—"but also Ali himself."

Julian hums deep in his throat just as his drink is placed in front of him. He reaches out and grips the glass tumbler, the black ink on the back of his hand flexing with his fingers. "Things change. Now you get to meet *me*."

CHAPTER 12

Julian

ONCE I MADE MYSELF KNOWN TO BE THERE IN ALI'S stead, I expected Alexander's countenance to change. For him to become more pliable and willing to grovel at my feet the way so many others do. Possibly for recognition to dawn in his eyes.

But if anything, the ire behind his gaze only grew.

"And who are *you?*" he asks haughtily.

"He's the bane of my existence," Yasmin pipes in.

I flash her a grin before focusing again on the man across the table who's trying to take what I've decided is mine.

"Or I guess you could call him my father's bitch, if that's more your speed."

My teeth grit until my molars ache at the disrespect, and if I didn't need her to experience what life would be like if she ended up with this idiot, I'd lash out, maybe drown her in a bathtub so I wouldn't have to hear her speak again.

"Forgive Yasmin," I say. "Despite her obvious beauty and rather large inheritance, she still has a nasty habit of being jealous."

Yasmin lets out a bark of laughter.

I turn my face toward her, tsking before I turn back to Alexander. "Hope you can handle it. Alexander Sokolov, I'm guessing?"

He nods stiffly, tapping his thick fingers on the table. "Yes."

"Interesting last name," I continue. "Russian?"

His jaw locks, eyes narrowing on me. "Correct."

I nod, throwing an arm around the back of Yasmin's chair. "Fascinating to have you so...*invested* in Ali's daughter."

"Mr. Faraci," a voice interrupts. I look over to see the hostess who led us to the table standing next to me with an apologetic look on her face. "So sorry to interrupt, but you had a call. A Mr. Godard requesting you call him back as soon as possible. He said he's tried to reach your phone."

I nod, irritated that Ian called the fucking restaurant when he knows I'm busy.

"Julian Faraci," Alexander says, recognition flashing over his face. "Of course. I've heard so much about you."

I hum because I'm sure he has. "If you'll excuse me, this will only take a moment."

Standing up from the table, I make my way through the hallway directly behind us and out the back exit to the private alley. It's a quiet night, other than the sound of cars rushing past on the street out front, and the stars shine brightly in the sky.

I glance up, noticing the full moon and how it spreads light across the cracks of the black pavement.

Withdrawing my phone from my pocket, I call Ian.

"Boss."

"You're already wasting my time."

"I thought you were just having dinner with the girl."

"Yes, and she's *important*."

There's a long stretch of silence.

"Ian, you're testing my patience."

"I know, I know," he rushes out. "But *this* is important. Tinashe's been blowing up my phone. He said Darryn Anders knows we're in their territory in Egypt, looking for the lost lamp. He isn't happy."

Annoyance bleeds through my posture as I toss my head back to stare at the sky, suddenly remembering that Tinashe tried to tell me about Darryn the other day before Ian cut him off and I hung up the phone.

"Christ, this is what we pay Tinashe for," I say. "To take care of these things before they become bigger issues."

Darryn Anders is an obnoxious man who has lots of money and lots of time on his hands. He's well known in the black market antiquity trade and is one of the main oppositions to people looking for the lost lamp. He's been doing several digs in Egypt over the past few years, and if he's upset that we're there and, even worse, knows we're looking for the lamp, then he could create problems for both me and Sultans.

And personally speaking, he's a prick and demands subservience from everyone he meets. I'm not inclined to give it to him, so I try to avoid direct contact whenever possible.

Sighing, I pinch the bridge of my nose. "Okay, I'll handle it. Is everything set to go with you and the boy?"

"Yeah," Ian replies. "We're on a plane tomorrow morning." He pauses, and before he even speaks again, I know what he's going to say. "I wish you'd let me stay with you. I don't do well in the desert. It's *uncomfy.*"

"You'd get in my way," I say back. "I need to focus on Yasmin, not on making sure you're comfortable. Egypt is where I need you."

"Who's going to run Sultans while I'm gone? You're prepared to go to all the meetings you hate and listen to all the bullshit instead of having me recap the important pieces after?"

"You hired Ciara, did you not?" I snap, irritated that he thinks *he* does anything close to running Sultans.

A deep sigh comes over the line. "Okay, boss."

Hanging up before he can say anything else, I walk back inside to where we were before, planning to try to hurry the dinner along so I can call Tinashe and make sure that Darryn won't be a problem, but I stop before I hit the table, shrouding myself in the shadows as I listen in on their conversation.

"I hope you don't mind," Alexander says, nodding to the plate of food that sits in the center of the table. "Do you enjoy oysters, Yasmin?"

She scrunches her nose, staring at the food like it's about to attack her. "No, I don't really like seafood."

Alexander tsks. "You should try this anyway. You might surprise yourself. You know," he continues, wiggling his brows, "they're quite the aphrodisiac. Maybe if you had a couple, you'd loosen up some."

Yasmin's spine stiffens.

It's surprising how much I enjoy seeing her body language shift and change right before she explodes. For the longest time, I didn't think she had the capability to speak out of turn. She was brought up with decorum bred into her bones, and she usually holds her tongue well, but once she came home from college, I noticed a shift. A spark that's simmering just beneath the surface, begging to be let out.

I should hate it, but I constantly find myself prodding the kindling instead, seeing if I can make it catch fire.

"That's hardly an appropriate conversation to have with a stranger," she snips back.

He laughs. "Please, save your faux outrage. I'm about to effectively *buy* you, sweetheart. Which, speaking of, when you have my last name, little outfits like these"—he waves his hand toward Yasmin—"are a no-go. I appreciate the view, but it's bad for my image. You're far too wealthy to dress so trashy, and my wife won't be flaunting herself around like a slut."

Fire bleeds behind Yasmin's eyes, her hands drawing into fists on top of the white linen table.

Good. Let her see what happens if she chooses to allow her father to pimp her out this way.

That being said, I can't allow the disrespect to stand. While I don't personally care if she's offended, she *is* here with me, and he's a fool to think I'll allow anyone under my protection to be talked down to. Besides, I've had enough of these games.

For some reason, this little twit of a girl breaks apart all my logic, splaying me open until I'm vulnerable and greedy, wanting immediate satisfaction and not being able to stop myself from demanding it.

I could continue to try and fight the desire, but honestly, my energy will be better used if I give in and adjust my plan to fit my needs. And my needs are suddenly screaming at me to make sure she knows that she has no choice when it comes to who she marries.

She'll choose me, or she'll learn what happens to the people who don't.

Bringing my phone up to my ear, I call her driver, telling him to pull around to the front, and then I make my way back to the table, bypassing my seat and placing my hand in front of her.

"Up," I say.

She looks at me with confusion, staring at my hand. "What?"

I shrug. "We're leaving. Unless you'd rather stay here, of course."

"No, I…" She trails off, looking back and forth between the two of us, before she slips her soft hand in mine.

I pull her to a stand and grab the shawl off the back of her chair, my fingertips ghosting across the skin of her collarbone as I wrap it around her shoulders.

"Unfortunately, Alexander, something's come up and Yasmin needs to leave. But stick around for a minute, yeah? I've got something for you."

He nods, waving us off with the confidence of a man who thinks he's already locked in the deal as he takes a sip of his whiskey.

I place my hand on Yasmin's back, leading her through the tables and out to the front where her driver is waiting.

"Don't *ever* bark demands at me like I'm a dog again," she spits when we reach the car, spinning toward me.

"Save your breath for someone who cares, gattina." I step in close, the tips of my loafers hitting her shoes, and I reach out, swiping a piece of her curly hair off her forehead. "If I tell you to sit, you'll sit. If I tell you to jump, you'll ask how high. If I want you to spin around in circles, then drop to your knees and suck my cock until I paint your pouty lips with my cum, you'll do it with a smile on your vapid face." Her mouth parts, and my thumb presses into her bottom lip as I lean in close. "And do you know why?"

"Because you're delusional?" she snips.

I chuckle. "Because if you don't, I'll stop being so generous and leave you to the likes of Mr. Sokolov inside. I bet he can't wait to try out the goods for himself. He seems like the kind of man who likes to taste test before he buys the whole meal."

She sucks in a gasp, her eyes growing wide with horror. "You wouldn't."

"Wouldn't I?"

Releasing her face, I reach behind her to pull on the door handle and push her into the car. I lean my arm on the hood and peer in. "Be safe getting home, Yasmin. It's dark out there. I'd hate for anything bad to happen."

I close the door behind her and watch as her driver pulls the car out into traffic. Then I spin around and make my way back inside to deal with *Alexander.*

"Everything okay?" he asks when I get back to the table.

I adopt a sympathetic look on my face, pulling my brows in and pursing my lips slightly. "Everything's fine. Yasmin just had some family matters she needed to deal with. You understand."

Alexander runs a hand over his blond mop of hair before nodding, his shoulders slumping. "We didn't even get to the main course."

Shaking my head, I reach out to pat him on the shoulder, although the touch makes my muscles want to shrivel up beneath my skin. "No worries. I'll make sure we take care of the staff."

It's not what he cares about, but propriety means he can't say anything without looking like even more of a tool, so he just nods and rises from the table, watching while I pull out the money clip from my back pocket and throw a small stack of hundreds down, enough to cover what was served plus a generous tip. I stop short when I see Yasmin's phone left on her seat at the table and dip down quickly to pick it up, sliding it into my pocket before following Alexander out of the restaurant.

Once we're outside, he hands his ticket to the valet. He rests his elbow on the valet stand, shifting slightly every few seconds from foot to foot while we wait, clearly uncomfortable with the silence of the night and the fact that I'm not filling it with conversation.

"I've heard of you," he notes.

"Oh?"

I slip my hands in my pockets and glance around, noting how the crowds outside are starting to thin. My fingers caress the metal of my staff as I glance back down at the fool who thought he'd get Yasmin's hand in marriage and ownership of the business that's mine in every way except for name.

"Unfortunately, I can't say the same."

It's not completely a lie. However, I did look him up the moment I left Ali, learning that Alexander Sokolov is the grandson of Oleg Sokolov, who up until three years ago was the minister of industry and trade in Russia.

Alexander doesn't have much of a name for himself, but his family ties are enough to make him important. Definitely enough to help Sultans barter deals with the Russian diamond trade in a way we've been cut off from in the past.

But it's risky, and I'm surprised Ali was so open to the idea of handing over the entirety of Sultans' shares to a man who could easily tear down his legacy and sell it off bit by bit.

A black Lamborghini with yellow trim and matte black wheels pulls around, revving like butter as it idles in front of us.

My brows lift, although I'm not truly impressed. I couldn't care less about cars; they're more hassle than they're worth.

I whistle. "This yours?"

Alexander beams, his smile blinding. "You ever seen one in person before?"

Shaking my head, I take a step forward, watching out of the corner of my eye while the valet lifts the doors until they look like wings and walks around the back of the car to hand Alexander the key. "Can't say that I have. I've always wanted one though."

Lies.

He stops, his face gaining a haughty look. "Not surprising. This is a limited edition. Only twenty of these coupes were ever made."

"I've got an Audi R8, but I bet this baby *purrs*."

He's such a slow thinker that I can *see* his brain working, his eyes shifting back and forth and his jaw twitching as he tries to work out something in his head.

"Want to take her for a spin?" He angles his face down. "As a passenger, of course."

My finger presses harshly into the metal of my staff still tucked away in my pocket, and I smile. "I thought you'd never ask."

CHAPTER 13

Yasmin

NO MATTER WHICH WAY I LOOK AT THINGS, IT ALL feels hopeless. Up until now, I've always had an out to this shitty situation, one that I didn't want to use but was still there as security, lingering in the background in case I needed to cave.

Maybe I should run straight to my baba's room right now and tell him everything, specifically the part where his pride and joy right-hand man, Julian, basically implied he'd let someone fuck me just to "test the goods."

But would he even believe it?

While he's *my* baba, I've spent a large majority of my life tucked away in boarding school and then university. Julian's been by his side every single day for almost a decade.

The thought of telling my father and having him not believe me or, worse, siding with Julian instead is like razor blades slicing through my insides.

And then there's Aidan. Sweet, perfect Aidan who has never done *anything* other than fall in love with the wrong woman. I can't help but feel like his life would be so much better if it weren't for me. I'll spend every second of tonight trying to convince him *not* to go to Egypt. Not to get involved with my father's company. We can figure out another way.

There's a part of me that wants to pick up the phone and vomit out everything to Riya. I know she's going to ask how tonight went, but this isn't something she can know. I've already dragged her into my bullshit enough, and knowing her, she'd try to do something wild to help and not let me handle things.

Besides, until this is resolved, I can't take the chance of putting her on Julian's radar. She's just another person he'd be able to weaponize against me, and I'm trying to lower his power over me, not increase it.

I shrug back on my oversize sweats and baggy Oregon State shirt, feeling a sense of comfort and familiarity being cozy in them while everything else in my life feels like it's spinning out of control.

Taking a deep breath, I try to focus on what I *can* control.

I can tell my father the truth about Julian's schemes and then about Aidan and me, even though the thought of it sends nausea rolling like a tide through my gut. I can say no to Alexander Sokolov. What an absolute pig. I'd rather stab myself in the eye than waste another second with him. I could take Julian up on his offer and fake an engagement with him to buy time.

But even as I think through all my choices, I know the best course of action is to suck it up and make an adult decision for *myself*, for once in my life, and accept the consequences of my actions regardless of what they might be.

Which means I need to make sure Aidan doesn't get on that plane.

I don't bother to unpin my hair from the style I had it in for dinner, leaving both that and my full face of makeup on as I rush out of my bedroom and down the hallways. It's quiet and dark, the only light coming from the underlit canvases hanging proudly on the walls and the motion sensor night lights that cast a dim glow when I walk by. I make it to the staircase that separates my wing from my father's, and right when I'm about to go down the steps and head to the staff rooms, I pivot, deciding to just peek in on Baba to make sure he's okay.

Bypassing the stairs, I head to the door to his bedroom, knocking and leaning my ear against the wood to see if I can hear him on the other side. My heart cinches tight in my chest when nobody responds, and my breaths start to come quicker.

I'm sure he's fine.

Maybe I should check just to be sure.

Sucking in a breath and holding it so I don't make too much noise, I reach out and grip the doorknob, slowly turning it until it unlatches and creaks open. I peek my head in to see him lying motionless in the middle of his king-size bed in the expansive room.

He's tucked under the red and gold covers, and it's not until I see the steady rise and fall of his chest that I let out the breath, nodding to myself as I close the door again, the soft click of the latch reverberating in my ears.

He's okay, just sleeping. He's fine. Everything's okay.

I hesitate before walking away, a large part of me aching to run into his room and wake him up, allow him to comfort me, because for most of my life, he was the only person in the world who could, but I stop myself. It would be selfish, and he needs his rest. And I need to speak to Aidan before I make any rash decisions anyway. If I see my father now, when I'm high-strung and anxious, feeling like I'm spiraling with no way out, then I'm afraid the words will pour from my mouth whether I want them to or not. One look at me and he'd ask what was wrong, and I wouldn't be able to hold back, breaking apart at the seams like a little girl who needs the comfort only her father can provide.

I make my way down to the staff wing and walk by all the closed doors, picturing the faces of the people who have worked and lived in our estate for most of my life. It hits me that I've never taken the time to get to know any of them outside of Aidan.

All these years, and I've never even taken the time to get to know his mom that well. At first, because I was a kid who didn't care, and then later because I was afraid of her knowing that we had grown into something more. I wasn't sure if she'd be angry at me and lash out by telling my father or by sending Aidan away.

It is odd though, now that I think about it, how he never pushed for us to spend time together, yet he's so eager for *my* father to know of him.

Now, I wish that she knew. That she could lend a voice of reason to whatever it is that Aidan and I are getting ourselves into, because it feels like I just keep digging us further and further into yet another hole that I can't crawl back out of.

Making it to the last door on the left, our usual meeting spot, I walk inside, expecting him to be there waiting already.

But he isn't.

I reach for my phone, realizing belatedly that it isn't in my pocket. I scrunch my forehead, trying to remember where I had it last.

At the restaurant, I think.

Shit.

I consider going back to grab it but decide against it, walking farther into the room and sitting on the small twin bed to wait for Aidan to show up.

Covering my mouth with my hand, I let out a yawn, deciding to lie down and rest while I wait for him. I'm sure he'll wake me up when he gets here.

Only he never does.

And I sleep the night away, only waking when the sunlight beams in through the small window on the far side of the room, sprinkling its rays across my skin with splashes of warmth.

Rubbing my eyes, I sit up slowly, trying to figure out my surroundings.

It's morning, clearly.

And Aidan never showed.

CHAPTER 14

Yasmin

I STILL CAN'T FIND MY PHONE, AND I CAN'T BRING myself to get in touch with Julian or that creep Alexander to see if they picked it up on their way out. On top of that, I still haven't seen Aidan, and there's a kink in my neck from sleeping on that lumpy twin mattress. And right now, I'm sitting at the high barstool at the edge of the kitchen island, listening to the TV drone on in the background, and downing enough coffee to keep normal people awake for a week.

But it's not doing the job for me.

My father walks in, his face lighting up when he sees me, and he walks over, sitting down in the stool next to me. "Morning, sweetheart. How'd you sleep?"

I paste a grin on my face even though I know it won't fool him and sip from my oversize mug. "I slept great. How're you feeling?"

My eyes soak him in as long as possible, cataloging every single feature and comparing them to how they appeared when I saw him last. Luckily, he looks the same, and I let out a deep sigh of relief that he hasn't gotten any worse. At least not physically. Not yet.

"I feel good. Ready for my tea," he says, glancing around.

Aidan's mom walks into the kitchen from the hallway, and my spine straightens as I take her in. She looks like she usually does, pretty and dressed in black slacks and a light-blue polo shirt, her blond hair pulled back in a bun. She pours my father a cup of tea and places it in front of him before bringing him the newspaper. I wait for some type of acknowledgment, although I'm not sure why I think she'd care to notice my existence. She never has before. But her son didn't show up last night, and there's a sinking feeling in my gut that things just aren't right.

Maybe Aidan talked to her, or she knows something and is here to pass along a secret message.

That's a wild assumption to make, of course, and like usual, she gives me nothing, not even a small glance before she's leaving again, disappearing down the hall off the side of the kitchen.

Dammit.

My stomach is in knots wondering where Aidan is and worried that something's happened. I just know he's been trying to get ahold of me but can't because I can't find my stupid fucking phone.

I glance down into my mug of coffee, trying to center my thoughts, but am distracted by the sound of a Sultans commercial on TV.

"Turn your love from in the rough to spectacular with a Sultans diamond."

I'm used to seeing ads for Sultans or going to different places and seeing our storefronts large and gleaming in the middle of the cities, so I don't pay it any mind. It isn't until my father picks up the remote and turns the volume up for the news that I lift my head, my interest suddenly piqued.

"The back roads of Badour are shut down completely, the Lamborghini unrecognizable from where it was wrapped around the tree."

"And what about the driver, Tom? Any updates there?"

"There's a search and rescue team combing the wooded area, but at this time, Diane, no bodies have been recovered."

The screen changes from the news reporters to drone footage of the country roads just outside downtown Badour, not too far from where we are.

"Looks like a nasty crash," I say.

My father hums before muting it and staring back down at his paper. "That's why I prefer other people to drive *you.*"

I hold back the annoyance at the reminder that I never learned how to drive, but it blossoms in full force anyway when Julian walks through the hall and into the kitchen like he owns the place.

Groaning, I tilt my head back. "Shouldn't you be working?"

He grins as he makes his way into the room, leaning his elbow on the island across from me and plucking a grape from the fresh fruit platter that was set out when I first came down.

"Just making sure you don't miss me too bad." He winks and then turns his attention to my father. "Good to see you up and moving around, old man."

"Hmm," Baba grunts, glancing between the two of us. "How did dinner last night go?"

"Yeah, speaking of, I thought you'd be there," I cut in.

My father's face softens. "I wasn't feeling too well."

"You could have told me at least."

He waves his hand in front of him like it's no big deal. "I didn't want you to see me that way."

I sigh, irritation nagging at my middle. "Baba, I want to see you in *any* way."

"Enough," he replies, causing me to jerk back at the harsh tone. "Tell me how last night went."

I place my coffee on the counter and fist my hands in my lap. "It went fine."

Julian isn't even paying attention, popping another grape in his mouth as he watches the drone footage of that Lamborghini crash.

"Fine?" my father repeats. "That's all I get?"

Shrugging, I look over to him. "He wasn't my type."

"He was a disaster, Ali," Julian interjects. "Honestly, I'm surprised you even set them up."

"He's an upstanding man, Julian," Baba argues. "I'd think you'd want someone in her life who knows how to present themselves around important people."

Julian's brows rise and he turns to face my father fully. "And why would that matter to me?"

"Because they'll own Sultans."

My lungs cramp, and a pregnant pause fills the air.

Julian's jaw twitches. "Ah, of course."

I watch Julian carefully, noticing the tensing of his body and the forced grin.

He clearly doesn't like that, and his offer to help me is exactly what I suspected, merely to help his own agenda. He doesn't want to help *me*; he wants what's being left to me.

Hatred swirls deep in my gut like a witch's brew, and I bite the inside of my cheek to keep from lashing out and saying something I'll regret.

Julian flicks his gaze to the TV again, nodding toward it. "I'm pretty sure that's the same car our very own Alexander Sokolov was driving away in last night."

"What?" I gasp.

My eyes lock on Julian's.

He smirks. "Sure hope nothing *bad* happened."

My mouth drops open, revulsion crawling through my insides like spiders.

"I'm sure it's just a coincidence," my father says, rising from his stool. "But I'll go put in a call just to double-check."

Julian murmurs his agreement. "Good idea, old man. He'd been drinking heavily. I tried to convince him to let me drive him home, but he wouldn't listen."

I sit with a dead stare as my father walks out of the room, shock filling up my bones and sticking me in place like I'm sinking into quicksand.

"Oh, come on, Yasmin. Don't look so surprised." Julian chuckles, popping another grape into his mouth.

"Did you do this?" I manage to rasp.

His brow lifts, and he makes his way around the island until he's standing directly in front of me, so close that his legs are on either side of my thighs. "I'm afraid death is part of life, gattina."

I narrow my eyes, something sick settling heavy in my gut. "What the hell is that supposed to mean?"

He shrugs. "Whatever you want it to mean."

My mouth is as dry as sandpaper, and I unstick my tongue from the roof, slowly licking my lips. I'm afraid to voice the next question, but I can't *not* ask. "Where's Aidan?"

"On a plane," he replies simply. "Happy as can be with a belly full of high-end champagne and the promise of a better life on the horizon." He pauses, tilting his head the slightest amount.

"He's with my assistant, Ian, who is loyal to a fault. Overeager to help me with any...*difficulties* that might get in my way."

I nod, even while my stomach drops to the floor, hopelessness filling me up like wet rocks. His implication is more than clear.

But is he really capable of that?

Of course he is. I'm no stranger to the darker side of my father's life and the company he keeps, despite Baba trying to keep me from it.

It's too late to go to my father. Julian has Aidan, and I have...

"Have you thought any more about my offer?" he continues, stepping in even closer and reaching out to cup my cheek with his large hand.

I swallow, forcing back the burn that's growing behind my eyes.

"Are you going to kill him?" I hate how weak my voice sounds, desperation clinging to every syllable.

His thumb brushes across my jaw, sending fear spiking against my spine. "Not if you cooperate."

My throat tightens and my heart beats wildly in my ears, but I force myself to look up and meet his eyes anyway. "What do you want?"

He smiles, his grip tightening until it stings. "You."

CHAPTER 15

Julian

"WHAT'S THIS?"

Ali's voice comes from the far corner of the kitchen, but I don't break my gaze away from Yasmin's face. In fact, I tighten my hold on her jaw, my thumb possessively caressing her cheek before releasing her and jumping back like I've been caught red-handed.

"Ali, I—" Running a hand through my hair to leave it tousled, I shake my head. "I can explain."

Ali's face is rigid as he stares between the two of us, his arms crossing over his chest. "Explain fast."

"Baba," Yasmin starts.

I cut her off. "I…I love her."

Ali's brows shoot to his hairline, and he steps farther into the room, his hand jerking out to steady himself on the counter. Although today he looks fine, I'm reminded how much weaker he is than normal.

"I'm sorry, old man," I continue, forcing sympathy into my voice. "This isn't how we wanted you to find out."

"Is this true?" His voice is incredulous, like he needs a second opinion. He turns his sallow eyes to Yasmin.

She doesn't reply for what feels like an eternity, her teeth digging into the corner of her lip instead. I step in closer to her, grabbing her hand and tangling her clammy fingers with mine.

Our eyes meet, and I swear to God I can feel the hatred radiating from her stare. I allow my grin to widen as I look down at her and wink. She frowns, tearing away her gaze until she's staring at the TV that's still showing Alexander's *unfortunate* crash.

Slowly, she turns her head until she's staring at her father.

"Yes," she whispers.

Satisfaction rushes through me like a waterfall.

Ali looks at me, his face scrunching in displeasure. "But you're so *old*."

I let out a chuckle. "Not as old as you, at least. We didn't mean for it to happen, Ali, but the heart wants what it wants." Bringing up our combined hands, I press a kiss to the back of hers. "Tell him, gattina."

She stiffens. "We didn't mean for it to happen, Baba."

"*When* did it even happen?" he asks. "How? Why didn't you say anything before now?"

She glances down at her lap, her voice breaking as she speaks, but her nails dig into the back of my hand until they slice through my skin. "I was afraid of disappointing you. And…I didn't want Julian's position in your life to be harmed."

Ali sighs, walking closer to her and taking her free hand in both of his. "And *this* is who you love?"

She swallows, glancing up at him and then looking away after only a few moments like she's unable to hold his gaze. "It is."

He blows out a slow breath and nods, leaning in to kiss her

forehead before he steps back and looks at the two of us. "Then he's who you'll marry."

I grin, my body buzzing with the thrill of success.

Yasmin visibly slumps, and I move my hand from hers, sliding it up her arm until it grips the back of her neck. She straightens immediately, pasting a wide smile on her face.

Leaning down, I press a kiss to her temple, speaking low so her father doesn't hear. "You've been a very good girl."

"What's wrong, Yasmin? Is this not what you want?" Ali asks.

Tears spring from her eyes, dripping down her face, and while I know they're most likely out of sadness or frustration, she does a good job at pretending they're from joy.

"I'm just happy, Baba." She shakes her head, reaching up to wipe the wetness from her cheeks. "I expected for you to be angry with me."

He nods, understanding pouring from his gaze. "I'm a man on the last leg of his life."

"Don't say that," she whispers.

His brows draw in. "It's the truth. Even if my footprints have been set in stone, *I* won't be here forever. I have no time for anger. I'd rather spend it finding peace. He's not who I would have chosen for you, sweetheart, but if you're happy, I'm happy."

Yasmin sucks in an audible breath, her entire body going rigid at his words.

I should feel vindicated, relieved even, that she didn't figure out he would have accepted her lover until now when it's too late and she's already played into my hand, but instead of feeling relief, my stomach twists violently. After everything I've given him, after everything I've done, I'm still not enough. He should be honored that I'm choosing his worthless daughter, and yet he's so blatant with his disregard.

It's a slap across my face.

Worse, it's a knife in my back. I swallow around the feeling of not being good enough, the same feeling that was responsible for many sleepless nights as a child, and push it so deep down that it's smothered.

It doesn't matter if I'm not his choice. I'm my *own* choice, and I'm the only person who's never let me down.

One day soon, I'll have complete control of Sultans, and I'll take joy in watching everyone who's ever thought I wasn't good enough choke on their words while I hold the universe in the palm of my hand.

"Now." Ali claps his hands together, moving back and staring at the two of us. "How about a wedding?"

"Tinashe, friend, tell me what the problem is," I ask, leaning back in my desk chair, peering out over the skyline of Badour from the wall of windows in my office. The sun is just setting, oranges clashing with pinks until the view creates a stunning glow across the tops of the shiny skyscrapers.

"Julian," Tinashe breathes out, sounding relieved. "Darryn is *not* happy that you're coming into his territory and trying to steal the lost lamp out from under him."

I grab a pen, tapping it on the desk, irritated that I have to deal with this situation at all. "Remind me again, old friend, why I pay you?"

There's a long beat of silence before his deep voice comes over the line again. "I'm not a miracle worker, Julian. I can get you a lot of places and make friends with a lot of people, but I am no genie. I can't wave my arms and suddenly make it okay for you to come in illegally and smuggle out relics from other countries."

I scoff, tossing the pen in my hand down, watching as it rolls across my desk. "Darryn Anders couldn't care less about smuggling relics. He practically coined the operation."

Tinashe clicks his tongue. "But he does care about someone else trying to beat him to the lamp. He's been there almost a decade looking for himself."

Sighing, I pinch the bridge of my nose. "And that's our problem how?"

"He wants you gone. Period. I'm just looking out for the people you have here on the ground. Darryn isn't known to be *gentle* with his points."

I shake my head, annoyance pouring over me like rubbing alcohol on wounds. The last thing I want to do is give in and reason with Darryn, but his resources there are much stronger and rooted in years of work, whereas ours is a newer venture. I need to be smart about this, treat it as a business deal instead of something I'm fighting against. Lull him into a false sense of comfort so that he doesn't cause us more problems down the road. Once I have the lamp, it won't matter. We'll leave the area, and he can't do anything else to get in my way.

"Does Jeannie know about this?"

Tinashe chuckles. "Jeannie knows about everything, Julian. That's why she's the lead."

My fingers tighten around my phone, annoyed that she hasn't said anything about Darryn Anders directly to me. Actually, I haven't gotten a single email from her since she told me about the new spot she wanted to look the other day, and if she already knew about Darryn, it's irritating she didn't include that in her update.

"Let me see what I can manage," I say.

Tinashe grunts and I hang up before he can say anything else. I bring up Ian's number and send him a text.

> Me: Do not do ANYTHING outside the compound until you hear from me. Take the boy there and stay put. I'll be very annoyed if you get yourself killed. And talk to Jeannie, figure out where we stand with the search. Ask her about Darryn Anders and why she didn't feel the need to tell us something so important.

Before I can even put my phone down, it vibrates again in my hand, and the bad mood that's been coiling around my back cinches a little tighter.

Mamma flashes across the screen.

Indecision weighs down my shoulders. I run my tongue over the front of my teeth, my fingers tap, tap, tapping on my desk as I watch the call go to voicemail. Only then do I let out a breath, guilt swirling in my stomach at the fact that I didn't pick up again.

I make a mental note to call her nurse, Jessica, and make sure she doesn't need anything, which she shouldn't. I put her up in a gorgeous four-thousand-square-foot home on the lake, giving her the best care money can buy.

And still, it's not enough to get her off my back.

A voicemail notification pops up and I press Play on speaker, my mother's voice filling the room.

"Vita mia, it's mommy dearest."

Her voice is low and soft, as though she can barely muster

up the strength to whisper, which only further proves I made the right choice in not picking up the phone. There's no escaping her doom and gloom when she wants to spread it to the world.

"Just trying to get ahold of you, you know? It's lonely here all by myself." She sighs. "Jessica says you're a busy man, but what type of kid is too busy to call his mother? Anyway, I hope I get to talk to you soon, and I hope you're not lying in a ditch somewhere, God forbid. Not that I'd ever be called if you were. It's like I'm a stranger even though I gave you life, but you know, that must not mean as much these days as it did when I was growing up."

Reaching over, I press a key on my computer keyboard to light up my screen, pulling up my emails as I listen to her drone on.

"I don't know if you care, since you can't even pick up the phone, but the doctors aren't sure how much longer I have left. It could be any day now, so I pray I get to hear your sweet voice again before it's too late. You're the only thing that keeps me going."

The need to check in on her surges through my chest, but it's anger that burns my heart. For years, her words would bleed into my conscience, make me think that time was limited and she was going to die. But you can only cry wolf so many times before people stop believing.

"Ti voglio bene, piccolo," she finishes.

Glancing down at my phone as the voicemail ends, I reach out, pressing the Delete button, a quick flash of guilt mixing in with the other emotions and making me sick to my stomach. Instead of focusing on the feeling, I jump up from my chair and leave my office, heading down to the bottom floor of Sultans' headquarters where we create the lab-grown diamonds.

We've only started manufacturing our own diamonds in the past few years, and it took a hell of a lot of convincing Ali that it would be worth it. He doesn't think they hold the same value, but it doesn't matter what *he* thinks. What matters are the consumers, and after the clean diamond trade act tightened regulations on conflict diamonds, lab-grown gems blew up in popularity.

People want to believe they're contributing to the *good* of the world instead of the bad, and synthetic diamonds are a way to market to that need.

Mainly, however, we use the synthetic diamonds to cut and polish the ones mined, and then we sell off a large portion of the rest to third-party sellers.

I walk down the aisles of the discolored concrete floor in the manufacturing warehouse, through the HPHT cubic press machines—giant light-blue machinery with six sides that apply immense heat and pressure to create the synthetic diamonds— and allow my mind to focus on the employees who are clearly aware of my presence, based on the way they're lingering on the edges of the aisles and not coming to greet me.

Other than the sound of the equipment and a faint beat of music from the offices in the far right corner, it's quiet.

Truth be told, I don't come to other departments often, but every once in a while, I make a surprise visit, just to ensure things are running as smoothly as the department managers tell me when I get the weekend reports. Normally, when I show up places, it disrupts the workflow more than helps, because people are on edge when I'm around.

Clearly.

But right now, I don't really care. I need the distraction from both the tumultuous emotions bleeding through my system courtesy of my nagging mother and from the annoyance of Darryn Anders trying to take what I want.

Something vibrates in my pocket and my footsteps falter. I reach in my pocket and pull out the phone, smirking when I realize it isn't *my* cell ringing but Yasmin's.

Riya flashes across the screen and I silence the call, slipping it back in my pocket, satisfied that it isn't the boy trying to contact her again. It was easy enough to break into her phone—having her father's birth date and hers isn't exactly a *difficult* passcode to guess—and once I did, it was child's play putting a stop to Aidan meeting her two nights ago. I simply pretended to be Yasmin and told him something had come up with her father, and when he replied, I left him on read. A tendril of satisfaction wraps around me when I realize that he hasn't attempted to reach out again.

Foolish boy.

But fortuitous for me, because I can't have him in my way. Especially when Yasmin is so close to becoming mine.

CHAPTER 16

Yasmin

I ORDERED A NEW PHONE, BUT IT WON'T GET HERE for another week.

Things have never been *more* obvious that while I had a fun time in college and boarding school and got along with mostly everyone, I never went out of my way to make lasting friendships with people I could trust beyond Riya, and now that I'm here, back at my home, I'm secluded and alone.

For the past hour, I've been sitting at my desk, switching tabs between trying to find a law firm that might consider going up against Julian and my father and a tab to sign up for a social media site.

One of the things my father asked is that I *don't* have social media, at least a public profile, because the daughter of a billion-dollar businessman who is touted as one of the most powerful men in the world shouldn't put herself in the limelight more than neces-sary. Personally, I've never felt the urge to be locked on my phone day in and day out, so I agreed without any issue, preferring to be behind the lens of my camera instead of on a social media app.

But now, my fingers hover over the sign-up button, trembling with indecision.

I'm not sure I'd even be able to find Aidan's profile, but I just want some way to be able to watch him when he's so far away in Egypt, see if he posts things so I can feel like I'm at least part of what's going on.

I imagine that Aidan must be worried sick and going out of his mind by now. Or maybe Julian's people have told him everything's fine. But if they're giving him messages, then there's nothing stopping them from telling him about the engagement, and the thought of Aidan hearing it that way and not knowing the full story makes me want to puke.

This is all my fault though. There's no one to blame but myself.

I should have been smarter with my decisions.

Ironic how now that I've been backed into a corner with no way out, I've found the courage I needed to tell the truth in the first place. But it's too late now. I won't put Aidan's life at risk.

And even though I can't wrap my head around it and don't have concrete proof, it seems that Julian had something to do with Alexander's death.

How many others has he murdered? Would he kill me? My father?

I can't take the risk.

But I'm panicking.

My father so easily believed that Julian and I were in love, that *he* is the man I want to marry, and I'm still reeling from the realization that he didn't even care enough to get angry.

Would it have been the same if Julian had no money?

Part of me hoped that my father would have seen through the facade. He's the one who's known me since birth, the one who should know me better than *anyone*, but maybe that's my fault for keeping so much of who I truly am from him for so many years, just to spare myself seeing the look on his face if he didn't like who he saw.

A knock sounds from outside my bedroom, and my hand jolts back from my laptop. I slam the lid closed, not wanting anyone to see what I was up to, and jump up, moving quickly across the room to the door. I grip the handle, cracking it open and peering through the small space it creates.

Julian's standing on the other side, his black button-down rolled up to his elbows and his forearm pressed against the side of the doorframe. My stomach flips and I huff a breath, annoyed my body is always betraying me when it comes to him.

"Time to pack, *princess*."

I open the door fully, stepping to the side.

"Don't call me that," I spit. "What do you mean, 'pack'?"

"I mean, grab some boxes and place whatever you wish to keep inside them. Then you use tape to close the top. I'd also recommend a Sharpie to mark what goes where, but if you want to live in chaos, I won't stop you."

Scowling, I cross my arms. "I'm aware of how to pack a box, Julian. I mean, why do you think I would pack?"

"Did you think I'd allow my wife to live somewhere other than my house?" He moves forward, and I stumble back. "To sleep somewhere other than my bed?"

Disgust sweeps through my middle. "I will *never* sleep with you."

He frowns, pressing a hand to his chest. "Devastated."

"And I'm not your wife."

He quirks a brow. "Yet."

Fire licks at my veins and I dart forward, my hand smacking across his face before I can control myself, a burn radiating through my palm as his head whips to the side.

I gasp, bringing my stinging hand up to cover my mouth, and I propel myself backward to create more distance, fear spreading through my muscles until I'm paralyzed. I can't believe I did that. I've never hit a person in my life.

Julian lets out a small chuckle, his face still turned to the side, black strands of hair sweeping across his forehead. He reaches up with his thumb and wipes a small drop of red bubbling on the corner of his lip from a gash my ring caused.

Slowly, he twists toward me, bringing that same thumb to his mouth and sucking off the blood.

Gross.

The words "I'm sorry" are on the tip of my tongue, even though I don't really feel apologetic. It's a habit, but somehow, I stop the words from vomiting out.

Things happen in a flash then. Julian moves forward quickly, grasping my upper arm until it cuts off circulation as he drags me farther into my room and throws me on my bed.

The breath is knocked from my lungs when I bounce off the mattress, and my heart beats wildly in my ears. Every single nerve ending is lit up and on edge as I push on the bed with my heels and my elbows, trying to shove my body back as far as possible. He continues to stalk toward me until his knee is pressing into the edge of the mattress, and he grabs my ankles and pulls until I slide beneath his frame.

He looms over me, pressing his weight on top of mine, his corded forearms flexing as they cage me in, resting on either side of my head.

From this vantage point, I can see the muscles in his jaw working and smell the clean linen of his clothes and the hint of spice from his aftershave. My stomach twists when he presses his chest and torso against me, forcing me to lie back.

I swallow heavily. "Wh-what are you doing?"

His hand runs up my side and my breath lodges in my throat, my body vibrating with the need to get away from him.

"Testing out the merchandise," he replies, his fingers feathering along my collarbone.

I make a noise in my throat, unwanted goose bumps sprouting beneath his touch. "You can't just *do* that."

He leans down, pressing a kiss to the juncture between my neck and my shoulder, and my thighs tense. I hate the way heat shoots through my body when his tongue touches my skin.

"I can do whatever I want," he murmurs.

"Not surprising from a man who thinks he's a god," I say through clenched teeth. I feel flushed, my body breaking out in a sweat from being beneath him, from lighting up in every goddamn place he caresses.

"That's right, baby." His hand wraps around my neck and my breathing stutters. "I'm *your* god."

I shove myself up on my elbows as far as I can go, which isn't far considering a man who's at least six six is resting his full body weight against me.

"You can make me wear your ring," I hiss, "and parade me around with your last name, but I will *never* bow for you."

He smirks. "We'll see."

Anxiety over what he'll do next digs into my sides and squeezes. "What's your aim, Julian? You want Sultans? Everything that *doesn't* belong to you?"

The pressure eases off my neck and he cups my cheek instead, his palm hot against my skin. "Hit me again," he murmurs, ignoring my question, "and you won't like the consequences. Understand?"

I scoff, twisting my head away.

His grip tightens, and he jerks my face back. "Tell me."

My nostrils flare, the anger breathing through my insides like a living dragon, but I shove it back, knowing that if I'm going to figure a way out of this, I need to cooperate.

At least for now.

"I understand," I force out.

He smiles, the sharp angles of his face softening from foe to friend. "Good."

Patting my cheek, he drops his hold and releases me completely, moving off the bed and running his tattooed hands down the front of his shirt.

"Now, listen carefully, because I don't like to repeat myself. You will marry me, you will take my last name, and you will be the good, dutiful, little wife that I know is buried deep down somewhere inside that head of yours."

Anger fills me up so quickly my fingers shake, but I clench the bedsheets and try to breathe through the fury.

"We will make everyone believe we're in love, and then when your father"—he pauses, swallowing so heavily that his Adam's apple bobs—"when he passes, you'll make a public statement that you have no interest in Sultans and as a belated wedding gift will be signing it all over to me."

"I'd rather die than leave Sultans to you," I snap.

He chuckles. "Be careful what you wish for, gattina."

My lungs cramp. *Is he saying he's going to kill me?*

"Play your part well and I'll let you ride off into the sunset with the boy."

My heart pounds against my rib cage, thoughts spinning wildly out of control. *Does he mean it?* Even as I ask myself the question, I know he can't be trusted. But what other choice do I have?

Marry Julian, give him Sultans, and then disappear.

Realization of what that would mean sinks into my bones, and I try not to let the desolation swallow me whole.

If I do this, then I'll lose everything my father begged me to keep safe.

But if I don't, I may lose everything else.

CHAPTER 17

Yasmin

I'VE BEEN HALF ATTEMPTING TO PACK UP MY belongings, not because I want to but because I have no choice. I went to my father's office, hoping to get a different resolution, to at least have him talk some sense into Julian or tell me it's too soon to move, but he wasn't there, and when I found him in his room instead, he refused to let me in. Shaina said he's becoming more lethargic, and he doesn't want me to see him that way.

I swallow back the nausea and walk into my closet, anger at the situation and frustration from feeling so goddamn helpless pushing me toward my racks of high-end clothes and reaching out to grab them while I scream.

Repeatedly I reach, rip, and pull down piece after piece until there's nothing left of my closet but piles of mess. And then there's me: my heart pounding wildly in my ears, sweat sticking my curls to my forehead, and a thick ball of anger lodged in my throat. Only the anger causes an ache that makes it feel a lot like grief.

The plush carpet cushions my fall as I drop to the ground,

feeling desolation once again creeping up and wrapping its long, icy arms around me.

Julian has, with one simple flick of his hand, wrapped golden shackles around my wrists. One simple tug and I'm helpless to do anything other than what he wants.

Maybe this is my penance. Maybe this is what I deserve, a lesson meant to teach me that every action has a *re*action and sometimes we have to deal with outcomes we don't want.

But it doesn't make it hurt any less. Emotions are rarely rooted in logic, so it's hard not to feel as though I've been betrayed by my baba. By the one man in the world who I thought would protect me from evil forever.

Sighing, I lean forward, pushing the mounds of clothes to the side to reach the pictures I have stowed away, hoping that I'll be able to find a silver lining, something that reminds me of my father's love. That he's always looking out for me, always doing what he thinks is best, even when it hurts me the most. Denim scratches against my wrist as I tear my way through the mess I've made, but eventually, I reach a shoebox and pull it forward, flipping open the lid.

My breath catches in my throat when hundreds of old photos stare up at me from the cardboard container.

I still take pictures now, but they're different, more reserved. I don't always have a camera on me like I did when I was away from home, and now... I've been so caught up in his illness and pleasing him that my passion went from photography to family, and it isn't until this moment that I realize it was like losing a piece of myself when I let that passion slip away.

Longing runs through me, making my chest feel hollow, and when I start to flip through the pictures, a small smile peeks through, despite how empty I feel inside.

Blurry images of me trying to take selfies before you could see yourself in the lens.

Riya and I at boarding school, school uniforms barely passing the regimented dress code as we stood on top of the cafeteria benches and sang into our milk cartons.

Nostalgia hits my gut like a battering ram, and my fingers tremble as I move faster through the forgotten memories. And then my hands stumble when I reach a photo of Aidan and me, lying in the backyard right outside the staff wing with snowflakes in our hair, rosy red on Aidan's cheeks and smiles beaming across both of our faces. I caress the side of Aidan's frozen face with my finger, trying to remember the moment. I must be around ten or eleven in the picture. It's a little blurry and out of frame from the way Aidan's holding the camera above our heads.

But it makes my heart squeeze anyway.

The snow hits me from out of nowhere. Icy, cold, and wet, smashing into my face and dripping off my chin.

I yelp, spinning around and diving behind the trunk of a tree, my breaths coming in heavy pants and my stomach flipping in excitement. I had hoped Aidan would see me out here and come to play. It's the entire reason I decided to make snow angels right outside the staff rooms.

I've been back on winter break for a few days, and this is the first time I've had a chance to come see him. Yesterday, my father took me to a special showing of Miracle on 34th Street, *which is my favorite movie, but today he has to work, and I woke up at the crack of dawn, bees buzzing through my whole body at the thought of coming down to this side of the estate today.*

Part of me was worried he wouldn't be here. Maybe his mom got another job or he had his own friends now to go and play with.

But as soon as the sting hit my face, I knew it was him.

Nobody throws a snowball like Aidan.

"Come out, come out, wherever you are!" *His voice is playful as he hollers through the yard.*

A warm feeling fills up the center of my chest, and I peek around the trunk of the tree, the snow crunching beneath my gloved fingers as I try to see him and stay hidden at the same time.

He looks taller than when I saw him last, his jacket too thin for how cold it is outside, and the tips of his bare fingers are red from holding on to the snow.

"I know you're there, princess," *he goads.* "You can run but you can't hide."

He glances my way and I dive back behind the thick trunk, my breathing choppy as it escapes in visible puffs through the air. I flatten my back against the bark, trying to remain as still as possible, but nothing and no one could wipe away the smile that's stretching across my face.

The crunch of shoes on snow gets closer, and my heart pitter-patters against my ribs, my frozen nose tingling in the winter air.

Suddenly, warm breath coasts across my cheek and I bite the inside of my lip to keep from squealing.

"Got ya," *he whispers.*

My eyes pop open, but before I can even take a step, he smashes a snowball right between my eyes.

"Oh!" *I yell, surprised.* "You big jerk!"

He laughs and stands up, jogging away, and this time, I shoot up after him, chasing him around the yard. He might be bigger, but I'm faster, and I tackle him quickly, taking us both clumsily down to the ground. I grab a handful of the snow right beside his head and shove it straight into his nose.

"Eat it!" I yell, giggling between each word.

"I give up! I give up!" he laughs back, picking me up by the waist and dropping me to his side.

It must be twenty degrees outside, but my chest is warm, spreading heat through my body, and I decide that this must be what pure happiness feels like, and I want to capture the moment forever.

I reach to the side of my neon-pink snow pants, unzipping one of the pockets on my leg and grabbing my disposable camera, the one I keep on me at all times just in case there's something I want to remember forever.

Before I can hold it up, Aidan grabs it from my hand, his other arm reaching out to pull me into his side. "Say cheese."

Aidan grins, his dimples creasing the apples of his cheeks and his smile wide, and right before he hits the button on top, he leans in, resting the side of his head against mine.

Butterflies erupt in my stomach.

I come out of the memory, my fingers coasting across our snow-kissed faces, the happiness so clear on both of them.

Shaking my head, I fold up the picture, slipping it in the side of my bra, wanting to keep it with me to give me something to hold on to today other than the sadness welling up in my sternum and spreading outward, infecting every single cell.

I wish more than anything that Aidan was here right now, that he could take me in his arms and tell me everything would be okay. If he were, I'd tell him how sorry I was for fucking everything up. I'd tell him how if I could, I'd take it all back and make different decisions, ones that wouldn't be made from my fear and cowardice. I'd thank him for sticking by me through thick and thin, always calming me down and reminding me of why I chose him in the first place.

To be honest, I would have bailed on myself a long time ago.

Tears spring from my eyes and pour down the front of my face, hot and messy against my cheeks, but once they start to fall, they're impossible to stop. So I stop fighting against the feeling and let it overwhelm me instead, until I can't see, can't think, can't feel *anything* other than the ache radiating from the center of my chest, pulsing with regret.

I cry for the loss of Aidan.

For Baba.

For myself.

I hiccup, wiping what I'm sure are black smears of mascara as I try to see through my now-swollen eyes. My legs tingle when I stand, numb from sitting on the closet floor. I move slowly but sure, my breaths stuttering as my nervous system tries to calm, and I walk out of my closet and grab an empty box, moving back to the piles of clothes and continuing to pack.

Because I have no other choice.

Acceptance of my situation stabs at my chest, and it splinters into a thousand pieces, washing away the foggy grief and bringing clarity.

Just because something feels hopeless doesn't mean it truly is. But to handle this, to even have a *chance* of figuring any of this out, I have to be smart. Cunning. I have to learn Julian's game and play it better than him so I can get rid of the son of a bitch for good *and* keep Sultans in the family.

My father is dying.

And I can't save him, as much as I wish I could.

But maybe I can save his legacy.

"What are you doing?"

My heart shoots to my throat and I spin from where I'm packing up the last box of things I want to take with me. I'm not sure *when* Julian wants me to move, but it's better to be prepared, so after I had my meltdown, I got my shit together and started to figure out what I wanted to keep out of Julian's reach and what I was okay taking with me.

This time, it's not Julian but my best friend in the doorway. "Riya, what are you doing here?"

I'm happy to see her, but the sight of her causes a crack in my newly formed shield and my bottom lip trembles, a burn starting to spread behind my nose and eyes.

Riya's face drops. "*Shit*, what happened?"

"He—I... He... I'm..." I stutter over the words, not sure how to say them, how to give her the truth without giving her *the truth*.

"What?" she cuts in, her hands going to her hips. "What did that asshole do?"

"You don't even know who I'm talking about." I laugh through the ache.

"Doesn't matter. If he makes you look like *that*"—she points a finger at my swollen eyes—"he's an asshole and I have no choice but to plan his murder."

I chuckle, but the gravity of the situation dims my amusement. *Does it make me a bad person if I wish we really could plan his murder?* I shake my head, dispelling the notion.

I'm not that kind of person. I'm not *him*.

"I don't have my phone," I say.

Her perfectly manicured brow arches. "Yeah, I got that when

you didn't call me back for the past two days. And you missed Sunday brunch."

Honestly, I hadn't even thought about our brunch. "Oh my god, Riya. I'm so sorry."

She shrugs. "I figured you not showing up was your distress call, so here I am. Now tell me what's wrong." Her eyes scan the room, widening as she sees the boxes scattered and the empty shelves. "Are you...*packing*?"

I nod, that ache stirring up again in the middle of my chest.

"I'm marrying Julian," I force out, refusing to meet her gaze.

She purses her lips. "By choice?"

My teeth clench to keep the truth from spilling off my tongue, but she sees through me anyway. I'm not sure why I even tried.

"*Not* by choice," she answers for me.

"It doesn't matter." I wave my hand like it can wash away the situation. "What is it you always say? If you can't get out of it, get into it? This is me getting into it."

She huffs out a noise, half laugh and half scoff, before her hands fly to her hips. "You're insulting as hell when you lie to my face like that." Riya moves until she's standing right in front of me, her hands coming up to rest on my shoulders, eyes locking on mine. "You jump, I jump, remember?"

"Please." I laugh even as tears brim on my lower lids. "Don't quote *Titanic* to me right now, Riy. I don't think I can handle any more pain."

But her actions have the desired effect, and I give in and start to talk. About how Aidan's life is at risk. How I haven't been able to find my phone to even send him a message. How Julian wants me to pretend that we're in love and how easily my father believed it.

And once the words start slipping from my lips, I can't stop, the heavy burden feeling a little less intense when someone else helps to shoulder the load.

"He's not a good person," I say. "And I don't—I don't know what to do. I don't even know what he's really capable of." Panic starts to wind its way around my spine, pricking my nerves like needles. "What if he hurts my father?"

"What if he hurts *you*?" Riya hits back.

I shake my head. "I'm not worried about me. I can handle myself. I just… I can't take the risk that someone else might get hurt *because* of me."

She nods, sympathy filling her gaze. "So what's the plan?"

Sighing, I walk over to my vanity and grab a silk scrunchie, pulling my curls off my neck. "Play along for now while I figure out a way to gain the upper hand. I don't really have another choice." I spin toward her. "I need a lawyer, or…I don't know, *someone* who's willing to go up against Julian so I can get out of this sham marriage and keep Sultans."

Riya sucks on her lips and nods, walking over to me at the vanity and staring at both of our reflections in the mirror. "I don't know if a lawyer would be able to get you out of this. Not many would go up against Julian Faraci. We need to come up with a different option."

"I don't know what to do," I whisper. "But I have to try *something*."

She hesitates, running her fingers through her hair before her eyes lock on mine. "Have you thought about the police? If he's out here causing car accidents and threatening you and Aidan, they really need to know, Yas."

I shake my head without a second thought. My father has police chiefs and district attorneys over for dinners and soirees all the time, and I know they're all on a first-name basis with Julian, happy to line their pockets in return for looking the other way whenever they need to do something less than savory.

"No, no cops," I say firmly. "Alexander's body hasn't even been found yet, and my father would never forgive me if I had the police sniffing around. Besides, I'm pretty sure most of them are in Julian's pocket anyway."

She huffs out a breath. "Then we'll find you a lawyer who doesn't give a shit."

A grin works its way across her face, even though her eyes are as dark and as serious as I've ever seen them. She holds out her hand, pinkie extended. I wrap mine around hers and her smile widens.

"Ride or die, bitch," she says. "We won't go down without a fight."

CHAPTER 18

Julian

THIS OFFICE IS SMALL AND CRAMPED FOR SOMEONE who's been a judge the past twenty years, with its blank white walls that have yellowed over time, offset by the dark wood furniture that Anthony McFarlane, the person I'm here to see, has spent a pretty penny trying to make more prestigious than it is.

Working as a municipal judge has its limits on grandeur, I suppose.

Right now, the size of the small room works in my favor, allowing me to see every single twitch of his face as he bumbles out worthless excuse after excuse for why he can't give me what I'm asking for.

"You don't understand," he implores, his small, framed glasses slipping over the large hump in the middle of his nose. "There's a mandatory twenty-four waiting period from the time of filing a marriage license to when we can perform the ceremony. Besides, I can't just draw one up and force her to sign. It doesn't work like that."

Nodding, I reach into the pocket of my suit, pulling out the small compact staff and pressing the button just beneath the top, the sound of it snapping to full size reverberating off the cramped walls. I flip the staff over the back of my hand, the smooth black metal feeling strong and sure as it lands in my palm. "I need for us to work together here, *Your Honor.*"

Beads of perspiration line the edges of his hair, his eyes flicking from the staff and back to my face. "Julian," he implores. "There's only so much I can do."

I take a step forward, the edge of his desk digging into my thighs through my black dress pants. "Remember when you came to me five years ago?"

His forehead creases as his entire stature droops in his chair. "Julian…"

"Ah, ah, ah," I tsk, reaching out until the end of my staff presses into his solar plexus. "Indulge me, old friend."

Anthony's mouth pinches shut.

"What was it again that had you rushing to me for help?" I tilt my head to the side.

He doesn't reply.

"It was your wife," I answer for him. "She was about to find those heinous videos of you bent over your desk like a stuck pig, getting pegged by your intern. How old was she again, nineteen?" I cluck my tongue. "Naughty boy."

His cheeks grow ruddy. "You promised to never—"

"And I haven't," I interrupt. "I used my connections, my *name*, to help a friend in need. Wasn't it that year I also gave you that stunning emerald necklace for your anniversary?" My smile drops, eyes narrowing as I dig the staff farther into his skin. "Or am I confusing that with the time you asked for those two-carat stud earrings for your mistress?"

He swallows, his Adam's apple bobbing.

"Doesn't matter, I guess. You made the right choice in coming to me for help. But you know, I feel almost guilty now." I laugh before cutting it off abruptly, my gaze burning through his.

The resounding silence is thick.

"Don't you want to know why?" I press.

"Y-yes," he stutters.

Leaning my torso over the top of his desk, I lower my voice to a murmur. "I never got rid of the tapes."

His cheeks turn pink, panic spreading through his features.

I move the tip of my staff from his chest, dragging it up his throat until it rests beneath his chin. I force his gaze to meet mine with a flick of my wrist. "I'd hate to see what would happen if they got into the wrong hands."

Withdrawing my staff, I start to flip it again, enjoying the way Anthony's eyes follow it around and around in my palm.

"But there's only so much I can do." My hand stops moving. "You understand."

His jaw muscles twitch, his body vibrating in his seat. "Give me an hour."

A smile spreads across my face. "I'm not unreasonable. I'll give you two."

Snapping back my staff, I close it and place it back in my pocket as I leave the room, walking through the stale halls of the Badour courthouse.

I move to grab my phone, my fingers ghosting across Yasmin's, and I smirk, wondering how badly she's freaking out over losing it. Three days ago when I told her to pack, she didn't mention it, and I'm sure by now she's figured it's gone forever.

If she's a good girl today, maybe I'll give it back. Once she's married to me legally, it doesn't really matter if she attempts to talk to the boy, and I've rigged her phone to send transcripts of everything to me anyway.

Picking my own cell from my pocket, I scroll past the new voicemail from my mother and dial my office's reception.

"Mr. Faraci," Ciara says. "What can I do for you?"

"I need you at the courthouse."

"Of course. I'll be there in thirty."

It takes her closer to an hour to arrive, and then another twenty minutes for me to tell her my expectations.

Don't speak unless she's needed, stay out of the way, and sign as the witness when Anthony asks her to. And above all else, *don't* breathe a word of it to anybody. The last thing I need is for the press to get wind of this and Ali to find out I've secretly married his daughter without him there. I need to tell him in person so I can spin it in my favor.

He's still alive, which means he can still change his will, and if he realizes what I'm doing, everything could go to complete shit.

But it's better to take the chance and make sure Yasmin is bound to me rather than give her time to second-guess her smart decision of playing along. Or even worse, to come up with some foolish plan and try to outsmart me.

I sent Razul, the bodyguard I've tasked from my personal security to be her shadow, to bring Yasmin from her house. Personally, I don't care if anything happens to her, but until everything is said and done—her father and her both out of the way—she'll be my wife, and I take great care in protecting my assets.

"So," Ciara starts as we lean against the wall outside Anthony's office. "*Married*, huh?" She picks at her pink painted nails.

I swipe through emails on my phone, ignoring her completely.

"And to Yasmin Karam?" she continues. "Now I get why you were so up in arms when I didn't let her in the other day. I didn't even know you were dating."

I glance at her out of my peripheral vision, my top lip sneering in disgust. "Since when is it a *receptionist's* job to know who her boss is fucking?"

She shakes her head. "It's not. You're right. I just…I don't know. I'm surprised is all."

"I don't pay you to care about my personal life," I reply. "I pay you to do what I say. Answer phones, schedule meetings, and when I say jump, you ask how high. That's *it*. Got it?"

She nods, moving her gaze to the ground, the toe of her blue-heeled shoe gliding back and forth on the tiled floor.

The sound of an elevator pings in the distance, click-clacks of high heels on hard floors reverberating off the walls. My eyes fly to the end of the hall just as Yasmin walks around the corner, Razul's large, bulky frame at her back.

She has a long black peacoat covering her body, the cinched belt making her curves look exquisite. Large black sunglasses cover her eyes entirely, shielding her gaze from my view. Her lips are a fire-engine red that match her manicured nails perfectly, and my eyes trail down her toned legs until they hit her black heels.

Her lips twist into a pathetic attempt of a smile as she reaches me, her head turning to nod at Ciara.

"Gattina," I say. "You look edible."

She doesn't give me a response, too busy untying the belt at her waist and slipping the coat off, handing it to Razul, who folds it over his arm and stands stoically behind her.

My cock jerks at the sight of her in a skintight, bloodred

dress, visions of what she looked like naked and splayed out in the throes of pleasure assaulting my mind.

"Hello, *husband*," she purrs.

My brows shoot to my hairline, but I recover quickly, smirking as I straighten from where I was leaned against the wall. "Not your husband yet, I'm afraid."

She looks around, pursing her lips, those black shades still blocking her gaze from my view, which annoys me. It's easier to tell what's going through her head when I can see her eyes.

"Is that not why we're here?" she asks.

I frown, making sure to put on a show for anyone who might care to watch. "I wanted to surprise you."

Her lips twitch. "Having one of your goons come to collect me and bring me to the courthouse isn't exactly stealthy, patatino."

A chuckle bursts out of me at the Italian term of endearment.

I'm sure she learned the word to irritate me, but if anything, it does the opposite, bringing a sense of nostalgia back, one that I haven't felt in years. My nonna—the one who never left Italy— used to call me patatino, her little potato, whenever I'd speak to her on the phone.

She was the only good thing in my life as a child, and even though I never got to meet her in person, I was devastated when she passed away. I begged to go to her funeral, but it was impossible. My father wouldn't hear of it, and even if he would have, we didn't have the money.

It was one of the first times in my life that I promised myself I would never grow up to be financially insecure.

Reaching out toward Yasmin, I link our fingers together, ignoring the way the touch sends an unwelcome tremor through me, and I bring up her hand, pressing a kiss to the back. "Learning Italian just for me? I'm touched."

Anthony's office door flies open, and he storms out, his beady blue eyes bouncing from me to Yasmin and then to the two people with us. He nods. "Ready."

"Excellent," I say, pulling Yasmin into his office.

"Where is my father?" she whispers, finally taking off her sunglasses and looking around.

"At home, I'd presume. This isn't about him."

Just like last time, her nails dig into the back of my hand until they cut through flesh.

I smother a hiss at the pain and tighten my grip until her skin blanches, bending down to ghost my lips across the shell of her ear. "Careful," I whisper before dropping her hand completely. Moving toward Anthony's desk, I look down at the shiny, new marriage license, picking up a pen and holding it out toward her. "You're more than welcome to plan the wedding of your dreams and have him walk you down the aisle. But this is about *us*."

She strides toward me, her eyes flicking between the pen and the marriage certificate on the desk's top. She moves and I wrap my free hand around her wrist, locking her in place.

"In time, you'll forgive me. I just couldn't wait another minute to tie us together. Until death do us part."

Swallowing, she jerks her chin, taking the pen from my hold and twisting toward the license.

My heart ratchets higher, slamming against my ribs as she leans over, her back arching slightly as she prepares to become mine.

I wasn't sure what I expected when she got here, but it wasn't this. I'm pleased things are going so smoothly, but I'm not naive, and her being so *agreeable* makes my hackles rise. Still, the scratch of ink on paper has never sounded so sweet. One step closer to Sultans becoming mine, just as much as Yasmin. She signs her name and then looks up at me, a dark look coasting across her features.

Her jaw tightens and I beam at her.

"What now?" she asks.

I smile. "Now, we get married, gattina."

Anthony stands at the front, his face drawn and somber as he officiates what must be the quickest ceremony in New York history.

Yasmin's mouth gapes when I pull out the 8.92-carat canary-yellow diamond, slipping it on her finger along with an eternity band, and she keeps a brave face when she slides the simple black ring on mine. But I can feel the tremor in her hands.

Stepping in close, I brush the tight, black curls away from her face. "Is this the part where I get to kiss the bride?"

I don't really *want* to kiss her, but she's been so docile and tame the entire time she's been here, and a part of me wants to see how much it takes to get her riled. To stoke that fire that I love to feel, just so I can imagine all the ways I'd love to snuff it out.

She runs her hands up the front of my torso, my abs tightening. I resist the urge to shove her away as she rests her fingers on my chest. I stare down at her, my body stiff as a board, nerves on edge from having someone touch me. I blow out a deep breath and she smirks as she rises on her tiptoes. If I weren't paying close attention, I'd think that she was enjoying this, but I see the flash of grief in her eyes right before her lips meet mine.

My synapses fire like an explosion, so intense it's almost painful, but I push through the feeling and wrap my arm around her waist, dragging her closer, my teeth sinking into her lower lip to anchor her to me.

Her lips part and I inhale her breath like it's stolen air.

My eyes are wide open and so are hers, a battle of wills that neither of us are willing to lose. My tongue slips against hers and she stiffens but allows the movement. And when I deepen the kiss, falling prey to the sweet taste of her mouth, her lids flutter before closing completely, her body relaxing against mine as she starts to kiss me back.

My stomach somersaults, my cock suddenly so hard it aches, and I fist the material of her dress, feeling—for the first time in my life—as if I can't get close enough. It catches me off guard, and I should be wary, take it as a giant red flag waving in my face, but instead, I'm lost to the new sensation of having someone touch me and not hating the way it feels.

One of my hands slips up her side, enjoying the way she gasps into my mouth, and I cup her jaw, my thumb pressing against her chin to pry her open further.

Christ.

A throat clears, and Yasmin and I jump apart, our hands dropping away from each other like they've been doused in acid.

Her hand flies to her mouth, her wide gaze filling with horror as she stares at me.

I force a haughty look, even though my insides are reeling. "No need to get shy, gattina. You're my wife now. Nobody will think twice if you take what's yours."

Her eyes narrow, but she lowers her hand and glances around, looking at Ciara, Razul, and Anthony. "I prefer to do things like that in private."

A slow smile spreads across my face. "Then let's go home."

CHAPTER 19

Yasmin

JULIAN'S HOME IS EXQUISITE, WHICH PAINS ME TO say. He's so revolting that in my head, I've built up everything else about him to be just as bad, so when he drove us through the hidden hills of Badour, past the iron gates and down the rows of trees that line his quarter-mile driveway, I was taken aback by the view, to say the least.

And now I'm in the family room that's just off the open kitchen, staring out at the lush forest that hides his mansion from prying eyes. It's a beautiful view, one that if this were any other scenario, I would bask in. The sun is starting to set over the tops of the trees, splashes of muted orange and pink breaking through the leaves.

But instead of enjoying the scenic moment, I'm trying to keep from throwing up.

I *kissed* him. Like, actually kissed him. My tongue was practically halfway down his throat. And I can pretend that it was nothing more than me playing the part—and to be fair, that's how it started—but I'm trying this new thing where I'm completely honest with myself. I have to be, or else my mind will get too muddled in the white lies to see the finish line and have a fighting chance of coming out of this on the other side.

And honestly…for just a moment, when he kissed me, I forgot where I was. Forgot who I was with.

My stomach heaves at the thought of Aidan finding out.

The sparkle of my new wedding ring glints off the dim recessed lighting in the family room, and I glance down, my heart squeezing at the sight. The ring itself is stunning, a yellow diamond cushioned between two trapezoid white diamonds. I don't want to think about what it means that the man I hate more than the world picked something so close to what I would have chosen for myself.

And it makes me so fucking pissed, because it's just another thing that Julian's ruined for me. I can't even take in its beauty without being reminded of the chains that are attached.

A champagne flute appears in my peripheral vision, and I tear my eyes away from my hand to look at Julian as he hands me the glass.

"A toast," he says.

My lips purse. "There's nothing to celebrate."

He sighs, his brows furrowing, and I take a moment to look at him. *Really* look at him. He's a magnificent creation, and I'd be lying if I said he was anything less. He's dressed down in a pair of jeans and a long-sleeve black Henley that's pushed up past his elbows, tattoos scrawled along the lengths of his arms and peeking through the collar of his shirt. His tanned skin has literally no blemishes, and it's like his jawline is cut from stone, framed with the perfect amount of stubble.

I hate how attractive he is. But I guess it makes sense that the devil would appear as perfection to lure away souls.

He sets down the glass I still haven't taken on a round end table that's next to the brown leather couch and then leans against the back, his eyes calculating as they stare at me.

"Things don't need to be as miserable as you're making them," he says.

I scoff, turning my face away from him.

"It's nothing personal, you know?"

"Spare me the bullshit," I reply. "We both know what this is."

Amusement sparks through his gaze. "Oh? Enlighten me."

My spine stiffens as I stare at him, turning my body to face him fully. "This is you trying to control *everything* to get what you want."

A Cheshire cat grin spreads across his face. "And what's wrong with getting what you want?"

"Hurting other people is wrong, Julian. And blackmailing me so you can make it out on top after my father dies is sick."

He straightens. "I—"

I cut my hand through the air. "Save the bullshit for someone who'll believe it. I'm not clueless, despite what you've always thought."

He crosses his arms.

Cocking my head, I take a step toward him, and then another, not stopping until I'm right in front of him, craning my neck to see every single speck of emotion that might flit across his face.

"Did you ever care about him at all?" I ask.

He lifts his chin. "Who?"

"My father."

His nostrils flare, the muscles on the sides of his jaw clenching as he grits his teeth.

"I bet you can't wait for him to die, huh? So you can swoop

in and steal everything that's rightfully his. What, you gonna kill me too?" I spit.

I don't mean to be so antagonizing—in fact, my goal was to be the opposite—but now that I've lit the fuse, my mouth is firing on all cylinders and there's no way to rein it in. It feels good to throw my verbal jabs, especially since it's the first time I've seen his blank exterior crack, small flashes of emotion blasting through like shooting stars across the sky.

His hand jabs out before I can blink, gripping my jaw so tight, my teeth cut into my cheeks, and he steps in close, his torso brushing against my chest.

Something jumps in the place our bodies meet, spearing through my middle and settling deep in my abdomen.

"Keep running that mouth," he rasps, "and you won't make it through the night."

I press up on my toes, our noses grazing. My stomach tightens. "I don't believe you," I whisper. "You need me too much."

His lips part, his eyes raging like a storm as his fingers twitch against my face. He releases me suddenly, and I drop back down onto my heels as he backs up until he hits the couch, running a hand through his tousled hair.

"I have work to do," he says, his blank expression firmly back in place. "Drink the champagne or don't, I don't give a fuck. But you will not leave this house, and you *will* watch the way you speak to me."

I swallow back the retort that's on the tip of my tongue, not wanting to push him further than I already have. I wasn't lying; I do think he needs me alive right now, but that doesn't mean he won't hurt me if I push him too far. I shouldn't be so willing to take that chance. Riya said she found someone who might be willing to work with me, and until I can meet with him, I need to play it smart, which means keeping my temper in check until I figure out what the hell I'm going to do to outmaneuver him. He may have me tied to him in name, but I'll die before I let him take my father's company.

"When can I get my things?" I ask instead. "You told me to pack, and I did, but the boxes are still at home."

He turns around and stalks out of the room, and irritation heats my veins at the way he just straight-up ignored me. But before I can even move to follow him, he's back, stopping next to the kitchen island that's facing the family room where I am. He places something on the top of the island before sliding his hands back in his pockets.

I walk over to see what it is, my breath catching in my lungs when I realize it's my cell phone.

My head shoots up, my gaze locking on his.

"This is your home now, Mrs. Faraci."

After Julian gave me my phone back, he informed me that despite his earlier threat of making me share his bed, he had set up a room for me that was on the opposite side of the house. He left shortly after without showing me how to get there.

But I navigated the expansive home without too much trouble, split between wanting to explore and wanting to immediately open my phone and try to get ahold of Aidan.

Aidan won out, and I made my way up the large staircase, choosing to go left instead of right when it broke in two different directions. After a few attempts, first running into a guest bathroom and then a large sitting room with floor-to-ceiling bookshelves and a glossy black grand piano, I found what I assume is my room.

If it isn't, he can come kick me out later, because I'm staying here.

It's soothing, if not a little creepy, how similar it is to my old bedroom at home—though I guess it's not my home anymore. The same four-poster bed with cream drapes, tied back on each end. The same style vanity and a full-length mirror tucked away in the left-hand corner of the room. There's a small desk sitting directly beneath the sheer-curtained window and a vase with lavender perched on the edge, creating a soft and pleasant scent.

Making my way through the space, I open the door to the left, which attaches to an incredible bathroom with a claw-foot soaker tub and an oversize shower that would easily fit five people.

The entire aesthetic of the place is gorgeous, and it pisses me off that I'm immediately feeling comfort in a strange place where I'm basically being held captive and forced to stay against my will.

Spinning around, my anger back intact, I move over to the sitting area that's to the left of the bedroom door, my hand gripping my phone so tight I'm afraid it might crack.

Plopping down in the chair, I let out the first full breath since I've gotten here and toss my cell down on the small round coffee table in front of me.

And then I sit there and stew, picking it up again before dropping it back down. Over and over, I repeat the motion, frustrated at myself that I can't seem to get it together enough to actually call Aidan. Something's holding me back, and I know it's the fact that now I have to tell him I'm married. My stomach pinches when I think about the "wedding," memory of the arousal that coursed through me when we kissed staining my body like ink.

I *want* to call Aidan, but visions of how he'll react slam into me, making me too nervous. I don't want to upset him or deal with the repercussions of how he'll respond.

Before I know it, an hour has passed, and I'm no closer to calling him, let alone looking through my messages, than I was when I first got the thing back.

What time is it in Egypt anyway?

My leg shakes and my teeth sink into my bottom lip, chewing until the skin breaks and the faint metallic taste floods my mouth.

This is ridiculous.

But what if he doesn't believe me?

What if he no longer cares?

Blowing out a deep breath, I snatch up my phone again and unlock the screen, seeing a few unread messages and a handful of voicemails.

My heart sinks the tiniest bit, because I won't lie, I thought there would be more. Regardless, I open the texts from Aidan, seeing him ask where I am and then a reply I absolutely never sent telling him that something came up with my father and not to come meet me.

My stomach churns.

Of course. That explains why he never showed up that night.

I know it was Julian, and it's honestly so par for the course for him to pretend to *be* me and then play ignorant like Aidan left without a word, and I'm reminded, once again, how he can't be trusted.

Still, after Aidan saying okay and that he'll miss me while he's gone, there's nothing. He's been there almost a week now and he hasn't tried to say a single thing.

But I know he's determined to win my father over by finding the lamp.

Anxiety clamps around my lungs and squeezes, making my vision grow hazy. *Everything's fine. He's fine. Julian won't hurt him unless I force his hand.* But even as I think it, I don't sound very convincing.

My fingers tremble as I type out a hasty text.

> Me: Hi, I'm so sorry I lost my phone and just got it back :(I hope you weren't too worried. How's Egypt? I can't believe I didn't get to say goodbye.

My leg shakes as I wait for a reply, but after ten minutes of staring down at my phone and realizing I'm not going to get one, at least not right away, I type out another message.

Before I can stop myself, I've sent a long string of texts explaining myself, trying to answer any questions that he might have before realizing that maybe I've said too much or the wrong thing, so I send another message trying to explain the previous one away. I finally send four more before forcing myself to put down the phone and walk away, knowing it's doing nothing but ratcheting up the high-strung energy that's coursing through my veins.

> Me: Are you mad at me? I don't like being so far away from you, it makes me nervous.
> Me: Any luck on the lamp?
> Me: I don't know what you've heard, but it isn't what you think. Can you talk?
> Me: I miss you.

I wait another few minutes before I groan, tossing my phone back on the table and deciding to break in my new shower. Anything to get my mind off the clusterfuck of messages I just sent.

The shower itself is incredible, and as the hot water cascades over my shoulders and down my body, I close my eyes and breathe deeply, trying to shake off the anxiety that clogs every pore. There's always been an incessant need inside me to please other people, to make sure that I'm well liked and that everyone around me is taken care of and happy, and although over the years, I've learned different coping mechanisms for easing the burden of my runaway thoughts, there's never been anything that's completely cured me of having to put everyone else before me.

I know it's a flaw, something that ends up putting me in more trouble than it's worth, but for the life of me, I don't know how to break it.

In fact, the only time in my life where I *haven't* felt the overwhelming urge to please somebody is when I'm around Julian.

My mouth sours at the fact.

Reaching out, I get some soap in my hand from the automatic dispenser on the wall and start to smooth my hands over my body, thinking about how different it feels when I'm around him and *not* concerned about whether he's thinking badly of me.

I hate him, of course. But underneath that, it's almost...freeing.

The thought makes my chest pinch tight.

Trying to refocus, I go back to the sham of a ceremony at the courthouse today, wondering how long it will take for a paper to run an article on the nuptials.

And then, before I can stop myself, as my hands brush over my breasts, I think about that kiss.

The one I haven't allowed myself to think of since it happened, because if I did, I'd have to admit that I liked it. But now, here in the safety of solitude, I give in and let my mind wander, if only to get some reprieve from the thoughts I can't control that are running through my head.

His mouth was soft. Softer than I expected, and I wonder if he'd be just as soft in other places.

My fingers ghost over my nipple, and I inhale sharply at the sensation. Slowly, I work my hand down the front of my body and slip my fingers over the top of my pussy, lightly brushing my clit.

A tingle surges through me when I apply pressure, and before I can stop myself, I'm imagining Julian on his knees, his tongue inside my pussy the same way it was devouring my mouth.

He'd be demanding, I just know it, but instead of it being a turnoff, it sends heat flaring through me, imagining him holding me in place and taking control of my pleasure the same way he controls the room whenever he walks into it.

I picture my fingers running through his hair, pulling on the strands until he groans from the pain, and my palm presses faster against my sensitive nerves, a slight moan escaping me into the air.

My muscles cramp and tighten, my body vibrating from the pleasure, and then I'm falling over the edge, my orgasm crashing through me and Julian's name leaving my lips on a shaky exhale.

It takes a few minutes for me to recover from the visceral experience, and when I do, the reality of my situation creeps back in, and I feel sick for what I've done.

Even though nobody will ever know except for me.

Despite my temporary lack of conscience and control, I exit the shower feeling slightly better. Showers always tend to cleanse away the negative energy clinging to my soul, and I feel more relaxed after the orgasm, as long as I don't focus on who I was imagining it was that was giving it to me.

I also don't think too hard about the fact that my exact type of shampoo and conditioner is already in there, and the lotion I like to use is stocked with backups in the cabinet to the left of the sinks.

How long has he been planning this?

Maybe he's the kind of man to always make things happen within a day. He's certainly powerful enough to snap his fingers and have people ready to serve, and while I know it should put me on edge that he's recreated almost every comfort from my home, I revel in the familiarity, even if it's only here to provide me with a false sense of security, one that I definitely shouldn't be feeling.

When I go to check my phone again, there's a new message. My heart skips as I open it.

Aidan: I miss you too. Can't talk, bill would be too much. Where'd you find your phone?

Frowning, I type out a reply.

Me: Julian had it. Is everything okay?
Aidan: You're still hanging around Julian? Princess, I'm taking care of everything here. There's no need.

I inhale a shaky breath, not knowing what to say. It doesn't feel right to lie to him, but I don't want him to lose faith in what we're trying to do, to lose faith in us. Not when my goal is still to be able to be with him freely.

Just as soon as I figure out how to get out of the mess I've made and meet with the lawyer Riya said she found. I have no intention of keeping the Faraci name.

> Me: I really don't want to talk about this on text.

Pausing before I press Send, I think about what I want to write. I could hold off on saying anything, but then, I'm not sure whether Julian's goons will tell him. And I'd rather him find out from me, even over text, even if he'll be mad, versus finding out from somebody else.

My stomach cramps and my hands grow clammy as I type and erase, then retype a message out.

> Me: I had to do something that you're not going to like. Something I didn't want to do. But it's to keep you safe, to keep everyone safe, and I need you to not be mad at me. I need you to understand.

Bile rises through my esophagus, and I swallow around the sour taste in my mouth, my stomach tossing and heaving.

> Aidan: You can tell me anything, princess.
> Me: I married Julian today.

And then I drop my phone, running to the toilet just in time to throw up.

CHAPTER 20

Julian

I'VE BEEN TRYING TO GET A HOLD OF ALI ALL WEEK, but he hasn't returned my phone calls and I haven't had a chance to stop by his house. He's been a ghost on email, having gone from working from home to not really existing within Sultans at all, and I wonder if he's taken a turn, one that has him unable to do things that require focus and energy.

A twinge of unease smarts in my chest when he doesn't answer *again* when I try to call, and my leg shakes beneath my desk. I'm not sure if he's just feeling worse for the wear or if he's avoiding my calls because he wasn't quite as accepting of my relationship with Yasmin as he made it appear.

Either way, I need to break the news that we're legally wed, and I want to do it in person.

Ending the call to Ali, I dial Yasmin's cell instead. She forwards it to voicemail, and I grit my teeth, taking a deep breath to keep the annoyance from suffocating every pore.

She's also been avoiding me; stubbornness obviously runs thick in the Karam family line. I haven't minded much, since I don't need her to do anything other than exactly what she has been, sitting in my house and sending message after unanswered message to the boy for the past seven days since we were married at the courthouse.

I haven't had much time to care about her silence because I've barely been home as it is. Sultans can only run for so long without me focusing on what's important there, and with Ian gone to Egypt, I've been up to my neck in meetings both within Sultans as well as after-hours meets in an empty warehouse I own on the outskirts of town with the Romanos, the Italian outfit that's based in New York. They supply us with the weapons we use to trade for access to the mines across the world.

And that's how this business works. Everything is a negotiation, and there's no true good and evil. The separation is an illusion created by those of us in power to keep the masses at bay and feeling as though there are people fighting for what's right.

But the truth is that one hand always washes the other, and I'm the water that rinses both clean.

In the few spare moments I've had, I've taken to pulling up her string of texts and call logs. She hasn't done anything crazy, other than act like a desperate girl eager to regain the attention of that street rat.

It *is* surprising how he's ignoring her, however. An odd one-eighty from the eager kid who was willing to turn the world upside down to prove his love just a couple weeks ago.

But I'm sure that when he returns home, she'll snare him again.

I remember peering at them through the thin slat of the door in the room where they used to have their secret rendezvous.

Blowing out a breath, I try to shake away the image of her naked body, but it keeps dragging me under, and as usual these days, I can't clear it from my mind.

Frustrated, I slam the phone down on the receiver, half-hard from just the singular thought of her, my hand running slightly over the growing bulge to temper my arousal.

It doesn't work, and instead of being able to move on with my day and clear her from my brain, I let her take over entirely. Closing my eyes, my palm rubs against my now painfully hard erection, imagining her beneath my desk, her soft hand being the one to tease me.

Would she beg for my cock? Choke on it?

Groaning, I unzip my slacks and pull out my throbbing dick. Gripping it at the base, I slowly roll my hand up the shaft, my heart racing and my stomach tensing from how good it feels.

I imagine Yasmin's pouty lips slipping over the head, her tongue flicking the slit on my tip and those perfect dark eyes staring up at me as she sucks me down.

My hand moves quickly, fingers tingling from how badly I wish I could grab fistfuls of her hair and slide into her mouth instead of the poor substitution of my palm.

Would she take me all the way down? Let me glide along her tongue and slip into the back of her throat?

My balls tense, heat collecting at the base of my spine, and I stroke faster, my hips thrusting up into my hand, wishing like hell that I could feel the wetness of her mouth and hear her gagging on my cock, the sparkle of her ring, proving to the world that she's *mine*, glinting in the lighting as she works the base of my dick in tandem with the strokes of her lips.

That last visual does it, and I grab a handkerchief just in time to catch the heavy spurts of cum that release into the rag, my vision dotting with stars.

Goddamn.

I can't remember the last time I've come so hard.

Blowing out a breath, I tuck myself back into my slacks, tossing the handkerchief into the bin beneath my desk, and reach up to tug at the roots of my hair.

Shaking off the momentary weakness, I refocus my thoughts on what's important, which is figuring out what the hell Ali is up to.

Yasmin should go with me to see him. It's the perfect opportunity for her to step up and show Ali that we're happier than ever. Picking up the phone one more time, I call her. She forwards to voicemail again. I press redial and finally she picks up.

"What?" She sounds angry.

"Get ready to go. I'll be there in thirty minutes, and I want you on the front steps waiting."

She sighs. "Where are we going?"

"To see your father."

I hang up, knowing that she won't pass up the opportunity, and walk out of my office, stopping briefly to look at Ciara as she types away on her computer. She looks frazzled, and if I had to guess, I would assume it's from the extra workload she's taken on ever since I've put Ian on the side mission of keeping the boy occupied. Ian didn't hire Ciara to be an assistant, but she's doing a surprisingly good job, and although I haven't mentioned anything, I plan to give her a raise when he returns.

She glances up at me from her computer.

"Reschedule my meeting with the PR department today. Something's come up."

She nods, her lips thin and her eyes downcast.

It takes forty minutes to get back to my house after sitting in traffic, and when I pull up around the circle drive, Yasmin is sitting on the front steps of the house, wearing black sweats that cinch around her ankles and a white hoodie, leaning back on her elbows.

The Audi R8 purrs as I stop in front of her.

"You're late," she complains as she slips into the passenger seat.

I sit and stare at her, one of my hands on the wheel of the car and the other resting on my thigh, my gaze involuntarily drinking her up like water in a desert. There's something about seeing her dressed down like this, like she just woke up from a nap and has nobody to impress, that has my chest tightening and my dick twitching.

"What?" she asks, her brows lifting to her hairline.

I'm thankful for the sunglasses that hide my gaze from her view. I don't need her knowing how much she affects me. Not until I figure out how to make the feeling go away. I would give *anything* to go back to before I spied on her and the boy in that room, because before that night, she was always just Ali's spoiled daughter. Too young and too annoying to even be on my radar. Now…

Things would be much easier for me if I wasn't suddenly attracted to her.

I put the car in park, leaning over the middle console, the side of my arm brushing against her chest. She sucks in a breath, slamming herself against the back of her seat. My face is almost directly in front of hers now, and the scent of vanilla overwhelms my senses as I reach around her.

"Wh-what are you doing?" she rasps.

Pulling on the seat belt, I drag it across the front of her body, the backs of my knuckles ghosting against her breasts as I buckle her in, then move back to my own seat, gripping the steering wheel so I don't do something completely out of character like grab her face and shove my tongue in her mouth.

She clears her throat. "Thank you."

I don't respond, my teeth grinding as I stare out the front windshield and drive onto the streets.

"We're really going to see my father?"

I nod, a tendril of worry creeping up my spine when I remember how long it's been since I've even spoken with him. "Have you talked to him?"

Her body slumps against the passenger door, her eyes glazing over as she stares out the window. "No, he hasn't answered his phone. But I've talked to his nurse. She said he's been sleeping a lot. And she's upped his pain reliever to keep him comfortable, so he's been groggy."

We come to a red light, and I take the opportunity to glance over, unable to ignore the melancholy bleeding from her features. It fills up the car and wraps itself around me, trying to drag me into its depth, but I won't let it. The last thing I need is to show weakness in front of the enemy. And even though lately Yasmin doesn't feel like it, that's what she still is. The enemy.

The one person who is standing in the way of what I want most.

So it doesn't matter that I empathize, just the slightest bit, with her sadness over losing her father. I won't *let* it matter.

"He doesn't like to have me around when he feels so weak," she blurts out.

It doesn't surprise me. Ali's always been a proud man, making sure he presents only the best version of himself in every aspect. It's something that I've always respected, revered even. Something I molded my own image around based on seeing him do the same.

There's a strange feeling inside my chest, making me want to say something to ease the hurt on her face, but I tamp it down, staying silent instead until we drive through the security at the estate's entrance and stop in the front circle drive right by the gaudy fountain.

I throw the car in park and am walking around and opening her door to offer her my hand before she can even unbuckle her belt, and when she slips her palm in mine, allowing me to pull her from her seat, my stomach flips.

She glances at me from under her lashes, a curious gleam coasting through her bright eyes. And she keeps stealing glances as we walk up the front steps together, our hands still entwined, my thumb rubbing against her wedding band.

"Put on a good show and I'll bring back the boy," I offer when we reach the door.

She exhales, staring at me with wide eyes. "You're lying."

"I'm not."

She lets out a sound, her hand flying up to her mouth to cover the noise. "So he's okay?"

"Why wouldn't he be?" I tilt my head.

"He's been quiet, and I just thought..." She shakes her head. "Never mind. I'm glad you haven't hurt him."

I play with the underside of her ring, my chest tightening from the look on her face. I don't enjoy the way she's making me feel bad for her, like I should care. Like I should try to make it better.

It's annoying, feeling like I need to be responsible for someone else's emotions. I'm still trying to break free from my mother's hold; the last thing I need is to add someone else to the mix.

My grip on her fingers tightens. "I told you that your time with me didn't need to be miserable. There's only one thing I want from you, and that's you to be *my* wife in public. I don't care if in private, you become his whore."

The grateful look on her face drops and she rips her hand away, scoffing. "Fuck. *You.*"

Then she opens the door and walks inside, her footsteps strong and furious as she marches down the hall to find her father.

CHAPTER 21

Yasmin

JULIAN AND I WALK THROUGH THE FRONT entrance and I'm stewing. Again. I don't know why I even tried to have a civil conversation with him.

"Put on a happy face, gattina, or I'll give you something to really cry about."

I glare over at him, wishing I could find the nearest sharp object and use it to stab him.

"I know what to do," I bite out.

"Clearly."

Smiling wide, I make sure to show all my teeth.

"Better," he says.

"It's because I'm imagining what it would feel like to kill you."

He smirks, his hand coming to the small of my back as he pushes me forward and around the corner toward my father's room.

I don't see my father's nurse Shaina in the hall before I'm slamming into her, my hands reaching out to steady myself and to keep us both from toppling to the ground.

"God, Yasmin, you scared me," she pants, jumping back and hunching her lithe frame over to catch her breath.

"I'm so sorry, Shaina." I can't help but laugh, the adrenaline of the moment wearing off and making me loopy.

Shaina stands up straight again, smiling wide, beads of perspiration dripping down the sides of her forehead and making her skin shimmer.

"Are you okay?" I ask, tilting my head, concern worming through me.

Shaina nods, her eyes flicking from me to where Julian's standing silently behind me. "I'm just fine. Your father had a fall, and he's not the lightest man to pick up. Took my breath away and gave me exercise, though, so can't complain too much." My heart squeezes, and it must show on my face because she reaches out and grasps my hand in hers. "I know it's hard to hear, sweetie. But it's just the natural progression of things. Better to come to terms with it than keep trying to…"

Her voice trails off when her gaze focuses on the giant ring sitting like a beacon on my left hand, her mouth dropping in shock.

I force a small smile, feeling Julian's ever-imposing stature come even closer to my back. "Is he up for company?" I ask, trying to keep things light even though internally, I'm screaming for her not to buy it.

For her to help me.

For *someone* to save me from this mess.

Shaina nods slowly, her eyes coming up to meet mine as she drops my hand. "I'm sure he'll want to see you for something like this. That's a beautiful ring."

I swallow back the pain and allow the anger at Julian for not even allowing my father to be there when I officially got married to fill me up in its place. What's the point of trying to trick him into thinking this is real if we eloped without him? Isn't this whole thing to convince my father to give everything to Julian anyway? I don't understand how pissing him off and excluding him will help that.

Although I *had* expected him to be much more upset at the fact that Julian and I were together at all, and instead, he surprised me with calm words and wisdom. So maybe I don't know this new version of my father as well as I'd like to think.

"Where is he?" Julian asks.

Shaina doesn't even spare him a glance, keeping her gaze locked on me before glancing behind her and then back. "He's resting in his room."

Nodding, I run my hand up her arm and bring her into a hug. "Thank you for doing everything you do. I know it can't be easy."

"Please," she replies, brushing me off and patting my back. "It's what I'm here for."

She lets me go and we smile at each other.

"Chop-chop, gattina. We don't have all day," Julian says at my back.

I inhale deeply, closing my eyes as I try to remain calm, because if I allow myself to get riled by him right before we go to see my dad, I might *actually* end up killing him. And that seems counterintuitive to proving that we're in love.

Moving down the hall, I reach my father's room first, knocking on his door and hearing a faint "Come in."

My hand trembles slightly as I turn the handle, because it's an overwhelming feeling to tell the man who I've always been afraid to let down that I got married to someone without him there.

I went through all this trouble to try and keep from upsetting him, and yet here I am coming full circle, about to disappoint him anyway.

His eyes light up when I walk in the room, and I force the smile to stick on my face even as my insides burn with grief as I take him in. He's lost a lot of weight, even though it's only been a week and a half since I've seen him. His face is gaunt, and if it wasn't for his beard, which is growing in nicely despite his body giving up the fight, he'd look almost skeletal.

There's a scent of Vicks VapoRub in the air, the menthol tang hitting my nose and making my eyes water, and his gaze is glossed over from him being doped up on pain meds to keep him from feeling the worst of the lung cancer breaking down his body.

"Yasmin," he coos.

"Hey, old man," Julian says from behind me, grabbing a chair from the small round table in the corner of the room. He drags it over to the bedside, and I expect him to sit down, but he surprises me, moving over to me instead and placing his hand on my lower back, ushering me toward the seat and helping me into it.

"Avoiding me?" Julian directs to my father as I settle into the chair.

My father's jaw stiffens the slightest bit, but then he blows out a deep breath and shakes his head. "I've just been feeling a little under the weather. Figured you had everything under control."

Julian nods as he pulls up the other chair right next to me, sitting down and crossing his leg over the opposite knee. "You know I do. Still, I'd like to catch you up on some things."

My father sighs, rubbing his forehead like a headache is forming. "Yasmin, give us a few minutes."

I move to stand, though everything in me wants to stay, even if it's just to be a silent bystander watching them talk shop. Every second I can spend in my father's presence I want to greedily grab up like treasure, because I don't know how many seconds we have left.

Julian's warm hands come down on top of my thigh, sending heat spreading up my leg and through my abdomen. My breathing falters at the feeling.

"Sit."

It's one word, but the command in it is unmistakable.

My father's eyes harden. "If you're here to talk business, she doesn't need any part of it. She's my daughter, not a business partner."

His words sting, the same way they always do, and I want to ask him why he's even bothering to leave me everything if he's so against me being any part of it, but I bite down on my tongue instead, jolting from the sharp prick of pain.

Julian nods, brushing his hands down the chest of his perfectly fitted black suit before meeting my father's gaze head-on. "And now she's my wife. Which means she's *my* partner."

My father's face starts to shift, anger becoming so prevalent on his features I can practically see the steam coming out of his ears. "*Wife?*"

"I know you must be upset," Julian continues. "And it's not fair that I took her from under your nose. Despicable, really. But what's done is done." He leans forward. "At least I waited until you approved the wedding before we did anything, old man. But honestly, can you blame me? Your daughter…"

He looks to me with such a genuine look of adoration that my heart skips.

Damn, he's good.

Asshole.

"Your daughter is *everything*. Surely you remember being in love."

I can't help the small huff that escapes when I think about Julian Faraci ever *actually* falling in love.

His eyes move back to my father's, and I follow the gaze, chewing on the inside of my lip until it stings. I expect a fight. After all, my baba isn't the type of man to go down without one, and his authority is law. The fact that Julian is so blatantly disregarding him and taking the power for himself so effortlessly is almost awe-inspiring to watch. If not absolutely terrifying.

Because if he can go against my father, who would *ever* go against him? *I need to talk to Riya.*

"There's no going back, so please, Ali, just be happy that she's mine." He leans forward.

My father sighs, his stare moving from Julian to me, his gaze like stone.

"Yasmin," he starts, his voice sharp. "How could you—"

"No," Julian cuts in.

The silence that blankets the air is thick, and I hold my breath, afraid that if I move, it will pierce the tension until it detonates like a bomb.

"You will *not* take it out on her," Julian continues. "This was my decision. The only thing she's done wrong is love a man she wasn't supposed to love and give in to his selfish, demanding ways."

My throat swells as I listen to Julian talk, gratitude, as misplaced and unwelcome as it is, surging through my veins and warming my heart. I've never had anyone stand up for me before, and even though it's not real, even though he forced me and is blackmailing me, there's a twisted sense of happiness that he's refusing to let me take the fall. He's protecting my relationship with my father as much as he can, even though he's the cause of all the strife.

I hate him just a little less in this moment, and it makes me sick.

There's a grunt from the bed, and I keep my gaze trained on my lap, not wanting to look up and see the rejection on my father's face. But he surprises me when he says, "I don't have the energy to be angry."

My head snaps up, relief pouring through me when I see nothing but acceptance in his eyes.

Julian's hand is still on my leg and his fingers squeeze my thigh. I reach down, slipping my hand beneath his and showing solidarity. He protected me in his own weird way, even though I'm not sure why, so I'll play my part to perfection, the way I know he wants.

"We can still plan a wedding," I chime in. "I want you to walk me down the aisle."

My father opens his mouth to speak, but instead, a rough cough surges up in its place, and the sound makes my insides jump and my fingers grip a little tighter onto Julian's.

The cough is harsher now than it ever has been before, and I feel useless, unable to do anything except sit by his side and watch him suffer through the pain.

My own chest feels like it's splitting in two the longer my father struggles to regain his composure, and it isn't until he has that I realize my other hand has grasped onto Julian's wrist, bringing his entire forearm to rest in my lap while my fingers hold on to him so tightly it blanches his skin. His thumb is rubbing soothing circles on my palm, and even though it's sick and wrong and everything I'm supposed to be against, I don't pull away from the comfort he's providing. It makes me feel a little less, and right now, sitting at my baba's bedside while his body fails in front of my eyes, I'd give anything not to feel.

My father recovers, wiping beneath his eyes and reaching for the glass of water at his bedside table. I jump up to grab it for him, but he stops me halfway there with a sharp glare.

"I'm *fine*, Yasmin. Leave it."

My heart drops. "I...of course. I'm sorry."

He sighs, leaning back against his pillows and rubbing his eyes. "I'm tired, and if you keep your *wife* in the room, I'm not able to talk. She doesn't need to be involved in the business, Julian."

Julian's quiet for a moment before leaning over and pressing his lips against my forehead.

I'm so choked up from everything that just happened, I couldn't speak if I tried.

"I'll only be a moment. Stay close so you can come back in and say goodbye."

Swallowing around the knot in my throat, I nod. And then before I can take another breath, his lips are on mine.

It's quick and chaste and shouldn't be anything other than a show.

But it throws my entire world off its axis anyway.

CHAPTER 22

Julian

I SHOULD BE IN THE OFFICE, DOING MY ACTUAL job of running a multibillion-dollar diamond conglomerate, something that I haven't done enough of ever since Yasmin took center stage in my life.

We're close to launching two new lines of jewelry, one for Christmas and one for Valentine's Day, and since Ian isn't at the office fielding the incessant questions and approving on my behalf things that I don't have time to focus on, there are mounds of emails and meetings piling up while I ignore them to be with her instead.

Take right now, for instance, when it's barely past five p.m. and I'm sitting in my family room, my body warmed by the crackling of the fireplace, as I watch her get drunk off my expensive whiskey.

"What are you looking at?" She squints at me, taking another sip.

I relax in the oversize chair, bringing my own glass up to my mouth. "You."

"Yeah," she sighs, throwing herself back into the couch. "You do that a lot."

"What?" I ask. "Look at you?"

"Mm-hmm." She closes her eyes, leaning her head against the cushions. "You never used to, not when I would have cared anyway. But now it's like...I can feel you staring and all I want is for you to disappear."

I frown, although I'm not sure why her words bother me.

Her gaze jolts open, her face turning toward me.

"So serious," she mocks. "You know, Baba used to say if you frowned too much, your face would get stuck that way."

"Fascinating," I drawl, taking a drink of whiskey and reveling in the burn as it blazes down my throat and settles in my chest.

"I could see you being a grumpy kid, I won't lie," she muses. "Got any pictures to dispel my theory?"

"Enough," I snap, not wanting to talk about my childhood.

She sticks out her bottom lip, scoffing and rolling her eyes. It's an immature thing to do, and my hand tingles, imagining what it would feel like to spank her ass and make her sorry for the disrespect. I take another sip instead, trying to shake off the feeling.

It goes silent after that because I definitely ruined the moment, and I'm about to leave her to continue drinking on her own when she speaks, her voice quieter than before.

"How do you remember then?" she asks.

"Remember what?"

"You know..." She waves her arm around. "All the good stuff."

I drain the rest of my glass and set it down on the end table beside me. "I'd rather forget."

Her brows furrow and she tilts her head, a curious gleam coasting across her eyes. The depth of her stare makes me uncomfortable, like she's peeling back layers that I didn't mean to expose and trying to find the broken little boy that's buried underneath.

She won't find him there. He disappeared with my piece-of-shit father.

"I love taking photos, but I haven't done it for real in years," she says absentmindedly.

"I've seen you with your camera several times," I note.

"Yeah, but it's not the same."

"A picture is a picture."

Her hands smack the couch and she scoffs. "And a diamond is just a diamond, right?"

I tip my drink toward her. "Touché."

She runs her fingertip along the bottom of her mouth, and my stomach jumps, wondering what her lips taste like with whiskey on her breath.

"You wanna know something?" she asks, a playful gleam in her eye.

I sigh, pretending to be annoyed although I'm anything but. "I assume you'll tell me regardless."

"I took photography courses in college." She smacks her hands over her mouth like she didn't mean to tell me.

"Wow," I drawl. "You're such a rebel."

She runs a hand through her hair, reaching to the table and grabbing her drink before gulping down the rest and placing the glass back down. "Yeah, well, my father doesn't know. But like… when I tell you I've never experienced true joy with *anything* the way I did when I was in a darkroom developing my own film?" She shakes her head. "I mean it. Now, everything is instant." She snaps her fingers. "Digital. But when I was alone in a room with no light, watching memories I captured form in front of my eyes…" She shakes her head. "That's the only time my mind would stop badgering me with uncontrollable thoughts."

My chest tightens as I watch longing peek through her face. I hadn't even known she was seriously into photography. I had always just assumed she was busy spending Ali's money and frolicking around the city on a flash-in-the-pan hobby she didn't really care about.

But that's not this woman in front of me, and now I'm wondering if the version of her in my head ever really existed at all.

"That's what you love about it? The silence?" I ask, suddenly desperate to know more about her.

She smiles softly. "I love capturing memories. Emotion that's usually fleeting being frozen forever in time. The wisdom in the gaze of a person who's lived a full life. The look in someone's eyes when they realize they're in love. The joy in their face when they're laughing at a joke. Photographs help us remember things we'd otherwise forget." Her grin fades. "I've been trying to take some of my father while I still can, but I have to sneak them in when he isn't looking. If he knew, I don't think he'd even *let* me take a snapshot to capture his last moments."

Her voice breaks on the last word, and an unwanted pang of sympathy hits me in the chest.

She gives me a pointed look, her eyes glossy from the whiskey and her unshed tears. "I guess he's like you and would rather just forget."

Leaning forward, she grabs the bottle of liquor from the coffee table, refilling her glass and taking a large drink.

"Your father loves you," I say. "He's just a proud man. You two really aren't that different. Both stubborn. Pigheaded.

Overachievers." I pause, not sure how she'll take what I'm saying but wanting to rile her up anyway. Dealing with her ire is better than dealing with her realness, and I'm uncomfortable with how much I enjoyed hearing about her passion. "You're more of a people pleaser than him though," I add. "Must have gotten that from your mother."

I expect her to shoot back with a smart-ass comment, one that will make me either want to murder her or bend her over and fuck the brat out of her, but she just nods, bringing the glass up to her lips again.

"Wouldn't know. Never met her."

"Yeah, well, consider yourself lucky," I reply. "Moms aren't all they're cracked up to be."

She tilts her head. "I can't imagine your mom. Tell me about her."

I smirk. "You can meet her if you like."

"Okay."

Chuckling, I stand up, my head spinning from the alcohol.

Shit. I guess it's gotten to me more than I originally thought, and if I'm feeling the effects, she must be hammered. Moving over to the couch, I sit down next to her, my fingers brushing against hers as I pull the glass of whiskey from her hand and set it on the table.

The energy in the room shifts, heat buzzing between us, firing against the side of my thigh as it rests inches away from hers.

My stomach tightens and I swallow as I stare at her face.

Goddamn, she's beautiful.

Slowly, I reach out and drag my fingers down her cheek until I'm cupping her chin. "How many times do I have to tell you to be careful what you wish for?"

Her tongue peeks out, swiping across her bottom lip, *so* close to where my thumb rests just beneath the pout of her mouth. I swallow hard, my stomach twisting into knots as I hold her stare, this weird tension spreading thin like a string about to snap.

Mentally, I go over every single reason why I should let go and walk away.

She's too young.

I'm planning to kill her.

She's not really mine.

I don't even *want* her to be.

But there's something stronger taking over, and that's what I listen to instead. Maybe later, I'll blame it on the liquor, but for now, I'm reveling in the moment.

Her perfect mouth parts and my thumb traces along its edges, my gaze dropping to the swell of her breasts as her breathing grows heavy.

"You're playing a dangerous game letting me touch you like this."

Her eyes flash and she leans in, resting the weight of her face against my hand. "Maybe I like a bit of danger."

Those words are my undoing and I unravel, leaning forward and brushing my lips against hers. She moans against my mouth, and our tongues meet, tangling and sucking and biting. It's messy and feverish, and I feel like I can't get close enough.

My hands reach out and wrap around her waist, dragging her into me until she's straddling my lap, the heat of her cunt settling on top of my cock and making it throb with the need to be inside her. My hand is still cupping her cheek and I press harder, cradling her face as I kiss the fuck out of her, lost in whatever this thing is that she's making me feel.

Her palms slide up my shoulders and around my neck until she's threading her fingers through the hair on the nape of my neck, and goose bumps sprout down the length of my arms. It's exhilarating, having someone touch me and not hate the way it feels.

I've never experienced it before. Never let it happen.

Suddenly, I'm desperate to feel her come. It's not a want, it's a *need* to know what it feels like to have her face flush with pleasure because of me, and not just because I'm watching.

My free hand glides down her torso, bunching up her shirt and slipping beneath the hem before moving back up, caressing her soft skin while I grip her hip and start to move her back and forth over me. She moans again, and I suck it down like water, savoring the unrestrained noises she makes as she grinds her pussy along the length of my dick.

I break my lips away, my hold moving from her cheek until it skates back into the curls of her hair, pulling until she bows backward, her neck exposed.

She inhales sharply, and my fingers flex in her hair, tilting her head to the side and leaning in to drag my lips across her throat. "*Fuck*, you're driving me wild." She's moving on her own now, rotating her hips in a slow and steady rhythm, and I push my hips into hers, letting her feel every inch of my cock as it strains against my zipper. "Do you feel what you do to me?"

Her mouth parts, and she leans more of her body weight into my hand.

"Answer me," I demand, my grip on her hip tightening.

"Yes," she breathes.

"You make me so fucking hard."

My tongue slips out at the juncture between her neck and her collarbone, and I groan at the taste of her.

"You like that, don't you? Knowing you drive me to the point of madness," I continue, moving the hand that's on her hip until it skims the top of her sweats, dipping my fingers beneath the fabric. "I can't work. I can't eat. I can't think of *anything* except spreading you wide open and slipping between your perfect thighs so I can fill you up."

Precum leaks from my cock at the image I'm painting, and I bite the inside of my cheek to keep it together. To not tear her clothes off and throw her on the floor, sinking inside her until she screams.

"You should tell me to stop," I rasp, my fingers dipping farther beneath the fabric of her pants.

"Stop," she whispers back. But her hands grip my hair tighter, twisting the strands until it stings.

I move my face up and my hand from out of her hair until I'm once again cupping her jaw. "If I *don't* stop, will you still hate me in the morning?"

Her movements halt completely, and she pulls back until we're locked in a heavy gaze. My cock pulses against her, so fucking close to coming just from her rubbing her sweet little cunt on my lap, and my hands—one on her face and one halfway down her pants—twitch with the urge to make her finish the job.

Her gaze shutters and she licks her bottom lip. "Probably."

I nod, resting my forehead against hers for one second.

Two.

Three.

And then I grit my teeth and pull away, dropping her and rushing out of the room.

I go straight to Isabella's enclosure, checking to make sure she's okay. Yasmin's presence has kept me from attending to her as much, and I want to make sure she isn't lonely. I don't see her in the enclosure, so she must be asleep or hiding, so I head to my room instead and then farther back into the en suite, throwing the shower on cold and jumping beneath the harsh spray, hoping the water will temper the fire that's blazing through my body, begging me to go back and claim what's mine.

It's *my* ring she's wearing.

It's *my* last name she has.

I close my fist and smash it into the tile, the pain grounding me enough to remind myself of what I really want.

And it's not her.

No matter how much it feels like it is.

CHAPTER 23

Yasmin

MY TONGUE IS STUCK TO THE ROOF OF MY MOUTH.

That's the first thing I notice.

Then, slowly, the thick, aching throb of my head starts to wake me up. Pulsing, beating, heavy stabs of pain that make me feel like someone hit me with a giant boulder, then ran me over with a tractor tire for good measure.

Groaning, I squeeze my eyes shut tighter, not wanting to open them. If I open them, then the vertigo might have a chance to set in before I even stand up, making my world spin and my vision blur until I puke.

Oh, man.

The back corners of my mouth turn sour, like I sucked on a warhead without the sweet aftertaste, my stomach tossing and turning violently even though I'm making sure to stay as still as possible in my bed.

The sheets are tangled around my legs, and I try to slowly jerk them free, my muscles tensing and releasing as I gingerly move my body and try to assess just how incredibly hungover I must be.

How much did I drink yesterday?

Finally, I get the courage to peel my eyelids apart, rolling to my side and adjusting to the bright light of the morning. Rays of sunshine splash across the room, and small kaleidoscopes of color reflect on a glass of water sitting on my bedside.

I scrunch my brows and then immediately regret the decision when it makes the pain in my head even worse.

But I don't remember bringing in a glass of water.

Swallowing around my cotton mouth, I push through the nausea and the general feeling of having died and reach out to grab the glass, the need for a drink overriding the fear of moving.

I take a small sip, my body crying in relief when it hits my tongue.

And this is why I don't drink outside of a glass of wine or champagne in social settings.

It's literally *never* worth it the next morning.

I'm a lightweight, and even worse, there hasn't been a single time in my entire life when I haven't gotten the hangover blues. I'm an overthinker on an average day, but add in the depressive episodes after binge drinking, and I'll convince myself that I should never go in public again, simply from ruminating over all the words and conversations I may or may not have had.

Regret runs thick through my veins, and I look for my phone, my eyes snagging on a piece of paper instead. There's a note set right next to the pain reliever, and I grab both, downing the pills without a second thought.

I go through everything that happened last night, reeling as I try to remember every single word that I'd said since we got back from my father's house and I raided the liquor cabinet in Julian's home.

Groaning, my hands fly to my face, my nails digging into my forehead as if trying to claw the ache away, the leftover embarrassment from everything that happened last night making me want to wither away until I'm nothing.

He must think I'm the stupidest girl on the planet. And that's probably because I *am*. Who else would find themselves in hell and make themselves at home with their quintessential captor? Even worse than that, I felt comfortable. Like I belonged. Like I could sit there forever, drinking Julian's expensive whiskey and watching him force a scowl so he doesn't break character and smile, and I could never care about anything else again.

But that was just the alcohol talking, and things always look a little different in the daylight.

I pick up the note, rubbing the sleep from my eyes to clear my vision. The nausea gets worse before I even read the words, because I just *know* it's from him.

Take the pills. Drink the water. Take a shower.—J

Rolling my eyes, I place the note back down on the table. *So damn bossy.* Like I wouldn't have done all those things anyway. Flashes of last night filter slowly through my brain, and while I should probably be thinking about how close he got to crossing a line we absolutely should never cross, instead I can't stop thinking about how he said he'd introduce me to his mother.

I can't lie and say I'm not intrigued at the idea of meeting her. To be honest, I had half convinced myself he was a weird anomaly, just showing up on earth as a raging asshole from birth with no parents to give him love. I try to imagine what his childhood looked like, since he was pretty tight-lipped about the whole thing, but I just can't picture him as a carefree little boy with innocence thrumming through his veins and giggles pouring from his lips.

Despite everything, a tendril of excitement grows inside me. I know I'll never work up the courage to ask about his family again, not now that I've sworn off drinking forever, so I hope that he meant what he said last night.

Honestly, it's the least he can do after forcing me to be his wife and then running away without letting me come.

I grab my phone, unlocking the screen, hope inflating like a balloon as I see a new notification, thinking that maybe it's Riya with some more good news.

Then the flash of guilt hits because it's the first time I *didn't* want it to be Aidan.

Doesn't really matter, I guess, because there's nothing from him anyway.

Again.

The cracks in my heart fracture just a bit more at the loss of him in my life. Regardless of the fact that I've done things with Julian I can't take back, I still love Aidan, and I still want to find someone who will break me free of Julian's grasp and let me live my life with Aidan instead.

I switch over to the unopened message.

Riya: We still on for brunch next week on Sunday morning? I've got some news, don't want to share over the phone.

Me: Yeah, if I can convince my master to set me free.

I smirk at the dark joke, trying to find some humor in this fucked-up situation, but all it really does is make me feel worse.

Tossing my phone back on the nightstand, I ignore the nausea that's teasing my throat, wishing like hell that pain reliever was instantaneous. All the inventions in the world, and yet we still have to wait twenty to thirty minutes to get rid of a headache. Dragging myself out of bed, I meander into the en suite bathroom, reaching into the large stone shower and flipping the water onto the hottest setting. Then I walk to the double sink, staring at the disaster of a girl in the reflection of the mirror.

Get it together, Yasmin. You're more than your current circumstance.

I move as slowly as possible while I strip off my clothes, the steam from the shower filling up the room, making it humid and hot. My hands grip the edge of the sink, and I lean down, resting my forehead against the cool white quartz counter, enjoying the way it feels against my sticky, clammy skin. I exhale and lift my head, staring at my reflection again as it distorts and disappears behind the steam of hot water, the mirror fogging completely.

Pushing myself off the sink, I walk across the cool tile floor and then step under the shower, enjoying the multiple nozzles that spray the water from every angle, plus the one directly above my head that rains down like a thunderstorm.

I give in to the feeling of the pelting water, leaning against the wall and bending my head until my hair is drenched, lines of liquid running down the side of my face to collect on the shower floor. I'll probably regret this later when my hair is a frizzy mess, but right now it feels so good, I'm finding it hard to care.

I'm not sure how long I stand there, hoping the water washes away the grime and scrubs me clean both inside and out, but eventually, I start to feel almost normal, and I flip around, leaning my back against the wall.

My hand sweeps across my collarbone, tickling the skin. I

continue the movement, back and forth, slowly feeling my body come alive beneath my own touch, my nipples pebbling even beneath the hot water. I move my fingers down, dragging my hands along the top of my chest until I cup both of my breasts, rolling my nipples between my thumbs and forefingers, enjoying the way sharp pricks of pleasure are sparking from my touch.

Similar to the last time I touched myself in the shower, I close my eyes and lean my head back against the wall, imagining Aidan in front of me, that *his* hands are touching me softly. He's the only other person besides Julian who has, and I refuse to picture the man I'm supposed to hate.

I bite into my lower lip as I keep working my way down, brushing my hand across the expanse of my stomach, feeling the skin pucker with goose bumps. The tops of my hip bones are next, and if I try hard enough, I can see the way Aidan would lean in, pressing a sloppy kiss to my body while he whispered sweet words into my skin. I sigh with happiness, getting lost in the fantasy as I ghost my fingers over my pussy.

The second I brush my clit, the image transforms, another set of eyes flashing in my head. It's brief and then it's gone, but it sends a shot of heat spearing through my middle like it's cutting me in half. My back arches off the stone wall and I let out a small gasp.

I don't know what the hell that was, but it felt good, so I do it again, applying more pressure the second time. My abs clench tight, and in my head, Aidan's soft hands turn into rough tattooed fingers.

No.

Shaking off the image, I try to force Aidan back into my brain, but my body is needy and my mind is rebelling, and the second I grasp my breast with my left hand and slip my right one through the wetness pooling between my legs, Aidan disappears completely, and dark, almost-black eyes stare up at me while he kneels on the shower floor.

A small moan involuntarily escapes me, my clit swelling beneath my touch as I start to move my fingers back and forth over the sensitive area, arousal coiling around the base of my spine and spreading like rolling fog.

I give in to the fantasy.

Something sharp and heady spears through my middle, my nerves on edge from every single touch. I remember the way it felt to have Julian's hands on me and his hard cock pressing against my center as I ground myself against him and listened to his dirty words against my skin. And then it flits to another memory of the heated look in Julian's stare when he was watching me through a crack in the door, his eyes like fire as my pussy got licked by another man.

My hand shoots out and pulls on a detachable showerhead, bringing it down until the water beats against my clit, and my breath whooshes out of me as my pussy spasms from the pressure.

God, that feels good.

I rotate my hips, grinding against the nozzle, the rhythmic pulses of the water making heat spread through my body like a wildfire. In my mind, Julian's not standing at the door anymore. Instead, he's walking into the room with that confident swagger that he always has, and he's standing next to me on that small twin bed, reaching down and palming my breast like it's his right.

I mimic the movement with my own hand, rolling the nipple between my fingers, my other hand moving the showerhead back and forth, the heavy water pressure teasing my sensitive nerves.

Julian leans down, his eyes locking on mine and his other

hand brushing along the side of my face, the way he always does. Pleasure skitters along my spine and my muscles tense.

"Come for me, gattina," he rasps.

And I do, my body exploding, wave after wave of euphoria spreading through every single part of me as I come harder than I ever have before, my legs shaking around the metal of the shower nozzle.

Slowly, my soul comes back to my body, and as it does, the regret starts to wind its way around my neck and squeeze, disgust hitting me full force in the gut.

I just got off to thoughts of my husband. *Again.*

And I liked it.

I am absolutely *not* in control.

CHAPTER 24

Julian

USUALLY, I'M NOT EASILY DISTRACTED. I'VE SPENT the hardest years of my life staying laser focused on my goals, which is why I've made it to where I am and why I've stayed on top.

I've built my reputation *and* turned Sultans from just another company into the empire it is today by being cold, aloof, and stubborn, and I have no interest in changing my ways.

But for the first time in my life, my mind wanders, and no matter how hard I try, I can't control it or drag it back to what I should be focusing on.

I'm sitting in a conference room, a dozen suits trying to gain my attention and keep me up-to-date on the latest batch of rough diamonds from Kimberley, South Africa, and I'm busy wondering what my little wife is at home doing and if I should take her with me to Egypt.

She might jump at the chance to see the boy, though I don't know if that will endear me to her or push her away. Or she might be too worried to leave the country with her father so ill, afraid that she'll miss his final moments.

To be honest, I'm not sure he'll let her be around for them either way.

By the time the meeting ends, I couldn't tell you a single fucking thing that went on during it, and I head straight to my office to check emails and leave for the day.

There isn't anything new, so I pull up the email from Jeannie that I received and press Reply.

> *Jeannie,*
> *I'd like an update on the new dig site and also on why you didn't make me aware of Darryn Anders sniffing around. Have it to me by the end of the day.*
> *—J. Faraci*

Shutting down my computer screen, I pick up my phone instead, realizing that I haven't heard from Ian in far too long to be comfortable and I'm putting an end to it now. He also hasn't given me an update on *anything* that I've asked from him.

"Boss," Ian's voice chirps over the line.

I sit in my office chair, leaning back and running a hand through my hair. "You sound chipper."

"Chipper? I sound *bored.*"

"How's the boy?"

I'm not sure why I ask him that first instead of asking about any developments with the lamp. Truth be told, I really don't care how he is; he could be rotting at the bottom of the Red Sea and I wouldn't blink twice. But having him alive and well is still paramount to ensuring Yasmin continues being agreeable. My stomach cramps at the thought of having to blackmail her to keep her at my side, but I don't let the feeling linger.

"Aidan is fine."

"On a first-name basis?" I ask.

"What, did you expect me to sit here and call him 'the boy' to his face?" he guffaws. "You know, I think we underestimated how much he despised working for the Karam family. He doesn't think very highly of Ali. Spends half his time talking to Jeannie—who, by the way, keeps disappearing and not letting anyone go with her—and then the other half of his time on the phone with his mom. And *I'm* doing okay too, thanks for asking, Julian. But it's fucking hot here. I swear to God, I'm practically melting. And we have five different archaeologists sitting around the compound, getting lazy and leaving dishes everywhere. You need to put people in line."

My lips twitch. "You're so dramatic, Ian." I laugh. "Things will all work out. I'll be there in a week and handle everything. We'll make sure everyone knows their place."

"I…you're coming here *yourself*?"

"Did I stutter?" I reply. "I need you to set up a meeting with Darryn Anders for me. Can I trust you to handle that?"

"I can do that." He pauses and then says, "I heard you married the bitch. Were you planning to tell me?"

"Watch your mouth," I demand, something hot and sharp serrating through my chest.

The other end of the line is deadly silent.

Shaking it off, I purse my lips, annoyed at my outburst. "That's my wife. I can't allow you to disrespect her."

"But she's—"

"The plan hasn't changed," I interrupt. "Set up the meeting.

And wait. You've been extremely disappointing lately. Don't let it happen again."

I press End, tossing the phone down in irritation before grabbing my jacket off the coatrack and walking out of the room to go home.

"Ciara," I call out right before I head to the elevators.

She perks her head up from where she's focused on her computer.

"I'll be out of town next week. Adjust my calendar accordingly. I'll need you to take notes at any meetings for me. Is that something you can handle?"

Her spine stiffens, determination filling her gaze as she nods. Smiling slightly at her eager attitude, I leave.

Thirty minutes later, I'm back home, pulling my Audi R8 into the oversize garage and parking at the end of the row. I don't see Yasmin creeping by the garage door until I'm out of the car and halfway there.

"What are you doing?" I ask as I step up to her, my eyes scanning her from head to toe, trying to see if she feels okay after what we did two nights ago and annoyed that I even care.

She glances at me and then back. "Debating on how pissed you'd be if I stole one of your cars and crashed it."

I smirk, slipping my hands into my pockets, my fingers brushing against my metal staff. "What's mine is yours, *wife*. But I'd appreciate it if you didn't crash. Insurance is a bitch."

Suddenly, she spins toward me. "Can you arrange a car to take me to brunch on Sunday? Like... with a driver?"

"Just take one. I really don't care." I wave my hand toward the row of them. "But if you're going out in public, Razul's going with you."

I expect her to fight against it. Her father didn't take her security half as seriously as he should have, considering who he is, but she does me absolutely no good if she dies before her father or before I forge a new will in her name.

"Well, *he* can drive, can't he?"

My brows lift, surprised by her reply. "Yes. Can't you?"

She scoffs, shaking her head. "Please, don't be ridiculous. What kind of twenty-three-year-old can't drive? I just don't *like* to."

I nod, watching her fidget from one foot to the other.

"Who are you going to brunch with?"

This time, her eyes flash and her jaw locks. I wonder if she realizes how much she gives away just by how her body responds to my questions.

"A friend." She brushes a curl out of her face.

"A woman friend?" I push. I assume it's the Riya name that incessantly called her while I had her phone and is now foolishly concocting some plan over text messages with Yasmin over how to best me.

She laughs, her eyes wide as she looks at me. "Don't pretend you care. We both know what this is."

I step in close to her, the tips of my shoes touching hers and her chest brushing against my torso as she cranes her head to keep my gaze.

"On the contrary, gattina. I care very much."

She licks her bottom lip.

I reach my hand out and wrap it around the back of her neck, my lips ghosting across her ear. "If you embarrass me by seeing another man in public, I'll take you over my knee and remind you of your place."

My hand drops like she's burning me, and I brush by her, lightly grazing her shoulder as I move inside.

I head back to Isabella's enclosure, not waiting to see if Yasmin follows behind and honestly not caring if she does. Stepping into the room, I walk over and open the side before moving to the chair that's sitting against the far side of the room. I wait to see if Isabella comes out and eventually she does, her body slithering along the floor until she curls at my feet, her head coming up to my leg. I reach down and give her a pet, an unusual feeling filling my chest.

"I'm a married man, Isa. Can you believe it?" I say. "But don't be jealous. You're still my number one girl."

Isabella's head rests on my knee and I know it's ridiculous to keep talking to her, but I do anyway. Over the years, she's become my closest confidante, my partner in crime, the only living being that I trust implicitly.

"Besides, she's temporary," I remind us both.

The words are bitter on my tongue.

CHAPTER 25

Yasmin

I'VE SPENT THE LAST FOUR DAYS PICKING RANDOM areas of the house to explore. It's not as big as my father's estate—not much is—but it's still large enough that I get lost.

Besides, it's rude that Julian hasn't given me a tour when he expects me to just sit here like a prisoner in solitude all day long.

There's the formal dining room off the foyer that leads into the kitchen. It's an open floor plan, which I like, opening to the family room that I've been actively avoiding ever since I drank too much a week ago and let the enemy get too close.

There's a large office on the other side, and I spent all Tuesday afternoon snooping around it, but most of the desk drawers were locked, so it got boring quickly.

Wednesday, I explored the rest of the rooms on my side of the house. There are three more guest bedrooms, a large library with floor-to-ceiling bookshelves, and the small sitting area in the back next to a baby grand piano. It's beautiful but looks almost completely untouched.

I've never really been a reader, but after spending the rest of the evening there getting lost in the classics, I think I might start.

Yesterday, I went on a walk around the grounds, needing to do *something* other than breathe in the stuffy inside air. I didn't venture too far, since we're way up in the hills and surrounded by trees. Plus, I don't do too well in nature for extended periods of time. I've never really been a "let's go camping" kind of girl.

Today, I'm finally going to venture into the other side of the house, try to find my husband's bedroom and see into the vulnerable side of Julian Faraci. It's the one place I've been wary of going, but if I'm going to find something that I can use against him, that's my bet of where it's going to be.

Besides, he *did* say that's what his is mine, and I'm going to take his words literally.

Being here, acting like I'm okay with everything that's happening until I can get away to meet with Riya, is a much longer game than I originally thought I was going to be playing. It's difficult, and my mind muddles up fact from fiction.

My entire life, I've been used to instant gratification. Used to asking for something and it being handed to me on a silver platter. I can admit that my privilege has gotten me far in life. But as I sit here, stuck in an empty house with no one here and no way to leave even if I wanted, I realize just how much the protective shield my father surrounded me with is more of a crutch than a blessing.

I've never learned simple life skills. I've never had to practice waiting for something and not having the ability to control when and how it lands.

This entire situation is the biggest lesson in patience.

I hate it.

I head across the hall, my hand sliding along the shiny wood banister of the open catwalk that connects the two wings, and straight back to the door that I *think* is Julian's room. Nerves jump and sizzle in my body, and I shake them off, annoyed that I feel like I'm doing something wrong. And maybe a little afraid that there will be repercussions I don't want to face if he comes home and catches me snooping.

My hand wraps around the doorknob and I push it open, half expecting it to be locked. It isn't, and I step inside, heat and humid air hitting me in the face.

Immediately I can tell this isn't his bedroom.

The lighting is low, but my eyes aren't paying attention to that. Instead, they go to the large enclosure on the far side of the room. It takes up the *entire* wall, and it has a glass front.

I walk closer, taking in the half logs scattered along the enclosure's floor and the large tree branches that look strategically placed throughout it.

A muted noise makes my heart skip and I walk closer, leaning in and squinting to try to see what the hell is in there. It's obviously an animal of some sort.

A hiss catches me off guard, my heart shooting to my throat. *Does he own a fucking snake?*

"She won't bite."

I scream and spin around, my hand flying to my chest. Julian is standing almost directly behind me. *How the hell did he come home without me hearing?*

"Don't *do* that," I complain, smacking him in the chest.

He smirks at me and walks over to the enclosure, peering into it like he's considering opening the thing. His hand reaches out and I jump forward, gripping his forearm.

"What are you doing?" I panic, my eyes growing wide. "Don't get it out!"

He chuckles but listens, drawing his arm back and twisting to face me instead. "She won't hurt you unless I tell her to."

"Oh, well, *that's* comforting." I side-eye the enclosure. I can't even see her; maybe she's a small garden snake or something. "What is it?" I ask.

"A twenty-three-foot python."

I sigh. "Of course."

He smiles. "Her name's Isabella. She was a gift from my father."

"Wow, a mom *and* a dad? Who knew you came from such a stable upbringing?"

His gaze dims, and when it does, something strikes against my chest, making me regret what I said, even though I shouldn't feel bad. He's the absolute worst and I need to keep remembering that.

Still, I make a mental note to never make fun of his family or childhood again. Right now he seems to be in a good mood, but I don't want to deal with him when he's not. I've had plenty of experience with him cold and aloof, and I can only imagine what he gets like when he's truly angry.

"Speaking of my mother," he says, "we'll go see her Sunday afternoon."

"Oh." My brows spike up. "Okay, um…does she know? About us, I mean."

He looks at me, amused. "She doesn't."

I let out a huff.

"You seem surprised," he says dryly.

"The opposite, actually," I reply. "Nothing about this moment is surprising. I absolutely believe you didn't tell your mom you got married, the same way I believe you own a giant predator snake as a pet."

His jaw ticks. "Lots of people have snakes as pets."

"What's it eat?" I peer over at the cage again.

His grin grows. "Rats. Mice. Lizards. Flesh of my enemies."

I scrunch up my nose. "You've got a sick sense of humor."

He laughs.

"So this is your hobby?" I wave my arm toward the enclosure. "Keeping pet snakes?"

He slips his hands into his pockets and rocks back on his heels, his head tilting to the side as he stares at me.

God, he's attractive.

A flash of heat scorches through me when I remember sitting on his lap and rubbing against him.

"I don't know if I have any," he says, interrupting my thoughts.

I shake my head, taking a step toward him. "Everybody has a passion, Julian."

"Martial arts, I guess."

My brows shoot to my hairline as I take him in. "You do martial arts?"

He nods, his chin tucking into his chest before he looks back up at me. "Since I was a little kid."

It's not surprising, really. His movements are fluid, and his aura is always calm, in control. A smile slowly appears on my face. "Will you show me something?"

He chuckles and straightens, walking toward me. He doesn't stop until he's directly in front of me, his hand reaching out to draw a fingertip down the side of my face.

His touch sends goose bumps down the length of my body.

"Maybe later, if you're a good girl," he murmurs, his voice low and raspy.

My stomach flips.

"What are you doing here anyway?" I ask, trying to redirect the conversation and ignore the way he's able to make my body go haywire. "I was starting to forget you even lived here, you're gone so much."

"I came home for you," he says simply.

My stomach jumps, and I fucking hate myself for it. "Why?"

He steps forward, clean linen and spice hitting my nostrils when he gets close. "Because, gattina, I'm going to teach you how to drive."

CHAPTER 26

Yasmin

"WHAT DO YOU *MEAN*? IF I DON'T STARE AT THE road, how do I know where to drive?" I cry out, frustrated and half-convinced that he's fucking with me.

Julian groans, throwing himself back in the passenger seat and running his hand through his inky black hair. "Listen to me," he grits out. "If you look down at the pavement directly, you'll crash. Just trust me."

I laugh so hard my stomach hurts. "*Trust* you? You can't be serious."

"I haven't given you any reason not to," he says, picking invisible lint off his shirt.

"Right," I snort. "Other than practically threatening to hurt Aidan if I don't behave. Forcing me to marry you and lying to my father, who is *dying*. And continually making me heel like your bitch to save the people I care about."

"Sounds to me like I've been nothing but honest." He shrugs.

"I—" Closing my mouth, I purse my lips.

He's not wrong, I guess.

"Try again," he soothes. "Just slowly press down on the gas. No need to get mad at it. She reacts better when you make her purr." He brushes his hand against the dash.

Rolling my eyes at how sexual he makes his car sound, I take a deep breath, glancing around to make sure the parking lot we're in is still empty. The last thing I need is for anyone else to see me try and fail at something most people know how to do.

Swallowing down the nerves, I do as he says, keeping my gaze trained in front of me instead of down at the road this time.

"Good," he says when the car rolls forward.

Pride sparks in my middle. *I'm doing it.*

I accelerate slowly, *very* slowly, as in we're going ten miles per hour tops. I'm going in a straight line and sitting in the driver's seat, and suddenly, I've never felt more independent and powerful in my life. Which in turn makes me feel silly, because it's such a simple thing.

"Perfect," he continues. "Now turn to the right. You want the car to follow you, not the other way around."

My left hand lifts from the wheel, gliding over the top to try to turn it.

The car loses control slightly, and I gasp, panicking and slamming on the brakes. My body jerks forward, the seat belt cutting into my neck.

I groan, frustrated, throwing my head back against the seat, the pride I just felt slipping away like sand through my fingers. "This is pointless. I'm clearly not made for driving."

"Do you always do that?" he questions.

"What?" I side-eye him.

"Give up so easily."

He doesn't wait for a reply, which is good because I don't have one to give him. Instead, I'm sure his question will just seep into my subconscious and fester there so I can overthink it later and wonder if he's right.

Leaning over, he reaches out, grasping my hands in his, his touch sending a shock through my system.

Flashes of my vision in the shower, with his rough fingers dragging down the sides of my body, make my skin heat. I rub my thighs together and clear my throat.

Dammit.

"Keep them here." He places my left hand on the wheel. "And here." Right hand on the right.

"You should stop touching me," I say, my voice low.

"Agree to disagree," he replies, slowly taking his fingers away.

My stomach flips, and it pisses me off because it keeps doing that, and I don't want to react to him at all. Besides, this is all just a ruse to keep me agreeable, I'm sure of it.

"You really don't need to try so hard," I bite out. "No one's around to see you."

"Is that what you think I'm doing?" He smirks. "Trying?"

I slap my hands against the wheel and the horn goes off, making my stomach surge into my throat and my heart skip.

He laughs. "Okay, that's enough for the day. Let's switch."

I don't argue, even though I really want to keep driving. Even more than that, I want to ask if he'll bring me back so I can try again. If he'll teach me more.

He's the only person who's seen me lacking and not just handed me whatever I need but given me the chance to learn it myself. It's different from what I'm used to, and I like the way it feels.

Opening the door, I move to slide out of the driver's seat. A hand appears in front of my face, and I hesitate to take it, not wanting my body to betray me again by reacting to his touch.

But this car sits *really* low, and I don't want to make a fool of myself trying to stand when he's clearly offering help, so I slip my palm in his, static energy shooting through my fingers and up my arm as I let him lift me from the seat.

I try to move my hand back, but he tightens his grip, pulling me in until his lips are by my ear. "If you think I've been *trying* with you, then you clearly don't know what a man looks like when he tries. I'll be sure to rectify that situation."

I suck in a breath. "Why bother?"

"Why not?"

He lets me go then, but the burn of his touch stays.

The sound of tires crunches on the loose gravel of the parking lot and I glance behind Julian to see a cop car pulling up.

My stomach cramps up tight. *Will I get in trouble for driving without a license?*

Julian's eyes flick from me to the patrol car, his jaw setting and his brows dropping down until that serious mask he wears so well coasts over his face entirely. It's dark and dangerous, and I'm reminded again why I don't let myself get on his bad side unnecessarily. He seems to let me get away with a lot of things that other people don't, but there's a reason why I don't fight with him more. Not when people's lives hang in the balance.

Oddly enough, even though I know I was technically doing something wrong, I feel safe with him here. I know that no matter what happens, he won't allow some local cop to have control over someone like him. This police officer might have a bit of power, but it's smothered entirely by the force that is Julian Faraci.

Julian's hand ghosts across the small of my back, sending a shiver racing up my spine. "Go sit in the car, Yasmin."

"Won't that look suspicious?" I look up at him. "I'd rather stay out here."

He glances down at me, the corners of his lips twitching, but his hand stays in place. "Suit yourself."

A car door slams and the police officer walks over, his hands on his hips, resting right over his gun. He takes in the scene, scanning the blacked-out Audi R8 and then Julian, and I wonder what it is he sees when he looks at us.

We're both in designer labels, with an expensive car, and Julian has tattoos that cover most of his body. I assume Julian knows most of the local police force, but when suspicion flits across the police officer's face and his fingers tighten over his holster, I second-guess myself.

Okay then. We must not look like anything good.

Julian's hand caresses my skin lightly, sending a comforting sensation through me. I lean into it.

"What's going on here? You realize this is private property?" the cop says.

Julian's brows lift and he glances behind him, over the empty parking lot and warehouse.

I hadn't asked what the warehouse was for; it's beige on the outside and large enough to fit several other buildings inside it, but there's no discernible name on the front, and I've been so distracted with driving that it hadn't crossed my mind to ask or to think we were trespassing.

"That's right," Julian replies.

"Odd place to be on a Friday afternoon."

Julian nods. "Teaching my wife to drive. Unfortunately, it's a skill she hasn't yet mastered."

The cop's brows raise, and he looks to me, his tongue peeking out to swipe across his chapped lips as his eyes strip me down.

Yuck. A single look and I feel more violated by him than I ever have with Julian.

"I don't know if I believe that." The cop laughs. "A man like you with a girl like her? Seems like she'd have a lot of *skills.*"

I hold back a scoff, crossing my arms over my chest instead. *What the hell does he mean by that?*

Julian's fingers twitch on my back.

"Unfortunately," the cop continues, "like I said, this is private property. You can't just loiter wherever you want, regardless of how nice the eye candy is while you do it."

"She *is* beautiful, isn't she?" Julian notes.

Julian doesn't spare me a glance, but my traitorous heart skips anyway at the compliment.

"Did someone call you to complain?" he asks.

The officer's bushy brown brows furrow. "That's none of your concern."

"Seeing as I own the place, I find it very concerning."

A small breath leaves me. I hadn't expected that, although I'm not sure why I'm surprised. Julian seems to have his hand in everything, the same as my father.

The cop, however, looks visibly shocked. "Let me see your license and registration, please."

Julian leans down and whispers in my ear, "Go get in the car, Yasmin."

Part of me wants to take the opportunity to tell him to go fuck himself for always thinking he can tell me what to do, but I realize now might not be the most opportune of times, so I bite the side of my cheek and do what he says.

I make my way toward the back of the vehicle, attempting to avoid the police officer, but he's standing right next to the car, and when I try to move around him, he steps in closer.

I jolt back, pasting a tense smile on my face. "Excuse me, please."

"How old are you?"

"Twenty-three," I reply.

"And you're here by choice? Just say the word and I can"—he lets his gaze wander again—"get you out of here. Take you with me."

"Officer." Julian steps up behind me until I feel the heat of his body at my back. "I'd recommend you stop questioning her."

"And why's that? Two of you alone out here, no one around for miles. Seems suspicious." He looks to me again. "He paying you for something, honey?"

His words smack me across the face, fire raging through my middle. I throw my hand up, showcasing the giant canary diamond. "We're *married*, asshole."

The officer's smirk drops. "Watch your tone."

"Yasmin." Julian's voice is sharper now. "Get in the car."

My stomach drops when the cop steps directly in front of me. "Now, I can't let you just disappear from my sight."

"You should," Julian cuts in. "If you value having it."

The cop frowns. "Is that a threat?"

Julian laughs, and I can't help but glance back at him. His hands are lifted in the air and there's a maniacal grin on his face. "You know, I'm sorry. It seems like you're getting the wrong impression about us. Let her get in the car, Officer. How else can she grab what you're asking for?"

The cop holds Julian's gaze for a long moment before finally stepping out of my way.

I blow out a breath, rushing by him, and right when I pass the jerk's side, he shifts, the length of his body brushing against mine.

A shiver of disgust rolls through me at the power play, and my footsteps quicken as I make my way to the passenger side, sliding into the vehicle and turning the rearview mirror so I can watch their interaction.

I can't hear what they're saying above low mumbles, but I do see Julian step forward, his tall frame demanding obedience from the short and stocky cop without even trying. Julian says something, and the cop jerks back, his face snapping down to something in Julian's hand before raising it again.

Slowly the cop nods, reaching out and taking whatever it was before walking away.

Julian slides back in the car and revs the engine, pulling out of the lot and driving away before the officer has even made it back to his vehicle.

"Everything okay?" I ask.

He glances at me. "Fine."

"Good." I nod my head, a dark tension wringing the air dry. "I didn't like him."

Julian chuckles.

I huff. "I don't know why you're laughing. Is sexual harassment *funny* to you? Didn't you see the way he stared at me? And he *touched* me. Like, what kind of person would literally hear you say you're my husband and then do it so blatantly?"

"A very foolish man."

"Yeah." Disappointment over the fact that Julian didn't care enough to do anything hits me in the chest. It catches me off guard, how much it upsets me, but I use it as fuel—a reminder that he doesn't really *want* me to be his spouse. That we may be married on paper, but not in all the ways that matter.

"He's lucky you don't really care," I pout. "One day he'll do that to the wrong person and not like the result."

Julian doesn't reply, but his hands tighten the slightest bit on the steering wheel and the muscle at the back of his jaw flexes.

I swallow down whatever I was about to say because clearly, he doesn't want to continue the conversation, and at this point, I'm just ready to go home and forget it happened to begin with.

"You sit over there." I side-eye Razul, who does nothing but grunt and get a table in the corner of the room, allowing me to go and see Riya for Sunday brunch without him overhearing every word I say.

He drove me here, but he hasn't said a word, most likely under strict instruction not to speak to me. It's fine. I don't really think we'd have much in common anyway, and although I didn't tell Julian because fighting him on anything while he can hurt Aidan is useless, I don't think I *need* a bodyguard.

My father never gave me one, and I grew up just fine on my own.

Looking around the restaurant, I see Riya sipping on a drink over in the back corner of the room, and I make my way there, sliding into the booth and eyeing the no-doubt alcoholic beverage already in front of me on the table.

"I took the liberty of ordering you a Bellini." She nods to the drink in front of me.

"Thanks." I smile, but I'm not touching that thing, especially since I'm spending all evening with Julian and his mother. Who knows what will happen if I don't have all my cylinders firing appropriately?

"Who's your sidekick?" she asks, jerking her chin at Razul.

I glance back at the bulky, grumpy man, who's sitting back in a chair across the room with his eyes trained on me. "My new watchdog."

Her brows lift. "Julian gave you security? Wow. How romantic."

"More annoying than anything. So what's the news?" I ask, reaching out to grab a piece of bread. It melts when it hits my mouth and I close my eyes at the taste.

"Wow, not even a 'how are you'?" she deadpans. "Julian's rubbing off on you."

The bread I'm swallowing gets stuck in my throat and I cough, my hand flying to my neck as I try to regain my composure.

"You okay?" Riya asks, her brow quirking.

"He is *not*," I rasp out.

"Yeah, I know… It was a joke, damn." She clicks her tongue. "Is it that miserable?"

"Even worse," I mumble, reaching back out to the basket of rolls in the center of the table and tearing off another piece. "He's being *nice*."

She gasps. "No! How terrible."

Scoffing, I throw the piece of bread at her. "Uh, yeah. It actually is. It's confusing, and I think he's just manipulating my emotions on purpose, and I don't know what purpose it's serving. It's not like it will make a difference. As far as he's concerned, he's already won, so what's the point?"

"Oh my god," Riya muses, her eyes calculating as she stares at me. "You *like* him."

"No," I snap. "Absolutely not."

She sits back in her seat, crossing her arms. "Don't lie to me, bitch. How dare you fall for the enemy and try to keep it from me?"

"I'm not falling for him. God," I complain. "He just...he confuses me."

She scoffs. "Please, you've *always* had a thing for the bad guy."

My mouth drops open. "I have not."

"Don't lie to me, Yas. I've watched *Die Hard* with you too many times to fall for that trick."

"That's different." I point a finger at her and squint. "Hans Gruber is the best villain of all time. He's not a real person."

"Right." She nods, her eyes wide. "You've got the real version of him as your man."

My stomach twists. "He's a fucking criminal hiding in a business suit, Riya. Who do you think I am?"

"Alleged criminal," she corrects.

I don't bother to tell her that Sultans is so much more than what it appears to the public. If I admit that out loud, then I have to admit my father is *also* a criminal and that both Julian and my father are just extremely good at hiding their nefarious deeds behind smiles and retail chains.

Nausea churns in my gut, remembering just who it is I'm dealing with in Julian and hating myself for how easily I forget when I'm around him. I've let him touch me, kiss me. I almost let him *fuck* me.

"Ugh, he's definitely trying to manipulate me. And I'm just like...a fucking helpless girl unable to do anything but bow to his demands and pretend that I'm okay with what's happening." I drop my head in my arms. "It makes me feel weak."

Riya sighs and reaches across the table, patting my forearm. "You're not weak, baby girl. You're smart."

I roll my head to the side and stare at her.

Her eyes flick back to Razul again and then to me, her voice lowering. "I talked to Aidan."

This gets my attention and I perk back up, my hands grabbing hers. "You're kidding."

She clicks her tongue. "Thought I'd call him up just to see if he answered, you know? Give him a piece of my mind."

"Okay." I nod, waiting for her to elaborate and ignoring the way it stings that he talked to her but won't even respond to me. "And?"

"We talked for a few minutes, and I told him that you were only doing what you had to. And he's out there, trying to find that lamp or whatever, so he's just been busy."

"Oh. Good." My stomach sours.

She winces like she's expecting me to fall apart right in front of her eyes, but surprisingly, even though knowing I'm not a priority *does* hurt, it doesn't sting quite as bad as I expected. It's a dull ache in my chest, not a sledgehammer to my heart. Although I'm not sure why he'd be so interested in finding the lamp still if I'm already married to someone else. Does he think he can still convince my father that he's the better choice?

"Hey, that lost lamp business is kind of crazy, huh?" she says, changing the conversation as she takes a sip of her drink.

"I don't really know much about it." My eyes flick up to her and I tilt my head. "In fact, how do *you?*"

"Aidan said it's worth, like, a billion dollars." She whistles. "Imagine what someone could do with that. No wonder your dad wants it."

My teeth sink into my lip. "Honestly, Riy, I couldn't care

less about the stupid lamp. It doesn't even matter anymore. It's not like Aidan can bring it back and we ride off into the sunset together. It's too late."

She nods. "True. There's still hope though. I found a guy, remember?"

I lean forward, my stomach flipping like I'm on a roller coaster. "Yeah. I was just afraid to ask."

Her eyes flick to Razul one more time. "You sure he can't hear us?"

I glance behind me and then back to her, shrugging.

"I got you a burner phone and programmed his number into it. His name's Randy Gazim. He's a lawyer right smack-dab in the center of New York City. He specializes in nasty divorces, and he *claims* to not give a shit about Julian Faraci or the power he has." She takes the linen napkin on the table and places it in her lap before wrapping it around something and sliding it back. "I figured you could try to text Aidan on here too, just in case you have extra eyes on your stuff or, you know, we could talk without worrying about who might look at your real phone."

My hand shoots out and I grip the napkin, feeling a lumpy object underneath. I drag it toward me and slip it into my purse, hoping that Razul didn't see. My chest warms.

She lifts a shoulder. "Listen, Aidan's really pissed, Yas. He's hurt, you know? But I told him you were trying to find a way out. And he…he said he hasn't lost faith." She nods toward the phone. "Text him. See what he has to say."

My heart catapults through my chest and slams against my ribs as I nod. "Thanks, Riya."

After brunch is over and I'm back in the safety of my room, I plan on doing just that.

CHAPTER 27

Julian

Razul: All is fine. She's with her friend. Will text when we're
on our way home.
Me: Woman?
Razul: Yes.

Closing the text on my phone, I place it on the folding table
I keep propped against the wall, outside the hanging plastic tarp
that covers the other 90 percent of the room, creating a transparent protective barrier over the walls and floor.

I've seen Yasmin snooping around the house the past week,
watching her from my desk at work on the security cameras that
she either doesn't realize I have installed or doesn't care about. But
she hasn't been in *this* room. Not that she'd be able to find it or
get in even if she did. It's locked with a high-level security system
and hidden behind one of the large bookshelves in the library.

I pull back the tarp and walk into the middle where a single
chair sits, that fucking piece-of-shit cop from yesterday bound
and gagged. His arms are strapped with rope to the arms of the

chair, his legs in a similar situation, and his face is turning a putrid shade of purple from the way he's trying to scream loud enough for someone to hear.

"Officer Tate," I start, my staff already in my hands as I flip it back and forth. "I want to thank you for coming out to meet me on such short notice. I understand how much time it took out of your day to be called back to that empty warehouse. And I know my trunk isn't the most *comfortable* of spaces, especially on these hilly roads to my home."

Smiling, I stop when I'm directly in front of him, satisfaction already burrowing in my stomach at the fear that's percolating in his small, beady eyes.

He makes another muffled noise and jerks against the bindings.

"Ah, ah, ah," I tsk, bringing up the staff to rest over the gag in his mouth. "You've done enough speaking."

I drag the end of the staff down from his mouth, over his neck, until it rests at his pulse point. I can't feel it, of course, but I imagine that it's beating rapidly, sporadically even. The thought excites me.

"I know what you're thinking. *How could I fall for it?* And you're right. It does make you incredibly foolish to think there'd be a wellness check needed in the same spot you were yesterday. But I promise, your trip isn't in vain. You see, my wellness *did* need to be checked." I chuckle, shaking my head. "My mental health has been incredibly unstable since we met."

Moving the end of my staff, I drag it along the top of his arm until it rests at his wrist. He tries to kick out, the chair itself moving violently against the floor.

He swallows, his gaze flicking to the end of my staff and then back.

"Curious about this?" I lift it from his skin for a moment before placing it back down. "I'll admit it's not the most practical weapon, but I have a soft spot for it. It's incredible what a staff can do when you're too weak to have a fair fight."

Thoughts of my childhood creep into the moment, remembering the first time I brought a staff home from the dojo.

"What the hell is that?" Mamma asks.

I freeze in place in the middle of my bedroom where I'm flipping the staff around. I keep dropping it when it skims the back of my hand, and the frustration has me in my room practicing ten times harder, just to make sure I'm the best at it. I don't know why I like the staff more than the nunchaku or short stick, but the second I picked it up, it felt right. Like it was made to fit in my hand.

But I never wanted Mamma to see because I'm afraid she'll take it. Use it.

I jolt out of the memory when Tate jerks in his chair again, the sound grating against my ears. My mood worsens from the memory, realizing that I'm going to visit her later tonight. And anytime I see my mother, she makes me feel two feet tall.

Right now, however, I feel like a god. I stand up straight, flipping the staff around until it's situated properly in my hand.

"Don't worry," I coo. "This will only hurt for a little."

I bring it down in a harsh stroke on his fingers, enjoying the sound of his bones breaking beneath the metal.

A muffled scream rings out and I breathe in deep at the noise, using it as fuel as I start an intimate dance of striking and twirling, my biceps burning from the muscle strain of quick movements as I beat him until he matches the black and blue of his uniform.

By the time I'm done, my chest is heaving, the exertion causing me to lose a bit of my composure. Laughing, I run my free hand through my hair to get the stray pieces off my forehead. "Your first mistake was not recognizing who I am."

His screams have fallen silent, perhaps from the shock of his injuries, blood spattering across the plastic tarp and over patches of his mangled skin.

I walk away from him and over to the edge of the strung-up makeshift plastic room, where I have my other tools laid out on the ground. I drop my staff in order to pick up my knife. When I turn back around, Officer Tate has tears streaking down his pathetic face and snot dripping from his broken nose, coating his upper lip and oozing down over the gag in his mouth.

My fingers wrap tightly around the handle of the blade, and I bend down, my free hand gripping the back of his neck.

"Your second mistake," I whisper, "was disrespecting my *wife*."

The knife cuts through his eye like butter, digging through soft and squishy cornea until it hits the back of his socket. Naturally, his yelling starts up again, more guttural this time, as though the pain is being wrought from the deepest parts of his fucked-up soul.

I revel in his screams while I bathe in his blood, and eventually he quiets for good.

Two hours later, both the room and I are clean, my hair still damp from a shower where I scrubbed remnants of Officer Tate off my skin.

My neck cracks as I let out a sigh of relief, the anxiety of my upcoming visit with my mother temporarily muted from the pleasant buzz that's left over after a kill.

Isabella hisses and I stare down at her in the enclosure.

"Don't look at me like that," I say when her beady eyes meet mine. "I warned him what would happen. It's a matter of respect."

Tate's body is splayed out in the bottom of her home, a few mice laid on top. She slithers over to it and slowly coils her body around the length of his torso, constricting tightly, not realizing that I've already incapacitated her prey, her jaw unhinging as she starts to swallow him whole.

I wait until her stomach is bulged from the large meal before I leave the room, making sure to lock the door behind me. I hadn't meant for Yasmin to see Isabella, and while I don't mind that she did, I don't want her asking questions about what type of meal is making her stomach extend the way it is.

Heading to the front of the house, I walk into my office, pouring myself a glass of scotch before sitting in one of the cushioned chairs by the window, soaking in the peace and quiet and trying to enjoy the last few minutes of peace before my mother undoubtedly ruins my mood.

My phone vibrates where I set it next to me and I glance down at the lock screen.

Razul: On our way

Sighing, I run a hand through my hair, tilting my head to the side until the entire length of my neck cracks again, and I guzzle the rest of the scotch.

If my mother finds out from someone else I've married, I'll never hear the end of it. And the guilt she already piles on is enough to bury even the strongest kind of man, so it isn't worth taking the chance.

Besides, I want to see how Yasmin fares against her. She's

been so docile and well-behaved; it will be interesting to see how she reacts to my mother, who will undoubtedly insult her.

My dick jerks when I think about her acting out, imagining bringing her back home and showing her what happens to naughty girls who step out of line.

I shake my head from the vision, willing my cock to go back down.

See, *this* is why I need the reminder. My body continues to play tricks on my mind, making me think Yasmin is here for my pleasure. That she's bound to me for *me*. But that's not the case. She's a means to an end, a loose thread that I'm going to unravel until there's nothing left and then toss in the fire to burn. And that means I shouldn't care if someone disrespects her or get angry at the audacity of the pathetic boy who keeps making her look so sad.

I shouldn't care at all.

And I need to figure out a way to remind myself that I don't.

CHAPTER 28

Yasmin

"STOP FIDGETING."

I frown over at Julian as I finish straightening my black pencil skirt. "It's crooked. I can't go into your mother's house with a crooked skirt."

"Well, it's fixed now, and you're distracting me," he bites.

"What crawled up your ass?" I scrunch my nose. "You're extra bitchy tonight."

His eyes narrow and his lips purse but he ignores me, walking up the sidewalk to a large home that backs up to a lake, with a brick exterior and stone archways. There's a chandelier in the high window above the front door, and purple plants are growing in the garden outside the bay window to the left.

"This is beautiful," I say, tripping over my feet as I try to keep up with him. "Does your mom live here alone?"

He doesn't answer, stopping when we reach the door.

Honestly, I'm kind of nervous about the entire situation, not sure what to expect from the woman who raised a man like Julian Faraci and not sure how I'm supposed to act. He's so touchy about his past, and I know that this is another opportunity for me to peer into the personal life of my husband, to see who he is and if there are any weak spots I can dig into and rip apart.

The burner phone Riya gave me is sitting underneath a pile of my clothes in my dresser drawer back at the house, a string of text messages with Randy Gazim waiting for me to get back to them and keep the conversation going.

He says he'll help me, that once I inherit Sultans, he'll draft up an annulment, help me go public against Julian and find both Aidan and myself protection so that we can be safe. He said that doing it now would be better, but I want to make sure my father doesn't know the lengths that his right-hand man would go to in order to betray him. He should be at peace when he passes, not worried about things that can be handled after he's gone.

It's a morbid thought, waiting for my father to die, one that has guilt and sadness commingling in my chest and compressing my lungs until they feel beaten and worn, but there's nothing else we can do except wait. I have to come to terms with it in order to make sure his legacy is protected in the end.

Julian's hand briefly touches my back and then retreats, and that brings me back into the moment.

I've noticed that Julian generally likes me to show affection in public or around people, including my father, who we're trying to convince that we're the real deal, but I don't know if that extends to his own mother. You'd think he'd let me in on what I'm supposed to do, but a large part of pretending to be in love with Julian is figuring out what he wants like I'm a mind reader. He just expects me to know. Another dickish trait of his.

Despite the nerves, though, part of me is excited to see him interact with someone he loves—although the jury's still out on whether he's even capable of the emotion.

When we reach the door, he doesn't knock; he just opens the matte-black handle and walks inside.

"Ma," he hollers.

His tone catches me off guard, and I hold back a laugh at how normal he sounds as I follow behind him through the large entryway with a staircase to the left and past the open dining room that already has food set in the middle of the table. The smell of oregano and something hearty hits my nostrils, making my stomach rumble in appreciation. I haven't eaten since brunch this morning, and the nerves of having to be around Julian *and* his mother at the same time have sent me into a bit of a tailspin, so I'm starved, and the food smells delicious.

We walk by a living room with a floor-to-ceiling stone fireplace, flames crackling, and then head to the right of the cream-colored couches and into the open kitchen.

A woman stands between the small island and a gas stove, her black hair with silver streaks pulled into a low bun on her head.

Right before she turns around, Julian reaches behind him and grabs my hand. *Tightly.*

My brows shoot up as I look at him, confused by how out of sorts he seems, an anxious energy radiating off him that normally doesn't exist. But when his mother faces us, I clear the expression, adopting a large smile and leaning in slightly to Julian's touch. Both because I'm trying to be convincing and because his mother immediately puts me on edge. Her face is stern, and her eyes are cold as ice. They zone in on our linked hands immediately.

"Ciao, Ma."

"Vita mia, come give your mother a kiss."

Her voice is strong and smooth like honey, and she's clearly not from Badour with the way she drops her *r*'s and elongates her *a*'s. I realize then that I have no idea if Julian is originally from here, and anxiety squeezes my insides tight, worried she'll ask me questions I don't know how to answer. Questions that any other married couple should know.

Whatever. It's not like I had a choice in the matter anyway, so if we look silly, then I'm blaming him, and he can deal with the repercussions.

There's a wooden spoon in his mother's left hand as she walks over to us, reaching up to wrap Julian in a hug. As she does, her left arm drops harshly, forcing my hand away from his.

My heart jumps and my fingers sting from the action, but I shake it off, telling myself that surely, she didn't do it on purpose.

She backs away from him, holding onto his biceps before reaching up to pat him on the face, then looks over to me. "And who is this?"

Julian shakes her off, grabbing me around the waist and dragging me into his side. "This is Yasmin."

"Yasmin." She lifts her chin so she's staring down her nose at me. "I didn't know my son would be bringing strangers into my home."

"Ma," Julian sighs.

"What?" she asks, her gaze swinging back to him. "You bring a girl here without warning me and I'm not allowed to ask any questions?" She turns toward me, primping the side of her already perfect bun. "Honestly, you'd think I'm chopped liver with the way he treats me. Barely calls, never tells me what he's doing with his life, and now here you are. A random girl I've never met." Her lip curls. "Maybe you're the reason he's been so distant."

I stare at her with wide eyes, extremely uncomfortable and insulted but also a little amused. She's talking to Julian like he's a kid, not like the formidable businessman he is. It honestly fascinates me a little, and I can't help the tiny smirk that lines my mouth when I turn to look at Julian, seeing him in a different light for the first time. It's hard to be intimidated by him when he's in this element.

"Is this new?" she asks, pointing her finger to me and then him.

"Not particularly," I reply after Julian doesn't say a word.

"And you never let me meet her?" she complains. "Typical."

"You're meeting her now," he says dryly.

"And for what? What if I died and you never even let me meet the girl you're seeing? You'd have to live with that for the rest of your life. Any day now, I could go, you know that? I don't have much time left. I've told you what the doctors say. Do you want that on your conscience?"

I inhale a harsh breath at her words, pain slicing through the hidden wounds caused by my father's illness.

"I'm—" I start, not sure what I'm going to say but knowing I have to say *something* so I don't break down into tears.

"She's your daughter-in-law, Ma. Congratulations," he throws out. "And you're not dead yet, so it looks like I made it in time."

Anger filters through me at how callously he brushes off her concern. If she's really ill, then I can't believe he's treating her this way. He should be over here, spending as much time with her as he can. At least she *wants* to see him.

Unlike my father, who's pushing me further away every day.

When she stares at me this time, I meet her gaze head-on. I don't know why, but this feels important. Like I'm aching for her approval and hoping she doesn't think I'm not enough.

Although, in the grand scheme of things, it really doesn't matter one way or the other. This marriage is going to end soon anyway, and it will be nothing more than a regretful memory, like a bad taste in my mouth that I wash away with water.

"Well." She smacks her hands on her thighs. "Dinner's ready. Probably cold by now with how long you took to get here."

And she turns around and walks away. Just like that.

I look at Julian, trying to gauge whether her completely ignoring the fact that we got married is a normal thing or if it's something we should be worried about, but his face is a shield, not betraying a single emotion.

We follow her into the dining room at the front of the house.

"You can sit here, Yasmin. Next to me, so I can get to know my new daughter." His mother points to a chair on the opposite side of where I'm assuming she expects Julian to sit, but Julian stops me before I can move, pulling out the chair next to him and helping me settle before pushing me in.

He sits down next to me and grabs my hand beneath the tablecloth, resting it on his knee, which is tapping out a nervous rhythm.

I glance down at our interlocked fingers and then up to his face, wondering if he even realizes what he's doing. It's not like his mom can see him holding my hand, so I don't really get the purpose. But I leave it because either way, he seems nervous, and I don't want to do anything to set him off.

His mother flicks her wrist at the buffet of food on the table. "Well, come on. Don't just stare at it."

Julian releases my hand then, placing it on his thigh before grabbing my plate, dishing up perfect portions of everything before setting it back down in front of me.

I stare at him, gobsmacked, before looking down at the food and then back up at him.

"What's wrong? Not enough? Too much?" he asks, slipping his hand back under mine.

"N-no," I stutter. "That's perfect." I pick up my fork and stab the leafy greens but pause before I take a bite. "Thank you."

Honestly, I don't know if anyone outside serving staff has ever plated food for me before, and it's a nice gesture, one that makes me feel cared for in a different way than I ever have been. Something foreign and warm fills up my chest, and I twist my fingers, sliding them between his and squeezing.

Funny how such a simple thing can cause such a cataclysmic reaction.

"Look at you two," his mother says, taking a large sip of her red wine. "So in love. Just like me and your papà were." She nods toward Julian. "Of course, he'd be less than impressed that you were starting a meal without saying grace."

His leg stops jittering. "Ma, stop it."

"What? I'm not allowed to talk about my husband now?" She tilts her glass toward me. "I wish you all the happiness I had."

Julian slams his fist down on the table, rattling the china and making my stomach drop. "That's enough."

I clear my throat, my heart pounding so hard against my chest that I'm afraid you can hear it across the room, and I pick up the glass of wine in front of me and take a large sip.

So much for never drinking again.

The bitter notes of the liquid make me cringe, but I swallow it down and gulp again, needing something to do so that I don't gawk at the scene happening in front of my eyes.

His mother—whose name I *still* don't know—flings her back

against the chair at Julian's outburst, bringing a hand to her chest. "Well, you can't say you don't have his temper."

Julian laughs, but it's hollow. My eyes fling between them, my hands growing clammy from how awkward I feel.

"Ma, you *really* don't want to test me right now. Okay? Can we just have a meal? Why is it always so hard to have a normal day with you?"

I expect her to give in. Julian's voice has dropped to that deep, smooth, and dangerous timbre, like a knife sharp enough to cut through bone.

"Who do you think you are, speaking to your mother that way?" she hisses.

Now my nerves ramp up for her sake. *Does she not know who her son is? What he's capable of?*

"You walk in here like a hotshot, dancing around in your Armani suits and toting your pretty new wife with a giant ring, and what do I get, huh? A smart mouth from a boy who used to be too scared of me to speak."

His jaw twitches, and he lowers his head, his nostrils flaring as he closes his eyes, pinching the bridge between his nose. He still hasn't let go of my hand, and he's squeezing so hard my fingers are starting to go numb, but I don't try to move.

"Mrs. Faraci, with all due respect," I start, trying to defuse the situation. "Your son is—"

"You know, if he were here—your father—he wouldn't stand for it. Whoop some sense into you and remind you who made you what you are." Her words soar across the air like finely aimed arrows, and I can tell the moment they hit their mark.

Julian tightens his fingers on mine for a second and then

releases me completely, the sound of his chair scraping against the ground as it echoes off the high ceilings and beige walls.

He leans over the table, his fists pressing on the top until his knuckles turn white. "No, Mamma. He'd whoop *you*."

My stomach is tangled in knots as I watch them, my fingers twisting together in my lap.

He reaches out and grabs my hand, pulling me forcefully up from the table. "We're leaving."

"Oh, okay, I…" I trail off as I regain my balance. He drags me away and I glance back once, not knowing if I should say goodbye or thank her for the meal or cuss her out for nagging her son instead of enjoying their time together. But I give her a pass, because if she's sick, then I'm sure she's confused, just like my baba, not wanting to lose the ones she loves yet not knowing how to approach them.

It's only a few seconds and then it's too late to say anything at all. Julian dragged me all the way out to the car, practically throwing me in the passenger seat and then driving like a bat out of hell off her property.

I sit ramrod straight, not even daring to breathe too loud. Anger permeates the car, buzzing like a hive of wasps.

Eventually, I open my mouth, then close it again, repeating the motion two more times before I give up. I have no clue what to say.

"Are you okay?" I finally muster.

He doesn't respond, jerking the wheel, my body jostling from the sharp left turn.

"You know," I continue, trying to get some type of reaction out of him, "your mom seems like a peach. It's no wonder you talk about her so much."

His mouth twitches.

I reach out before I can stop myself, my finger poking into the side of his face. "Look at that. Your face *isn't* stuck after all."

He snaps his head to the side, chomping his teeth like he's trying to bite my hand, and I squeal, pulling it back and slamming it to my chest.

I'm not sure why this sudden need is here, aching to make him feel better. Maybe it's because I didn't like the look in his eyes or the obvious strain that he and his mother have. Maybe it's because I could tell there are things from his childhood that I could never imagine for myself. Or maybe it's just because in this moment, I don't hate my husband as much as I should. Whatever it is, I grab on to it with both hands, hoping that it doesn't slip through my grasp.

"You're an animal." I laugh.

"Oh, gattina." He sighs, smiling broadly now. "You have no idea."

CHAPTER 29

Julian

I'M LOSING COUNT OF HOW MANY TIMES I'VE LET Yasmin touch me unprovoked, and I hate the way it feels.

It feels like comfort. Like a warm blanket on a cold night. Like I *don't* hate it at all, which makes it a very big problem for me.

Dinner with my mother went differently than I expected, but it's in my nature to constantly underestimate her. I knew things would be interesting, had expected the disrespectful tone of voice and the way she pricks and prods, trying to make me snap. But I hadn't expected *my* reaction to the way she so callously disregarded someone I chose to spend the rest of my life with.

Forget the fact that it isn't real, that I'm blackmailing Yasmin to even spend time with me. My mother doesn't know that, and a *normal* mom—a good mom—would have had more to say than "let's eat dinner."

In any other situation, I'd let her get away with it. But a strange new protective energy waved its red flag in front of my face, warning me that if I didn't get us out of there, I was going to ruin everything. Ma would deserve it, but like usual, there's something tethering me to her even after all these years, an invisible rope that frays more with every example of disrespect, every time she brings up my childhood, acting like I don't remember how all my scars are from her.

But it's still there, and it's still connected, and I don't know how to make it snap in half.

It hurts that she couldn't even pretend to care about me bringing home a wife. I had expected her to get angry, not bitter.

God knows why.

"You know," Yasmin says, sitting on the family room couch in that black pencil skirt and silk blouse, slipping her heels off. "That went differently than I expected."

I roll the glass of scotch around with my wrist as I take her in, the fireplace warming up the air and the fall leaves outside the wall of windows adding a warm feel to the space as the sun sets behind the tree line. Walking over to the couch, I sit down, placing my drink on the coffee table and grabbing the sole of her foot, running my thumbs up the arch.

She moans, her eyes fluttering, and then like she realizes what she's doing, her hand flies to her mouth, an embarrassed look crossing her face.

I smirk.

"Can I give you some advice?" She tilts her head.

My thumb presses against her heel. "I'm sure you'll give it whether I want it or not."

A thoughtful look passes over her face. "If your mother's as sick as she says she is, then you should try to work out whatever you two have going on before it's too late."

My hands stop their motion, dropping her foot back to the couch. "Advice *not* taken, thanks."

She scoffs, crossing her arms. "She said she was dying, Julian. People do weird things when they're facing their own mortality. Look at my father." Her voice softens at the end, a sad look ghosting across her eyes. "You can talk to me, you know? If you're struggling with her being sick. If anyone knows what that's like, it's me."

She leans in, her arm reaching out for mine. I jerk back, and she sighs and drops her hand.

"She's been dying for twenty years."

Yasmin gasps. "What?"

"She's a liar, gattina. A fake. She'll do anything to get what she wants."

Her gaze narrows into slits. "Wow, must run in the family then."

She's not wrong. The apple doesn't fall far from the tree, and everything I am, the people I've had to hurt in order to get to where I am, are only because of the ones who raised me. I am my mother's son. In almost every way.

I pinch the bridge of my nose, her statement sending irrational anger surging through me. "You should go to your room."

Deadly silence.

And then a shoe flies toward me, missing me by an inch. My back slams into the arm of the couch and I look at her, unamused. "Real mature."

"I'm so *sick* of you telling me what to do," she grits out.

"There's the little brat who's been missing." I cross my arms. "I was wondering when you'd stop pretending you were some well-mannered woman and let your true colors shine through."

"Oh, well, forgive the fuck out of me," she spits, leaning forward until she's close enough to jab her finger into my chest. "Sue me for trying to make the best out of the cards I've been dealt. The cards *you've* dealt me."

I stay stoic, looking down at her from where she's practically on top of me, telling myself that she's not worth my time. That she's nothing more than a necessary and *temporary* annoyance. Even though the heat of her body has my cock growing hard and my hands tensing with the urge to grip her by the hips and show her just how much I could make her enjoy being told what to do.

"God forbid I try to make this shitty situation that *you* put me in more bearable. Do you know what it's like?" Her voice breaks and she drops her finger, closing it into a fist and slamming it into her own chest, digging in like she can rip out the hurt herself. "My father is dying, Julian. He's really, he—he's *dying*. And all I want to do, all I can think about doing, is being with him. But instead, I'm here, getting wrapped up in *you*, the person I'm supposed to hate."

She sniffs, and I clench my jaw, my hands curling into fists at my sides to keep from reaching out.

"Life is so tough, isn't it, gattina? Such a hardship to be so spoiled."

"And that's the fucked-up part, isn't it?" she cuts in. "I know. I *am* spoiled. I never had to learn to drive. I never had to learn to cook or how to fold my own clothes. I never once had to worry about learning a life skill or a trade because why would I ever, in a million years, need to work for a living? And that is a prison in itself. It feels like I'm stuck at the top of a bell tower, hidden away, and never let out to see the light. If you can't see that, if you're not capable of empathizing, then I don't know why I'm even talking."

I clench my jaw.

"My father tried to auction me off to the first prick who came along, because he knew I wouldn't be able to make it on my own," she continues. "And he's right. And I bet you love that, don't you? Having me here at your mercy and knowing I can't do shit for myself."

"Poor little rich girl," I hiss, leaning in until our gazes lock. "You have no clue what it means to struggle, no idea what real trauma is. So sorry you've had to deal with your caring father while living in a twenty-thousand-square-foot mansion, handing you the world, and having him *love* you too much to want to leave you."

Tears well in her eyes, making them even more beautiful. More raw, maybe.

"Truly, how can you survive it?" I ask, my voice rising with sarcasm. "Must be so *hard* having a stable, healthy relationship with him."

"Don't take it out on me because you treat your mother like shit," she bites back. "Let me tell you something, Julian. If you don't make amends now, if you don't at least try, when she does die? You'll regret it the rest of your life." She pauses, looking at me with disgust. "But I guess it's to be expected from a man who bleeds evil."

"That's a little dramatic," I reply.

She reaches out to push against me.

I grab her wrists instead, locking her in place against my chest.

"You're the devil, Julian Faraci. And I hope you burn in hell."

I press in close, until my torso barely ghosts across her body, rage pulsing through my body to the beat of my heart, filling up my bloodstream until I'm seeing nothing but red.

I move quickly, dragging her by the wrists until her body flies forward and drapes over my knees. She squeaks in surprise and then starts to struggle against me, but my forearm locks against the small of her back, small zips of pleasure zinging down the length of my cock as she writhes on top of my dick, making it so hard it strains against the zipper.

My other hand flips up that tight black skirt she couldn't stop touching earlier, exposing the smooth apple of her ass cheek, prime and ready to be punished.

I bring down my hand without a second thought, the slap reverberating through the room and off the walls. My cock jerks to attention as I rub my fingers across her flesh, soothing the area.

Glancing toward her, I loosen my forearm, realizing that she isn't fighting against me now. She's just prone, on her stomach, her elbows sinking into the couch cushion and her breathing so heavy, I can feel it escaping from her lungs.

"It's far past time somebody taught you how to shut that mouth of yours," I murmur, smoothing my hand over the flesh.

"Did you just *spank* me?"

I bend down until my lips ghost across the shell of her ear. "If you want me to stop, tell me to stop. Otherwise, I'll do it again, gattina. Over and over until your ass is so sore, you can't sit for days and your sweet little pussy begs for a taste too."

She sucks in a breath, her torso fidgeting against my lap, and my stomach tightens, enjoying her reaction. I pause, waiting to hear what she says, but the silence rings louder than ever, just the way I knew it would.

"Now, apologize."

"Go fuck yourself," she sneers.

Smack.

The sting radiates through my palm as my hand once again smooths over the cheek.

Her body jerks as she tries to free herself from my hold, but

I don't let her escape, instead pressing her firmly down until my dick pushes into her stomach.

"I'd rather fuck *you*, wife," I murmur. "But little brats who need to learn their lessons don't get things unless they play nice. Now." My fingers dance over the reddened area of her ass. "Be a good girl, and do what I say."

She twists her head to see me, fire blazing in her eyes, her pupils dilated and desire sneaking through her features. She can pretend she doesn't like this all she wants. We both know the truth. This is what she needs.

And I'm the man who can give it to her.

"I'm not sorry," she whispers.

My cock pulses at her disobedience.

Smack. Smack. Smack.

Three more slaps in quick succession and she sinks deeper into my hold, her grunts morphing into moans.

"Julian," she breathes. "Please…"

My fingers dip between her thighs, running along the lace of her underwear, her pussy dripping so much it drenches the fabric. "You know what I want."

"I'm sorry," she finally says, grinding herself against me.

"What's that?"

"I'm sorry," she repeats.

I lean down and press a soft kiss to the reddened area on her ass cheek. "You're so sexy when you behave."

Relaxing my forearm, I expect her to move, but she doesn't, choosing to stay in her prone position. The moment itself is vulnerable, and I move to wrap my arms around her body, dragging her into me to hold her tight against my chest.

It's odd, to…*cuddle* like this. But what I did was intense, and while I know she enjoyed it, I also know it's important to make sure she knows she did well.

That she pleased me.

We sit that way for a few minutes, and then I move her to the side, making sure she's comfortable on the couch. Her arms reach out to bring me back. "Where are you going?"

"Don't move." I push her hair back from her face. "I'll be right back."

She hums, her eyes glazed, and I head down the hall and to the medicine cabinet, grabbing the arnica cream to make sure she doesn't bruise.

Walking back over, I see she hasn't moved from her position, and she twists her head toward me, smiling softly.

I stand in front of her, tapping her thigh. "Up."

She moves without complaint, and I put her back over my lap, lightly rubbing where I spanked before opening the cream and spreading it on the area.

"When I was three," I start, "I got a stuffed animal. A hand-me-down teddy bear from some kid who lived around the block and didn't want it anymore. It was dirty and used and already coming apart at the seams, but it was *mine*."

Yasmin pulls back slightly, her face turning toward me and her eyes growing wide at my admission.

"My father came home that night and saw me with it. I was afraid he'd take it from me, so before he could, I ran to my room and found a hiding place, beneath the slats in my tiny little bed." My throat swells with the memory and I swallow around the pain. "I didn't even make it back out before I heard my mother screaming and him yelling at her for treating me like a girl. For raising her son *wrong*."

"Oh my god," Yasmin whispers.

"He never took it out on me though. It was always her. She didn't make me enough of a man. She didn't cook dinner right. Sometimes the way she was breathing just annoyed him, I guess. It was *always* her fault." I grit my teeth, my nose scrunching against the burn growing behind it. "But my mother is a vengeful woman, and she knew who was really to blame." My eyes go unfocused, and I stare at the wall behind Yasmin, the memories so vivid it's like I'm there. "That was the first time I remember my mother beating me. Hours after her own pleas quieted and my father had gone back out to the bars, I was lying in my bed, that stupid fucking bear cuddled tight against my chest. And she came raging in, dried blood around her nose, a shiner on her face the size of New York, and my father's belt wrapped around her fist." I lift up my shirt from my torso, pointing to a small scar, one of many that are hidden beneath the ink. "She liked to use the metal end. Really get her point across." I let out a small laugh. "There were tears in her eyes though, and she promised it would only hurt for a little. But that's the thing about abuse, I guess. The pain always lasts even after the bruises fade."

A tear escapes from the corner of Yasmin's eye, and I drop her wrists, reaching out to swipe it away, letting my thumb drag down her perfect face.

"When you're a kid, you don't really know any better. The only thing you *do* know is that she's your mom, and moms are supposed to love you. To be your safe space. Not the other way around. I just wanted the best for her, even after she was the cause of so much pain."

"Julian..."

I hush her, my fingers never stopping their motion on her

skin. "So you see, I *wish* she would die. To free me from this guilt that lives inside me, festering like an infected wound, knowing that if maybe I had just never existed, she wouldn't have had so much strife."

Emotion, thick and volatile, floods through me, pouring into my chest and filling up my veins until I can't think straight. It's too much. Too strong. And I need to do something to make it go away.

Yasmin spins around on my lap and I let her, her face staring up at me with a new look in her glossy eyes, one I've never seen. I'm not sure if I like it there or not.

My fingers follow the trail of wetness on Yasmin's face until I'm cupping her chin and lifting, dragging her into me.

"If I'm the devil, amore mio, cast stones at the one who made me."

And then I kiss her.

CHAPTER 30

Yasmin

MY HEART SLAMS AGAINST MY RIB CAGE, TRYING to leap out of my chest and soar into his, and I'm not quite sure why it's happening or how to stop it. Maybe it's to soothe what Julian feels like may be broken or to simply comfort the vulnerable little boy locked inside.

Either way, I don't have much time to process what he said before his lips are on mine, stealing the breath from my lungs like he needs it to survive.

And I've been kissed before, but the way Julian devours me—like he can't stand the thought of staying away for another second, like I'm the *only* thing he needs and nothing will get in his way—shows me that maybe I've never truly been kissed.

There aren't butterflies in my stomach. No soft pitter-patters of flapping wings or gentle flips. Instead, he causes an inferno, raging through my system and disintegrating me.

My fists unclench as his hands grip the sides of my face possessively, both of us no longer able to fight against whatever this is that's been slowly steeping for the past couple of weeks.

Now it's pulling us both under, and it feels so good I don't care if it makes me drown.

I moan into the kiss, my eyelids fluttering closed as his tongue slips against mine, his hands tilting my head like he needs to get deeper, to taste *more*. It makes my stomach drop and twist like I'm on a roller coaster, and I sink into his hold, my arms wrapping around his neck, fingers digging into his hair as I try to get as close as possible.

Somewhere, in the back of my mind, I know that logically, I should be pulling away. That I should be fighting whatever this is between us and making sure I don't fall for what I know is just another manipulation.

For a second, Aidan flits through my thoughts, guilt for what I'm doing trying to seep into the moment, but then I remember that he wants nothing to do with me. And to be honest, nothing with Aidan has ever felt like *this*. The thought is gone as quickly as it came, the passion coursing through me washing Aidan away like he was written in chalk and not carved on my soul.

Besides, it's been a while since anything has felt *good* in my life, so as selfish as this might make me, I'm going to grab on with both hands and hold on tight. I'm going to take the temporary respite while I can.

He tilts my face, breaking his lips away and dragging his mouth down the expanse of my neck, his teeth nibbling and sucking on every piece of bare skin he can find.

This doesn't feel like a one-time thing.

It feels like ownership.

The thought sends a spear of heat through my middle, making my back arch and my body fall further into him.

His hands move from where they were cupping my face,

grazing down my sides and causing my breath to stall and goose bumps to prickle beneath the silk of my shirt.

He wraps his arm around my waist and pulls me closer until not a single centimeter is left between us, his cock pressing against my torso, thick and *large* and something that I'm suddenly desperate to feel.

Before I can overthink it, I reach out and run the palm of my hand from the base all the way up, reveling in the way his body stiffens and his breathing stutters from where he's still nibbling on the crook of my neck.

My pussy throbs, wetness seeping into my black lace thong, and I imagine what he would feel like slipping between my legs. I bet he would split me apart, dominate every single part of me.

Make me feel loved and secure and whole, even if just for the moment.

He groans but moves his own hand in between us, halting my movements and bringing my arm back up to his chest. I ignore the slight stab of rejection I feel when he does, and then he's spinning me around quickly, lifting me up as he stands until I'm sideways in the air.

I gasp, letting out a small squeal as he maneuvers me exactly how he likes, forcing me to bend over the edge of the coffee table. My elbows ache when they slam into the carved wood, and my knees sink into the purple and gold Persian rug beneath us.

His hand skims up the length of my spine, sensing a shiver racking through me. I lift my head up and am about to turn to look him in the eye, but his palm wraps around the back of my neck and forces me down until my cheek is pressed against the table and my body is supple and open beneath him.

"You are *so* goddamn beautiful, do you know that?" he

murmurs, his free hand caressing my calf and gliding up slowly, massaging the muscle as he does.

My breathing comes in small puffs of air, delight at his compliment filling up my body and sending warmth through me as his fingers play with the hem of my skirt that fell back down when he moved me to the table. Slowly, painstakingly, he pushes it up until the material is bunched at my hips and the cool air kisses the skin of my ass.

His palm feels strong and rough as he grabs a handful of the cheek, muttering something Italian under his breath and then smoothing across the skin.

He moves then, the thick length of his erection pressing against me and making my body ache for more as he leans his upper half across my back, his lips ghosting across my ear, the heat of his breath sending a shiver down my spine.

"Tell me you like my hands on you, gattina."

The words soar through my throat and try to tumble off my tongue, but I sink my teeth into my lip, not wanting to give in, not wanting to give him the satisfaction of being able to demand everything from me when he's already got me splayed out and dripping for him like this. Besides, when I rile him up, he likes it. I can tell because even through his pants, his cock stiffens when I don't do as he asks.

My fingers dig into the wood of the table next to my face, tempering the urge to reach down the front of my bent-over body just to relieve the throbbing ache that's pulsing between my legs.

I think I might die if he doesn't touch me soon, but I still don't want to give in.

Smack.

A sharp sting radiates across my right ass cheek and my teeth bite harder into my lip, the taste of copper flooding my mouth. He smooths over where he just hit, and the anticipation of what he'll do to me next sends a buzzing through my body, my muscles tensing and butterflies exploding in my stomach, fluttering so intensely it feels like I might fly.

It's never felt like this before.

"When I ask you a question, amore mio, I expect you to answer it." Another smack of his hand in the exact same spot, followed again by him caressing the already tender skin.

He's still holding me down by the nape, but now he moves his touch, skimming it upward until his fingers are tangling through my curly strands and fisting my hair. His other hand teases the lace of my underwear before gripping tightly and pulling.

I feel the rip on the skin of my hips before I hear it, and then the panties are gone and I'm exposed, at his mercy, and I've never felt so alive.

His fist tightens in my hair, and he pulls, a harsh stab of pain radiating on my scalp that sends a shock of pleasure straight between my legs.

My body bows as he brings me up, my back coming flush to his front, his chin resting perfectly in the crook of my neck as he forces me to lean my head against his shoulder.

His right hand moves up to the front of my blouse, repeating the tearing motion, buttons popping off my silk shirt and scattering on the rug as he rips the fabric easily, like it was made for his hands.

My chest heaves as I'm left in nothing but my bra, and soon that's gone too, thrown somewhere on the floor, and then I'm completely naked, my nipples pebbled and begging to be touched.

"Where's that smart mouth, *bad girl?*" He cups my right breast in his hand while he pulls roughly on the makeshift ponytail he has clutched in his other fist. "Don't want to give it to me now?"

His fingers pinch my nipple before he holds my entire breast in his hand, manipulating the flesh until the pleasure turns into torture, the ache between my legs intensifying from his touch until it becomes almost too much to bear.

"Please," I pant out.

"Sei bellissima quando implori."

My body vibrates, and his palm dances down the front of my torso until he's hovering directly over where I need him most, his hand cupping my pussy like it's his.

"I could do so much to make you scream," he purrs.

His middle finger slides along the seam of my pussy, my clit throbbing from the ghost of his touch as he drags it all the way down to my entrance, dipping in just a little to tease the outside of my hole.

I moan, my muscles giving out as I practically collapse against him, his front remaining plastered to my back as he plays with me like I'm a marionette dancing on his strings.

"But you like my hands on you," he states. "Be my good girl and tell me how it feels."

"I hate it," I say, biting my lip even harder.

He moves and smacks my pussy, the sharp sting radiating all the way down my legs, my body shaking from how badly I want him inside me. To ease this ache. He removes his touch, bringing his palm up to my face, my wetness glistening on his skin as he rests his fingers against my lips.

"Your wet cunt doesn't lie, gattina."

His finger parts my mouth and forces its way in. I whimper, my tongue wrapping around his digit as I lick myself off his skin.

"That's my girl, sucking yourself off me like a desperate little slut," he rasps. "You can taste the truth, can't you, baby?"

I nod against him, so turned on I don't even *want* to fight it anymore. I just want to do whatever he says so that he'll make me come and I can keep feeling this way forever.

He removes his fingers from my mouth, and I wantonly whimper in protest.

His hold on my hair loosens, hand moving to wrap around the front of my throat now, my pulse pounding so heavily I'm sure he can feel it.

"Say it," he demands.

"I love it when you touch me. *Please*," I beg, my legs trembling.

My body is so on edge that everything feels heightened. The air is cool as it whips against my overheated skin, the rug scratchy as it digs into my knees. My pussy is aching as his hand finally gives me what I need.

His thumb rubs my clit and immediately my vision grows hazy, so lost in the pleasure I wouldn't be able to see the forest for the trees, and when his fingers slide effortlessly into me from how drenched I am, I let out a loud moan, my head dropping back against shoulder. His other hand tightens around my throat, being careful to avoid my windpipe.

He's done this before. Jealousy whips through me like a tornado, but just as quickly as it came, it's gone, my stomach tensing as he rubs against my sensitive nerves.

"So responsive," he murmurs . "You feel like fucking heaven, and I've barely touched you."

He starts a rhythm, his fingers plunging inside me and curling until they hit a spot that makes me cry out, and right when they do, his thumb presses against my swollen clit, making pleasure swirl through my middle and pool in my core.

My arm flies up behind me to wrap around his neck, because if I don't hang on to him, I won't be able to hang on at all, and before I can stop it, I'm muttering, "Please, Julian, *God.* I need... I need—"

"Such a good little wife when you're dripping on my hand and begging for me to fuck you."

My pussy spasms around his fingers.

"Is that what you want, amore mio? You want me to pry your thighs apart and slide myself so deep inside you that you'll feel me for days?"

My teeth slam into my lips, trying to keep from telling him, to make him drag the answer out of me, but I'm too far gone to fight.

"Yes," I plead.

"Yes," he repeats. "You'd come all over my dick like my perfect girl, wouldn't you?"

He disappears from between my legs, the pressure on my neck easing as he moves both hands and grips my hips. He picks me up from where I'm bent and spins me around, perching my ass on the edge of the table, his fingers digging into the meat of my legs as he forces them as wide as they'll go.

I breathe deeply, watching this powerful, dangerous man on his knees before me, and my pussy clenches at the sight.

He moves in, his nose running along the inside of my thigh. "I'm going to fuck you with my tongue until you soak my face."

I swallow, my mouth dry and heart beating so hard I can feel it in my ears.

His breath coasts across the top of my already sensitive clit, and it throbs.

He skims a finger along my slit, dipping just the tip inside me. "Deny me what I want, and next time I'll tie you to this table and torture you until you scream. Do you understand?" He peers at me from between my legs, his pupils dilated and his cheeks flushed.

He can pretend he's in control all he wants, but I see the way this is affecting him just as much as it is me.

"I understand," I breathe.

"Good girl."

And then he's on me. He doesn't waste time being soft and sweet. His tongue and mouth work me like he's ravenous for my taste. I cry out, the pleasure squeezing my insides tight and spreading through my limbs, tighter and tighter until it feels like I'll burst.

I grip the strands of his hair, pulling harshly as a loud noise escapes my mouth, my back arching off the table and my legs resting on top of his shoulders.

He continues his assault, the feel of his tongue licking and his mouth sucking while his fingers work in and out of my pussy the best kind of torture, and before I know it, I'm already on the edge.

He's built me up for so long that I can't last. I won't. It's fucking impossible.

I've never felt anything like this, so all-consuming and like I'm going to die if I don't get to come.

"Oh *god*," I moan.

"That's right, amore mio," he coos, releasing my clit from his teeth. "Let Him hear your screams."

He dives back in, and then I'm coming, my vision going black and my legs pressing so tightly against his head I'm surprised he can breathe, a groan ripping from my throat and permeating the air.

Through it all, he never stops licking me, working my pussy as I ride the high, and easing down to soft nips when I start to come back to earth.

It isn't until I become so sensitive it hurts that he finally pulls away, his face glistening with *me* as he gives me a grin.

My hands fumble as I reach out to grab him wherever I can, pulling him up and over me until his body covers mine, the fabric of his shirt scratching against my overheated flesh. I surge up, capturing his lips, sucking myself off his tongue, and he grunts, his body weight falling to rest on me.

I love the way it feels. And I know that I shouldn't, but right now, I'm lost.

"Fuck me," I beg against his mouth.

He shakes his head even as he kisses me back. Pulling away slightly, he rests his forehead against mine, his heavy breaths coating my lips.

"Are you mine?" he asks.

His question cuts through my chest and settles in my heart, fracturing the already breaking pieces. I suck in a breath, my body freezing. I can't answer that.

I won't.

Because regardless of how I feel right now and what just happened, it doesn't change anything.

Not really.

Being his means letting go of everything else, and I'm just not willing to do that.

He swallows, his Adam's apple bobbing as he nods against me, and then he's gone, my body chilled from the loss of his touch.

I lie there for a long time, coming to terms with what just

happened. And then slowly, I stand up, grabbing my ripped clothes off the rug and heading to my room.

I'm not sure what makes me do it, but I head straight to the burner phone, pick it up, and unlock the screen.

1 new notification.

My chest tightens as I open the text to reply to my lawyer. Only the message isn't from him.

CHAPTER 31

Yasmin

THINGS DON'T LOOK THE SAME IN THE DAYLIGHT.

That's the first thought that crosses my mind when I wake up in a foreign room with silk sheets beneath me and the most comfortable mattress I've ever laid on.

It takes me a few seconds to come to fully, rubbing the sleep from my eyes to figure out where I am.

Sitting up in the bed, I look around, blinking.

This must be Julian's room. It's filled with sleek modern furniture, and this is the largest bed I've ever seen. It screams masculine yet lacks any defining personality.

I smirk at the thought but then quickly remember why I'm here and what happened last night, and the amusement drains away.

Did he move me here in the middle of the night?

It's the only logical explanation, because I remember falling asleep in my own bed, my chest feeling like it was splitting in two from the conflicting emotions going on inside me.

I wonder if anyone else has ever had the pleasure of being in here, but the second the thought crosses my mind, my stomach cramps, so I push it away, convincing myself that I really don't care.

The urge to jump out of his bed and snoop through his belongings is strong, but now it feels heavier, like there's a bigger sense of betrayal somehow. Although after opening the burner phone last night and reading a message from Julian's "employee," snooping is low on the list of things I've done behind his back.

I know I should regret what happened, that I should be beating myself up and claiming it was a mistake, but the truth of the matter is that I don't really regret it.

For the first time in my life, my mind was clear, my body was free, and all my problems disappeared. At least for a while. I felt safe. Cared for. *Wanted.* Desired. And that's not to say I've never felt those feelings before, but having that type of attention from Julian Faraci is like being used to cloudy days and then being blasted by the sun.

I'm not sure how I'll go back.

But I *have* to go back.

Just like everything else I should come to terms with but am choosing not to, I push the feeling down, ignoring it, deciding to enjoy the delicious strain of my sore muscles and the memory of what it felt like under his tongue.

Arousal heats me slowly from the inside out.

I stretch out in the bed, raising my hands above my head and sighing at the way it relieves the sleepy tension from my muscles. Then I push the covers off me completely, slipping out of the side of Julian's bed and padding through the room until I hit his en suite.

Glancing around, I wonder if maybe he's here, but there's no sign of him, so I decide to make myself at home. He wouldn't have brought me here if he wasn't implying I had free rein to do what I wanted.

The second I see the master shower that takes up the entire length of the far wall, with multiple showerheads from a thousand different angles, I know I'm going to be using it.

I waste no time, stripping off my pajamas and making my way to the shower, turning on the water and watching with excitement as the multiple different showerheads light up and spray water.

There's a main one, just like there is in my room, that sits on the ceiling, creating a rainfall effect on your head when you step under the spray. It has a removable head beneath it, attached to the shower wall. Beyond that, there are spouts on the sides, spraying from all directions. I've never experienced anything quite like it, and I'm immediately immersed in the sensory overload of it all, allowing the heat of the water to cascade over my skin and relax my body even more.

Rude of him to not tell me this shower was here the whole time.

There's an automatic dispenser on the right-hand wall, and I reach my hand underneath, the smell of Julian's soap filling the air. Closing my eyes, I hum under my breath as I start to wash my body, my breath hitching when I run my palms over my sensitive breasts. My mind starts flashing memories of the night before, how Julian's hands moved me where he wanted like I was a doll there for his enjoyment. How he demanded things of me and held me down while he made me come, yet made every single second about *my* pleasure.

I never knew that being handled that way would be such a turn-on.

It's always in the shower that visions of Julian make me want to come.

When I brush my fingers across my clit, a shudder racks my body. Slowly, I rub back and forth over my pussy again, a sharp sting of pain mixing with the pleasure when I pinch myself, trying to recreate the feeling from last night, but it falls short.

A throat clears and I gasp, my heart flipping and my eyes shooting open, my hand flying away from between my legs.

Julian stands there in the middle of the room with nothing but gray sweatpants and a smirk on his face.

I'm caught so off guard at the sight of him without a shirt that I don't even say anything, instead just letting my gaze roam the length of his body. I've never seen him look this way, and if I thought he was dangerous in a suit, he's *devastating* when he's just up and out of bed.

Both of his arms are entirely covered with tattoos; they sprawl across his shoulder blades and drip down his chest. In fact, it's easier to find spots of him that *aren't* showing skin than parts that are. There's a snake's head that starts on his left hand and wraps around his entire arm, coiling up over his shoulder blade. It's the largest of all his pieces, and my eyes are transfixed on the art.

His stomach is toned, because *of course* it is, and his eyes are like fire behind thin, silver wire-frame glasses.

My stomach jolts.

He runs a hand through his perfectly mussed black hair. "Don't stop on my account."

"You scared me," I complain, my palm pressing against my chest to calm my speeding pulse.

His eyes blaze down my body, and even through the steam, I feel exposed, lit up like a firework without a single touch.

What is he thinking? Is he regretting last night? Wanting it to happen again? Gloating because he has me exactly where he wants me?

He shakes his head. "You make it hard for a man to leave when you look like that."

My heart flips at his words. I'm not sure why his compliments affect me in such a visceral way, but the most selfish part of me hopes that he never stops.

"So don't," I reply.

He swipes his tongue across his bottom lip. "Duty calls, gattina. And Razul is here to take you to your father's."

Confusion swims through me and my forehead scrunches. "Why?"

Julian tilts his head. "Don't you want to see him?"

Sadness, that nasty emotion, reminds me of its presence again with a sharp tug around my chest. "Yes, of course," I whisper.

He's quiet then, letting his gaze sweep over me one more time. "I'm leaving for Egypt tomorrow morning for a few days. I'm hoping you'll come with me."

Egypt.

"Oh," I reply.

I don't really know what to say. Before last night, I would have jumped at the chance to see Aidan, but now...now things have changed, shifted. And going to Egypt with my fake husband who I let fuck me with his tongue and seeing the man I thought was the love of my life but who now feels like a distant memory is confusing to say the least.

"But go see your father first. Check in with him, see how he's faring. If you don't want to leave him, I understand."

I'm surprised he's giving me the choice, but I'm grateful for it either way. I don't know if I *can* leave with my father only having a limited amount of time left. I'd never forgive myself if he died while I wasn't here.

But if I stay, I doubt he'd let me see him at the end anyway.

"I'll be leaving from the office in the morning, so if you

choose to come with me, Razul will bring you to the airport after you wake up. Otherwise, I'll see you when I get back."

I nod, watching him turn around and leave without so much as a goodbye. This shouldn't be a big deal; it's just a short trip, and I'm honestly surprised that he's willing to let me stay alone, so far out of his reach.

But it feels heavy, like something will fundamentally change regardless of what I decide. A thick sense of foreboding creeps up my spine and doesn't leave.

Not through the rest of my shower.

Not when I call Riya and fill her in on what happened last night.

And not when I finally pull out the burner phone and bring up the message that's been nagging the back of my head ever since I read it.

Unknown number: You don't know me, but I work for Julian. I took this number from Aidan's phone because I know you need some help.

My fingers shake as I type out a reply, a sick feeling rolling through my stomach.

Me: Who is this?

I get an immediate reply.

Unknown number: A friend. Come to Egypt when your husband does. I can help.

The words from the last text are seared in my brain and stay there even an hour later when I'm in the car with Razul, going to see my father.

He's awake and on the main patio overlooking the pool, a cup of steaming tea beside him when I get there.

It's a beautiful morning, the crisp autumn air breezing through the trees that line the property, wind chimes clinking together in the distance, and the sun sparkling down on the heated pool that hasn't been covered yet for the winter.

Something pulls in my chest as I walk over and sit down next to him, the cushioned chair soft beneath me. I don't say anything at first, and neither does he.

This is different. *He* is different.

But I guess facing your own mortality will do that to a person. "Baba."

He jumps slightly, his tired eyes swinging over and widening when they meet mine.

I've been told that right before you die, you straddle the worlds, one foot in this one and one foot in the next. It makes my stomach cinch up tight when I think about how far gone out of this life he has to be to not have noticed I was here.

"Yasmin, what are you doing here?" he asks. His voice is worn and soft, barely above a whisper.

"Baba, how many times do I have to tell you?" I choke out, trying to stem the tremble in my voice. "I'll *always* be here."

A soft smile plays around the corners of his lips, and he turns his face forward until he's staring out again at the view.

"Nice morning," I manage.

He nods. "One of the prettiest."

We sit in silence for a few more minutes, and even though

I've spent the past few months lying to myself—even though I've raged and fought and tricked my mind into believing it isn't true—right now it's impossible to ignore.

He's *dying*. And there's not a damn thing I can do.

A sharp, searing ache pierces through my chest at finally acknowledging this for what it is.

With clarity comes pain. With acceptance comes grief.

I've been running away from both for quite some time.

Fingering the ring on my left hand, I say, "I'm sorry you didn't get to walk me down the aisle."

He sighs, reaching over and patting the top of my forearm. "I've had a lot of time recently to think on who I am. Who I've been as a man. A husband. A father."

His words are a punch to the gut. "You've been a great father."

"We both know that's not true. I've been what I knew how to be." He shakes his head. "But sometimes what you know isn't enough. And not acknowledging my need for growth, so I could become the father you deserved, the one who was *present* and not just a name on a check, that's something that will haunt me into the afterlife."

"Baba," I whisper. "You did the best you could."

"If I had done the best I could, I would have noticed you and the man who's like a son to me falling in love right before my eyes. But I missed it all. My selfishness and greed made me think I knew what was best instead of trusting that you had grown into a strong woman."

I inhale sharply, because never in a thousand years did I think we would be having this conversation. My father has always been stuck in his ways. The fact that *this* is what he's grieving over, that he thinks he missed something that was never there, makes it difficult not to pour out all the secrets I'm holding close to my chest just so I can alleviate his guilt.

But I stop myself, because even if he could help me be free of Julian for good, even if he *didn't* miss anything between us, he still missed me falling in love. Still disregarded my feelings to honor his own.

And if he's taking the step to acknowledge where he failed, the least I can do is allow him to feel the pain of his actions so he can let them go and find peace before death, no matter how much I wish to take them away right now.

Tears spring up behind my eyes, and I let them fall, small sniffles coming from my nose as I realize that it took my father on his deathbed for me to truly feel *seen*.

Again, I waver on what to say. I could tell him that Aidan is the one I really love, that I need his help and I want to be free of Julian. I now know, for the first time in my life, that if I did lay everything on the line, my father wouldn't look at me with disappointment.

I'm also not sure if all of it would still be true.

So I don't say a word. Because if my father is coming to terms with his innermost feelings, maybe I should do the same.

And this marriage doesn't feel fake to me anymore.

Not like it did. So maybe I won't go to Egypt. I won't meet this mystery "friend." I won't see Aidan. Maybe I *won't* keep talking to Randy Gazim.

"Thank you, Baba," I murmur.

"Are you happy, Yasmin?"

His question hits me in the center of the chest, and I chew on my lip as I think of how to answer. A few weeks ago and I would have said no. I don't think I would have had it in me to lie to him when he's being so open and vulnerable with me.

But now...

Now I'm confused. Because while there's still a profound sense of sadness and grief when I think about the state of my life, there are moments that peek through the clouds, sprinkling bits of sunshine down. And yeah, they feel like happiness.

And all of them include Julian.

I clear my throat. "Of course."

He sighs, nodding. "Good. That's all I want."

"Julian wants me to go to Egypt on a trip. But I think I'll stay here with you instead."

He sighs. "I love you more than the world, Yasmin, but go with your husband to Egypt. I'll still be here when you return."

The way he says it like a command leaves no room for debate. I could waste my breath arguing, but it wouldn't make a difference, and if I pushed, I'd only be faced with a locked door from a stubborn man who doesn't want me to see him wither away.

I swallow, ignoring the way my throat swells. "Promise?"

"Promise," he says. "I'm tired. I think I'll go lie inside and rest."

He pushes himself to a stand, and I move with him, reaching out and hugging him like it's the last time I ever will.

He kisses my forehead and whispers his love, and somehow, even through the deep sickness in my heart, I manage to do the same.

And then I leave my father in peace and walk out the door to pack before going to meet my husband.

CHAPTER 32

Julian

I SLAM THE PHONE DOWN, IRRITATED THAT ONCE again, Ian isn't answering my calls when he works for *me*. I grab my cell from the corner of my desk and scroll through the latest text messages, noticing a disturbing pattern of me having to check in with him repeatedly, when before it's always been him blowing up my phone.

He's never given me reason to doubt him, but I'd be a fool not to take notice of the change.

My fingers fly over the keys as I type out another message to him, anger brewing in the bottom of my gut. If I had known he was going to go AWOL at the same time that Jeannie did, I would have convinced Tinashe to stay in Egypt and oversee the boy himself.

Me: Ian, you have two minutes to call me back before I fire you and give Ciara your job.

I grit my teeth and watch the clock count down, hoping that

he remembers I never bluff. I have no time for people who want to play games. While I wait, I glance down at the papers that were just couriered to my door and flip through the pages one more time, staring at the fake signature of my wife signed on the dotted line and backdated to the day of our marriage.

My finger pops out and rubs along the edge of the piece of paper.

Will of Yasmin Karam-Faraci.

It's always been the plan. Marry the girl. Let Ali die. Kill her and take everything that was supposed to be mine.

Only now, it doesn't feel as euphoric as I imagined it might. It feels like confusion. A giant war waging inside my mind and body. Everything I've always wanted clashing violently with my newest obsession.

The phone rings and I pick it up.

"Boss."

"How nice of you to check in, Ian."

I lean back in the chair, rocking slightly as I twirl a pen around in my hand, the smooth plastic rubbing against my skin as it slides through my fingers.

"Just getting things ready for you to be here next week."

Telling him that I'll be there earlier is on the tip of my tongue, but I decide not to at the last minute. There's something fishy going on, and I want to see what it is.

"So you've contacted Darryn."

There's a shuffling on the line and he clears his throat. "Yeah, yep. Everything's all good. He's willing to meet with you. How are things there? With the bi—the uh, the wife?"

Absentmindedly I twist the ring on my left finger, a sharp stab of *something* piercing through my chest. "Things are going according to plan here. Don't worry your pretty little head about that."

"Good."

"Good," I parrot.

"Is there... I mean, do you need anything else from me?"

My brow quirks. "I have the will."

"Perfect. So now what?"

His question irritates me, although it's a valid one to ask, and I snap at him. "*Now* you focus on finding that fucking lamp so you can come home. And then you wait to see what I decide to do."

"What's there to even decide?" he asks. "You have the will, you married the girl, so either wait until the old man croaks or kill him yourself."

"Watch your mouth. You know better than to say ridiculous things over phones."

"Of-of course, boss. I'm sorry," he stutters.

"I'll see you in a week. Try and stay out of trouble until then."

I hang up the phone, fresh annoyance rushing through my veins from talking to Ian and having him ask so many questions I can no longer answer. And then my mind goes back to her.

Yasmin.

She's all I can fucking think about.

I breathe through the tension in my back, rolling my shoulders and trying to ease the sharp, throbbing pain as my phone vibrates, a text flashing with my driver telling me he's out front. Opening the right-side drawer in my desk, I drop in the papers, slamming it closed and walking out the door.

My stomach is in knots, wondering if Yasmin will choose to stay here with her father or come to see the boy.

I'm under no illusion it would be for me.

Forty minutes later, I'm on the plane, the engine rumbling beneath me as I sit in one of the four oversize chairs on the left-hand side.

It's a gorgeous aircraft, one that I've been using for the past five years after I bought it for Sultans. An upgrade from the last one, and it made travel much more comfortable with the bedroom in the back—not that I'm ever able to sleep on planes—and the long cream couch on the opposite side of the chairs with a large flat-screen TV hanging in front.

Travel isn't something new with my position, and I've made flying almost like a second home, despite the fact that it's not something I really enjoy.

I nod at the flight attendant who brought me a club soda on ice and glance at the text from Razul saying they're on their way.

She's coming.

Part of me is surprised she's willing to leave her father when we both know he could go any day. He's been extra reclusive the past month, especially with the business side of things, but I was almost sure that she'd be too afraid to not be here in case things went south.

I suppose I was wrong.

Selfishly, I'm glad.

And this will be good. She'll reunite with the boy and I can witness them together, the puppy love in her eyes and the heart-break aching to be soothed in her soul, and watch him sweep in and erase whatever weird thing has been happening between us.

It's what I need. A slap in the face, a cold reminder that even if I was able to trick her into staying with me—*force* her into it—nothing when it comes to Yasmin and me is real.

Even if it feels like it is.

Even if she's the only one who's seen my darkest parts and still decided I was worth a shit.

Or maybe even that was an act all for *him*. To ensure the boy's safety when she knew I had the power to kill him in an instant. I have been hanging him over her head, and even though we haven't spoken about my blackmail recently, it doesn't change the fact that it's there, like a concrete wall directly between us.

A heaviness settles in the center of my chest, and I clink the ice cubes in my club soda, wishing it was something with alcohol to wash away the ache.

A car door slams, muted outside the thick windows of the plane, but my heart jumps anyway, knowing who it is. Foreboding wraps around the base of my spine and spreads through my limbs, but I ignore the way it feels.

This is *exactly* what needs to happen. I'm getting too lost. Too soft. Too unfocused.

It's preposterous, really.

Yasmin walks through the door of the aircraft and around the corner, her footsteps faltering when she sees me. Her gaze swings from the large TV and living area to the hallway that leads to the bedroom in the back.

"Wow, this is nice," she breathes, moving toward me and sitting in the chair directly across from mine, her camera plopping in the seat at her side.

I'm happy to see that she brought her camera. Knowing it brings her so much happiness makes me want to glue it to her side and make sure she's never without it again.

I tip my head. "Gattina."

Her hands run down the side of the chair, letting out a

contented sigh as she feels up the buttery leather. She smiles at me and my chest pulls tight.

"Patatino," she replies.

I smirk because I can't help it, shaking my head slightly as I take a sip from my drink.

"Is this big plane all yours?" she asks, looking around again.

"Nope," I state. "Actually, it's yours."

Her brows shoot up. "I've never been on this plane in my life."

"Your father has."

She eyes me carefully, nodding. "Well, that would make it *his* and not mine." She pauses, her tongue peeking out to swipe across her bottom lip. "I really have no interest in taking all the things that were once his, you know? I'm just doing it because it's what he wants. And I owe it to him to keep his legacy in the family."

I clench my jaw to keep from spitting out something hurtful, something about the fact that it must be nice she at least gets the choice, but I hold it back, realizing the anger isn't for *her*, it's for the deep wounds caused by Ali's disregard when I've given him everything. But I suppose that's my fault for placing my mentor in a father role when he never asked to be.

Click.

My head raises up, seeing her placing her camera back down again.

She grins. "Sorry, couldn't help it. You looked pensive and I wanted to catch the moment."

"Why didn't you major in photography?" I blurt out.

All I've ever heard from Ali about his daughter is how much she excels in her education and how proud he is to have her, but he's never told me about her photography, and I wonder if he even knows.

Even worse, it makes me want to know what else she dreams of, what she craves, where her passion lies. I've spent years assuming I know everything about Yasmin Karam, but lately, she's shown me that I never really knew anything about her at all.

She laughs. "Can you imagine? My father would never have wanted a daughter with a *photography* major."

I purse my lips. "Does a degree in photography even exist?"

She nods. "Bachelor of fine arts in photography. I actually looked into the program before I went, but..." She trails off, shaking her head.

I hum, taking a sip of my drink and watching her as she glances down at her lap and picks at her nail.

"Do you want a tour?" I ask.

"What's to see?" She shrugs. "We're on this plane for, like, ten hours, right? I'll get to it all eventually."

She settles in, resting her head against the back of her chair, and closes her eyes. Just after takeoff, she falls asleep.

She looks uncomfortable, so I slam my laptop closed after having gotten an hour or so of work done and move to sweep her up in my arms. She stirs but doesn't wake completely, instead snuggling up against my chest as I carry her like a new bride down the back hallway and into the bedroom, tucking her in and running my hand down the side of her face.

I sit next to her and watch her sleep, counting every breath she takes and the way they make her chest rise and fall, how her lips part ever so slightly and her lashes flutter like she's in the middle of a dream. And eventually, my lids flutter closed and I fall asleep too.

When I wake up, it's to the feeling of someone staring at the side of my face.

"Hello, wife," I say without opening my eyes.

She huffs, and the mattress dips and jiggles when she scrambles back. "It's weird to talk to people without your eyes open," she says.

I peek a lid open and twist my head, looking at her mussed-up hair and sleepy gaze. "No weirder than watching me sleep with your nose almost pressed into my face."

Her teeth sink into her lip. "Yeah, well, sue me. How did you know I was there anyway?"

"I'm a man of many talents." I smirk, stretching out my arms and placing them behind my head.

"Humble as ever," she says with a snort, falling back until she hits the pillow. "No wonder you had to blackmail me to be your wife, since your huge ego doesn't leave room for anyone else."

It's the first time she's said it so plainly, but I don't mind that she did. Better for her to remind us both of that fact now, before things get even more confusing.

Still, we only have a few hours left until she sees the boy again, and the feeling that rushes through my veins and cramps up my insides makes me desperate to spend the rest of my time on the plane reminding her how much I can give her that he can't.

I don't focus on the reasons *why* I want to show her, just that I do.

Rolling over quickly, I grab her by the waist and drag her underneath my frame, my hips slipping perfectly between her thighs. "Would you like me to prove it to you?"

Her eyelids flutter and I press into her, letting her feel how hard I am and how much I'd love to sink myself inside her.

She lets out a small moan, her arms flying to wrap around my neck. "Prove to me what? That you have a big ego?"

I smirk. "That too."

Dipping down, I run my nose along the expanse of her neck, breathing in her scent, desperation filling my veins, wanting to make the time we have here last forever.

I don't *want* to give her back. Even temporarily. I'd rather keep her in this bubble we've created, one where she lets me touch her and I don't hate that she's touching me, and we can pretend, even for a little bit, that this is more than what it is.

The thought of losing this new feeling, of letting the boy have even a little piece of her makes me murderous.

"When we get to where we're going," I murmur into her skin, "I'm going to fuck you with my tongue until you can't breathe."

Her back arches and she pushes herself against me, and even through our clothes, it's the best thing I've ever felt. My hands glide up the sides of her body until our hands meet, and I tangle our fingers and place them above her head, pinning her in place while she grinds her pussy on my dick.

I bite the inside of my cheek, heat spreading across my abdomen and down my thighs at the way she's working my cock, aching to rip off her clothes the way I did before and sink inside her so I can fuck her raw.

"Needy little slut," I rasp, accenting the words with a thrust.

She whimpers, her fingers tightening around mine.

"So eager for a real man, aren't you, *wife*?" I continue, my mind growing fuzzy from the pleasure.

Her legs come up and wrap around my back, dragging me down into her until we're flush together, my body weight on hers, and our mouths sharing the same air.

"Fuck me," she begs. "*Please*, Julian. I need you."

And *goddamn*, I'm desperate for it.

I run my nose across hers, our lips brushing just enough to send my heart slamming against my ribs.

"Are you mine?" I ask.

She sucks in a breath, the passion that was weaving between us suddenly doused like a wet flame.

The slight hesitation is all I need to know.

The ache in my chest spreads, a sharp pain that throbs like a deep bruise.

I release her hands like they're lava, moving from the bed and readjusting my hard-on as I walk out of the bedroom altogether.

CHAPTER 33

Yasmin

TEN HOURS ON A PLANE AND THREE IN THIS JEEP
with a random man driving us, and my mind still feels alert like
I've been shot in the heart with adrenaline.

Or maybe it's just pain.

My brain wars from one extreme to the other, split between
wanting to smooth things over with Julian and reminding myself
that he's the reason everything went to shit in the first place.

And my stomach is already tied in a thousand knots from the
thought of seeing Aidan again after so much has happened and
figuring out who the hell this mystery texter is.

Not that I think they'll be awake right now. It's two in the
morning wherever it is that we are, which I couldn't tell you if you
paid me to. I've never been to Egypt, and this trip isn't exactly for
sightseeing.

With every mile we drive, the nausea grows stronger, my legs
shake faster, and the nerves in my stomach jumble a little more.

Julian's been cold and aloof since we've landed.

Since he asked if I was his. *Again.*

And honestly, how *could* he ask that?

Even worse, how could I want to tell him yes?

It isn't fair. Not when he's taken away the choice entirely. I'm his whether I want to be or not.

And until that situation resolves, how can he expect me to figure out what's real and what's some fucked-up version of Stockholm syndrome?

But this Julian, this man sitting next to me with eyes like obsidian stone and a scowl that tries to turn you to ash, this is the Julian I knew as a girl.

I hadn't realized how much he had changed with me until he flipped the switch back.

A swell of emotion surges in my chest, caught between wanting to beg him to just *look* at me and being thankful for the respite, because if he's out of the equation, I won't have to balance the way I'm confused over him with the anger I feel at the things he's done.

I lean my head against the cool glass window, watching the urban streets turn to desert sand, and eventually, after what feels like hours of driving on empty roads, there's a large warehouse-type building in the distance, with several smaller buildings sprinkled around the edges. The entire thing is surrounded by a fence, signs in both English and Arabic on either side of the opening to the drive that warn people not to trespass.

Finally, we come to a stop directly in front of the building.

The driver gets out of the Jeep and moves to the back, unloading our bags and taking them inside, and I sit still, my hands wringing together in my lap, waiting to see what Julian's going to do next.

He doesn't say a word, just unbuckles his seat belt and gets out of the car, so I follow suit, the quiet night air kissing my cheeks as I do. My muscles sigh in relief when I stand up, and I take a moment to stretch, trying to ignore the random pains from so much travel.

The sky is pitch-black other than the lights from the building, and I don't know that I've ever seen stars shine so brightly in the sky.

There's so *many* of them.

"Where are we?" I finally ask, glancing around.

Julian doesn't even spare me a glance. "This is the compound."

"Yeah, I got that, genius. I meant where in the country?"

He cuts me a sharp glare, and a thrill sparks in my veins. *Finally, some attention.*

"That doesn't matter."

I roll my eyes, because I know he hates it when I do. "Well, that narrows it down."

He spins toward me fully now, his jaw tensing and his gaze hard and cold. A slight twinge of fear drips through my middle, but it's muted by the racing of my heart, excited to have his attention on me again.

"Let me make this perfectly clear," he says, his voice low and controlled. "You are not here for vacation. You are not here to sightsee. It doesn't matter *where* we are because you're not to leave this building."

I scoff, walking toward him with my arms crossed. "The fact that you think you can treat me like shit and then still tell me what to do like I'm a child is truly mind-blowing."

I'm not really upset; I'm trying to rile him up on purpose.

Just for fun.

Just to see how much it takes for his icy exterior to crack and give me back *my* Julian.

I lift up on my tiptoes, my nails scratching against his chest and our faces coming close enough for our noses to brush. "Better get it together, patatino, or else the people here will think you're my daddy and not my husband."

He chuckles, deep and dark, his head tilting as he stares down at me, reaching out with his veiny hand and cupping my cheek. "If I want to be your *daddy*, then I'll take you over my knee again."

My eyes flutter, leaning into his warm touch.

"If I want to be to your husband, I'll keep you at my side."

His thumb caresses my cheek.

"And if I want to be your lover, then I'll kill the boy you *love*."

There's something about the way he says that last sentence that has my focus snapping into place, wondering if maybe he's so hot and cold, if the reason why he's suddenly so *desperate* for me to tell him that I'm his is because he's worried about Aidan.

About the boy who's held my heart for years. The one who he had to manipulate in order to get us apart, and the one who up until a couple of weeks ago, I was sure I wanted to spend the rest of my life with.

Of course.

If the situation were reversed and I was in Julian's place, wouldn't I feel the same?

My mind flashes back to the plane. To the night before. All the small moments in between. The ones that we shouldn't have had but couldn't escape.

Somewhere along the way, things shifted for both of us, changing from something that I had no escape from to something I ache to escape *into*, and if that's happening for me, wouldn't it make sense that's it's also happening for him?

He's not a morally upstanding man, but then again, neither is my father, and I've looked past all the things I've known Baba to do because of how much I love him, so what's stopping me from admitting that what I'm feeling for Julian could be something true, despite the way it began?

I tilt my head, watching him in an entirely new light.

Maybe this is real for him, the same way as it's starting to feel real to me.

He starts to move, to turn away from me and the conversation, but I'm not letting him off that easily. Not when he's put up these walls that keep me locked out, when I know that he's really hurting inside.

Suddenly, the questions of if I'm *his* make perfect sense, and it isn't until right now that I let my defenses down fully, letting go of everything I was angry about, all the heavy, sick emotions, and allowing myself to admit that I care for him in a dizzying, painful type of way.

In a way that I've never felt for anyone else, not even Aidan.

My husband.

The man I'm supposed to hate.

He spent his entire childhood having to put others first without ever getting the love and attention of being chosen back. So of course he's putting up walls.

Of course he's turning away.

I'm sure all this terrifies him as much as it does me, and it's realizing that—realizing he's having to deal with his feelings for me in the only way he knows how—that has me running after him to grab his arm.

He stiffens but stops in his tracks, and I move in front of him, craning my neck to stare into his eyes. My heart slams against my chest, teetering on the edge of a cliff, and I don't know what I'm supposed to say, but I do know that I don't want to be like my father, waiting until I'm on my deathbed to come to terms with my emotions and where I've failed the people I care about. And I don't want to be like Julian's mother, taking everything I can get from him and never giving anything in return.

I cup his face, his stubble scratching the palm of my hand.

He flinches, but he doesn't push me away, his nostrils flaring as he stares down at me.

"You *stubborn*, silly man."

Sliding my fingers up his jaw, I cup the back of his neck, lifting on my tiptoes while I drag him down until his forehead rests on mine.

"Don't you know I'm yours?" I whisper.

His breathing is heavy, and his eyes close in a long, slow blink.

My stomach flips, and my soul bleeds, wondering if I'm too late. I should have just said it on the plane when he asked, but I wasn't sure until this moment.

When it felt like I had lost him, even though he was standing at my side.

"It's easy to get lost in something when you're cut off from everything else," he says, straightening up and pressing a chaste kiss to my temple. "Tell me again when we get back home, and maybe I'll believe you."

Then he grabs my hand and pulls me behind him to walk inside.

CHAPTER 34

Julian

NOBODY IS AWAKE WHEN WE WALK INTO THE main building, most likely because it's the middle of the night. I haven't been back here since Sultans bought the place, after I convinced Ali we should be the ones who found the lost lamp and that we needed housing for the archaeologists to use as a base in between their excavation digs.

I had forgotten how much of a warehouse it felt like on the inside, but the tin walls and the high ceilings with exposed beams are warmed up by the furniture that's now placed throughout. Plush couches and a few oversize bean bags are centered around a flat-screen TV, and high bamboo stools are placed beneath the kitchen island.

It's an entirely open floor plan, no separation from the long rectangular dining table to the kitchen to the living room.

There are two small hallways, one on the right side that leads to two bedrooms and a bath, and then another hallway on the left with the main bedroom. No one uses that unless Ali or I make the trip, which until now, we haven't.

There are three small cottages that surround the outside of the main common area, where the archaeologists can live comfortably and with a sense of privacy. It hasn't been a cheap endeavor to find this relic, but it's one that, if we do, will be worth the cost.

I walk Yasmin straight through the main area without showing her around, both because it's the middle of the night and also because she's whipped up a violent storm with her statement that's raging through my middle and showing no signs of calming.

The largest part of me wants to take her at her word, wants to brand her and fuck her and breed her, just so she can never take it back. I have this indescribable urge to make her say it again and then tie her to me in every way that's left, all the ways that would make it impossible for her to leave.

But she's playing a game I'm not sure she's mature enough to handle, so I won't believe that things with us have truly changed until she spends some time with the boy. That way, I can watch and see her body language and decide whether she's playing me for a fool or if she's truly just as confused as I am.

The thought alone is enough to make me murderous.

However, it's better to come to terms with reality now than to give myself false hope. I've never been someone's first choice, and I'm not deluded enough to believe that God will show me any favor now.

Men like me don't get into heaven and we don't get second chances.

When we reach the bedroom, I lead her inside and finally let go of her hand. I point to the en suite. "Shower." To the closet on the right. "Clothes." To the mattress. "Bed."

Her gaze follows, and she chews on her lip, nodding.

I point to her now. "Stay."

"Woof," she barks.

Amusement trickles through my frayed nerves, and I smirk. "Cute."

"You're not staying?" she asks.

I shake my head. "Work to do."

She purses her lips, and I can tell she has more to say. I *want* her to say it, to convince me to let go of what I think needs to happen and just take her right here and now. But if I do that, then I'll lock her in this room, kill the boy so he can't even see her, and then take her home and make her promise to never leave.

And something tells me that would undo any slight chance we may have.

My mind wanders to the will I had made and stowed in my desk drawer back home. I know I'm not going to be able to go through with killing her. I've known for a while now and just haven't allowed myself to think about the fact that when it comes down to it, the things that used to be important to me pale in comparison to her.

I don't give a single fuck if I inherit Sultans.

Couldn't care less about the lost lamp.

Not as long as I get to keep her.

Spinning around, I leave the room before I do something I shouldn't, my chest burning and my throat tight.

I walk back outside and around the front of the building, making my way down the sandy paths that lead to the small cottages, heading to where Jeannie stays. She never replied to my last email, and I'm done playing the waiting game. I put her in this position as the lead archaeologist, and I can take it away just as easily.

Walking up to the front door of the small house, I knock on the dark blue door, pulling out my staff and elongating it so I can flip it around in my hands.

The front window to the left is covered by dark drapes and I notice someone peeking through the edges, thinking I can't see them peering out.

I slip my free hand in my pocket, waiting patiently, even though I'm counting down from thirty until I break down the door myself and force her to answer. I'm sure she was asleep, but I don't care.

Right before I hit zero, the door swings open and Jeannie stands in front of me, her eyes wide awake and her bright-blue hair tangled in a messy bun on top of her head.

"Mr. Faraci," she mumbles, her cheeks growing pink.

I smile and force my way past her until I'm standing in the small living room. "Jeannie, you disappoint me. I put you here"—I pause and wave my arm around the space—"yet you ignore me like you have no one to answer to."

She shakes her head, her fists tightening at her sides. "No, Mr. Faraci, I swear…I just, there's nothing to tell."

I quirk a brow. "So you haven't had any luck with the new dig site?"

She swallows, and I don't miss the way her eyes dart around nervously. "No."

"And Darryn Anders?"

"He's an annoyance, but even he didn't know about the new place I found. He's just been around the other spots, making it hard for us to get any work done."

She swallows again, nodding her head, her feet shuffling on the plain shaggy carpet.

"Why are you so fidgety?" I demand, annoyed at the way she can't stand still for a second. "Do I make you nervous?"

Her forehead scrunches and her tongue peeks out to swipe along her chapped bottom lip. "I just haven't been feeling so great. Nothing that a good night's rest won't fix."

I tilt my head as I watch her. *Something's off.* "Do you need to take a leave of absence?"

She snaps her head up to meet my gaze. "No. Everything's fine. I promise, I just…I'm on my period. You know how it is."

"No," I drawl. "I can't say that I do."

I take a step closer, watching as her entire frame tightens like she's waiting for me to strike. I bend down until she's forced to crane her neck to look me in the eyes.

"Despite how disrespectful you've been by not replying to my emails, I *do* care about your well-being. If you have something to tell me, if there's something going on, now is your chance."

She's quiet for a few moments before her movements cease and she stiffens her jaw. "No, Mr. Faraci, everything's fine."

I don't believe her for a second, but I know a losing battle when I see one, and she isn't planning to tell me anything that's worthwhile.

"How has Ian been treating you?" I ask instead, pivoting the conversation.

She's about to come apart at the seams, which makes me think that things are *not* going well.

Her entire body straightens, her jaw locking up tight. "I'd appreciate it if you'd remind Mr. Godard that I don't work for him."

My brows rise. "Technically, you do. You work for *me*, and Ian is here on my behalf. Is he the one causing you problems?"

She swallows audibly and shifts her head to the side,

breaking our eye contact. "He just makes a mess of things is all. He doesn't help."

I sigh, nodding as I slip my hands in my pockets. I'm beginning to think that being here entirely is a bust. For everyone involved. Ian isn't pulling his weight, and clearly my lead archaeologist needs some time off.

Originally, I was here to ensure things were still on track, but with every second I stand here, it sinks in that maybe I should just let everyone pack up and go home.

Maybe it isn't worth it after all.

What's the point of it anyway? I don't care half as much for the lost lamp as I once did, and it's becoming a headache that's starting to cause too many issues for me to handle. I don't want to meet with Darryn or search anymore. He can have the lamp. I have enough already.

"Pack up your things, Jeannie," I say suddenly.

The words slip from my mouth before the decision has fully formed in my head, but once I say them, I don't pull them back.

A shocked expression washes over her face. "Are you... firing me?"

I shake my head. "No. I'm closing down the compound entirely."

Stepping closer to her, I place my hand on her shoulder. She flinches and my stomach jolts, not enjoying the way it feels to touch someone other than Yasmin.

Her eyes meet mine and I try to adopt an empathetic expression. "Go home. Get some rest. You've done good work for me, but it ends here."

She licks her bottom lip and nods slowly.

And I turn around and walk out the door, heading back to

Yasmin, a large weight feeling as though it was just ripped off my shoulders from my decision.

───────────

When morning breaks, I'm in the kitchen, a cup of hot coffee in my hands, the memory of Jeannie and how on edge she was last night playing on a loop in my head. There's something going on that she isn't telling me, and I'm going to figure out what it is. Maybe she's been here too long, working too much.

Ian and the boy's voices start filtering down the hall, and I lean nonchalantly against the edge of the counter, waiting for them to get around the corner and notice me.

An ache pulses between my eyes as I watch them with their heads bent together, talking like they're old buddies whispering secrets. I take a sip of my coffee, my gaze following their every move.

I clear my throat.

Ian's eyes fly over, his body jerking straight and his gaze going round. It's just for a moment and then he recovers quickly, adopting a confident swagger as he moves toward me. "Boss, you're here early."

"Surprise." I take another sip of my drink.

My eyes flick to the boy, something hot and sharp stewing in my gut.

"Mr. Faraci," he mumbles, not willing to meet my eyes.

I ignore him, turning my attention back to Ian as he moves to stand directly next to me, so close it makes my skin itch. I had forgotten how uncomfortable his lack of personal boundaries made me.

Small pitter-patters of footsteps come from the left, the energy shifts, and I know Yasmin is here before I even see her.

Her gaze is trained on me as she walks into the kitchen and a smile breaks across her face. My heart flips because *goddamn*, she's beautiful when she's like this. All sleep mussed and messy.

A sharp intake of breath across the room draws her attention, and her footsteps halt before she gets to me.

Gusts of green whip through my insides and I look away.

"Aidan," she breathes.

Ian watches me with a curious sheen.

"What?" I snap at him.

"Your meeting with Darryn isn't until next week," he replies, sipping from his own mug of coffee. "That's when I thought you'd be here."

"Doesn't matter. We're leaving anyway. Cancel the meeting." My gaze drifts from Ian to Aidan and Yasmin, now standing right in front of each other, emotion I'm choosing to ignore in both of their eyes.

Yasmin yawns into her hand, and I start to move, grabbing a cup of coffee, but then Aidan walks around the island and does it himself. My stomach cramps, flames exploding in my middle and scorching up my throat.

He grabs creamer from the fridge and mixes it into her cup before walking over to where she is and placing it in her hands.

I purse my lips, watching and waiting, curious to know if she's going to speak up about him making it wrong. I knew her coffee preference by heart after the second day of living with her. He's been with her for years and still doesn't know.

She smiles as she takes it, looking down into the mug and saying a soft "thank you." She doesn't bring it to her lips.

"Why'd you come early?" Ian asks.

"Because I can." I turn around and grab another mug, pouring a fresh cup of coffee before dropping two sugar cubes in the bottom and mixing it with a stirrer.

"Wait," the boy's voice cuts in. "We're *leaving?*"

Spinning back to face them, I walk over toward where Yasmin stands, briefly casting a quick glance to him. "Yes."

I pull the mug full of heavy cream from her hands and place the new cup there instead before moving back to where I was and dropping it in the sink.

The boy frowns as he watches Yasmin take a sip, humming at the taste. His eyes flick down to where my wedding band sits and then over to the giant diamond on her finger.

He moves until he's standing in front of her, shoving his hands into his pockets, his brown hair falling into his eyes.

"*Princess*, can we talk?"

I clench my fists to keep from reaching out and choking him to death.

She locks her stare on me, her mouth parting slightly and indecision weighing heavily in her features. And I see the yes in her gaze before it falls from her lips.

My teeth grind so forcefully, I feel a molar crack.

I pretend I don't notice when they walk out the door, not looking back at me once.

CHAPTER 35

Yasmin

I COULD TELL THAT JULIAN DIDN'T WANT ME TO go with Aidan, could see it in the way he was trying to act like he wasn't paying attention. In the way that muscle in the side of his jaw twitched, the way it always does when he doesn't say what he really wants to.

But it's something I need to do regardless. One, because even though the way I feel about Aidan has shifted and changed, he's still the first love I've ever held. He was still my best friend growing up. And my chest still hurts when I think about losing him.

And also, despite what Julian might think, if he doesn't let me bandage the wounds with Aidan, he'll never believe me when I say that I choose him. There will always be a doubt, niggling in the back of his mind, wondering if I would have gone back if only I had been given the chance.

That's not healthy for either of us.

I follow Aidan through the small hallway on the right into a small bedroom with a full-size bed. He's clearly made himself at home; there are clothes strewn over the back of the desk chair in the corner, and the bed is unmade and messy. A corkboard is hung up on the wall, things tacked to the front. Walking over, I peer at them, curious to see what he's been up to here while he was ignoring me and my heart was breaking over all the things I had to tell him but couldn't get through to say.

There's nothing except a map and a few written notes. I lean in closer, taking a look at what they say.

Last night was fun, with a heart and the name Jeannie.

"That isn't what it looks like," Aidan says from behind me.

My hands slip into my back pockets as I spin around to face him, shaking my head. I believe him, but it wouldn't matter if I didn't. "It's okay if it is."

He's on the other side of the bed, his hands on his hips and his brows drawn in. He sucks his bottom lip through his teeth before releasing it with a pop. "Because you love him?"

The question catches me off guard, my heart careening off the precarious cliff it's been teetering on, spinning and flailing as it drops to the floor.

"Because I hurt you when I married him," I answer. "And hurt people *hurt* people."

He nods slowly. "Jeannie's an archaeologist here. She was a friend…kind of. But the past few days, she's been different. Off-kilter. We spent a night together watching funny movies and talking about things we missed from back home. That's all."

"Okay," I reply with a small smile.

"So you trust me?"

"What?"

"Do you trust me?" he asks again.

I shrug. "Trusting you hasn't ever been the problem, Aidan."

"Would it have hurt you?" he continues. "If it *had* been more?"

"Knowing we got to this point so easily hurts me." I swallow around the knot that's forming in my throat. "I was forced into marrying Julian, and if you had just listened, you would know that I hadn't given up on you. On *us*."

"Don't play that card with me," he scoffs, his eyes squinting as he shakes his head. "You weren't a martyr in our relationship, princess. You *never* stood up for me or us. To anyone. It was always me, screaming into the void, begging you for a fucking chance." His hand slams against his chest. "Don't be so surprised that I thought you had picked the better offer."

His words sting, but I know they're true.

"Don't you think that means something?" I ask. "That we were willing to jump at the chance to trick my father, but neither of us were willing to actually sit down and talk when it mattered?"

He shrugs.

"I want someone who believes in my love for them."

He sighs, running a hand through his hair. "Princess, you have to *show* someone you love them in order for them to believe it."

My brows shoot up, clarity smacking me in the face and leaving behind a sting.

Aidan is right. Only it's not him who I want to prove it to.

Not anymore.

And maybe it never really was. When I think about Julian being in Aidan's place, if he were the one I knew my father wouldn't approve of, I don't think there's anything in the world that would keep me from standing at his side and fighting for the right to love him.

My breath whooshes from my lungs at the realization.

"Do we still have a chance?"

His question surprises me because for me, this is closure, and I thought it was the same for him.

"Aidan…" I shake my head. "So much has happened—"

"It's barely been a month, Yas." He walks around the bed and rushes toward me. "I don't want to give you up. I'm *not* giving you up."

I let out a humorless laugh, a dull throb pricking my middle. "I'm not *yours*."

Turning around, I start to leave, suddenly desperate to find Julian.

To tell him that I *see* him.

That I think I might love him.

Right before I get to the door, a harsh grip spins me around, Aidan's cold and chapped mouth slamming to mine. I freeze in shock, but it's only for a second, and then my hands are flying up to shove him off.

Before I can, a throat clears from behind me.

I push Aidan away, and when I twist to see who it is, my heart drops, panic weighing on my nerves like a hundred-pound weight.

Julian stands there staring at us, a stoic look on his face, his eyes sharp and glossy like ice. His hands are in his pocket, forearms flexing.

"Julian," I breathe.

He forces a thin smile. "Don't let me interrupt."

CHAPTER 36

Julian

IT DOESN'T MATTER.

I don't care.

Why am I surprised?

My mind is being pulled into a thousand different directions as I turn from Yasmin and the boy to leave, storming across the living room of the common area until I reach the bedroom.

I throw open the door to the room I share with *my wife*, pacing in front of the bed, my fingers gripping my hair so tight it feels like I'll pull out every strand.

Logically, I know she wasn't kissing him. I saw her spin around and the way she didn't respond. Emotionally, it doesn't fucking matter.

The thought of him having tasted her, having *touched* her while she's wearing my ring makes me violently angry, and it's taking every single ounce of self-control to not go back there and rip his tongue from his body.

Groaning, I run my hands down my face as I try—and fail— to convince myself one last time that it doesn't matter. That she can choose him, and I'll survive, the way I have every other time I wasn't someone's choice.

Go get her.

Stay.

Fuck.

I smack the sides of my face and stalk toward the door, about to find her and grab her caveman style, throw her over my shoulder, and spank her ass until it's black and blue for thinking that I'd ever let her leave.

But the door flies open before I can, and there she is standing on the other side, looking like a goddess sent to hell. She storms in, her eyes blazing like a thousand suns, and she slams the door behind her.

"Just who the fuck do you think you are?" she asks, marching up to me and shoving her hands against my chest.

I reach out and grasp her wrists, halting her assault. But really, I'll revel in the pain as long as I get to touch her.

"You don't get to *do* that," she spits. "You don't get to see something and leave before we talk."

"I'll do whatever the hell I want," I grit out.

She huffs. "Classic Julian Faraci. So afraid of letting the little boy inside heal that you throw up walls and shelter him from even living."

Anger punches me straight in the gut. "Watch your mouth."

"You watch *yours*," she hisses.

I tighten my grip on her wrists, her glare stripping every pretense away until I feel naked and vulnerable beneath her gaze.

"I'm trying to do what's best for you," I bite out. "And sometimes that means walking away."

"Well, I'm sick and tired of every man in my life thinking

they know what's best for me." She struggles in my hold, trying to break free so she can shove at me again. "Guess what, asshole. There's this little thing called free will. You should try to let people have it."

I bite back the amusement that's trying to break through the rage, my cock hardening from the way her body is squirming against me. I adjust my hold on her, walking her backward, energy wrapping around us like a rope and pulling tight until it's hard to breathe.

Her back slams against the closed door and I press myself flush to her, the soft curves of her body fitting perfectly against the hard planes of mine, separated only by her arms, which are being held in my grasp between us.

Dipping down, I rest my lips against hers, not kissing, just existing in the same place, her breaths becoming my oxygen. *If I stand here for long enough, I wonder if I could fill myself with her.*

"I'm no good for you, gattina. I bribe and blackmail and kill. I will hurt you. I *have* hurt you."

"I don't care," she whispers. "I forgive you."

Shaking my head, frustrated that she doesn't get the point, I move her hands until they're above her head, pressing them tightly into the wood of the door. Her chest brushes against my torso, moving in and out with her unsteady breaths of air.

"You should," I reply. "That boy out there, he's got history with you that I'll never have. Moments that will forever live in your memory, snapshots you've taken to freeze the feeling for when you start to forget." I press my lips to hers, drowning myself in the torture of almost tasting her the way I crave. "He's got all your firsts, and that's something I won't ever get. But I don't want them," I whisper against her mouth. "I don't care to have your awkward moments or your shaky promises and your fumbling hands. And do you know why?"

"No," she breathes, her eyes glossing over with tears.

"Because I don't love you like he does."

She whimpers, twisting her head away. I drop one of her hands, ignoring the way she immediately tries to shove me back, and I grip her cheek tightly, angling her so I can press my face against the side of hers, my lips ghosting across her jaw. I'm pinning her to the door with my body, and her hands are fisting the fabric of my shirt, clenching and releasing, like she can't decide if she wants to drag me closer or push me away.

"My love for you is dangerous."

A heavy breath whooshes from her mouth, a tear rolling from her eye, dripping over the back of my knuckles. I move, pressing a kiss to her wet cheek to soak up her cries.

"I would kill anyone who looked at you. Anyone who dared to even *breathe* too close."

Her body shakes against mine.

"I want your blood and your anger and your violence and your lust." My thumb brushes against her bottom lip. "I want your smiles and your tears and your insolent fucking mouth."

She pulls me in until there's no space between us, her breasts grazing against my torso with every shaky exhale.

"I want to reach into your chest and hold your heart in my hands, making sure it only beats for me," I rasp. "But I don't want your firsts, Yasmin. I want your forever."

She lets out a cry, her hands clawing into me like she can't get close enough, but I resist, jerking back as I fight against her hold. I move my other hand up until I'm cupping her face, making sure she meets my eyes.

"You're an angel, gattina. And I'll break your wings just to keep you by my side. So do us both a favor and walk. The fuck. Away."

I release her then, but before I can even move, she's on me, her mouth slamming into mine, her limbs wrapping around me as she jumps into my arms. She bites and sucks and licks, and I give it back in equal measure because after everything I just said, after I've cut myself open and bled out on the floor at her feet, she's still here.

And I don't have the will to fight it anymore.

"Stop telling me what to do," she demands in between her kisses.

I grin against her lips, my hands gripping her ass to hold her tightly to me as she breaks her lips away and licks down the side of my jaw, then sinks her teeth into the skin of my neck. I groan, my cock pulsing.

"You think I'm not the same?" she says into my skin.

Pulling back, she looks at me, her eyes wide and open and so fucking beautiful it makes me lose my breath.

"I want your laughter and your tears and your smiles too." She brushes a finger against my lip. "I want your broody stares and your fucked-up morals and your obnoxious need to always tell me what to do."

My body warms, blood pumping so fast I feel like my heart might explode from my chest.

She looks me in the eye, gripping my jaw with both of her hands, her legs still wrapped around my waist. "I'm in love with you, Julian Faraci. And I would burn the world myself if it meant I could keep you by my side."

Something cracks open in my chest, flooding through my insides like rushing water, clearing away everything else that ever mattered outside of her.

I spin us around and slam her down on the bed, ripping her clothes off clumsily, unable to focus on anything other than the need that's raging through me, pulsing with the beat of my heart to *take her, fuck her, claim her*. My fingers dig into her sides and glide up her body, tearing her sleep shirt off her supple frame.

Her nipples are pebbled and fucking perfect, and I need them in my mouth immediately, so I lean down and suck one of them between my lips, swirling my tongue around the nub and sinking in my teeth because I want to hear her moan.

She responds beautifully, her back arching and her hands flying to the back of my head, pressing me further into her skin. My cock pulses, precum beading from the tip and soaking into my briefs.

My other hand moves down her sternum, tracing patterns on her torso before reaching the hem of her sweats and sliding the soft fabric down her legs, my mouth never losing its rhythm on her breast.

She lifts her hips and I draw her underwear down next, tossing them somewhere behind me, needing to see her naked and splayed out before me like an offering.

Because that's what she is. That's what she's doing.

Offering herself to me.

Finally, I release her nipple, pulling back and tearing myself away from her hold, sitting back on my legs and gazing down at her.

I've had her sweet cunt in my mouth and her taste on my tongue, but this is the first time I've seen her completely naked.

She's so beautiful it hurts.

"Julian," she pleads, squirming on the bed, her eyes heady.

"Don't interrupt me while I'm staring at my wife," I purr, unbuckling my belt and lowering my pants until my cock pops out, hard and aching.

Reaching down, I grip my shaft, the length jumping in my palm when I imagine what it will feel like to slip between her legs and bury myself inside her.

"I like it when you call me that," she says, biting on her lower lip.

I smirk, nudging her legs farther apart as I move closer, and then I reach forward with my free hand, pulling on her chin until she lets go of the skin.

"Don't mar these pretty lips, amore mio," I say, hovering over her and skimming my mouth across hers, my cock twitching in my palm. "I have plans for them."

She reaches out, her fingers playing with the buttons on my shirt. She undoes them one by one, and I breathe deeply, allowing her to slip it off my shoulders and run her fingers across the expanse of my chest.

Pinpricks of feeling skate along my skin with her touch, and I fight against the intrinsic urge to push her away, to hold her down and control the situation.

She runs her hands over my shoulders and down my arms until she grips my cock, her palm covering my own. "Show me how you like it."

I release my shaft and let her fingers wrap around it, the feel of her on my skin making my body buzz. I cover her hand with mine, moving us slowly up the length of me and then back down, my nuts drawing up from the visual of her beneath me and stroking my cock.

More moisture beads at the tip and she swipes her thumb over the head, smearing it down the sides and using it as lubrication as my hand falls away and she takes over jacking me off.

"You're so big," she states.

I stop her movements, grabbing her fingers in mine and pressing her hands above her head, the same way I had them earlier when we were up against the door. Leaning down, I flatten my body to hers, her heart beating against my chest and her breaths puffing out against my lips as my cock teases the wet entrance to her pussy.

"And you'll take every inch, won't you, good girl?"

Her hips thrust up, trying to get me inside her, and *fuck*, my eyes roll back in my head from just the thought of sliding into her wet cunt.

"Fuck me like a whore," she moans, running her slit along the length of my cock, making it drenched from her arousal.

"You're not a whore."

Her legs push against my frame and then wrap around my back, pulling me into her, my dick lined up perfectly at her entrance, and her eyes lock on mine. "I'm *your* whore."

Jesus.

And that's all it takes to send me off the rails. I push forward with my hips, sliding inside her, her pussy wrapping around me like it was made to fit my cock.

She moans, her mouth gaping and her eyes rolling as her back arches.

I lean down as I start a rhythm, pulling out slowly before slamming back in, going insane with the need to be as far inside her as I can get, my hands pressing hers so harshly into the mattress I'm sure it's cutting off circulation.

"Harder," she pants, her hips moving in sync with mine.

I release her fingers, dragging my palm over her hair and down her face until I've wrapped it around her throat, squeezing on the sides just enough to lift her off the bed, making her lips hit mine with every forward thrust.

"You take my cock so well, gattina."

There's a sheen of sweat on both of our bodies as I fuck up into her, and my heart pounds against my rib cage as I piston my hips, pleasure building at the base of my spine and curling outward until my muscles tense up.

"I'm about to come inside you," I say, my fingers flexing around her neck. "Fill you up and make sure it sticks, so I can tie you to me in every way and make sure you never leave."

She whimpers, her legs trembling from where they're wrapped around my back, urging me forward every time I drive deep inside her.

"Would you like that, amore mio?"

She groans, her mouth parted in ecstasy.

The walls of her pussy clench around my dick, and my balls tighten in response. My other hand finally lets hers go and tangles in her hair, my palm cupping the side of her face tightly. I bend down and press a hard kiss to her lips. "Tell me you want my cum. Beg for it."

"Fill me up," she begs. "I need it, Julian, please, I—"

And then she's coming, her cunt squeezing and releasing my shaft, a scream escaping from her pouty lips as she plasters herself against me.

Her words are my undoing, the vision of her swelling with my child and being bound to me forever too much for me to take.

My body tenses and then releases in an explosion, and I push myself as deep as I can go, feeling my cock pulse with heavy throbs as I come deep inside her, collapsing my sweaty body on top of hers.

Our hearts syncopate, beating in time, and I rest my head on her chest, her fingers playing in the strands of my hair as I wrap my arms around her.

I've never felt so content.

And this feeling? I don't want it to leave. I won't ever let it go.

Because it feels like she's *choosing* me.

And she's the only one who ever has.

CHAPTER 37

Yasmin

I CAN'T SLEEP.

My body is sore and my heart is at ease for the first time in what feels like forever. For all intents and purposes, I *should* be able to rest in my husband's arms, knowing that he's actually mine.

Even though how we started isn't ideal.

I trust him now. I believe what he says when he tells me that he loves me, because the way I feel, the way that we went from hatred to this? There's nothing else it could be. I thought I loved Aidan, but he never made me feel the way Julian does.

And maybe he's too dangerous. Maybe he's all wrong. Maybe I'm being naive for allowing myself to love the man who blackmailed me into marriage, but I've spent my entire life being a people pleaser, and I'm done ignoring the darkness inside me that understands everything that Julian is.

And I'm finally taking Riya's advice and doing something for myself.

Glancing at the clock, I roll out of the large king-size bed where Julian is sleeping peacefully next to me and tiptoe over to where my bag is, picking up my camera. I make my way out of the room and through the common area, sighing as the crisp night-time air whips across my face as I open the front double doors.

It's a beautiful night, and I wrap my light cardigan around my arms as I make my way down the small path that leads between the small cottages and start taking pictures of the sky. I'm so lost in the moment, the serene quiet that's blanketing the air, that I don't hear the footsteps behind me until they're *right* there.

I grip my camera tighter, walking farther down the path and hoping they disappear, but they don't. My heart shoots to my throat and I exhale heavily before turning around.

Someone's following me.

But it's difficult to see in the dark, so it isn't until I squint my eyes that I'm able to make out their features.

She has bright-blue hair and chipped nail polish on her fingernails, holding something in her hands that's covered in a dark purple cloth.

"You know, stalking is considered a felony," I yell.

She ignores me, continuing to move closer until she's standing directly in front of me.

Her eyes glance from me to the cottage on my left and then to the one slightly in front of us, less than a hundred feet away.

"I've watched you today," she says, her voice low enough that I have to strain to hear. "And I needed to get you alone."

My spine stiffens, and I glance around, suddenly wishing that I hadn't snuck out without telling Julian where I was.

"And you are?" I question.

"I'm Jeannie."

Recognition flickers through me, remembering she was the one Aidan was telling me about. "The archaeologist?"

She nods, licking her lips, her hands gripping whatever she's holding tighter to her chest. She looks around again before she steps in closer, and I stumble back, putting a hand in front of me.

"What do you want?" My voice is sharper now, because seriously, what the *fuck*?

"I'm the lead on the excavation dig in Kharga."

"Okay." I look down at the box in her hands. "And what's that, Jeannie? A present?"

She glances around her again, anxious energy pouring off her body, her fingers digging into the edges of the box until I'm afraid her nails might split down the middle.

"I found something," she whispers. "Something that can help you. Aidan told me about what Mr. Faraci is forcing you to do, and I...it isn't *right*."

My head tilts to the side. "What do you mean?"

"I'm the one who texted you."

Another step closer.

Recognition flares through me. "You're the employee of Julian's."

She bobs her head.

"Well, I appreciate that, but it won't be necessary anymore. I love my husband."

She barks out a laugh and shakes her head, like she doesn't believe me.

I look at her closely. *Something's off.* "Are you okay?"

Again, she glances around before she maneuvers the covered box she's carrying to her side and reaches out to grip my arm tightly.

I suck in a breath, but before I can scream or do *something*, her words stop me in my tracks.

"You shouldn't trust them," she warns.

My brows rise. "Who?"

"They always talk too loud. Men, you know?" She shakes her head. "They get cocky…messy."

"Are you talking about Julian?"

She swallows, huffing out a breath like my questions are frustrating. "And his goons. Ian, his assistant? He gets drunk and lets things slip."

Her fingers rip into my forearm, breaking the skin. I jerk back, hissing from the pain, a small trail of blood oozing from beneath her grip and dripping onto the ground.

"They'll kill you. Do you hear me? Once they get what they want, they're going to *kill* you."

My stomach deep dives to the floor, my heart slamming against my ribs.

"I can help you," she says again, nodding down to the box. "*This* can help you. Barter for your freedom."

Irritation swims through my veins because this woman is doing anything but giving me answers, and quite frankly, she's freaking me the hell out. "I don't *need* any help. I promise, I'll be okay."

A door opens from one of the cottages in the distance, and her gaze flies behind me before coming back to mine with a frantic look.

"I found it," she whispers. "Nobody knows. And you shouldn't tell them."

My forehead scrunches. "Found *what?*"

She reaches out, handing me the box. "The lamp."

I'm not sure when Julian had time to arrange things for everyone to leave, but the next day, we're loaded up and ready to go.

We're outside the main building's entrance, Julian's arm wrapped around my waist possessively, hugging me to his side while we listen to Ian complain about not being on the private jet. And I'm reeling on the inside, my eyes watching as the driver throws my suitcase into the back. The one that has the lost lamp.

God, what the hell am I supposed to do with it?

I was tempted to take it straight to Julian, but something held me back. I don't know who has eyes and ears here, and if it's that easy for Jeannie to overhear people talking, then I don't want to risk someone else finding out what I have. I can just tell him when we get back home.

"I don't understand. We're all going to the same place," Ian complains, crossing his arms as a driver loads his and Aidan's luggage into the back of the car. I watch him closely, Jeannie's warning whispering loudly in the back of my mind.

"I want time alone with my wife," Julian replies. "There are things we'll be doing that I'm sure not *all* of you would like to hear."

His eyes flick to Aidan, and I elbow Julian in the side.

"Don't look so glum, Ian. At least I put you in first class," he says.

Ian scoffs, throwing his hands up and storming over to the car, sliding into the back seat. Aidan follows, pausing just before he sits down, his hand on top of the door and his eyes locked on me.

He looks downtrodden, and a small pang hits my chest, because I know that nothing between us will ever be the same.

I don't hold any hate toward him, just a profound sadness for what we lost. He was my first love, my first everything, and while I don't know how things ended up this way, I have to believe it was for the best.

Maybe one day we'll be able to stay friends, after the hurt has healed. And really, I have Aidan to thank. If it wasn't for him loving me, I wouldn't know the difference. Because my love for Aidan is like a warm sunny day, and my love for Julian is a blazing inferno.

"Remember what I said, princess," Aidan says.

Julian's hand tightens around my waist, and I reach up, pressing my palm to his chest, sliding it over and turning his face toward me, bringing him down into a kiss.

It's probably a bitch move to do right in front of Aidan, but my concern is with the man I chose. He's waiting for the other shoe to drop, but I'm going to show him all the reasons why it won't.

We break apart and I move toward the car, glancing around one last time to see if I catch a glimpse of Jeannie. But she's like a ghost, and she's nowhere to be found.

My stomach churns, hoping like hell that nothing happens to the lamp, and I'm freaking out that I didn't hide it well enough. I have no idea how we're going to get it through customs, but right now I only have the mental capacity to freak out about one thing at a time.

It isn't until Julian and I are on the private plane that I think about it again. I'm sprawled out on the couch, drinking sparkling water, watching him stare at something on his computer screen, a slight crease forming between his brows beneath his reading glasses.

"Are they going to check our bags?" I ask.

I probably shouldn't just blurt it out like this, not when there are flight attendants and pilots and a number of other people around to hear, but if I don't at least figure out the customs situation soon, I'm going to puke.

Julian glances at me from over the rim of his silver frames. "Would you like them not to?"

I shrug, standing up and walking over to him, maneuvering myself between the table and his legs and plopping myself down in his lap, my arms wrapping around his neck.

His hands grip me immediately, strong and sure, and a spark of desire rushes through me from the touch.

Leaning in, I press a kiss to his neck. "I don't want anyone touching my things but you."

He hums, his fingers running up and down the length of my spine. "Then they won't."

Relief flows through me, because I know that if Julian says they won't, then they *won't.*

"You know, this was really a shitty vacation," I muse, sinking deeper into his lap. "You didn't take me to a single place to sightsee, and on top of that, now we're here on this big plane with a huge bed, and I'm still here"—I lift my eyes to look at him—"wearing all these clothes."

He smirks, but I feel him growing hard underneath me. "Some of us have work to do. Diamonds don't sell themselves."

"You have hundreds of employees to sell them for you," I whine. Sighing, I stand up and sink my teeth into my bottom lip. Shrugging, I start to walk to the back bedroom. "Guess I'll just take care of things myself then."

He's on me before I can blink.

Large hands wrap around my waist, flipping me over his shoulder. I squeal, my stomach rising and falling like a roller coaster as he takes me to the bedroom, closing the door with his foot and throwing me on the bed.

His face is serious and his hands go directly to his belt buckle. "Time to put that smart mouth to work, gattina."

I grin like the cat that got the cream.

He moves to stand at the edge of the bed, lowering his pants so his thick cock bobs in the air, his veiny hand gripping it at the base and stroking it all the way from the length to the tip. "Crawl to me," he growls.

I shake my head, feeling playful.

He tilts his head. "That's one."

My heart skips. "One what?"

"One orgasm you won't get."

My mouth drops open. "That's not fair!"

He strokes his cock again, and my tongue swipes across my bottom lip as I watch him touch himself.

"Life's not fair." His words are punctuated with his eyes moving to the edge of the bed where he wants me. "Crawl to me, amore mio. Show me how bad you want it."

Rolling over until I'm on my hands and knees, I do what he's asking, slowly crawling across the bed, my hands sinking into the plush comforter as I stare at him from under my lashes and make my way across the bed until I reach where he is.

He presses his free hand against the back of my head. "Good girl."

And then he drags my face forward and presses his dick against my lips.

My tongue peeks out, swiping at the salty liquid beading at the tip, and I hum at his taste.

"Suck it."

I don't argue this time, too desperate to feel his thick cock stretching my mouth. There's a large vein that runs up the underside of his length, and the thought of it pulsing on my tongue while he shoots his cum down my throat makes my pussy clench. I wrap my tongue around the head of him, planning to tease him until he cracks, but before I can, he fists my hair and pushes me forward until he's hitting the back of my mouth. My eyes water and my hands splay out on his lower abdomen as he holds me there, his cock slipping down my throat inch by inch. I make a humming noise, even though it's difficult not to gag from the sheer size of him.

His other hand comes up to cup beneath my chin, stroking softly. "Breathe through your nose, baby."

I do, and it helps, and then he's pulling me back off him until he pops out of my mouth completely, a thin string of spit connecting the tip of his cock to my bottom lip.

"Are you okay?" he asks.

Nodding, I lean forward again, my hand gripping the base of him as I suck him deep, taking him all the way down to the base of his cock and creating suction on the way back up until my cheeks hollow. He doesn't force me down again, allowing me to go at my own pace, and I double my efforts, wanting to feel him as he unloads everything he has on my tongue.

"*Fuck.*"

One of my hands moves to his balls, lightly scratching against the sensitive flesh while I'm bobbing my head down the length of his cock, and they jerk in my hand.

I'm so wet, I can feel it pooling in my panties, and I start to reach down to give myself some relief, but before I get there, the grip on my face tightens.

"Do *not* touch yourself."

The command in his tone is unmistakable and I listen, not feeling like disobeying this time, because I don't want him to punish me even worse.

"You look so perfect like this," he says. "With your makeup

smeared and your pouty lips wrapped around my dick. I bet if I asked you to choke on it, you'd slide that pretty mouth down my length until you were gagging like a greedy little whore, wouldn't you?"

A thrill sparks through me at his words, because I've never been talked to like that. Everyone has always walked on eggshells around me, and I never realized until him how much I needed the opposite.

I pop off him, my hand messy with saliva from where I reach up to continue stroking him. His dick throbs and satisfaction rushes through me.

He's close.

"Fuck my face," I beg. "*Please.*"

His eyes flare at my words and he doesn't waste a second, gripping my hair so tightly it pulls at the root as he slips his length past my lips and drags me up and down his shaft. His hips thrust and he hits the back of my throat forcefully. My eyes water and my nose burns, but I push through, swallowing around him and drawing him in deeper.

"That's my girl, amore mio. You were made for sucking my dick."

Pleasure zings through me at his words, my hands reaching around his hips and grabbing onto his ass, feeling his muscles flex as he uses me like a toy.

I'm so wet that my panties are completely soaked through, but I remember what he said about not touching myself. Not letting myself come.

Julian's breathing grows heavy and his eyes glaze over, his thrusts becoming erratic.

I moan around him, and that's all it takes. His cock starts to pulse in my mouth, hot cum shooting down the back of my throat, and I flatten my tongue along the underside of his shaft, feeling that vein throb rhythmically with every drop.

It's sexy, and it makes me ache from how badly I want him inside me.

"Swallow it all, gattina."

I do, letting him slip out of me after and opening my mouth wide so he can see I didn't waste a drop.

He groans, bending over and kissing me, his tongue tangling with mine until I'm sure he can taste himself, and then he breaks away and cups my cheek, his thumb smearing the wetness that's left on my lips.

"You are so fucking perfect. And so fucking *mine*."

He swoops down and lifts me, cradling me in his arms and plopping me back on the bed, tucking me in and smoothing down my hair. He spends the rest of the plane ride catering to my every need: bringing me a drink, making sure I have food, combing my hair, and whispering that he loves me.

It's nice, and when we finally make it home, I'm floating on a cloud of bliss, wondering how he could have gone from someone I hated so vehemently to *this* so quickly.

But the good feeling doesn't last, because before I even get up the stairs, I'm checking my voicemails, and Shaina's voice comes on the line.

Her tone is soft and soothing, and the second she speaks, I just know.

Dropping the phone from my hands, I spin around from the foyer of the house, meeting Julian's eyes.

He stops short and then nods when he sees the tears that I'm trying to keep at bay brimming.

Julian doesn't waste any time, taking me to the estate himself, and when we reach my father's bedroom door, Shaina is there, looking at us with tears in her beautiful big brown eyes.

Emotion burns through my chest, a heavy ache settling in deep. I open my mouth to speak, to maybe ask how he is or what I can do, but my breathing stutters the moment I do, grief welling up like a tidal wave.

Julian's arm wraps around my waist and pulls me into his side, giving me silent support while he presses kisses to my temple.

"He's asleep," Shaina says without me asking.

"Will he wake up?" I force out.

She shakes her head softly.

My heart splits.

She walks toward me, reaching out and grasping my hand in hers. "But he can hear you. And I know he's been holding on until you could make it back."

A tear drips down my face, my throat so swollen I can hardly breathe. I nod, spinning around to look at Julian.

He cups my cheeks, wiping away the tears before they can hit my chin.

"I don't know how to do this," I whisper, my voice cracking.

Sighing, he presses a kiss to my forehead before leaning away and staring directly into my eyes.

"There's nothing for you to do, amore mio," he soothes. "Just walk in there, hold his hand one last time, and say goodbye."

My face screws up as tears fall without me being able to stop them, my breaths stuttering from the pain that's shredding my chest in two.

I nod, backing away from my husband, and I walk toward my father instead.

One last time.

CHAPTER 38

Yasmin

MY FATHER PASSED AWAY WITH ME STILL IN THE room.

It took hours, but the second I told him it was okay for him to let go, he did.

I spend the rest of the night crying, deep, guttural sobs that tear up my soul and make me feel like I'll never be whole again.

And honestly, I don't think I *will* be. Losing a parent is like losing a limb. There's a part of me that will always be missing now that he's gone, an ache that will never be filled. I loved my father with everything that I am. I gave up my own dreams and ambitions just to make sure he was happy, looked forward to every summer I'd come home, just to be able to breathe the same air.

He was my everything.

And it wasn't until he faced his own mortality that he became the man he truly wanted to be, and somehow, even though I won't get to experience the relationship that could have been with that version of him, I'll have to find peace in the fact that at least *he* made peace with himself.

And now he can go be with his love, my mother.

But none of that makes it hurt any less, because he's still not *here*.

Julian didn't leave my side all night. And I know that even if he doesn't say it out loud, he's hurting too.

He loved my father, regardless of whether he'll admit it.

And when he tries to stay home with me the next morning, I push him out the door, telling him that he needs to go on with life like things are normal. I need him to be normal, because if he isn't, then my whole world will fall apart. I still haven't told him about the lamp, but I will. Tonight when he gets home.

I'm fortunate enough to have had time to prepare for my baba's death, but it doesn't make the loss any less overwhelming.

I spend the morning sitting outside on the back patio, taking in the crisp autumn breeze and closing my eyes as it kisses my face, wondering if I can feel my father's spirit in the air if I only try hard enough.

But even through the grief, the world keeps spinning.

Clicking my tongue, I spin the burner phone around in my hand on top of the patio table, staring blankly at it. I suck in a deep breath and open it to the texts I've exchanged with the lawyer, Randy, rereading everything and letting my choices cement even further in my head.

I don't need him anymore, and if I'm going to be with Julian for real—truly *choose* him—then I have to make sure Randy doesn't think I still want to move forward with our plan to annul things.

Me: Hi. I want to thank you for being so helpful and willing to go up against my husband, but there's been a change in plans and I won't need your services.

I press Send, that familiar swirl of anxiety at doing something for myself squeezing my stomach tight. The phone vibrates quickly.

Randy: Understood. I'm here if you change your mind.

And just like that, it's over. I breathe out a sigh of relief and stand up from where I'm sitting, stretching my arms over my head, trying to ignore the heavy weight of sadness that's pressing down on my chest when I'm reminded that my baba is gone.

Something my school counselor used to tell me was to write out my feelings in a journal or as a letter, any way that would help me process them so I don't bottle them all up inside and let them build until they explode. I've never tried it before, choosing to find my therapy behind the lens of my camera, but now the urge to take a picture isn't there, so maybe journaling will work.

I walk down to Julian's office to find a blank piece of paper and a pen.

When I get there, I stop along the bookshelf, running my fingers along the framed photo of him with my father, both of them grinning as they hold up a large uncut diamond. My heart squeezes tight, and a few stray tears drip down my face. I press my fist to my chest, trying to stem the throbbing ache.

Moving along, I go sit behind his desk, glancing around. Reaching for the right-side drawer, I open it, looking for a piece of paper and a pen. I grab some random papers with writing, moving them out of the way, but my breath catches when I see a flash of a name.

My name.

A sick feeling weighs down my chest.

"Don't trust them."

My breathing stutters, and I scoff, shaking my head and convincing myself it was a trick of the light. Trust is paramount in a relationship. And I do trust Julian.

Frowning, I glance at the papers again, unable to stem the urge to just peek and see.

I pull out the papers.

I read.

And my already broken heart shatters completely as it falls to the floor, ripping through my very fucking being on the way down.

Will of Yasmin Karam-Faraci.

"They're going to kill you."

I drop the papers from my hands like they're on fire, my stomach tossing like I'll throw up if I stay in one spot.

Maybe the will is a mistake.

Maybe it's from back when he first started blackmailing me, before things changed.

All these things are possible, and I want to hear his explanation for every one. But not right now. Not like this, when my feelings are so raw and I feel so ripped open and betrayed.

Was *everything* just a game to him?

I know I won't get any relief until I find answers. I breathe deep, trying to find my center and not react out of shock. I've spent my entire life running away from problems, and it hasn't gotten me anywhere good.

It's what got me in this mess in the first place.

I slide down the desk and just sit on the floor for a long time, staring down at the pages that say if I die, everything is left to Julian, and it isn't until the doorbell rings that I come out of my daze, standing up and trying to hold myself together long enough to walk across the foyer and answer it. I'm sure my eyes are puffy and I look like a disaster, but I can't find it in me to care.

I don't even know who would be here in the first place.

Opening the door, I find Julian's assistant on the other side, his eyes dragging slowly up and down my frame.

"You look like shit," Ian states.

I move to the side, letting him in, even though now everything in me is screaming to keep him far away. *Is he here to kill me?*

"My father's dead," I reply blankly.

Ian spins around to stare at me, his gaze growing round. "Excuse me?"

I tilt my head. "You didn't know?"

He swallows, his hands sliding into his pockets as he glances around. "No. Where's Julian?"

My forehead scrunches. "At the office. With you, I thought."

He shakes his head slowly. "No. I came here to find him."

"Call him, I guess," I state, trying to keep my body from visibly trembling from the nerves. "Make yourself at home." I wave my hand around. "I have to make a phone call."

I leave him in the foyer and walk up the stairs back into Julian's room, my heart beating out of my chest as I grab my phone and call Riya.

She doesn't answer, but I leave her a message, peeking behind me and making sure my door is fully closed.

"Hey, Riya." I keep my voice a whisper. "I need your help so call me back. I have this…" Groaning, I run a finger over my curls. "I don't know what to do. Baba died," I choke out. "And then I found a fake will for *me*, and…maybe I should be calling Randy, but I need you to come get me out of here. I have that lamp, and

I don't know what to do. It was one of my father's last wishes to find it, and I just—I'm not sure who I can trust. So call me back. *Please*."

I puff out my cheeks, place my hands on my hips, my phone digging into my side as I try to find my center. I head out of the room and down the hall, passing by Ian as I make my way into the kitchen.

"Do you want some tea?" I twist back around as I ask the question, but I never hear his response.

Because all that's next is sharp, blinding pain across my skull, and then silence.

CHAPTER 39

Julian

I HATED LEAVING YASMIN THIS MORNING. SHE spent the entirety of last night crying, and I spent mine trying to come to terms with the fact that the only man who's been any kind of positive influence on my life is gone forever.

Everything I was trying so hard to take from him seems pointless now.

It was *his* legacy.

I've just left his lawyer's office, having had him draft up a prenuptial agreement, one that protects *her* assets, not any of mine. I don't care if she takes me for all I'm worth. She could burn Sultans to the ground with me inside, and I'd die happily, knowing she was queen of the ashes.

But I need to show her that for me, this is real. My penance for being so blinded by greed for so long that I couldn't see the forest for the trees.

She's under no illusion of what this started as, but I want to make sure she knows that if she isn't in my world, it isn't worth living.

She's changed me for the better. In all the ways I care to change, that is.

I'm not sure that she'll ever realize the impact she's had on me. I'm a powerful man, and I've worked incredibly hard to get to where I am in life. To pull myself from rags to riches and make something of myself.

There's a type of confidence that comes along with that, a sense of pride that I feel, one that I don't think anyone can take away from me.

And the only person who can is about to no longer have access to my life.

I thought about driving to my mother's house and seeing her in person one last time. All night long, as I was holding Yasmin in my arms, comforting her loss of her father, I imagined what it would feel like if the shoe were on the other foot.

If I lost my mother suddenly, would I cry? Would I feel pain?

All that came was longing for the freedom it would provide.

She doesn't deserve my time in person. I'm protecting myself and the little boy who's still living and breathing somewhere deep inside my soul from ever dealing with her abuse again.

People only have the power you give them, and I'm done giving her mine.

She picks up on the second ring.

"Do you remember when I was little?" I ask instead of saying hello. "And you had to take me to the hospital because I had a broken femur?"

"Are you not even greeting your mother now?" she complains.

"Just answer the question."

"I don't know. You were sick a lot back then."

"No." Anger bubbles like a cauldron deep in my chest. "You

don't get to do that. That femur break was from when you stomped on my leg so hard it fractured, remember?"

"I don't want to talk about this," she interrupts.

"You were mad because I got straight As on my report card and it was the first time ever that Papà said he was proud."

She scoffs.

"Proud of *me*. Not of you," I finish, disgust filling me up until it bleeds from my pores. "You always were a jealous bitch."

"How *dare* you—" she starts.

I cut her off. "I'm no longer interested in entertaining this relationship."

She lets out a laugh. "Please, Julian. I'm your mother. *Family*."

I won't lie; her words have the intended effect. They sink into me like hooks, trying to reel me back in, but then I remember what real family is. What it feels like when someone chooses you over everyone else.

My family is Yasmin, and that's all I'll ever need.

"For years, I felt responsible for you," I say.

"Good," she replies.

I shake my head, my eyes growing glossy and my stomach burning like acid. "Five years old and I was your protector. But who was there to protect *me*, Ma? Huh?"

"Look, vita mia, I've made mistakes just like anyone—"

"You can keep the house, although I doubt you'll be able to afford it. But we're done. Do you hear me, Ma? We're done."

"You'd cut your own mother off?"

"You have *no* idea what I'm capable of." My fingers dig into the side of my phone. "Contact me again or bother my wife, and I'll pay you back for every single pound of flesh. Don't push me, Anita."

I hang up the phone, blowing out a sigh of relief and running a trembling hand over my face. Invisible chains lift from my shoulders, breaking the tether I felt to her for so many years.

Some people say that family is family, blood is blood. But *I* say that toxic is toxic, and no one is more important than my inner peace, even if it means I lose them for good.

I've tried not to bother Yasmin too much today, giving her the space she needs to feel whatever it is she's feeling and grieve, but the few text messages I *have* sent her have gone unanswered, so there's a niggling feeling that's curling around my middle, urging me to hurry home and make sure that she's okay.

I pull into my garage and walk inside, noticing immediately that the house feels *off*, and that gut feeling that I've had all afternoon about Yasmin grows stronger. I walk through the back hallway from the garage and go immediately up the stairs, walking to our bedroom and peeking inside. I don't see Yasmin, so I turn back around and walk into Isabella's enclosure, making my way over to where she's lazing on one of the tree branches.

She looks fine, and Yasmin isn't here either, so I turn around and walk back out, making my way through each of the rooms, my heart ratcheting higher into my throat with every step.

My hand goes to the pocket of my pants, and I pull out my staff, elongating it as I check the spaces, just in case. I can't imagine anyone would be able to come in without being *let* in, my security system is far too advanced, but I can't shake off this feeling, and I'm not going to be foolish and walk through without a weapon.

She's not in any of the rooms upstairs, so I make my way down the steps and head to my office, walking through the door and around to my desk, noticing there are papers on top when I didn't leave them there.

My heart drops to the floor, panic suffusing every single pore of my body when I see what's laid out.

Will of Yasmin Karam-Faraci.

I swing around and rush out of the room, now worried that she left of her own volition. I haven't had time to explain how things have changed, how when I fell for her, I fell out of love with the idea of power, because she gives me everything I've been missing instead. I hit the entrance to the kitchen, my foot crunching on top of a small piece of green glazed clay.

What the hell?

My stomach twists as I look down at the ground and lift the sole of my shoe up, noticing pieces of a vase that's usually in the corner of the hallway stuck beneath my foot.

I take a step farther into the room, the panic of thinking Yasmin left being replaced with something far more sinister when I see the vase is smashed into a hundred pieces on the floor. Drops of blood trail over the ground, and my mouth goes dry when I think about Yasmin lying somewhere, broken and bleeding.

Another step forward, and I see a phone, tossed haphazardly as though it flew from someone's hand. I bend over and grab it, then twist and head back to my office, pulling up my computer, an unbearable agony mixing with the anger that someone thought they could come into *my* house and hurt *my wife.*

I bring up the security cameras and watch.

And when I see Ian smash her over the head, dragging her out to his car, bloodied and unconscious, fury races through my veins like an avalanche.

CHAPTER 40

Julian

"BOSS."

My fingers grip the phone so tightly that it creaks from the pressure, and I breathe deeply, trying to keep calm even though my blood is pulsing with the need to find Ian and murder him slowly.

"Where is she?" I bite out.

Ian chuckles.

For the first time in as long as I can remember, I feel helpless, lost to the demands of someone I foolishly trusted for years, never thinking that he would betray me. But I should know by now that people are fallible, and even the ones who I think will choose me still won't put me above themselves.

"She's fine. And it's pathetic you care. Who have you turned into, Julian?"

"If you *touch* her…" I pause, my throat swelling from the panic of not being able to see her, touch her, feel her.

I would rather light myself on fire than allow her to experience another ounce of pain because of my selfishness and greed.

"Oh, *please*. You've grown soft," Ian hisses. "And the most disgusting part is that I saw it coming from a mile away. Knew it was happening from the second you chastised me like a child for calling the bitch what she is."

I clench my jaw so tightly my mouth aches. "What do you want?"

"The lamp, obviously," he drawls.

My brows draw down in confusion.

"I know she has it, and while I would have loved to stick around and search your house myself, time was of the essence. But if you want the girl, you need to give me the lamp. Simple."

I shake my head, because Yasmin having the lamp? Impossible.

Her phone vibrates on the table next to me, and I glance down as it lights up, *Riya* flashing across the screen.

"What are you talking about? She doesn't have the lamp. Why would she?"

"I know what I heard," he says. "And I don't care to hear your theories. They frustrate me. I'd hate to take it out on her. I have years of repressed aggression that you wouldn't let me get out, just dying to be set free."

Bile rises in the back of my throat. "I'm going to enjoy killing you."

He laughs again. "You've always been so dramatic. Isn't that what you said to me once? Well, boss, let's see just how *dramatic* I can be. We're at the warehouse. You know, the one where you stow the guns to trade for diamonds? I wouldn't call for backup or else Sultans will go down in flames when I show them everything illegal you have going on here."

I laugh darkly, murderous rage thrumming through me until it bleats against my skull. "I don't need backup to find you, friend."

"You have until the end of the day. Darryn and I will be waiting."

Click.

Darryn. Fucking. Anders.

I should have known. I throw my phone across the room. If she did have the lamp, then I will tear this house apart to find it. Darryn and Ian, that traitorous little fuck, can have it as long as I get her back.

Her phone vibrates again, and I silence it, but then the doorbell rings. Groaning in frustration, I walk to the front and swing it open, then stop short when a pretty woman is standing there with her hand poised to knock on the door.

She lifts a brow and looks me up and down. "You're not Yas."

Impatience wrings my nerves tight, because I don't have time for this, but she doesn't give me the opportunity to send her away as she pushes past me and walks inside, looking around.

"Where is she?"

"Who the hell are you?" I hiss.

She looks at me and points a finger at her chest. "I'm *Riya*. Yasmin's best friend. She never mentioned me?" Scoffing, she shakes her head. "Typical. Listen, I don't know what you did to her, *Julian*, but she called me in a panic."

I clench my jaw, remembering the will that was laid out on my desk, my heart fracturing with the thought that she's hurt somewhere, *because of me*, and thinking I was planning to betray her this entire time.

Racing forward, I grip Riya's arms tightly. She screeches and fights in my hold, but I tighten my grip. "Did she tell you about a lamp?"

"Get the fuck off me, dude."

"Listen." I shake her slightly. "This isn't a time for games.

Someone has taken her, okay? They're *hurting* her. And if I don't get the lamp to them, I can't save her."

She stops fighting, suspicion blazing through her eyes. "How do I know to trust you?"

I swallow around the thick knot in my throat. "Because I love her. *Please.*"

She's silent for a few minutes before she nods, licking her lips. "Okay, yeah…yeah, she said she had the lamp."

The words aren't even fully out of her mouth before I'm dropping her arms and racing up the stairs into our bedroom, ready to tear the world apart to find it. My eyes immediately zone in on her suitcase, remembering her not wanting anyone to look through it except for me.

Slamming it down on the ground, I rip open the top and dive my hands into it, my fingers hitting a hard object almost immediately. My breath whooshes out of me as I pull out the silver case, Sultans' logo on the front, and I bring it to my lap.

Jesus Christ. How did she even get this?

My hands shake as I open it, seeing the object that's been my desire for years for the first time and a note tucked into the side of the case.

Keep it safe. Use it to gain your freedom.—Jeannie

Of course. Jeannie must have found it and given it to her when we were in Egypt.

I stare at the object I've been lusting after for years, expecting to feel a pang of *something.*

It's gold and dusty, and jewels encrust almost the entire perimeter. It's beautiful.

But I feel nothing.

Hollow.

Because none of this means anything if I don't have *her*.

Snapping the lid closed, I shoot to my feet, knowing full well that I may be heading to my death but willing to accept the consequences as long as I can make sure she's okay.

I storm back down the hall with the case under my arm and stop short when I see Riya is in the foyer with Aidan.

"What the hell is he doing here?" I snap.

She shrugs, her eyes wide and panicked as she runs a hand through her hair. "I called him when I couldn't get ahold of Yasmin. I was worried, okay? And turns out I should be."

Suspicion races through me as I meet the boy's stare. "Leave."

"Look, we all love Yasmin here," Riya cuts in. "Just let us help you. We're not leaving until we know she's okay."

I blow out a frustrated breath. "Fine. Stay here. She'll need you when she comes back."

"And where are you going?" Aidan yells out as I walk away toward the garage.

"I'm going to save my *wife*."

CHAPTER 41

Yasmin

MY HEAD IS POUNDING AS I SIT AGAINST THE WALL with my hands tied behind my back and a gag in my mouth.

Dried blood drips down the side of my face, and I can feel a pulsing ache on the top of my head where I'm sure there's a contusion.

My stomach rolls and heaves, making me want to puke, but since there's a gag in my mouth, I try to hold it back, not wanting to throw up and have to swallow it down again.

Julian's piece-of-shit assistant, Ian, is pacing on the other side of the large warehouse—the same one that Julian brought me to when he taught me how to drive—and he has a gun in his hand as he talks on the phone, using his arms to punctuate whatever point he's trying to make.

There's another man here too, and I can only see him out of my peripheral vision from where I've been hog-tied and leaned up against the wall. He's older, graying at the temples, and has on a khaki shirt and dark jeans. He's flipping a gun around in his hand too, like he's bored and waiting on something.

I'm not sure what it could be.

Ian hangs up the phone and walks over between me and the mystery man.

"He's coming," he says.

The man perks up. "How do you know?"

Ian glances toward me, his eyes narrowing. "Because he *loves* her. He'll bring the lamp, don't worry. I know Julian like the back of my hand."

Surprise makes my heart clench because I had assumed Julian was in on this. I should have known better, should have trusted in what we were feeling and everything he said.

He *loves* me. And he's coming to help.

The man nods sharply. "You better be right."

"Darryn, I told you back in Egypt. There's nothing to worry about. He's changed. Gone soft. He'll bring the lamp to free the girl, and there's nothing he can do to get both."

"That's not *entirely* true."

My heart shoots into my throat, my eyes swinging to the front of the warehouse where Julian stands, a long metal bar in one hand and the silver case that holds the lamp in the other, his stature strong and sure like he doesn't have a care in the world. My stomach tightens even as a tendril of hope weaves its way through my middle and squeezes.

He came for me.

Ian twists around, grinning wide. "Boss, glad you could make it." His eyes drop down to the case. "Is that the lamp?"

He moves forward until he's directly in front of Julian, but Julian backs up a pace, flipping that long bar over the back of his hand so quick I can barely see it and shoving it into Ian's chest roughly.

Ian stumbles back, the hand that's holding his gun coming up to rub at his chest before he points it at Julian, his arm shaking visibly even from where I am across the room.

Panic wraps around me, and I try to scream through the gag, but only a muffled noise comes out. Julian's eyes flick to me, taking inventory of my body quickly before going back to Ian.

"This is all dreadfully disappointing," Julian drawls, his gaze going over to where the other man sits, leaned back against the wall like he's watching a movie. "Hello, Darryn."

Darryn smirks. "Julian Faraci. Shame we had to meet this way, but it's business." He stands up, grabbing the gun he has sitting next to him and walking toward me. "You understand."

Julian's head tilts. "Of course."

Cold metal presses against the side of my head, and tears escape down my cheeks, my chest caving in on itself, because no matter what I've gone through in my entire life, I've never felt as powerless and weak as I do in this moment.

"Hand over the lamp, Julian. Don't make me hurt the girl."

Julian swallows, and I see a flash of panic in his eyes as they meet mine.

My stomach sinks, my lower lip trembling beneath the cloth gag.

Julian walks forward, bypassing Ian completely, and drops the lamp's case on the floor in the middle of the room. "Have it then."

"You, you traitor!" Ian yells, kicking the ground. "You'd give up everything we worked for so easily, for *her*?"

"It would seem you're being very hypocritical right now, Ian." Julian takes a step toward him. "I'm not the one pointing a gun at his boss."

Another step.

"You betrayed me," Ian spits. "I was loyal to you for years. And the second you get a warm pussy and a bitch who does as you say, you drop me like I'm nothing?"

Julian takes a deep breath, flipping that metal bar around the back of his hand like a baton. "Now, Ian. I've warned you about what would happen if you disrespected my wife."

Ian laughs, waving his arms in the air. "I have the gun, asshole. I could kill her and fuck her dead body in front of you, and there wouldn't be shit you could do."

"I fell in love with her, and I won't apologize for it." Julian looks at me. "I'm not sorry for loving you. I'm only sorry it took me so long to realize that I did."

My heart squeezes, and I know without him even explaining the will that he never would have gone through with it. Not after everything we've shared.

Not that it really matters now anyway.

"We had a plan," Ian hisses.

"Plans change. Surely you realize, Ian, that I would never let you harm her."

Ian's eyes darken. "You don't get to call the shots anymore."

Julian nods, glancing toward Darryn, who is standing over me with his gun digging into my temple. "And I suppose you talked Ian into this sometime in Egypt?"

Darryn shrugs. "What can I say? He came to me for a meeting and left with a new friend instead. Look, we don't want to hurt your wife. I just want the lamp. And you'll have to die, of course, to make sure you don't cause any trouble down the line."

No.

Darryn's attention goes to where Julian set down the lamp, and I take the opportunity, because I can't *not*, thrusting my head as far as possible into his hand and knocking the gun out of the way.

It scatters on the floor, and then there's commotion.

A loud yell, and then a stinging sensation on my hair as I'm jerked harshly to a stand.

I whimper, my eyes squeezing shut from the pain.

Suddenly, I'm knocked over again, a high-pitched scream echoing through the tall ceilings of the warehouse, and I land on my side, a heavy throb radiating up from the fall. I roll over and see *Riya* on top of Darryn, her fists slamming repeatedly into his face.

I should feel relief, but all I feel is more panic that she's here.

In danger.

Because of me.

She must have followed Julian.

Groaning, I try to sit, but I can't with my hands and feet tied together, so I roll onto my back instead, inhaling a sharp breath at how broken my body feels when I do. There are loud noises all around me, but my hearing is muffled, my brain foggy from the abuse.

"Princess," a whisper comes from my right, and then I'm being jostled again and put into a sitting position. Aidan is crouching in front of me, his jaw tense and his eyes dark and heavy.

His hands float down my body, and I suck in a sob that wants to break free because I don't know what the hell is going on, but I *do* know that the people I love most in the world are all here, trying to help me, and I don't want any of them to die.

He gets the gag off my mouth, and my jaw aches as I suck in deep breaths, flinging my head over to where Julian is staring at Aidan as he unties me. One hand comes free and then the other, blood rushing back in and making my fingers tingle.

"Aidan?" I gasp. "What—How?"

"We followed Julian." He jerks his chin over to Riya.

I start to nod but before I can even focus on what he means, a sharp shot rings out in the air, and time freezes.

Riya falls to the side from where she was punching Darryn, clutching her stomach, blood pouring through her fingers.

"No!" I scream, grief welling up inside me at the sight. I start to struggle against the rope, Aidan working to try and get them off my ankles. "No, *please*," I sob.

There's a scuffle to my right and I turn my attention there, seeing Julian flipping that metal bar and slamming it into Ian's legs, his knees cracking as they hit the concrete floor, his gun flying from his hands.

Despair surges through me when I look back to my best friend who has sunk back onto the floor, and I can't think, can't see, can't *breathe* from the pain that feels like it's ripping me in two.

The second my ankles are free, I'm crawling over the cold ground to where Riya is, trying to wipe away the tears with my trembling fingers.

"No, no, no," I repeat as I make it to her and press my hands against hers to try and stop the bleeding. "You can't do this. You're not *allowed* to do this, Riy."

There's commotion behind me, but I couldn't care less what it is, trusting that Julian has the upper hand. I need to focus on my best friend, who's bleeding out on the floor in front of me.

Suddenly there's a presence at my back and Julian crouches down, his hands grasping me and turning me to him so he can check on me. "Are you okay?"

"I–I—," I stutter through my tears. "Please, Julian. *Help* her. I can't…I can't lose her too, *please*—"

There's a groan from close by, and Julian grows rigid when a gun presses against his temple, a bruised and swollen Darryn standing behind him.

Darryn spits, blood dripping on the floor around him. "Don't make me hurt anyone else."

Julian ignores him, and I'm barely coherent from the panic that's splintering apart my insides. He cups my face in his hand, his jaw set and his eyes clear. "Remember what I told you? My love for you is dangerous, amore mio."

I shake my head against him, pressing my hands farther into Riya's stomach, my fingers slipping in the blood. "I can't let this happen. I can't let—She can't *die*."

"I can't save you both," Julian continues. "*Go.*"

I'm not even able to comprehend what it is that he's saying or what's happening or *why* he's doing this. "No, Julian, *please…*"

He looks behind me and nods sharply, his head pushed to the side when Darryn presses the gun harder against his temple. "I'm being *very* generous with my time here, Julian. I don't have to kill them, just you."

And then there are arms wrapping around me from behind, Aidan dragging me back, away from the two people who I love most in the world.

"No!" I scream, fighting against Aidan's hold. "Don't do this!"

Julian's face is solemn as he drops his head, his hand twitching on the ground as it wraps around that metal bar he's been carrying since he walked in.

"You can't save them, princess," Aidan grits out against my flailing body. He grunts, pausing for a moment and jostling me in his hold as he bends down on the floor and grabs something before he drags me outside.

A shot rings out in the air, and I slump against Aidan then, grief creeping through my veins and cooling my blood until everything ices over and I go numb.

My father is dead.

Riya is close to dead.

Julian is dead.

Aidan puts me in the car, and I hiccup through the pain, staring blankly ahead of me as he does. A flash of silver catches my eye, and if I could feel anything at all anymore, maybe I'd care that somehow through it all, Aidan got the lamp.

But instead, I just feel numb.

We're in some small cottage on the edge of Badour, and for the past few hours, Aidan has been trying to get me to eat.

"Princess, you *have* to eat something."

A tear drips down the side of my face, and I twist my head away from where he's holding out a piece of pizza, looking to the side.

"I can't," I whisper.

He sighs, running a hand through his hair as he tosses the pizza down on the end table next to the bed. "Everything will be okay. We're together now, and we have the lamp. Things will be just fine."

My chest feels like there's a black hole spinning in the center, growing larger with every breath I take, sucking everything into its path and leaving behind a blank type of numb that blurs all the harsh edges.

"Sure," I whisper, staring blankly at the wall.

Julian loved me. And now he's dead.

And Riya…

How is it that I got here?

All the things I've learned in the past few months still end up with me losing everything that matters, so what the fuck is the point?

Aidan stands up, the couch creaking when he moves, and he walks over to grab his phone off the desk in the corner, the lamp sitting in the case next to him like it's just another piece of furniture.

"Princess."

I ignore him.

"Princess," he repeats. "Look at me."

I don't. I *can't*. Looking at Aidan reminds me of everything I've lost, and it makes me sick. *He* makes me sick.

He sighs, walking over and pressing a kiss to the top of my head. "I'm going to make a couple calls. I'll be back."

The front door closes behind him, and I sit in silence for a few moments before his words filter through me. *A couple calls.*

Who the hell would he be calling right now? Doesn't he care at all that Riya just died? That we went through an insanely traumatic experience, yet he's prancing around and making *calls*.

For the first time since I've gotten here, something pierces through the dark fog that's encased me, and I feel angry.

Shooting up from where I was on the bed, I walk over to the front door, cracking it open and heading outside to find him so I can scream at him and ask him who the hell he is, because clearly he isn't the same boy I grew up with and loved.

I don't see Aidan, but when I take move forward, his voice filters from around the corner.

"Yeah. She's broken, Mom. I can't get her to agree to anything right now."

I suck in a breath. *Is he talking about me?*

"Yeah, everything went to plan. Darryn and Ian handled it. It was messy but… I know it's dangerous, Mom, but I told you everything is fine. We don't need Darryn or Ian now, and we definitely don't need Sultans anymore. I've got this lamp, and I'm telling you, it's worth enough. Let me just take care of things here, and I'll come grab you."

His words hit me in the chest, and I stumble back a few steps, my insides curdling and withering away like dying leaves fallen from their branches.

We don't need Sultans anymore.

Rushing back inside the cottage, my heart beating in my throat and my stomach tied in knots, I scramble to grab the lamp, not willing to let yet another person take advantage of me.

I may have lost everything, but I won't let him take this from me too.

And *fuck* him for playing me for a fool. For all these years? God, the thought of how gullible I must be punches through my stomach, making nausea churn in my gut.

Reaching the end table, I stumble over my feet and grab on to the silver case, the metal rough against my fingers, and then I dive into the pocket of Aidan's bag, searching for *something*. Money or anything that will help me get out of here and far enough away to safety.

My fingers brush against cool metal and my heart stutters as I wrap my hand around it and bring it out of his bag.

A gun.

Oh my god. Who *is* he?

"Princess."

His voice jolts me out of my daze, and I spin around, seeing him standing in the doorway, his eyes wide as they flick from the gun in my hand to the lamp in my other. He walks in slowly, his hands held out in front of him as he closes the door and moves toward me.

"What are you doing?" he asks.

My arm shakes violently as I raise the barrel and point it at him, tears blurring my vision. "Was any of it real, Aidan?"

He tilts his head, acknowledgment that I overheard him filtering through his gaze. "Let's just take a second here."

"Answer me!" I yell, my frayed insides unraveling until there's nothing left.

He swallows, placing his phone down on the table slowly. "You have to understand, Yas…my mom and I, we've lived our lives with nothing."

My nostrils flare from the burn building behind my eyes, because finding out that the man I thought I loved for most of my life was just using me to get my fortune is the icing on top of this fucked-up cake.

My father was right when he told me to be wary.

"So this whole time, everything between us was just what? You using me to get my fortune?"

He licks his lips and moves closer. "I care about you."

And with that, I'm done.

Done people-pleasing and living for others. Done giving a fuck about anything other than the sorrow that's shredding apart my soul until it withers and turns into an unrecognizable lump of charred remains.

"Put the gun down, princess," Aidan coos, walking up to me

until the barrel is pressed against his chest. He runs his hands over mine gently. But then they tighten and he bends my wrist until it feels like it might break. I let out a harsh yelp and stumble, but I tighten my hand around the gun, even as he tries to wrench it from me.

"I don't want to hurt you," he huffs out as he fights me for control.

I lose it, flinging myself forward and bashing my head against his face, a sharp pain radiating through my skull as he rears back, blood pouring from his nose.

My arms shake as I pull up the gun and aim it at his chest.

"You don't have the power to hurt me anymore, Aidan."

And then I pull the trigger, feeling nothing as he falls to the floor.

CHAPTER 42

Julian

THE PLASTIC TARP CRINKLES BENEATH MY FEET AS I walk back and forth, staring at the two men who thought they could walk into my house, hurt my *wife*, and get away with it.

Isabella slithers around my feet, hissing.

Darryn is unconscious, the gun wound to his side slowly stealing his life away. Unfortunately for him, it will only make the pressure of Isabella's coiling body worse. He should have known that I wouldn't allow him to walk away after he used Yasmin as bait. As soon as I saw she was out the door and being dragged to safety, I moved, spinning my staff around and busting his kneecaps. When Darryn fell to the floor, his hold on his gun slipped, and he injured himself. Makes my job easier, I suppose, but I'd be lying if I said I wouldn't enjoy this more if he was conscious for what I'm about to do.

Ian, on the other hand, is bloodied and broken but alert, eyes staring out of his mangled face as he watches me slowly pace in front of them. They're both stripped naked, their backs facing each other, tied together with rope as they sit on the floor.

Isabella doesn't enjoy the taste of cotton.

"This is truly an unfortunate situation," I muse, my footsteps stopping as I stare at them. "I don't care that you tried to take the lamp or that you *crossed* me. Predictable, really. Textbook, almost. The thorn in my side and the greedy assistant banding together to try and outsmart the man they love to hate." I smile. "Unfortunately for you, that man has a vengeful spirit and a pet he doesn't like to let go hungry."

Bending down, I stroke Isabella's head. Ian jerks as much as he can with no working limbs, muffled sounds coming from his bruised and bleeding mouth.

"Luckily, I have a soft spot for the people I've cared for, even when they choose to hurt me." I purse my lips. "It's a complex, really. One that I'm just now working on overcoming."

I move closer until I'm directly in front of Ian, his eyes locked on mine, wide and filled with terror.

He gurgles, blood trickling from the side of his mouth.

"But then you touched my *wife*." Standing up straight, I walk over to where the box of mice sits, a bone saw directly next to it. I click my tongue, looking back and forth at the two. "Decisions, decisions." I pick the bone saw, gripping the large handle and making my way back to Ian. "What was it you said?"

Taking the tip of the saw, I press it into his inner thigh, dragging it slowly across the meat of his flesh, enjoying the way his broken body jerks from the pain.

"You said you would *fuck* her dead body, is that right?"

He tries to speak, but his lips are so disfigured from the way I beat him with my staff that it's hard for him to talk.

"Don't worry." I move the saw over to rest on top of his puny dick. "This will only hurt for a little."

A sharp slice through the rubbery flesh and a tortured scream later, his useless member falls to the ground, severed from his body, blood gushing from the wound. I move quickly, realizing that he'll likely pass out soon from the pain or maybe the loss of blood, and grab his severed cock, prying his mangled lips open, shoving it in his mouth as his eyes roll back in his head, his body jerking wildly before he stops moving all together.

Standing up straight, my hands sticky and red, I crack my neck, looking at the two pieces of shit who thought they could threaten Yasmin and live to tell the tale.

I walk back over and pick up the box of mice, dropping the bone saw, now stained with red, before making my way to the two unconscious bodies. I'm not sure if they're alive or dead, but at this point, it doesn't matter.

I dump the rodents in their laps and spin toward Isabella, lifting a brow. "Hungry?"

Isabella slithers up to them, curling around their limp frames.

I don't leave until I'm sure they're both dead.

And then after a long shower where I scrub away my sins, I head to the guest room where I have my on-call doctor tending to Riya.

She'll be fine, thankfully. Just a long recovery and a lot of rest.

I'm walking past the foyer and to the stairs when the front door slams open, causing me to spin around, my stomach tightening.

Yasmin stands in the doorway, her hair a tangled mess and her clothes dirty and torn. But she's here. And she looks shocked to see me.

She stumbles into the foyer, bruised and bloody, the silver case with the lamp tucked under her arm.

"Yasmin," I breathe, frozen in place.

Her mouth drops open, a sharp cry ringing from her lips as she drops the case and rushes into my arms, throwing herself at me.

I close my eyes and catch her, pulling her flush against me as her limbs wrap around my body and she sobs into my neck. "I thought…I thought you were dead," she says.

"Shh," I soothe, running my hands up and down her spine, my chest feeling like it might explode from having her in my arms again. "You think I'd allow death to come for me when I knew you were out there with another man?"

She presses kisses all over my neck and my face and then pulls back, staring at me. "How could you send me away? How could you *do* that to me? You said you'd never let me leave."

I sigh, tensing my arms around her. "I would do anything for you, including setting you free. Don't you get that yet?"

She sniffles, shaking her head, her fingers tickling the nape of my neck. "I don't want to live if it isn't with you."

Slowly, she slides down my body, and I push her back, holding her by the arms as I take her in, my eyes desperately covering every inch of her to make sure that she's whole. That even though she's been through an incredible ordeal, she isn't too broken for me to piece back together.

"How did you get here?" I ask, rubbing my palms up and down her body to check for broken bones. "Where's the boy?"

"I took a cab. And Aidan's dead."

Her voice is monotone, and I jerk back, my brows shooting to my hairline. "Come again?"

She seems apathetic about the entire thing, which is not like her, but I let it go, realizing that she lost her father, thought she lost her best friend and her husband, and now has lost the first boy she ever loved. She's allowed to disassociate for a while if she needs. I'll be here in the end to bring her back.

"I'm so sick of people telling me what to do." She shrugs. "And he wouldn't let me leave, was going to hurt me and take the lamp, so I did what I had to do." She pauses, staring up at me from beneath her lashes. "I'll need your help cleaning it up."

I brush her hair away from her face and nod. "I'll take care of it."

She swallows, looking down at the floor. I reach out, tipping her chin up so her glossy eyes meet mine. "Would you like to see your friend?"

She gasps. "Riya's alive?"

"She is."

Now tears *do* escape her eyes, and she covers her mouth with her hands, nodding. "You saved her. You sent me away so you could save *her*."

It's true, even though it almost killed me to watch the boy take her away, kicking and screaming. I couldn't focus on saving her best friend and subduing Darryn at the same time as long as she was there too. It had to be one or the other.

And I couldn't let her lose another person who she loves, even though it meant setting her free and having to trust that she'd come back home.

I cup her cheek, bringing her into me. She smiles, rising up on her tiptoes and brushing her mouth across mine.

My chest warms, heart beating harshly against my ribs.

I've spent my entire life feeling less than. I spent countless years and killed numerous people, all to work toward gaining the upper hand and becoming something more.

Who knew this whole time, all I ever needed was *her*.

My wife.

And she makes me feel like the most powerful man in the world.

EPILOGUE

Julian

YASMIN IS GLARING AT ME FROM WHERE SHE'S resting in our bed.

It's been two months since the disaster that turned into our new beginning, and in that time, things have finally started to calm down.

Riya is out of our house now and back on her own, almost completely on the mend.

Aidan was added to Isabella's meal over the next week after I hunted down where he had her in some small house that he somehow got out in the hills of Badour.

And the lamp?

We buried that with her father. It wasn't ever something he truly ached for the way I once did, but it seemed fitting he be the one to keep it in the end anyway.

Cathartic, both for me to let go of my past and for Yasmin to be secure in how I see our future.

And the only future for me is *her*.

"What did I do now?" I ask, glancing at her through the mirror by our dresser as I adjust my cuff links.

"You were planning to kill me," she says.

I purse my lips, walking over to her, the mattress dipping beneath me when I sit down.

"We've talked about this." I reach out and press my hand against her cheek.

She scoffs. "Yeah, well, what are we supposed to tell people when they ask how we got together? Oh, my husband is a *romantic*. He forced me into marriage and then drafted up a fake will so he could kill me himself and inherit everything that's rightfully mine."

I smirk.

"But don't worry," she continues. "It all worked out in the end. I have a magical pussy and he just couldn't stay away from the siren's call."

Leaning over, I press a kiss to her lips. "That's true."

She grins, shoving her hands against my chest. I reach up, gripping her wrists and dragging her underneath me, my body hovering over her frame until she's flat on her back.

"Care to show me more about this *magical* pussy of yours?" I press my erection into the heat between her thighs.

She moans, giggling as she wraps her hands around my neck.

Happiness races through me, and I still can't quite believe that this is my life. That I'm hers, and she *chose* me.

"If people ask, tell them the truth. That your husband is a greedy, selfish man who tied you to him and won't ever let you go."

"Promise?" she asks.

"I do." Tapping my hand on her side, I move back, my cock twitching at the way she protests, trying to pull me back in. "Up. I have a surprise."

Her eyes lighten and she jumps out of bed, tangling her hand in mine as I lead her out of our room and to the new space I had built off the garage.

I told her I was renovating the garage to make space for another car because I didn't want her to get nosy, but the truth is that I was building something for her. Preparing for this moment.

My stomach jumps in anticipation as I lead her through the house and to the new room, maneuvering her in front of me when we reach the door off the garage. "Go ahead, open it."

She looks back at me with a curious expression before she opens the door and steps inside, a gasp leaving her mouth as she spins around and takes in her new darkroom.

It took a lot of research and a month and half to complete, but finally it's done.

"You built this for me?" she asks, her back still toward me.

I take the moment to drop down to one knee, waiting for her to twist back around. "I did. Do you like it?" I ask.

"Like it? I lo—" She spins, her hands covering her chest when she sees me lowered to the ground. "What are you doing?"

I reach out and grip her hand, my thumb brushing on the underside of her left ring finger, the metal of her wedding band cool against my skin. "I told you once that I don't want your firsts, but I have a confession to make." My heart skips with nerves. "I lied."

Her bottom lip trembles as she stares down at me, her fingers squeezing mine.

"I want your awkward moments. And your fumbling hands." I slide my hand from hers, up her side until I'm gripping her hip, and I pull her into me, my face pressing against her stomach. "I want your laughter and your love and your endless fucking light.

I'm a greedy man. A selfish one. And I want it all. I want the rest of your firsts *and* your forever."

"Julian," she chokes out.

I shake my head, pressing a kiss to her torso and hugging her to me. "Tell me you're mine."

She drops down until she's on her knees, her hands flying to cup my jaw, forcing my eyes on hers. "I'm yours, Julian Faraci. I choose *you*."

Our mouths crash together, and my heart flips and flies, feeling like it might explode through my chest.

"Thank you for my darkroom," she says against my lips.

I pull back from her face, feeling my love for her fill me up until I can hardly breathe. "Don't you know yet, gattina? I would do anything for you. Burn this life down to the ground and build a whole new world if you demanded it."

She grins, pressing her lips against mine one more time. "To a new world then."

"*Our* new world."

EXTENDED EPILOGUE

Julian

IT'S BEEN A QUICK AND PROSPEROUS FIVE YEARS since the death of Ali. After the dust settled on the chaos from the search of the lost lamp, Yasmin and I spent the rest of the year focusing on healing the wounds between us, the ones that were born from our unfortunate start.

But nothing about our relationship has ever been *normal*.

I offered her a real wedding, but it didn't hold her interest, not after her father wasn't there to walk her down the aisle, so instead I took her to a private island and we had a month-long honeymoon where we forgot the world entirely, creating our own cocoon of happiness.

And then when we returned, we started running Sultans. Together. She's a quick learner, and while she leaves most of the actual work to me, she's there behind the scenes, ushering us into a new era, one that keeps her family's legacy alive and keeps me as the CEO of one of the most powerful conglomerates in the world.

We *did* end up getting into the antiquity trade, and we've also finally been able to do business within the Russian diamond market, centering Sultans as *the* most powerful and prestigious diamond producer in the world.

My dick twitches at the memory of yesterday, when we stopped by the newest Sultans retail chain just outside Brooklyn after hours and she sucked me in a room full of sparkling jewels, making me hold her face to my groin while I shot my load down her dirty little throat.

"Mr. Faraci," Ciara's voice interrupts my daydream and I clear my throat, my chair creaking as I lean forward over the conference table and tap my fingers on top of the papers splayed out in front of me, showing new designs in honor of Sultans' fiftieth year.

"This all looks decent. Send it to my wife and get her okay. You know she's the one who cares about the aesthetics more than me."

Standing up, I button my suit jacket and leave the room, heading back to my office and clearing the day's emails before going to pick up Yasmin for her event tonight.

She's becoming quite a household name in the photography world, although she insists she doesn't want to make it a career. Her work is frequently displayed in galleries around New York City, and tonight they're hosting an event in her honor. I'm sure once we're there, Riya will be stealing all her time. Ever since her best friend recovered from her gunshot wound, she's been around like a gnat, one that I've had to get used to because my attempts at keeping her away have been wildly unsuccessful. Over time, I've gotten used to her and have even tried to bring her on as a lawyer for Sultans, but she's turned me down on numerous occasions, saying she doesn't like to work for criminals and would rather spend her time building her own practice.

I open my briefcase for the first time today, slipping in a few important papers to take home, and pause, my stomach tightening and blood rushing to my groin when I see a pair of fire-engine-red lace panties lying on top.

I groan when I pick them up and bring them to my face, inhaling the sweet scent of Yasmin's pussy.

I'm going to fuck her until she can't breathe when I get home.

Rushing out of the office, I head to my car and make the normally forty-minute drive in twenty minutes. Parking in our garage, I head to her darkroom first, pressing my ear against the door and listening to see if she's there. I don't want to open it and mess anything up if she is, but it's silent, so I'm assuming she's in the house.

I find her in the kitchen, her juicy ass on display in tiny cotton shorts as she waltzes around the island making what looks like chocolate chip cookies. Isabella is curled up in the middle of the floor, and every so often, Yasmin reaches down and pets her.

She's humming to herself and dancing around to whatever song she's playing in her head, and I lean against the wall, slipping my hands into my pockets, my eyes feasting on the vision.

Goddamn, she's perfect.

And mine.

When she turns around, she sees me and she jumps, her hand flying to her chest with a yelp.

"God, Julian, why do you always *do* that?" she complains. "Such a Peeping Tom."

I smirk, straightening and stalking toward her, my hands coming out to grip her around the waist. She comes willingly, jumping up and wrapping her long legs around my hips, her hot cunt pressing against my already straining erection. I press a kiss to her lips as I walk with her into the family room, my tongue tangling with hers as I deposit her on the Persian rug in front of the fireplace.

Wasting no time, I rip her shorts off before she can protest and dive into her glistening pussy, her scent and her taste overwhelming me.

My cock grows, begging me to let it out and sink inside her, to let her walls suck on my shaft the way I'm sucking on her clit until I fill her up with my cum.

"You taste so sweet, gattina," I say between nips.

She attempts to sit up, but my arm flies out, pinning her down, my other free hand smacking across her swollen cunt, a sharp slap that I know will send her into the stratosphere.

Yasmin loves being spanked.

"Stop moving," I demand.

She jerks even harder against my hold, a devious flare coasting across her perfect face. Heat collects at the base of my spine when she disobeys me so openly.

I press my forearm more harshly against her middle until she's plastered to the floor and incapacitated entirely. "Does my little brat need to be taught a lesson?"

My fingers tease her hole, her wetness coating them as I slide inside, finger-fucking her slowly. Leaning back down, my tongue swipes out across her clit, swirling in a slow circle, enjoying the way her pussy walls clench every time I suck it in my mouth between licks. Her entire body tightens, and I know she's seconds away from exploding, so I pull back, using my hands to grip her hips tightly as I flip her around until she's on all fours.

"*No*," she complains.

"I want to feel you gripping my dick when you come, not my fingers," I reply, unbuckling my belt and dropping my pants. I stare at the way she's splayed open, her tight little asshole and dripping cunt on display for me as she rests on her elbows and knees.

My cock bobs free and I stroke it from the root to the tip, my sack tightening from the touch, already on edge from seeing my wife so vulnerable in front of me.

I reach out and run my fingers along her pussy, from the top of her slit down to behind her hole, drenching my hand in her arousal.

"Such a greedy whore, amore mio." Moving forward, I rest the tip of my throbbing dick at her entrance, teasing her as I slip it forward and run the length of my shaft along the outside of her cunt until I'm sliding against her clit.

Her body trembles and she pushes back against me, her ass slapping into my hips, which makes my cock jerk, precum leaking from my tip and mixing with her own wetness.

My hand slowly glides up her back, over the cotton of her oversize shirt, ghosting along her spine until I'm fisting her hair and dragging her body up until she's plastered against me. Her breathing is heavy and my shaft jerks as it rests between her thighs.

I pull back slightly and thrust forward, the feeling of my cock sliding against her, so close to where it belongs, making my muscles contract and sweat bead at my brow.

My fingers tighten in her strands and tug sharply, making a heavy breath escape her pouty lips, my other hand dragging down the front of her until I'm cupping her pussy.

"This cunt is mine," I state, my lips ghosting across the juncture between her neck and shoulder.

"*Please*, Julian."

"Have you been a good girl, baby?" I place a small kiss to her skin and move my cock back slightly until I'm poised at her entrance. "Only good girls get my dick."

"Yes," she breathes, her hips rotating against me.

"What a filthy little liar." My fingers tighten in her hair and I tug sharply, pressing my lips against the shell of her ear. "Good girls don't leave their panties in my briefcase where anyone can find them."

Her body trembles against me, and I move my hips forward, my cock splitting apart her lips and sinking inside the smallest bit.

My abs tighten.

"Is that why you're prancing around here in those little shorts with nothing underneath? To tease me until I can't think about *anything* except the way it would feel to be balls deep in your sweet little cunt?" I push forward again, my dick sinking into her another inch. "Tell me what you want, gattina."

She tries to push against me, but I tighten my hold on her body, keeping her in place.

"I want you to fuck me like I've been bad."

"Your wish is my command."

Releasing her hair, I throw her body forward, her elbows caught by the purple and gold fabric of the rug beneath us, and I'm on her quickly, deep inside her before she can blink, my cock spasming from the feel of her warmth encasing every hard inch of me.

I start a brutal and punishing rhythm, my hips slamming against her, watching the way her ass jiggles with every single thrust. My hand flies down and cracks across the meaty part of her cheek, and she cries out, fucking me back so well I'm already seeing stars.

This isn't going to last long. I'm too wound up from the day and too turned on from the feel of her perfect pussy massaging my length.

My palm moves until my fingers are sliding down the crack of her ass, rimming around her tight little hole.

"I'm going to fuck you here," I say, pressing the tip of my thumb past the tight ring of muscle. "Tonight when we get back from your photography event, I'm going to spread you open and force myself into this tight little space, fucking you up the ass until my cum leaks out of you."

Her walls contract around me.

"You'd like that, wouldn't you, little slut?"

My breaths are coming harsher as I thrust in and out of her while I tease her back entrance, and when I slip my thumb in entirely, her entire body seizes, locking up and forcing my balls to draw into my body. I lose control, cum surging through my shaft and shooting deep into her instantly. My vision goes black while I unload inside her, and she's *vibrating* on my dick, which only prolongs the pleasure until I feel like I might pass out.

I collapse on top of her, slipping out of both of her holes and pressing kisses to her neck, my lungs begging for air.

"I love you, Mrs. Faraci."

She hums, lying flat against the floor, both of us too satiated to move.

"I love *you*, husband."

Flipping her over until my body is pressed against the front of hers, I press a long kiss to her lips. "Tell me you're mine," I whisper, my heart squeezing tight in my chest.

Her eyes fill with so much love it hurts, and she reaches up her hand, running her fingertips along my face.

"I'm yours, Julian Faraci. And you're mine."

Another kiss to her lips.

"Forever?" I ask.

"Forever."

Character Profiles

Julian Faraci

Name: Julian Faraci

Age: 36

Place of birth: Brooklyn, New York

Current location: Badour, New York

Nationality: Italian American

Education: Business degree

Occupation: COO of Sultans (a diamond empire)

Wealth: Multi-millionaire

Eye color: Dark brown

Hair color and style: Jet black, slightly messy

Body build: Tall (6'6") and fit

Preferred style of outfit: Suit

Glasses?: Yes, only when reading, silver framed

Any accessories they always have?: A compact metal staff that
was custom made

Level of grooming: Impeccable

Health: Healthy

Handwriting style: Cursive and pretty but not extremely legible

How do they walk?: Confident

How do they speak?: Drawls like he has all the time in the world. Deep voice. Very charming when he wants

Style of speech: Normal

Accent: American

Posture: Perfect

Do they gesture?: Yes

Eye contact: Always

Preferred curse word: Cunt

Catchphrase?: It will only hurt for a little

Speech impediments?: No

What's laugh like?: Low and deep

What do they find funny?: He'll let you know when he figures it out

Describe smile: Charming, more of a smirk than a smile

How emotive?: Not very

Type of childhood: Extremely traumatic. Had a father who beat his mother and a mother who beat him. He spent his childhood protecting his mother and aching for her love but only being met with abuse.

Involved in school?: No. Named most likely to amount to nothing in the yearbook.

Jobs: Started in the mail room at Sultans and worked his way up by getting a degree in business, proving himself useful at Sultans, and killing the people whose positions he'd take

Dream job as a child: Becoming the most powerful man in the world, who in his eyes was Ali Karam, the CEO and owner of Sultans

Role models growing up: Ali Karam

Greatest regret: Allowing his mother to control him for so long

Hobbies growing up: Hapkido martial arts

Favorite place as a child: The dojo

Earliest memory: His mother coming into his room with a bloody face and beating him with his father's belt

Saddest memory: Too many to pick one

Happiest memory: Falling in love with Yasmin

Any skeletons in the closet?: Many

If they could change one thing from their past, what would it be?: Allowing his mother to have so much control over him

Describe major turning points in their childhood: His father gifting him Isabella and then Julian using her to kill him

Three adjectives to describe personality: Unhinged, manipulative, determined

What advice would they give to their younger self?: People only have the power you allow them to have.

Criminal record?: None on paper because he has the police in his pocket, but he is heavily involved in criminal activity and is also a serial murderer

Father:

Age: Deceased

   Occupation: Owner of a dry cleaning business

   What's their relationship with character like?: Julian resented him because he was never around, and when he was, he spent his time beating his mother and making his childhood a living hell.

Mother:

Age: 60

Occupation: Does nothing but live off Julian's money

What's their relationship with character like?: Toxic and abusive. He feels a responsibility to her that spawns from his childhood, and she is a narcissist who doesn't truly know how to love anyone other than herself and uses/abuses him.

Any siblings?: No

Closest friends: Ali and Ian

Enemies: Darryn Anders

How are they perceived by strangers?: Dangerous and powerful

Any social media?: No

Role in group dynamic: Leader

Who do they depend on:

Practical advice: Ali

Mentoring: Ali

Wingman: Ian

Emotional support: Nobody

Moral support: Nobody

What do they do on rainy days?: Work

Book-smart or street-smart?: Both

Optimist, pessimist, realist: Realist

Introvert or extrovert: Extrovert

Favorite sound: Bones breaking underneath his staff

What do they want most?: To be the most powerful man in the world

Biggest flaw: His need to prove that he's worthy because he was never chosen by anyone in his life and allowing that trauma to bleed into his aspirations as an adult

Biggest strength: His determination

Biggest accomplishment: Becoming the COO of Sultans

What's their idea of perfect happiness?: Owning Sultans and proving everyone in the world wrong about how important he is and that he's worthy

Do they want to be remembered?: Yes

How do they approach:

Power: Demands it

> **Ambition:** Most important thing
>
> **Love:** Doesn't have time for it
>
> **Change:** Adapts

Possession they would rescue from burning home: His snake, Isabella

What makes them angry?: Disrespect

How is their moral compass and what would it take to break it?: Nonexistent

Pet peeves: People not listening to him, people not choosing him or giving him the respect he deserves

What would they have written on their tombstone?: Here lies Julian Faraci, the man who chose himself.

Their story goal: His goal is to realize that love is what makes him powerful, that material things and ruthless ambition, while good in their own right, won't ever fill the void that he had from his childhood and growing up when he was always cast to the side and punished for things that weren't his fault. His feeling of never being worthy or being chosen is what drives him, and by the end of the story, he will realize that Yasmin *did* choose him, and he feels more fulfilled than he ever could have dreamed. His goals shift from finding the lost lamp and centering Sultans as both his and the most powerful force in the world to making his entire world revolve around Yasmin and making her happy because she is what is most precious to him.

Yasmin Karam

Name: Yasmin Karam

Age: 23

Place of birth: Badour, New York

Current location: Badour, New York

Nationality: Lebanese/Iranian American

Education: College psychology degree

Occupation: Jewelry heiress

Wealth: Billion-dollar inheritance

Eye color: Brown

Hair color and style: Dark and curly

Body build: Normal height and curvy

Distinguishing features: Pouty lips and fierce eyes

Preferred style of outfit: High-end turquoise or red pantsuits and dresses, or else her oversize Oregon State shirt and sweats to lounge in

Glasses?: No

Any accessories they always have?: No

Level of grooming: High

Health: Healthy

Handwriting style: Almost perfect

How do they walk?: With confidence

How do they speak?: Normal speech and proper when it calls for it

Style of speech: Regular

Accent: American

Posture: Good

Do they gesture?: Yes

Eye contact: Sometimes

Preferred curse word: Fuck

Catchphrase?: She doesn't truly have one although she enjoys calling Julian patatino

Speech impediments?: No

What's laugh like?: Light and airy

Describe smile: Blinding

How emotive?: Very emotive. She has outbursts because she can't hold it in, and when she does, it manifests as anxiety.

Type of childhood: Extremely pampered, wealthy, grew up in boarding schools and only came home for holidays and summer

Involved in school?: Yes, but only because she lived there. Named most likely to be the richest in the yearbook.

Jobs: None

Dream job as a child: Photographer

Role models growing up: Her father

Greatest regret: Not standing up for herself

Hobbies growing up: She's always loved photography

Favorite place as a child: At home in her father's office, sitting on his lap while he taught her about diamonds

Earliest memory: Her third birthday

Saddest memory: Learning her father was terminally ill

Happiest memory: Being a child and playing snowballs with Aidan

Any skeletons in the closet?: No

If they could change one thing from their past, what would it be?: Learning to stand up for herself sooner

Describe major turning points in their childhood: Her father becoming ill

Three adjectives to describe personality: Spoiled, naive, people pleaser

What advice would they give to their younger self?: Sometimes, it's okay to be a little selfish, and you have to be wary of everyone's intentions.

Criminal record?: No

Father:

Age: 58

> **Occupation:** Billionaire businessman, owner and CEO of Sultans

> **What's their relationship with character like?:** Very strong relationship. She is terrified of disappointing him and loves him more than anything.

Mother:

Age: Deceased

> **Occupation:** None

> **What's their relationship with character like:** Never had one

Any siblings?: No

Closest friends: Riya and Aidan

Enemies: Julian

How are they perceived by strangers?: Pretty and pampered

Any social media?: No, because her father requested she didn't have any

Role in group dynamic: People pleaser

Who do they depend on:

Practical advice: Riya

> **Mentoring:** Her father

Wingman: Riya

Emotional support: Riya and Aidan

Moral support: Riya

What do they do on rainy days?: Take photos

Book-smart or street-smart?: Book-smart

Optimist, pessimist, realist: Realist

Introvert or extrovert: Introvert

Favorite sound: Her father existing

What do they want most?: To be free to love whomever she wants

Biggest flaw: Her need to please people

Biggest strength: Her loyalty

Biggest accomplishment: Standing up for herself

What's their idea of perfect happiness?: Any moments with laughter and love and family

Do they want to be remembered?: No

How do they approach:

Power: Doesn't need it

    Ambition: Average

    Love: Aches for it

    Change: Doesn't like it

Possession they would rescue from burning home: Her shoebox of photos

What makes them angry?: Her father not letting her know anything about Sultans because she's a woman

How is their moral compass and what would it take to break it?: It's bendable because she grew up around morally bankrupt people, and although she has standards and morals, she would break them for those she loved.

Pet peeves: Being treated differently because she's a woman

What would they have written on their tombstone?: Here lies Yasmin Karam. She was free.

Their story goal: Yasmin starts off as a wealthy, pampered, sheltered woman who is terrified of disappointing others (especially her father) and who aches to be free to love the person she chooses instead of feeling trapped in her need of having her father's approval. Throughout the story, she will realize that what she thought was love wasn't and that sometimes it's okay to be a little selfish, that standing up for yourself is what keeps your life happy and full, and that by *not* speaking up and doing scary things even when they may disappoint others, you can cause way more problems for yourself. By the end of the story, she will have found her own voice and live for herself truly for the first time, which will be the freedom she's always ached for and never known how to get.

JOIN THE MCINCULT!

EmilyMcIntire.com

The McIncult (Facebook Group):
facebook.com/groups/mcincult
Where you can chat all things Emily. First looks, exclusive
giveaways, and the best place to connect with me!
TikTok: tiktok.com/@authoremilymcintire
Instagram: instagram.com/itsemilymcintire/
Facebook: facebook.com/authoremilymcintire
Pinterest: pinterest.com/itsemilymcintire/
Goodreads: goodreads.com/author/show
/20245445.Emily_McIntire
BookBub: bookbub.com/profile/emily-mcintire
Want text alerts? Text MCINCULT to 833-942-4409
to stay up to date on new releases!

Acknowledgments

The first thank-you goes to my sensitivity readers who gave me invaluable help and incredibly in-depth read-throughs of this novel. Sarosh from Tessera Editorial and Salma: Thank you for your time, your willingness to help, and your dedication to ensuring that I wrote this book with authenticity and care.

To my husband, Mike: The man who does everything behind the scenes. Stickers, merchandise, kid duty, dish duty, dinner duty, working out plots, and supporting me while I live my dream. I love you. Thank you for loving me too.

To my best friend, Sav R. Miller: You already know and I say the same thing in every book. Thank you for being my rock. Here's to the smokies. Love you and wouldn't want to do this without you.

To my editor, Christa, her assistant, Letty, and the rest of the Bloom Books/Sourcebooks team: Thank you for pushing me to become a better writer, talking me out of my spirals, and making my dreams become reality. This book wouldn't be half of what it is without you.

To the McIncult: Thank you for being my biggest supporters and loving the words I write. Forever grateful for us finding each other.

To *all* my readers, new and the OGs: Thank you for taking a chance and picking up my books. For reading until the end and getting lost in the worlds I create.

And last but certainly not least, to my daughter, Melody: You are now and always will be the reason for everything.

About the Author

Emily McIntire is an international and Amazon top-fifteen bestselling author known for her Never After series, where she gives our favorite villains their happily ever afters. With books that range from small town to dark romance, she doesn't like to box herself into one type of story, but at the core of all her novels is soul-deep love. When she's not writing, you can find her waiting on her long-lost Hogwarts letter, enjoying her family, or lost between the pages of a good book.